Margot Pickard is married and a mother to an amazing son, Michael, who together with his beautiful wife, Adriana, created five adorable grandchildren. Following a long career in the marketing and communications industry, she retired and left city life behind for a more rural existence, where she finally made time to pour her passion for words onto paper.

This work is dedicated, first and foremost, to my mother, Kathryn, who instilled in my siblings and me the passion for and power of words and reading. She is a remarkable woman, in so many ways, and I'm incredibly fortunate that she chose me to be her daughter. I must also thank my favorite sister, Linda, and our dear friend Marylou, who agreed to review the original draft and provide their honest feedback, with assurances that no harm would come to them. I'm happy to report that they are alive and well, and willing *'to take another one for the team.'*

Margot Pickard

RED TEDDY BEAR CANDLES

AUSTIN MACAULEY PUBLISHERS™

LONDON • CAMBRIDGE • NEW YORK • SHARJAH

Ordering Information:
Quantity sales: special discounts are available on quantity purchases by corporations, associations, and others. For details, contact the publisher at the address below.

Publisher's Cataloging-in-Publication data
Pickard, Margot
Red Teddy Bear Candles

ISBN 9781643785561 (Paperback)
ISBN 9781643785578 (Hardback)
ISBN 9781645368120 (ePub e-book)

Library of Congress Control Number: 2019914115

The main category of the book — FICTION / Thrillers / Psychological

www.austinmacauley.com/us

First Published (2019)
Austin Macauley Publishers LLC
40 Wall Street, 28th Floor
New York, NY 10005
USA

mail-usa@austinmacauley.com
+1 (646) 5125767

I would be remiss if I didn't acknowledge Warren MacDonald for his wisdom, experience, and encouragement. Thank you, my friend.

Prologue

She's being kept within the too tiny confines of a holding cell deep within the dank, dark bowels of an old courthouse, awaiting yet another day of her trial. The only daylight she has absorbed over the past few days is what little filtered through the tinted and barred windows of the police van that shuttles her between the jail and the courthouse.

Time crawls. Second after second. Hour after hour. She's fighting to keep control. Control over her mind and its erratic thoughts. Control over her body and its want to twitch. Control over her very life.

How had it come to this? How had it all gone so wrong? Where had she gone so very, very wrong...this time?

One thing she knows for certain, though...she'll never make the same mistake again, just as she never did after that last mistake. This was a new mistake, though. A different mistake. And one must always learn from one's mistakes.

If nothing else, Mama had taught her that lesson...and taught it well.

The Formative Years

A teddy bear is a furry friend
whose love and support never end.

Keeps your secrets, never lies,
friendly, fuzzy, cozy, wise.

Tell it your secrets, it'll keep them well.
You don't have to worry, it won't ever tell.

— *Jon Wimer*
Excerpt from Teddy Bears and Good Friends

Chapter One

'Ms. Foster, you are the defendant's aunt, is that correct?' the cocky, immaculately dressed criminal defense attorney, Blair Scott, asked the woman who now occupied the witness seat at the front of the courtroom.

'Yes,' Ms. Foster answered. 'Megan's mother was my older sister,' she added, but quickly changed her mind, 'sorry, I suppose I'm to now refer to her,' she looked briefly toward the defendant, 'as Jessica, but she was born Megan and I've always called her Megan.'

'I'm sure the court won't object to you referring to your niece by the name you know best, Ms. Foster.' Mr. Scott smiled easily at her, nodded his head with encouragement that she was doing fine, and continued, 'and would you please describe for the ladies and gentlemen of the jury what your sister was like, both as a person and as a mother to Ms. McCallum.' Mr. Scott gestured toward the defendant, his client, who sat tensely at an overbearing desk behind him, her hands twisting anxiously in her lap, her eyes not daring to look at anything, nor anyone. Just the floor; her go-to place. Her lungs struggled to maintain steady breaths, while her chest rebelled against the intensifying *thumpidy thump* of her heart. She can do this. She *has* to do this.

'My sister, Suzie, was always a very free spirit…that's what our mother used to say about her,' she admitted. 'I don't think she did things on purpose to get into trouble, though. I just think she had such a curious nature, she wanted to try things for herself. It didn't matter if someone told her she might get hurt or that she might get into trouble, she'd just go ahead and do it anyway, because she wanted to find out things for herself. She never could nor would rely on just the say-so of others.'

Ms. Foster took a moment before she continued, 'Suzie always seemed to be in such a hurry to grow up, and never really made time for dolls or toys and such. But she loved to watch television, especially those old black and white movies. You know, the ones where the handsome young hero rescues the beautiful maiden.' Ms. Foster's eyes wandered for a moment, the smallest hint of a smile on her lips as she recalled distant and oh-so-different memories.

'Please go on, Ms. Foster,' Mr. Scott prompted her.

'As she got older, Suzie became a real handful for our parents. She'd stay out all hours of the night and constantly skipped school to the point where she was expelled for good. So, at 17, she went looking for a job,' Ms. Foster recalled. 'She wanted her independence.

'I thought my parents were angry then, but a few months later, Suzie came home and announced she was pregnant.' Ms. Foster shook her head. Not about that particular incident itself, but because it was the spark that had ignited all the emotional fires that were to come.

'We honestly thought that, although it was far from an ideal situation, maybe this would be the making of Suzie. Maybe this would force her to grow up and settle down,' Ms. Foster continued. 'And it did…at least for a while anyway. She married the boy who got her pregnant, but it wasn't long before he realized he'd made a terrible mistake and one night he just disappeared, never to be seen nor heard of again,' she remembered. 'About two months later, our Megan was born,' Ms. Foster paused and looked directly at the defendant, a smile lighting up her face. 'She was absolutely perfect, in every way. I used to tell people that when she had a messy diaper, you'd open it and there the mess would be, perfectly wrapped in a little pink box that was neatly tied up in a matching pink bow, just waiting every time,' she laughed to herself quietly, as did most of the courtroom. 'That's how adorable she was…*is*,' Ms. Foster added with conviction, looking at the jury to make sure they had heard her. 'Is,' she repeated in an almost whisper-like voice, her self-confidence suddenly wavering, but she forced herself to carry on.

'Unfortunately, as Megan grew, she found herself alone and lonely most of the time. Her mother made it abundantly clear that she preferred the company of men, whether they were tall or short, dark-haired or blond. In other words, it didn't matter.' With each word she uttered, Ms. Foster's emotions ascended, growing louder and stronger. 'Just as long as they had enough money in their wallets and a penis in their pants!' she spit out the unexpected words. Her face flushed at her out of the blue and completely out of character choice of words.

Scott was momentarily caught off guard by her blunt remark but recognized and appreciated its immediate value. There was no uncertainty left in anyone's mind within the entire courtroom as to where her sister's interests had lain, *literally*.

Scott remained silent. He was counting. Four was the number he most often counted to, silently of course, while he waited for a jury to catch up, to keep up. *One. Two.* And just enough time to whet their hopefully increasingly curious appetites. Wanting them to want more. *Three. Four.*

'Ms. Foster,' he continued, 'can you please tell the court what happened on the night of June 6, 1990, with respect to the defendant, your niece, Ms. McCallum.' He once again gestured toward the young woman who sat mannequin still behind him. He was using every opportunity to influence the jury's perception of his client. To form a bond, however fragile it might be, between the accused and her peers who sat before her, judging her. Ultimately tasked with determining how she would live…or *if* she should live.

'Yes, sir,' Ms. Foster assured him. 'My sister, Megan's mother, knocked on my door late that night demanding that I open it and let her in. I barely had the lock off when she burst in through the door, dragging poor little Megan behind her, and told me I had to watch her for the night because she had something important she had to do,' Ms. Foster recalled.

'And how was your sister's temperament that night…her overall mood?' Scott asked.

'Well,' she thought for a moment. 'She did seem quite angry about something, but also strangely excited at the same time.'

'And was that the first time your sister had shown up at your door with Megan in tow at such a late hour and left her there with you?' the attorney questioned.

'Oh no, sir,' she verbally baulked at the thought. 'I made sure I was home every day right after work, because I never knew when Suzie would show up with Megan, and I wanted to make sure I was always there for her, someone had to be there for Megan,' she added almost in the form of a question, looking directly at the jury as if soliciting their endorsement and not just their understanding that she had done the right thing.

'Was there anything different about this particular night? About this particular visit?' the attorney asked as he subtly maneuvered himself into a position that left his witness with no option but to look directly at the jury.

Slowly, she raised her head, but her eyes were shut tight. She took a deep breath and only then could she open them and force herself to look directly at the jury, as she had been instructed.

Tears once contained behind pale lids succumbed to gravity and slid down her cheeks, falling to their silent deaths in her lap.

'After Suzie left my house that night, I took Megan into the kitchen and asked her if she was hungry, because she most likely hadn't been fed. She didn't seem to want anything, so I asked her if she wanted me to read her a story. But she didn't want that either, which was unusual, because she always loved to read with me. The only thing Megan said that night was that she wanted to lie down, go to sleep and…and to make everything go away,' she added hesitantly, as though still trying to decipher the meaning of those last few words, even after all these years.

'So, I took her into the bathroom to run her a bath, because she was quite a mess. That's when I realized something was terribly, horribly wrong,' she almost whispered.

'What did you discover in that bathroom, Ms. Foster?'

She didn't want to say the words. She didn't want to remember the beginning of what could now be the end. The end of Megan. The end of what was left of their family.

Ms. Foster lifted her chin high, hoping that it would force her lips apart, causing the words to simply fall from her mouth. Then she wouldn't actually have to say them. Then perhaps she wouldn't be held responsible for them.

But she's going to have to, out loud. She is going to have to breathe life back into the very memories she thought she had suffocated and put to death years ago.

'There was…I found a small bloodstain on Megan's underpants.'

Chapter Two

Megan is her bait. The lure Suzie dangles in front of men with just the hint of a two-for-one deal for anyone with enough cash and body parts to step up. The men don't ever touch Megan. But they do defile her with their wanting eyes and lust-filled thoughts.

Megan is familiar with the night's routine. It always began by watching Mama and her shaky hands apply cheap makeup to a face that had been used, abused, and discarded so many now unmemorable times over the years. The results remind Megan of the picture of a funny clown she once saw in a magazine. Mama has bigger than life red lips and huge, round rouge dots on her cheeks, and wayward smudges of darkened charcoal outlining her eyes, making them appear even more battered than perhaps they already were. Megan giggles.

But slowly Mama's hands begin to settle down with each swallow she takes from the bottle that always stands guard at her side. Mama calls it her 'pretty potion' because it changes her from an 'ugly duckling into a beautiful swan,' one that everyone wants to be around, that everyone adores, that everyone wants to touch. Wouldn't Megan 'like to be a beautiful swan, too?' Mama wants to know and puts the bottle up to Megan's lips. Mama promises her she will be. One day. *Soon.*

Whatever is in the bottle looks just like water, but to Megan it never ever tastes like water. And water shouldn't smell, should it? Every drop causes her baby blues to blink in reaction to its bitter taste, while the warm, slow-moving glow of the liquid spreads strangely throughout her body. Tears inevitably threaten to drown her eyes, but she always rescues them at the very last second by gently wiping away the droplets with the back of a tiny, tentative hand.

Soon, it's time for Suzie to choose an outfit for herself. The second most important prop of the evening. It has to be just so. Not too slutty, but suggesting the possibility. Not too classy, but rather just a girl working her way up in the world...'or down, I should say,' she adds huskily under her breath, followed by a self-appreciative snort for her bawdy humor.

Megan giggles again. She doesn't know why. 'Here, have another sip, baby doll.' Suzie forces Megan's mouth open with one hand, while tipping the lip of the bottle and some of its contents into her mouth with the other. 'This will make you even happier, I promise.'

Standing in front of a full-length mirror, Suzie tosses aside the towel she had chaotically swathed around her. She's trying her best to like what she sees, but it's not working. She holds fatigued pieces of lingerie in front of her in an effort to determine which one will best shore up her free-falling features. Or, perhaps more importantly, which one will ultimately be the easiest to remove when the time comes?

Add a two-sizes-too-small sweater in a color meant to clash with her too-short-too-tight skirt and the melding of the two results in drawing attention to both and the fatty masses that bloat defiantly beneath them.

A pair of black come-fuck-me boots, some second-rate bling, and a swipe to her less-than-perky-but-still-ample cleavage from the free peel-off perfume sample she had helped herself to from a neighbor's mail slot the previous week.

One last inspection in the mirror: a pat to the hair, a fingertip dab to the corner of her mouth where the lipstick refuses to hang on, a pretend smile looking back at her.

'Mama's going to get you ready now,' she says as she turns and reaches for the child. By now, the alcohol has done what it was intended to do. Megan is pliant and compliant.

Suzie props Megan up on a stool in front of the mirror and slowly removes her clothes, piece by piece, taking the time to admire every soft, youthful feature of her shape. *Something that time itself had methodically and meticulously robbed her own body of,* Suzie thinks bitterly. Her envy never tires of the near flawlessness of that young and beautiful age.

She takes a brush from the bedside table and begins to arrange Megan's long golden curls, draping them carefully over one bare shoulder, then the other. One solitary strand of soft coils is left to cascade freely down her back, tickling the little hollow at the top of her buttocks.

Megan giggles. She can't seem to help giggling. But, it's okay to giggle, because she knows it's almost time for one of Mama's special plays. She knows, because she has her pretend costume on now.

* * * * *

'For the past seven months, you have spent time with the defendant, Ms. McCallum, is that correct, Dr. Fitzgerald?' Blair Scott addressed the world-renowned forensic psychiatrist who now sat in the witness box.

'A great deal of times, yes,' the doctor confirmed.

'Can you please explain for this Court what the expression *one of Mama's special plays* meant to Megan...*for* Megan,' the defense attorney asked as he began what he knew would be one of the most difficult examinations of this entire proceeding. Not because of the witness himself, but rather the graphically repulsive content of his testimony.

The doctor shifted slightly in the seat. The time had come. He knew what he was about to say would crash head-on into the psyche of every person in this room. It couldn't be helped, but it would help Ms. McCallum. That was what mattered most.

'Suzie McCallum, Megan's mother, was what I would consider to be an extremely wounded human being, although unfortunately I will never have the opportunity to fully understand why that was,' he added with professional regret.

'Suzie McCallum used her daughter to attract men. Not for Megan, but rather for herself. As the years passed and her looks began to decline, I believe the more desperate Suzie became for attention. Any kind of attention,' the doctor added quietly. 'She was no longer the star of her show, so to speak. Megan was.

'She carried a picture of Megan around in her purse and, if she met a man in one of the bars she frequented and thought he could sexually and financially satisfy her, Suzie would inevitably take Megan's photo out and share it.'

The attorney stepped back to the defense table, withdrew a photo from a file, and approached the witness. 'Is this the photo to which you are referring, Doctor?' Scott asked as he held it up in front of the witness.

'Yes,' the doctor confirmed.

'For the record, Your Honor, this item is marked as Defense Exhibit F,' he said as he took the photo, deliberately stared at it as he walked over to the jury panel and slowly handed it to the foreman.

How does a sane mind process such a visual juxtaposition? He had anticipated a reaction. Perhaps even a shocked reaction. He got what he wanted. What he had hoped for, and more.

One woman cried silently; her mouth overpowered by the handkerchief tucked in a fist. A man did his best to stifle an audible sound, yet it nonetheless escaped. Was it an inhale or an exhale? Did it matter?

Each jury member struggled to process the image of a beautiful little girl with vacant, blue eyes and a pretend smile trapped for all eternity staring back at them.

'*What hidden treasures await,*' the picture whispered. The insinuation was obvious. The little girl, oblivious.

'And what was the true purpose behind this photograph of Megan, at least as far as her mother, Suzie McCallum, was concerned?' the attorney asked the doctor, knowing the jury had probably drawn its own, and most likely accurate conclusion. But nothing hammered a point home for a jury more than hearing the words.

Hearing the words spoken by an expert was the equivalent of using a sledgehammer. While the blow may be unsettling, the result was unambiguous.

Chapter Three

The man lets his eyes take their time. He appreciates the photographer's attention to detail. How she lies on her stomach atop a plush, white, faux fur rug. A cozy fire in the background, casting a sensual glow around her. How her legs are crossed at the ankles, up in the air behind her. The toes poised and posed. 'Hats off to the photographer,' he raises his glass to no one.

How her head is tilted, ever so slightly, to one side. The right side. How her wrists come together, bound to each other with a strand of big, pretend white pearls.

Fingertips crowned with pretend nails finished in a French style fan out, five on either side of her face. Her chin resting on inverted, supportive palms.

Big blonde curls cascade from the top of her head, snaking their way around her body. Beneath her body, her naked body.

He takes another swig from the glass he's been holding out in the air, momentarily forgotten. He's been distracted. Fair enough.

He lets the fluid slide unhurried along the lengthy shaft of his tongue, the ice having long melted from the heat in his hand. His body temperature rising, fueled by an ember now slowly smoldering deep inside him, gaining strength.

He turns to the woman sitting next to him. 'Does she take after her mother?' he wants to know. He looks her up, then down. He already knows the answer. That's a big *no*. Her tits, no longer having the confidence, or perhaps just lacking the courage to face the world are seeking solace in the hollows of her armpits.

And it's hard for him to work out just where her ass stops and her thighs start, or is it her thighs stop and her ass starts? Whatever it is that's swathing the shabby bar stool next to his, it's a large load. No matter which direction you come at it. Period.

Tonight's her lucky night, though. He's found the bottom of enough drinks that she's about to validate that well-known one-liner. What was it again? The one that still makes him laugh out loud. Oh, yeah. *'The more I drink, the better she looks.'* Fuck, he really does love that one. And isn't it the truth? It is in this dump, anyway. He signals the bartender 'Another' as he holds up his glass.

The bartender pauses and looks back at the man, then at the woman sitting next to him. *Fuck.* 'And whatever it is the lady's drinking.' Sarcasm seeps into his tone and he waves a dismissive hand in Suzie's general direction.

Suzie slowly leans in to the man. Her lips just inches from his ear. 'Like mother, like daughter, huh? Why don't you come home with me and find out for yourself,' Suzie answers in response to his last question, challenging him in what she hopes is her finest licentious lilt.

Suzie had left Megan alone in their apartment just a few blocks away. Not really asleep, but more an induced slumber, compliments of the alcohol Suzie had plied her with less than an hour ago. Suzie has no intention of staying here long. She just needs time to find tonight's toy. She's hoping she has. This one looks like he could be fun to play with…for a while anyway.

'My daughter and I are putting on a special play tonight. Would you like to come and watch? Or maybe you'd prefer to take part?'

Her tongue slowly traces the upper ridge of her top lip, then the bottom. She thinks it's sexy and inviting. The man turns away. To him, it's neither. It's disgusting. She's disgusting.

On the other hand, the little girl in the picture is anything but…

* * * * *

Mama's thumb and go-fuck-yourself finger work furiously together in an effort to get her attention. 'Hey.' *Snap. Snap.* 'Hey.' *Snap.* 'I told you, good things come to those who wait, didn't I. Now come and say hello to my special friend, baby doll,' Mama's gin-saturated words wash across Megan's face like a rancid rag, rousing her unkindly.

'He really wants to meet you. He says baby dolls are his absolute favorite thing in the whole wide world,' she says, her arms spread wide as if to encircle a cosmic orb that had magically suspended itself in front of her. She begins to laugh.

Laughing is good. It disguises the pain. While alcohol fuels the laughter. Laughter multiplied by alcohol equals less pain. It's a simple equation. Easy to remember. Even easier to apply. Literally *and* liberally.

Suzie takes Megan by the hand. She is a beauty already at just eight years of age. Megan's blonde locks hang long and full with soft coils that relentlessly tickle her just above her buttocks. But this time, it doesn't make her giggle. Something tells her that it wouldn't be right to giggle this time. Standing in front of a stranger…a *man* stranger. Her little body naked.

'Well, now. Aren't you a pretty little thing,' the man's voice is little more than a restrained growl as he kneels down in front of her. It may appear to be a child-friendly gesture, but his only aim is to get closer. Hopefully take 'a more hands-on approach' as the saying goes.

Suzie recognizes the vein of lust as it pulses to life, throbbing against the zipper of his skin-tight denim jeans. She can't wait for it to be exposed, but only to her. She can't wait for it to explode, but only in her. First things first.

21

Suzie takes Megan by the hand and roughly delivers her to a once-overstuffed-now-understated chair hiding in the dark shadows of a corner. What does the chair know?

Suzie's taking her away from the man. She reminds him 'only looking...no touching.' Suzie has a few boundaries. Perhaps 'a few' is a bit of an exaggeration. She has that one, though. She's pretty sure.

Megan turns around, stands on tippy toes, and eases herself up onto the chair, carefully settling in to a position she knows so well. She has, after all, been made to practice it often. An elbow perched like so, here. A hand draped delicately just there. One leg tucked under her. The other bent at the knee, tipped slightly to the right. Just enough to suggest a better view might be possible, if one were so inclined.

Next, Megan turns her attention to her hair. She divides the curls to either side of her face, loosens her hold, and lets the gentle tresses stream down. Past her yet-to-blossom breasts. Past her teeny, tiny waist to its intended destination. A sentinel for her virginal crevice.

'You look so pretty. Mama loves your pretend costume,' Suzie whispers into her ear as she bends down to tame one unruly lock. Megan giggles. Silly Mama. Funny Mama.

Suzie's focus now turns to the man. *Fuck.* He hasn't taken his eyes off of Megan. But, he will, she assures herself as she works her body over to an old radio that's hanging precariously from its rusted finishing nail roost halfway up a wall.

She twists a knob and it comes to life with the sleazy sounds of a has-been Latino orchestra. Her body begins to move. No, no, it's more of a ripple effect. It seems to propel itself, once it gets going. Forward, side to side, back, repeat.

Now she has his attention. He's paying attention now.

Suzie dances over to a cupboard to retrieve a bottle of...whatever. What she drinks tonight is the least of her concerns. What she hopes to put in her mouth tonight, well that's a different story.

She takes a long pull from the upended bottle that's being strangled by its neck in her hand. Her eyes closed tight so that absolutely nothing detracts from the exquisite sensation she gets from the alcohol's slow-burning passage down her throat, leaving a mantle of warmth behind.

She stands in front of him and offers him the bottle. He eagerly accepts. Anything to pacify the flames now engulfing his three-piece genital suite.

She runs her hand slowly down her body, as though following the path and pace of the liquid fuel as it meanders on its way. Down...down to that place. The place that always hungers, yet is never satisfied.

Her hand works its way up under her skirt, lifting the hem higher, a little higher. More and more. There, she touches it. The softness and the nakedness. She loves the feel of a shaved-clean pussy. It reminds her of Megan's. Smooth. Virginal. Or in her case, hopefully not quite so obviously used.

She lifts the same hand. Inserts her middle finger in to the back of her mouth and slowly, deliberately pulls it out. A red teddy bear shaped candle with a lit wick protruding from the top of its head casts an eerie flicker around the room from its precarious perch atop an upended wooden crate. The saliva that now wets her finger glistens in its wake.

She retraces her hand's previous journey. Down, under her skirt, slipping the wet finger inside herself. It's not enough. It's never enough.

The man's nose lifts slightly, buoyed by the first whiff of the familiar, intimate scent of a woman. Mere inches from his face. It finally draws his attention away from the little girl who sits across the room from him, looking at him. Eyes wide. Eyes vacant.

He suddenly lashes out and seizes the wrist of the hand Suzie has up inside her, never taking his eyes from hers that are looking back at him. Have been looking at him the entire time. They're wanting. They're pleading. On the threshold of begging.

He pulls on her hand and her finger slips easily from the moist darkness. Slowly, ever so slowly, he leans in, opens his mouth, and welcomes the taste. Licking and sucking up every last slippery trace of the vaginal nectar.

Megan has been watching. She's not interested, though. She's seen it before.

She's tired and lets her eyes go away behind closed lids. If only she could make the sounds go away, too. But she has a secret. When she's asleep, everything magically goes away. Even Mama…for a little while anyway.

Chapter Four

'Yes,' Dr. Fitzgerald confirmed in response to the defense attorney's last question, 'Megan was in the same room the entire time her mother and the man were engaged in sexual activities.' He was struggling to keep his voice unemotional and steady. He was only offering his professional opinion. He was not here to influence the jury one way or another through his own emotions regarding this case. 'Not just this man, but any man her mother brought back to the apartment.'

He paused and took a sip of water from the glass beside him.

'Megan's mother would pose her, naked in a chair, directly across the room from a pull-out futon where Suzie and her date would eventually have sex,' he continued. 'Megan was, in reality, just a prop for Suzie.'

'Could you explain what you mean by that, Doctor?' Scott asked.

'Megan's mother must have struggled with debilitating self-esteem and had probably convinced herself that she could no longer attract a man, let alone arouse him on her own even if she did,' he continued. 'She knew Megan could. Megan became a living doll for Suzie. Something she could play with. Something she could dress up. Something beautiful she could put on display for her dates, always with the suggestion that Megan may be part of the evening's entertainment. But only if they satisfied her needs first,' he added.

'And to your knowledge, before the night in question, the evening of June 6, 1990, had any of the men ever touched Megan?' the attorney put the question to the doctor.

'I don't believe so,' the doctor stated. 'Megan's memories of her childhood are very vivid up to the time she reaches the age of eight. Based on that, it was and still is my opinion that the events of that night had such a profound effect on Megan's psyche that it literally blocked access to any memories of that night,' he added.

'Are you saying she had amnesia, Doctor?' the attorney inquired, wanting the jury to know the difference. It would be imperative that they understood the difference.

'No, no,' the doctor responded without hesitation. 'The memories were still there. They weren't lost, nor had they simply vanished,' he added. 'They were blocked. Locked away somewhere within Megan's being...her mind...waiting to be let out. Waiting to be freed, if they ever would or could be.

'From that moment on, everything Megan did was as a result of that night. She approached almost any situation in her life in the same emotional state as that night. By doing so, she protected herself psychologically,' Dr. Fitzgerald explained. 'You see, if a person expects and prepares for the worst, then they don't ever allow themselves any false hope. They never set themselves up for failure, let alone disappointment.'

Scott walked over to stand directly in front of the jury box. He could reach out and touch any one of them. He took his time, looking at each jury member's face. He waited for some form of awkward eye contact from each before moving on to the next.

'Doctor, how does one 'free' these locked-away memories?'

'Well, they are not so much 'freed' as they are 'released,' he began. 'In most instances of repressed memories, they first require some sort of action. A trigger, if you will.'

The attorney wasn't sure the jury had grasped the doctor's analogy. 'What sort of trigger, Doctor? Can you give the jury an example of what you mean?' he asked.

'Certainly. It could be as simple as a familiar aroma that triggers or brings back memories of grandma's kitchen, or a song one hears that takes him or her instantly back in time to a specific place or event, such as dancing to that very song with someone special at the senior prom,' the doctor explained.

But Scott wanted the jury to know, to fully understand, that it wasn't just about little old ladies and long-lost sweethearts. There was a much deeper and darker side to repressed memories.

'Dr. Fitzgerald,' he tried a different approach, 'isn't it also true that these triggers, as you refer to them, can dredge up not-so-wonderful memories?'

'Most definitely,' Dr. Fitzgerald assured the court. 'There's a reason these types of memories are locked away in the first place,' he explained. 'For example, say a person is either personally involved in or perhaps only witnesses a horrific incident. Not everyone, or more accurately not every mind, is capable of processing let alone coping with what has happened or what it has seen, so it protects itself by taking that memory and in essence, locking it up and throwing away the key, or at the very least, burying the key.'

'And do these repressed memories always surface, Doctor? Does every memory have a trigger…or a key?' Scott asked.

'No,' Dr. Fitzgerald offered. 'It actually takes a relatively strong trigger to unlock memories, particularly those of a horrific nature. Or a series of triggers where each one may not be strong enough on its own, but when brought together or occurring in succession become a formidable force that can then activate those memories.'

Scott paused, allowing the jury time to process the doctor's words.

One. Two. He was in no hurry. *Three. Four.*

'In your opinion, Dr. Fitzgerald, did someone or something finally pull Ms. McCallum's trigger?'

'In my opinion, it was not just someone or something, but rather a series of triggers. Ms. McCallum had locked away so many horrendous memories, it was only a matter of time before her mind could no longer cope with them, let alone contain them.'

* * * * *

She remembers the face now.

Now she remembers the stale, alcohol-laden smell of his breath, heavy and up close. Remembers his hands, the pain, and the blood. *Tic.*

But she didn't always remember. For the longest time, her mind hadn't allowed her to remember, because remembering it might have led to reliving it. She knew she wouldn't survive it a second time. Her mind had been protecting itself…protecting her.

It hadn't wanted Megan to remember how she had been awakened from an imaginary world where she had been riding atop a big white unicorn as it silently soared over vibrantly painted fields of giant flowers, its wings beautifully presented to a gentle wind.

Hadn't wanted Megan to remember how she had opened her eyes to see a man standing in front of her, his hands roughly kneading his swollen private parts. How his eyes had a look she didn't think she had ever seen before. Knew for sure she didn't recognize.

How it took her a few seconds to really come awake. How it took her another few to realize Mama wasn't there. To grasp that she was alone, with *him*.

How she had covered her little ears with little scrunched-up fists, trying desperately to hush the unnatural noises that were beginning to ooze from his ugly mouth.

Didn't want her to remember how she hadn't been able to move. How she froze. How she didn't know exactly what it was that was making her so very anxious, so very frightened. How she had no idea what it was she should be protecting herself from or preparing herself for.

Nor could her mind let her remember the image of his body as it started to quiver, then shudder. The noises intensifying. How he held his breath, threw his head back, his whole body writhing. How she thought that maybe he was sick.

How he let out an agonizing cry. How she was certain that he was sick, because his private part was crying…weeping thick, jelly-like tears. On the chair, on her, on the little red teddy bear candle another of Mama's 'special friends' had given her just a few weeks ago.

Her mind couldn't let her recall how his final scream made her finally scream, too. How he threw a large hand up to her mouth, covering it completely. How she struggled to breathe. How he told her to shut up or she would wake Mama and how very mad Mama would be. Now, she wouldn't want to make Mama mad, would she?

How his hand over her mouth was replaced with his mouth over her mouth. His teeth gnawing; his tongue probing; his hands eventually relaxing their grip on her shoulders, only to move down to separate the blonde curls, revealing what secrets lay beneath. Awaited beneath.

Her mind never wanted her to discover the truth about how the man had squatted down on his knees in front of her. How he reached out and slowly spread her legs wide…wider. How a hand once again came up to cover her mouth, before the other reached for her. Telling her all the while how pretty she is. How he wants to touch her, to feel her…every inch of her.

Didn't want her to be reminded of where he had put his face, down between her legs; or how she felt when his tongue suddenly darted out, down between her legs.

How she didn't giggle. Couldn't. How his hands had made the blood come, down between her legs. How that was the first time she met Jessica.

Chapter Five

'Why is it no one ever reported this incident to the police, Ms. Foster? Children's Aid? Or to anyone, for that matter?' the defense attorney addressed the witness.

She swallowed. Her conscience threatened to choke her. 'I didn't report it, because I really wasn't sure what had happened,' she tried to explain. 'I gave Megan a bath right away, which I now know was absolutely the wrong thing to do. But, at the time, all I could think about was getting her cleaned up.'

'Did Megan tell you what had happened to her?' Scott asked.

'No. I asked her a number of times, in different ways so I wouldn't upset her or scare her, but she never said a word,' her voice now little more than a murmur.

'And did you ever find out what really happened that night?' he wanted to know. Everyone wanted to know.

Ms. Foster looked down and gently shook her head. 'No,' she admitted, 'not until this trial.' Scott paused. Here it came. The question that would establish a pattern—the pattern of lies—lies Megan's mother wove from the fragile threads that must have been unraveling in her own mind. 'Did you ever confront your sister? Megan's mother?'

'Of course,' she snapped at him, then reminded herself that he was not the enemy. He was here to help Megan, to save Megan.

'Yes, I absolutely did,' she replied much more gently. 'I put Megan to bed right after her bath, but I didn't want to leave her alone until I was sure she was asleep. I thought it might take a while, but Megan closed her eyes and almost seemed to force herself to sleep. That's when I got on the phone and started calling everywhere looking for Suzie. I tried her apartment first, but there was no answer. So, I called around to some of the bars I knew she went to, but she wasn't at any of those either. I left messages for her everywhere.'

She took a moment to let another tear slide. They hadn't stopped since she took the stand, but she no longer tried to trap each one in a tissue. There were too many.

'Suzie finally showed up at my place the next day. She had come to pick up Megan, but I told her I wouldn't let Megan go with her until I knew what had happened the night before,' Ms. Foster said.

'Suzie asked me what I was talking about. *"What happened last night?"'* she asked me.

'I told her about the bloodstain. About how Megan hadn't said a word since she dropped her off. How withdrawn she seemed.'

'And what was Suzie's response?' the attorney probed.

'*"Oh, that,"* was all she said, as if it was nothing. She told me that Megan had been playing in the living room with a friend of hers while she was taking a shower, and that Megan had simply fallen and scraped herself, *"like all kids do."'*

'And did you believe her, Ms. Foster?' the attorney asked.

'I wasn't sure, at first,' she admitted. 'But Suzie started to cry. Then she screamed something at me about how could I possibly think that she would ever let anything happen to Megan. To her baby. To *our* baby.'

'So,' Scott asked quietly, 'nothing was ever done? Nothing further ever came out of it, as far as Megan's mother and her boyfriend at the time were concerned?'

'No,' she simply whispered.

The defense attorney wasn't finished. He needed to make one more point. It was a harsh point, but he had to keep the jury focused on his client. He needed them to remember this incident. Because it was the first. The first of many. He needed them to understand that this one experience was the genesis. The embryo that began to grow ever so slowly inside Megan. Inside a molested mind that sat atop an equally molested body. Waiting for its next feeding. And it would come.

'Was anything ever done to help Megan? Did anyone take her to a doctor to confirm any injuries from that night?' he pressed. 'Did anyone ever seek out the help of a child psychologist when Megan stopped talking altogether for the next several years? Did anyone question why Megan's mother suddenly took her out of school, saying she was going to home school her? Did anyone do anything when she became even more withdrawn as she got older?'

There was nowhere for her to hide from the regret. No way for her to sufficiently disguise the '*if only I had done something*' guilt.

Her eyelids dropped from the weight of shame. 'No,' Ms. Foster quietly confessed.

* * * * *

Megan's mother had done something about it, though. She smelled an opportunity.

She remembers waking to find a man lying next to her. She hated this part. The fucking 'morning after.' The vile breath. The funky tang of musky body juices fused together on sheets that lay strewn about. Random, raunchy recollections.

Why wouldn't they just leave when they were done? *Fuck*, why couldn't she remember to kick them out before she passed out?

Only it wasn't yet the morning after. What had disturbed her? Something had dared to resuscitate her from the depths of an addiction-provoked slumber. That something was taking a big risk.

She lay still for a moment, listening intently for a sound. Any sound that might help identify the guilty. Isolate the offender. There, she heard it again. Weak, muted, mew-ish? A kitten?

She staggers from her bed. 'Here puss, puss,' Suzie whispers as she rounds the corner into the living room. 'Here pussy, pussy.' But the sight that greets her is not the one she expects.

What's the big chair doing on its side? Why is the wooden crate upside down in another corner? How did the little red teddy bear candle end up smashed to pieces on the floor, its decapitated head with its penetrating eyes staring right at her, its rounded body nowhere to be seen? *Must have been quite the party*, she compliments herself.

Suzie hears the noise again. Somewhere off in a corner. She gets down on her hands and knees. Silently, she creeps along. It's coming from behind the overturned chair that's ahead of her. Slowly…slowly she puts one paw-like palm in front of the other on the floor beneath her. One knee crawling ahead of the other. Closer. Closer.

'Come out, come out, wherever you are,' she tries to singsong the childish phrase, but it comes out sounding too much like a ghostly, horror movie chant instead. The kind that sends chills slithering up one's spine. Then right back down again.

She rounds the big chair. It's not a kitten at all. It's Megan. Motionless. She doesn't register that she's heard Mama. Doesn't acknowledge that she's even aware of her surroundings. Her head hangs down. Matted curls hide her face. She holds a little pillow to her chest, bony arms encircling it. Squeezing the very life out of it. The decapitated body of the red teddy bear candle clasped in one tiny fist. Her eyes are shut tight. If she can't see anyone, then maybe no one can see her either, especially *him*.

It is then that Suzie notices the red stain on the inside of Megan's thigh. She reaches out to touch it, but Megan recoils even further behind the chair and buries her face in the pillow she now clutches for dear life.

'What happened, baby doll?'

Megan's eyes only seek out the safety and emptiness of the floor beneath her. Floors have no eyes. Floors never pass judgment. They only ever listen.

Her new friend Jessica was a very good listener, too. She had stayed with her and comforted her all night.

Suzie dresses herself first, then Megan. Quickly. Quietly. She leads a silent Megan down the stairs of the apartment building and puts her in the back seat of the man's car that sits waiting for its owner in the dark parking lot outside. They are going to 'go for a drive' but Mama needs to 'do something first.' She'll be right back and to be very quiet, like a good baby doll.

She returns after a while, the man in tow. Groggy, scruffy, pissed off. Not at all aware, yet, of what was happening. Hazy memories; a bruised hand; aching balls.

Suzie opens the passenger door to shove him inside and the automatic light illuminates the interior. He sees the little girl, curled up, huddled on the floor behind the driver's seat, head down, eyes hidden, arms wrapped around herself so tightly her little hands are almost touching each other behind her. A flash of something red in one fist.

His memory creeps and crawls its way out of a trance and into the truth. The truth about what happened. The truth he felt sure the little girl would never, ever reveal. They had had a private little chat and come to an understanding. He had spoken and she had come to understand that he would hurt her if she ever opened her mouth. She had taken his warning to heart and refused to speak to anyone. For many years after that night, just to be sure.

Suzie insists on driving. She tells him she wants to take him to a 'special place' she knows, but first she needs to drop Megan off at her sister's so they can finally have some 'alone' time. He wants to know where they were going. She smiles a pretend smile and tells him just to sit back and enjoy the drive. They'd have plenty of time to talk later. 'Get some rest, you're going to need it,' she winks at him.

After dropping Megan off at her sister's house, they ride in silence for almost an hour. He is good with that. He doesn't feel like talking to her or to anyone. He will soon learn that he was only ever expected to listen.

Suzie eventually stops the car beside a small lake hidden deep within a remote, wooded area. Quiet. Deathly quiet. Deadly quiet. *The kind of quiet befitting the occasion,* she thinks.

She gets out of the car and walks slowly to the water's edge. She lights a cigarette and waits…waits for him to come to her, and he does.

She speaks first. 'Ever been in jail?' she wants to know.

He's taken aback, but decides to play along. 'No.'

'I wonder what it's like. Ever been curious if it's as bad as former inmates say it is?'

'Not really,' he disagrees.

'Guess you wouldn't be in too much of a hurry to find out, then?'

His mouth is suddenly dry. His stomach queasy. A small shiver shoots up his spine. She takes his uncomfortable silence as a 'no' and gets to the point.

'The big question is, what's your freedom worth? I hear that in prison, child molesters are the lowest of the low. Pond scum,' she spits. 'So, what's it worth to you to not have your asshole reconstructed over and over and over again on the cold cement floor of some lonely shower stall inside a maximum security prison?'

It was just a few days later when Mama went out and returned home several hours later driving a new used car. She was wearing a new outfit, too. She got a lot of new outfits that year. A lot of new things.

Too bad for Mama, though, that her latest conquest possessed the cowardice to commit suicide about a year later. The local newspaper said that, 'although there was no suicide note on the deceased when he was found hanging from a rafter in his own garage,' authorities subsequently learned that he had dug himself into a serious financial hole over the past year, all without his wife's knowledge. The official report concluded it was this that had most likely prompted his decision to take his own life. 'Well now, that was inconsiderate of him,' Suzie grunted after reading the article. '*Fuck.*'

It was also about this time that Suzie realized she couldn't get through a day without her new best friend, the divine Miss Ecstasy.

Chapter Six

Blair Scott shocked everyone with his next question, as was the intent. 'Dr. Fitzgerald, to your knowledge, who first gave Ms. McCallum drugs?'

An audible, mass murmur filled the courtroom.

'Based on my sessions with Ms. McCallum, I believe it was her mother who first gave her drugs,' the doctor answered. 'At some point in time, Suzie no longer found as much relief in alcohol as she used to and had graduated to something that would enhance the effects of alcohol.'

'What was her drug of choice?' the attorney asked.

'Her drug of choice, although it is my opinion that she most likely never turned anything down if it were offered to her, was Ecstasy,' Dr. Fitzgerald answered.

'And what is Ecstasy, Dr. Fitzgerald?'

'Ecstasy is a synthetic, psychoactive, or mind-altering, drug with hallucinogenic and amphetamine-like properties. It is known for its energizing effects on one's body, as well as for its ability to distort time and perceptions of situations that occur around the user,' he explained. 'However, one of the most sought-after effects of Ecstasy is the enhanced enjoyment the user gets from physical experiences.'

'By physical experiences, do you mean actual physical contact, such as touching, Doctor?' Scott was guiding the way with the help of his carefully mapped out questions. He was taking everyone exactly where he wanted them to go.

'Yes,' the doctor agreed.

'So, would it be fair to say that sexual intercourse itself might be considered the ultimate physical experience for Ecstasy users?'

'Absolutely,' Doctor Fitzgerald agreed again. 'Hence, the name. For some, engaging in sexual intercourse, and most especially achieving orgasm, while under the influence of this drug, is, to put it simply, the best. Uncontaminated delight. *Pure ecstasy.*'

Scott was leading the jury through a maze of facts. Methodically dissecting this judicial puzzle. Explaining each piece, because each had a special story. Putting each piece in its place, because each occupied a specific space. Then, moving on to the next.

'What are the psychological effects of Ecstasy, Doctor?' Scott asked.

'There are a number of concerning effects, including confusion, depression and sleep problems, to much more serious consequences such as overwhelming anxiety and severe paranoia,' he explained.

'On average, Dr. Fitzgerald, the most intense effects from the average dose of any drug usually last anywhere from three to four hours, is that correct?'

'Yes, more or less. Although there are a number of factors that can certainly influence the length of the effects, such as the amount taken, if it was taken in combination with another drug or alcohol, the stature of the person taking it, etcetera. However, unlike a lot of other drugs of this type, the effects from Ecstasy often last for several weeks afterward,' he explained. 'There have also been a number of recent studies supporting an earlier theory that the effects of Ecstasy can last years and even continue into one's life later on.'

Scott was quiet. He was counting. Waiting. Giving the jury an opportunity to catch up to the reality of where his questions were heading, if that were even humanly possible.

If not, he might sacrifice the full significance of what he was about to ask. He might squander this slap-in-the-face moment he'd been waiting for. Working toward.

'Doctor,' the attorney moved in, closer, 'how old was Ms. McCallum the first time her mother gave her Ecstasy?'

* * * * *

She's floating across the wooden floor on pretend ballerina tippy toes. Her body movements inspired by a rhythm only she can hear. She's *happy*. No, no, she's more than that.

Megan needs to find the right word. It's important that she first identify and then accurately label the feeling. She usually categorizes her feelings as either *happy*, *uneasy*, or *terrified*. Not so much for how they make her feel, but rather for the likely consequences each represents for her.

For example, '*happy*' is her favorite category, but it is also her most elusive. She rarely allows herself to put her feelings into that category, because the consequences inevitably lead to other categories like *disappointment*, *depression*, and disappointment. It had taken years, but she had finally broken the cycle of expecting something positive by applying this method to every aspect of her life.

Tonight's routine was, well, mostly routine. There was one difference though. Mama had insisted on making a special 'pretty potion' just for Megan. How had she categorized that particular feeling at that particular moment? *Uneasy*? Yes, that was it.

Mama left a while ago, uttering her predictable leave-taking as she went. 'I won't be long. Make yourself pretty, baby. That's Mama's little doll.'

Megan knows Mama won't be long. She's never long. Never long enough. She wonders who this evening's special guest is. Who's Mama's flavor of the week? Or does she still have an appetite for last week's buffet?

An answer isn't necessary, because it didn't matter. It never mattered. It never matters what Megan thinks. What she feels. Or what she has to say. So, she's taught herself not to do any of them. At least not out loud, if anyone else was around. But Jessica cares what she thinks. Everything about Megan seems to matter to Jessica.

At the moment, though, her whole being feels like she's just gathered together her greatest pleasures in life, mixed them in with her favorite foods, and eaten everything all at once. It's an amazing feeling. It's a new feeling. She simply must give it a special name, a special category. But, what?

Curious, euphoric waves of heat envelop her body, making the touch of clothes on her skin suddenly oppressive. Abruptly unbearable.

She begins to remove them. Piece by piece. Like Mama does.

She stands in front of the full-length mirror and stares at herself, like Mama does.

She releases the clip from her hair and lets it down. Not like Mama does. That's one thing Mama can't do. Mama can't let her hair tumble down in big, soft curls to tickle the little hollow at the very top of her buttocks. The sensation still makes Megan giggle. After all these years. After all these times.

Mama had also encouraged her to add a few colorful touches to her pretend costume over the years. Big red lips, big red polka dot cheeks, and big blackened eyes just like Mama.

Time to take her place. An elbow perched here, like so. A hand draped delicately there. One leg tucked under her. The other bent at the knee, tipped slightly to the right. Always enough to suggest a better view might be possible, if one were so inclined.

She brings the curls from around the back of her neck and lets the tresses stream down. Past her now succulent breasts. Past her now perfectly sculpted waist to its intended destination. A sentry for her now ripened, womanly crevice.

By age 17, she had transformed into a swan. Just as Mama had promised. Apparently, an extraordinary swan, too. One everyone wanted to be around. One everyone wanted to touch, like they used to do to Mama.

Megan giggles. She can't seem to help giggling. But it's okay to giggle, because soon it will be time for another one of Mama's special plays.

Megan hasn't noticed that Suzie finally returned. Hasn't noticed that Suzie is not alone. Has noticed that Suzie is seldom alone. Mama's thumb and go-fuck-yourself finger are working furiously together. 'Hey.' *Snap. Snap.* 'Hey.' *Snap.*

'What's the matter, doll?' Mama's voice tears into her private moment. 'What are you giggling about?' she wants to know. She needs to know. She wasn't going to allow herself to feel left out...of anything.

'What's better than happy, Mama?' Megan asks. 'What would you call the best feeling you've ever had in your whole life?'

'That's an easy one, baby doll,' Mama answers. 'I call it Ecstasy.'

'Ecstasy.' Megan surrenders the word to her psyche for a moment.

Yes, she likes it. She likes the feel of the word on her tongue. And isn't it amazing how it sounds just like it feels?

EC-STA-SSSSSSY.

Chapter Seven

'When did Megan come to live with you, Ms. Foster?' Scott asked. 'How old was she?'

She didn't need to guess the answer or pretend to know it. She was more than familiar with it. In fact, she knew the answer, intimately.

'Megan was 17. It was January 1, 2000. The start of the new millennium,' she remembered the answer all too well. The answer lived in her mind. It had taken up permanent residence, alongside all the others. It was crowded.

'Would you tell the jury the circumstances that led to Megan coming to live with you,' he was still leading. Everyone was still following, even though they had no inkling yet of their final destination. They didn't seem to care. It was the journey that fascinated them, disturbed them…disturbingly fascinated them.

'I woke to a knocking sound. It was about midnight. I remember the time, because I looked at the clock beside my bed thinking that the noise was probably coming from a nearby New Year's Eve party or maybe fireworks.'

'And what was the source of that noise, Ms. Foster?'

'I realized someone was knocking on my door. I got up right away, because I thought it might be my sister. I was hoping she had changed her mind about going out and was dropping Megan off to spend the night with me.' If only it could have been. If only it would have been.

'Who was at your door, Ms. Foster?' he was gentle. He knew she was tired. He knew she was fragile. He knew he needed her.

'There was a detective. I believe his name was Detective McNeill, as well as two police officers,' she offered. 'The detective asked if my name was Linda Foster, and I said yes. Then he asked if I had a sister named Suzie McCallum. I must have said that I did, because he asked if they could come in and speak with me privately.'

'Why were they there, Ms. Foster? Why had they come to see you?'

She was close to numb. A lifetime of emotions had been sucked from her in just the few short days since the trial began. 'The detective said that he had some unfortunate news regarding my sister, about Suzie,' she recalled. 'He told me she was dead.' No tears. No blinks. No nothing.

'Did the detective tell you what had happened to Suzie, Ms. Foster?' the lawyer continued, once he was sure she was able.

'He said she had apparently taken an overdose.' There, there it was, the awful truth and the life of an awful waste…the waste of Suzie.

'And what about Megan, Ms. Foster?' he asked. 'Where was Megan throughout all of this?'

'That was my first question to the detective, Mr. Scott,' Ms. Foster answered quickly. 'Once the news about Suzie finally sank in, I became frantic about Megan. I asked him where Megan was. *Had something happened to Megan, too?*'

She remembered the panic she felt at that very moment. She wanted to know the answer, and yet she didn't want to know the answer. She wanted to know, because it might help put her at ease. She didn't want to know, because once the truth was revealed she may never again be at ease. Another one of life's cruel, little ironies.

'The detective told me that Megan had been rushed to the hospital in an ambulance. That she had apparently also overdosed,' she admitted. The news had stunned her. 'I remember telling him that he must be mistaken, because Megan didn't do drugs. Wouldn't do drugs, let alone drink alcohol,' she recalled. She never imagined she'd know now what she didn't know then.

'How did the detective respond to that, Ms. Foster?' the defense attorney asked.

She shook her head in disbelief. 'He said it was no mistake. Megan was in the hospital at that very moment being treated for a drug overdose.'

'And was there something he wasn't able to tell you, Ms. Foster? Something he couldn't tell you about what had happened to Megan that night?' Scott prepared the jury. *One. Two.*

'Yes,' she eventually acknowledged. 'The only thing he couldn't say was whether or not it had been self-inflicted.'

Three. Four. 'By self-inflicted, Ms. Foster, did he mean that Megan may have attempted suicide?'

* * * * *

No, no. They have it wrong. She hadn't tried to kill herself. She hadn't wanted to be dead. She had only wanted to sleep. At most, nothing a good stomach pumping couldn't fix.

She can clearly make out the hushed conversations taking place around her, but keeps her eyes closed. If I can't see them, then they can't see me, she reminds herself. But she does listen intently, intensely.

'Excuse me, Nurse, how long do you think it might be before we can talk to her?' she hears a man voice ask and a pleasant female voice respond.

'The problem won't be getting her to talk,' the nurse voice answers. 'The problem you're going to have is comprehending what she says. Her mind is pretty chaotic at the moment and will be for probably the next 24 hours, at least,' she explains. 'Her memory is erratic. Completely unreliable.'

'No, *no* it's not,' Jessica's mind silently screams. 'But, you're right, nurse voice. I'm not ready to tell what happened. Well, that's not quite true. I'm just not ready to tell *exactly* what happened.'

Chapter Eight

Out of 365 of them every year, this was by far Mama's favorite night: New Year's Eve. She went all out on this night. Well, all out on herself at least.

She bought a new shimmery black dress. More of a gown, really. It was nice, even on Mama.

Tonight, Mama's hair is no longer skunk-striped from graying roots, but freshly colored, blow-dried, styled, and heavily sprayed into place.

Her makeup had been augmented for the night. Besides the usual, cut-price smudges, Suzie added a little something special: false eyelashes.

Not the kind you'd see normal women wear, delicate and sensual, discrete and understated. Of course not. They are bigger, much bigger, which immediately and always translates to '*better*' to Mama.

They remind Megan of butterflies. Butterflies that had landed on Mama's eyelids. Every time Mama blinks, they flutter. Every time they flutter, Megan giggles.

She's already had one of Mama's 'pretty potions' earlier in the evening. Mama says she can have an 'extra potion' tonight. It's a special occasion. Mama's bringing two guests home tonight.

Mama's thumb and go-fuck-yourself finger work together. 'Hey.' *Snap. Snap.* 'Hey.' *Snap.* 'Baby doll, bring your glass over to Mama. We'll have another drink, just us girls, before I go and get our special guests,' she insists.

Megan watches Mama accept her glass. Watches Mama pour the clear liquid into it. Watches Mama take a small container out of the drawer in the table beside her. Slowly takes the cap off. Shakes two pills from the container. Drops one pill into Megan's glass and the other pill into her own. Watches Mama use the straw to swirl a long to stir   stir   stir some more.

Watches Mama hand her glass back to her, now filled with the 'extra special potion.' 'Cheers, baby doll,' Suzie puts her own straw to her lips and sucks hard, long, eagerly.

Megan watches Mama put the container of pretty pills back in the drawer. Watches the drawer close. She makes a mental note, then makes a decision.

Mama leaves, but not before uttering the time-honored, 'I won't be long. Now, make yourself pretty, baby. That's Mama's little doll.'

She knows Mama won't be long. She's never long. Never long enough.

She readies herself for tonight's guests. She instinctively begins by removing her clothes, piece by piece, like Mama does.

She stands in front of the full-length mirror and stares at her body, like Mama does.

She adds a few colorful touches to her pretend costume. Big red lips, big red polka dot cheeks, and big blackened eyes just like Mama.

No butterflies on her eyelids, not like Mama.

She sits down in a big chair, releases the clip from her hair, and lets it fall.

She knows the drill. An elbow perched here, like so. A hand draped delicately there. One leg tucked under her. The other bent at the knee, tipped slightly to the right. Always enough to suggest a better view might be possible, if one were so inclined. She can't remember any of Mama's guests ever declining.

She brings her blonde curls from around the back of her neck and lets them stream down past her breasts and her waist. The curls are purely for show now. Window dressing. She no longer needs a sentry. There's nothing left to protect.

One of Mama's '*friends*' had made her into a complete woman. About a year ago, now. Whether she had wanted to be or not. Whether she had been ready to be or not.

Mama knew about it. Mama told her it was no big deal. It was going to happen sooner or later. Then, Mama had welcomed her to '*the club.*'

She didn't know what '*the club*' was, but remembers the category of her feelings at that exact moment. It had been that rare and elusive '*happy*' category. She was happy, because she liked the idea of belonging to something, not someone.

But, right now, Megan has other things on her mind. She and Jessica were working out the final details for this year's New Year's resolution. But, unlike last year's, this one wasn't all about them. Wasn't purely selfish. They wanted to do something special for Mama.

Megan had to admit to herself, though, that last year's resolution was, by far, her best. It was going to be hard to top that one, although this one did have so much more long-term potential.

She'd worked hard on last year's resolution. Worked hard to do it right, to get it right, and she had. It had taken her months and months of practice over the past year, but she had finally done it.

Megan had allowed Jessica to send her adrift somewhere in her psyche. Far, far away. Jessica had finally forced the meek-mannered bitch into the shadows.

Megan had been weak, useless, and pathetic.

Jessica had come calling, again. But this time for good. Jessica now had full control over the body, the mind, the thoughts, even the twitches.

The best part was, no one had suspected a thing. Mama's not the only one who can put on a play. All Jessica had to do was sit there, quiet and subdued like Megan. 'Yes, Mama.' 'No, Mama.' *Fuck you, Mama.*

This is going to be Jessica's first real New Year's Eve; her coming-out party, so to speak. She wants to make it memorable. Truly special.

She decides to greet Mama at the door with a drink upon her return to the apartment. As any dutiful baby doll would naturally do when her Mama triumphantly returns with her latest sexual conquest.

Jessica picks up the glass Mama left behind, empty, on the table. She unscrews the cap from a whiskey bottle that's apparently now just guarding Mama's chair, waiting for her imminent return. Whatever. *Boozed-up bitch.*

She pours the liquid slowly, but only halfway. She doesn't want any of it to spill. She doesn't want even one little droplet of her very own, very special mixture to be wasted.

She opens the drawer in the table. Pulls Mama's little pill container out, opens the container, and counts 18 pills into the palm of one hand. With the other hand, she selects one pill at a time, 'One for Mama. One for me.'

Again. 'Two for Mama. None for me.'

One more time. 'A whole bunch for Mama, so none left for me. Oh, dear.'

Mustn't forget to stir.

She giggles. *Fuck.* She still hasn't quite got Megan's laugh down pat. She tries again. That's better.

'Tonight, you're going to star in my special play, Mama.'

* * * * *

'Detective McNeill,' the defense attorney began, 'can you please walk us through the events of that evening, New Year's Eve, 1999, beginning with the 911 call.'

Detective McNeill didn't need to refer to his notes, although they were right there in front of him. He knows the case, inside out, upside down. When he's awake. Mostly when he's asleep, though.

That particular night, he had been less than an hour away from going off duty when his partner had sounded. He had been looking forward to a quiet evening with his wife. Just the two of them, alone. A private New Year's Eve party.

The 911 call had come in at 11:04 pm, made by an anonymous male caller who simply said that an ambulance was needed right away and gave the address. Hung up. He never said what the problem was. Never gave his name.

An ambulance had been dispatched. Detective McNeill and his partner had been notified at almost exactly the same time.

They arrived at the address given, located the specified apartment, and were greeted by a partially ajar front door with dread-filled darkness beyond it. Detective McNeill had entered first, gun in hand. The only sound was coming from a radio playing somewhere within.

He announced their presence. 'Police.' No response. 'Police.' Again, no response.

He and his partner entered cautiously, flashlights scanning ahead. Working their way down a small hallway, past what appeared to be a bottle-strewn galley kitchen, around a corner to a cramped living room. The beam from Detective McNeill's light suddenly captured an image. A scene neither would ever forget. Not because they hadn't tried. Again and again.

There was a woman lying face-up on top of a soiled, pulled-open futon. She was naked, arms stretched out at her sides, legs spread wide, and her clean-shaven pussy fully exposed.

He checked her breathing: none. He checked her eyes: open and blank. He checked her lips: blue. Checked her mouth: foamy. Her pulse: nonexistent.

That's when he noticed there was something else in a corner of the room. But it wasn't just a 'something.' It was a 'someone.' It was another body. What appeared to be a teenage girl, slumped over in a chair directly across from the futon on which the first victim lay. She, too, was naked, exposed.

He checked her breathing: shallow. He checked her eyes: pupils dilated. Checked her mouth: clear. Her pulse: weak.

The girl had immediately been tended to by the EMTs and transported to the hospital.

The woman had eventually been tended to by the coroner and transported to the morgue.

Chapter Nine

'Was a full autopsy performed on Suzie McCallum?' Blair Scott inquired of the coroner who now sat as his witness.

'Absolutely, as is required when an individual dies under unusual circumstances,' the coroner stated. 'We did a full pathology workup, including the usual tissue samples, and blood samples for toxicology purposes.'

'Did you determine a cause of death?'

'Yes,' the coroner confirmed. 'Not only did Suzie McCallum have a blood alcohol level three times over the legal limit, but the findings also concluded that she had ingested a large quantity of the drug known as Ecstasy.'

'And was it the combination of the two that resulted in her death, Doctor?' the attorney asked.

'Indirectly, yes,' he explained. 'I believe Mrs. McCallum had been lying on her back, most likely close to unconsciousness at that point, and choked on her own vomit.'

'What else did your findings reveal about Suzie McCallum that night, Doctor?'

'She had recently engaged in sexual intercourse,' he said matter-of-factly. 'We recovered semen.'

'So, Suzie McCallum had sex just before she died?'

'Yes, she had. In fact, we discovered two individual DNA profiles,' the doctor confirmed.

'You found two? Suzie McCallum had sex with two different men just before she died? Is that what you're saying, Doctor?' the attorney knew the answer already, but he was so looking forward to the jury hearing it.

'That's correct,' the coroner confirmed. He was adding yet another special piece to the puzzle, fitting it perfectly into its specific place.

'Doctor, what were your official findings as to the cause of Suzie McCallum's death?'

'Aspiration as a result of excessive alcohol use mixed with what, in my opinion, was an overdose of drugs, specifically Ecstasy,' the coroner stated.

Scott faced the jury panel again, even though his next question was directed at the witness.

'How did you determine that it was an overdose, Doctor?'

'Most street tablets of Ecstasy contain anywhere from 60 to 90 milligrams of the drug MDMA. MDMA is the acronym for methylenedioxymethamphetamine. The problem with street Ecstasy is that it can contain just about anything, because it is most often manufactured in secret labs by individuals who by no means qualify as anything even remotely considered to be chemists.' He paused.

'The standardized measure for expressing and comparing the toxicity of a chemical is called LD50. LD50, or Lethal Dose 50, is the amount of substance that, when administered as a single dose, kills 50% of the test population,' he explained. 'Based on that standard, it would have taken approximately four or more Ecstasy tablets for Suzie McCallum to reach LD50.'

'And how many do you believe she had taken, Doctor?'

The coroner looked at his notes. He always found himself referring to his notes when it came to this one particular detail, because it still shocked him. He needed the black-and-white proof. 'Based on our findings, Suzie McCallum had ingested somewhere in excess of a dozen Ecstasy tablets.'

'Excuse me, Doctor. I'm not sure I heard you correctly,' Scott affected a dramatic, shocked posture for the Court. 'Did you just say that Suzie McCallum had taken at least 12 tablets of Ecstasy?' He waited for the confirmation. It didn't come. Even better.

'No, that's not actually what I said, Mr. Scott,' he corrected firmly. 'What I said was that Suzie McCallum had *ingested* approximately a dozen Ecstasy tablets. I didn't say she had *taken* a dozen Ecstasy tablets.'

'Ingested, taken. Tomato, tomata. Is there a difference, Doctor?' the attorney asked.

'There is, particularly when it involves a suspicious death,' he explained.

'What are you suggesting?' the attorney continued. It was all he could do not to take a moment to congratulate himself. This couldn't be going any better than if he had scripted the doctor's testimony himself.

'I'm not suggesting anything, Mr. Scott,' the coroner stated. 'I'm telling you that in a suspicious death where an overdose either directly or indirectly contributes to the cause, a determination must be made as to whether or not it was self-inflicted, hence 'taken' or if the person unknowingly ingested it.'

One. Two. Three. Four.

'In other words, Doctor, whether it was a suicide…or a homicide.'

* * * * *

She drifts in and out of consciousness for the better part of a day. She remembers hazy images of white, indistinguishable figures floating around her. Are they angels? *Fuck.* Is she dead?

No, she wasn't dead, because if she really was, she wouldn't hear the bits and pieces of strange conversations taking place around her. 'Conversations that contain information that angels probably didn't need to know, wouldn't need to know,' Jessica's mind decides.

The soft nurse voice explains to another harsher male voice how Megan is doing. What her toxicity levels are today.

How the nurse voice calmly and knowingly answers each of the other men voices' questions. Had Megan woken up? Had she said anything? Had the toxicity reports come back yet showing exactly what was in her system? Was there alcohol? Were there any traces of drugs?

She hears the distinctive 'snap, snap, snap' of a binder releasing its three-ring talons. Her body involuntarily twitches. She then hears the successive flapping of paper pages back and forth on a harried flight. Finally, an answer.

According to the nurse voice, Megan had a blood alcohol level only slightly over the legal limit. Not a huge concern.

However, in the nurse voice's opinion, the real worry was the level of Ecstasy. Megan had enough in her system to have potentially killed her. She was one very lucky young lady, indeed. They all agreed.

Jessica had to agree, too. She was lucky.

Lucky that she was smarter and could think so far ahead of most everyone else. Lucky she was the very proud recipient of physical attributes that allowed her to seduce her way into most things, or even better, out of them. Lucky that she was prepared to do whatever it took to survive, to take control, to win.

But what is giving her the biggest high at this very moment, as she lies there, eyes closed, chest barely rising, her mind so easily pretending, is what she hears the voices say about Mama.

The nurse voice asks someone if it is true. Had Mama taken an overdose? Had she tried to kill herself? Had she been trying to kill Megan, too? Had she swallowed a handful of Ecstasy?

Fuck. The voices aren't yet giving her what she wants. She doesn't want to know if Mama had tried to kill herself. She couldn't care a less if they thought Mama had intentionally taken an overdose. And as for the handful of Ecstasy, no, no, no. *Fuck. It wasn't just a handful, people. It was 17 to be exact,* Jessica wants to say out loud, but knows she mustn't. Can't.

She knows it was 17, because that's the number she counted out, specifically, intentionally. One for each miserable, fucking year she had spent with Mama.

What she wants the voices to say is whether or not Mama is dead. Is she free? Free of Mama? Free to be Jessica forever?

A machine that sits discretely next to her bed, monitoring her heart, suddenly comes to life, its electronic beat quickening. It's going to give her away. She can't control her heart rate. Can't quite control the rush she is feeling. But the nurse voice unwittingly gives her an out.

'Megan,' the nurse voice says. 'Megan, can you hear me?' mistakenly thinking the increased monitor activity signaled her awakening.

'Megan,' she hears, her thoughts momentarily stalled. She simply decides to listen, 'there's a Detective McNeill here who would like to ask you a few questions. Do you think you could open your eyes for a bit and speak with him, hon?'

She keeps her eyes closed. She needs another moment to pull herself together. Well, to pull Megan together, really. She has to become Megan without actually becoming Megan. She has to get this right. She won't get another chance.

She allows her eyes to open, fluttering gently. That's good. That's exactly what Megan would do, ever so gently. A look of bewilderment spreads across her face. A visibly shaking hand reaches up to cover her mouth in alarm. A weak voice cries out, 'Where am I?' Mama? Where's Mama?'

Not a dry, fucking eye in the room. She really should get herself an agent. That was one Oscar winning moment, Jessica girl.

That is also the moment she finds out. The moment they circle round her hospital bed and tenderly hold her hands in theirs. That is the exact moment she learns Mama is dead...*finally*.

That is also the exact moment when everyone in the room believes the heart monitor spikes erratically as a result of Megan's sudden and uncontrollable grief that slowly turns to hysteria, then climaxes to the very brink of irrepressible laughter.

Poor Megan, they all think. *What an unfortunate girl.*

Chapter Ten

'Detective McNeill, when were you finally able to speak to Ms. McCallum?' Blair Scott asked.

'My partner and I spoke to her the day after she was admitted to the hospital. January 2,' he indicated. 'Unfortunately, we weren't able to get much from her,' he remembered.

'Why was that, Detective?'

'When we informed Megan of her mother's death, she became hysterical and had to be mildly sedated. When she had calmed down a little, we explained to her that we were not there to upset her, but we did need to ask her some questions to help us figure out what had happened,' he explained. 'We asked her what she remembered about that night. But she couldn't remember much. She remembered getting ready for the party with her mother. She remembered her mother mixing one of her 'special potions,' then her mother leaving to go and meet some friends. After that, she says she remembers nothing,' he added.

'So, she didn't remember her mother returning with any guests?'

'No,' the detective answered.

'She didn't recall if she had any more to drink or not?'

'No,' once again the detective concurred.

'She didn't remember having had sex with anyone that night?'

'No.'

'She didn't remember having had sex with two men that night, is that correct?' the attorney pushed.

'Yes,' the detective affirmed. People shuffle in their seats with growing discomfort from the rapid-fired questions, each one more unsettling than the last. The extent of what happened that night was revealing itself. Slowly. Painfully.

The attorney approached. 'Detective, can you please tell this court what you believe occurred that night. What you believe happened?

'None of us will ever know with absolute certainty, but we believe that Ms. McCallum's mother intentionally mixed Ecstasy with alcohol in a drink she then gave to Megan.'

The attorney interjected. 'Are you aware of whether or not that was the first time Megan's mother had made her one of her "special potions"?'

'I believe she had done it before. On more than one occasion.'

Out of the corner of his eye, Blair Scott saw more than half the jury members make quick notations in their notepads. It was a good sign. They were really paying attention to every detail.

'My apologies for the interruption. Please continue, Detective,' the attorney said.

'We believe when Suzie arrived back at the apartment that night with the two men she had picked up at a local bar, things immediately got out of control. The men turned their attentions to Megan right away and I believe Suzie became jealous. She probably thought Megan was an eager and willing participant, because she never resisted. Never objected when the men started to touch her. We believe that both Suzie and Megan were so intoxicated that neither was fully capable of realizing what was actually happening to either of them or to the other,' he explained.

'We also believe that both men had sex with Megan first. Most assuredly without her consent and most likely without her full knowledge, because of the effects of the alcohol and drugs. Megan was probably very close to unconsciousness by the time her mother returned to the apartment with the men,' he added.

'I feel there are two possible scenarios for what happened next. It was during that time that Suzie either absent-mindedly began feeding herself Ecstasy and chasing them down with alcohol, or intentionally took them. Either way, she took them, one after the other, as she watched the men rape her daughter,' he added with barely contained restraint, 'and did absolutely nothing about it.'

He paused to take a sip of water from the glass to his left, then continued. 'By the time the men finished with Megan, we believe Suzie was on the verge of passing out. But the men didn't care. They each took their turn with Suzie and it is during this time that I believe she must have vomited and subsequently choked to death.'

'And do you believe, Detective, that it was one of those men who made the 911 call that night?' Scott asked.

'I do,' he confirmed.

Scott stopped. Thought for a moment, then asked what everyone else in the Court had to be thinking, must be thinking. 'Detective, based on the evidence you have and your many years of experience on the police force, especially with the Homicide Division, do you believe that the defendant, Megan McCallum, was intentionally drugged?'

'I do.'

'And is it also your belief that Suzie McCallum was the person who drugged Megan?'

'Yes.'

Two down. Two to go.

'Is this Court to also understand that it is your conclusion that Suzie McCallum, whether intentional or not, is responsible for her own death?'

'Yes.'

'And my final question, Detective,' the attorney promised. 'Is it also your determination that Suzie McCallum's one intention that night was to kill her own daughter?'

'In my opinion? Without a doubt, *yes*.'

Chapter Eleven

Just a few days after being released from the hospital and into her Aunt Linda's care, the detectives came to the house to explain to Jessica what they believed happened 'that night.' They wanted her to hear it first, to try to understand it before anyone else, before everyone else.

It was also only a few days after she learned she'd never have to go back to Mama's apartment again. Just a few days after she had become used to the sparks that tasered her mind every time she heard '*poor Megan*' or '*that unfortunate girl*' whispered behind her back.

Her Aunt had asked her to please go to her room while she spoke privately with the detectives, 'there's a dear.' She hadn't asked her to close her bedroom door, though. She hadn't told her not to listen.

Nor did Aunt Linda say that it probably wasn't in good taste to smile when the ugly details of Mama's death were discussed. Or high-five the air when she heard them express their sincere sympathy to Aunt Linda because 'poor Megan' had been an undeserving victim of her mother's 'disturbed behavior.'

But it wasn't all misery and misfortune for dear Aunt Linda. They also brought with them a silver lining. They wanted her to know that they couldn't wait to see who Megan would become. What she would become. After all, she had survived horrific experiences, and therefore, must be destined for great things. She's special.

Her Aunt had then summoned her to the living room to tell her why the detectives had come. They were going to close out their file now, because they had all the information they needed. Mostly, they wanted to thank her personally for all her help.

They said how nice it was to meet her, to get to know her. How they admired her, how strong she is, and how brave she was.

They wished her all the best.

They let her know that they are always 'here' for her, should she ever need anything. Or, if by any chance, she remembered something and 'just wanted to talk.' Anything at all from '*that night*' that they're still all so sorry about.

The smile she returns is vague, mechanical, pretend. After all, she had had a great teacher. One of the best. She had had Mama.

Everything seemed almost too easy. Everything was coming together so perfectly.

Jessica had less than a year to master being Megan and then she would be out of here. She was biding her time, just waiting for her 18th birthday, the universal benchmark of freedom.

She wasn't just sitting around and waiting, though. She'd been a busy girl, a very busy girl.

She was going to make a fresh start, a new start. Settle in a place where no one knew her *or* Mama.

She must be patient, though. She'd come so far. Been through so much in such a short time, especially for 'someone so young' as everyone was constantly reminding her.

When she turns 18, she'll find some place far away where she can finally let the true Jessica out for good, or bad. It would all depend on how pissed off she was by then.

* * * * *

'Ms. Foster,' Blair Scott asked, 'after Megan came to live with you, how long did she stay?'

'She was with me for a little over ten months. Until just after her 18th birthday,' she answered.

'And during that time, what was Megan's demeanor like? Her behavior?'

Ms. Foster shrugged her shoulders subtly and answered. 'I don't know. She seemed remarkably good, under the circumstances.' She thought back. 'She was quiet, but then she was always pretty quiet as a child, too, so that didn't seem unusual.'

'And following the New Year's Eve incident, Ms. Foster, did Megan receive any psychological counseling?' the attorney asked.

'Oh, yes,' she assured the court. 'I insisted. She had a one-hour session every other day for the first month after the incident, then it became less frequent as time went on and the psychologist felt she was improving.'

'Did Megan's psychologist ever contact you over the course of treatment to give you a report on her progress?'

'Yes, as her legal guardian, I was very much involved,' she confirmed. 'I believe we spoke at least a few dozen times.'

'And what was the general nature of these conversations?'

'Well, she said she thought Megan was making remarkable strides, but obviously had some challenges ahead of her,' she explained. 'Megan was still quite reserved, but the doctor felt that was just her basic nature. Time and trust would help bring her out of her shell a little more. She just needed time…time to heal.

'The last time I met with the psychologist, she wanted me to know that she felt it had been a blessing of sorts that Megan had passed out that night, because she couldn't remember most of what had happened. Wouldn't probably ever remember most of what had happened,' she was grateful for that, at least. 'The doctor felt that, that was why Megan was handling everything so well, dealing with things so well, because she had no actual memory of most of it.'

The lawyer took a moment to consult his notes. 'Ms. Foster, there came a day when Megan said she was ready to move out. To be on her own, is that correct?'

'Yes, it wasn't long after she turned 18. She came to me and said she loved me, she appreciated everything I had done for her, and that I would always, always be a huge part of her life,' she remembered fondly. 'But she felt it was time to move on with her life and to get on with her life.'

'Did Megan know what she wanted to do? What she was going to do?'

'Surprisingly, yes,' her Aunt recalled. 'She had apparently put a lot of thought into it before speaking to me...and effort, too. She applied to a very good university and was excited because she had just been accepted.'

'What program had Megan been accepted into?'

'Psychology, of all things,' she said. 'Megan thought it would help her get better. To become a better person, she said. And in turn, she could help others.'

'Had Megan discussed her 'plan' with the psychologist? Did she feel Megan was ready to take such a big step?' the attorney asked.

'She was reluctant at first, but Megan met with her several times and finally convinced her that she was ready to at least try, if she were just given the opportunity,' she recalled. 'She said she had earned the right to at least try.'

'So, the psychologist finally agreed, then?' Scott wanted to hear the words. He needed the jury to hear the words.

'Yes, she did. She said Megan had obviously put a great deal of thought into her future. A future that seemed to have an unmistakable purpose and a carefully planned sense of direction, although Megan never fully elaborated on what those were. She just kept assuring us she knew what she was doing and to trust her.

'The psychologist felt that Megan's decision and ability to set goals and follow through on them demonstrated that perhaps she was ready. She believed that by going off to school, Megan would be taking a healing step along her continuing road to recovery and eventually she gave Megan her blessing,' she added.

'And where was it, Ms. Foster, that Megan was going to continue her studies?' Scott asked.

'It was on the other side of the country. Might as well have been the other side of the world, because even being an hour away from her was going to be too far for me,' she smiled, unconvincingly, pathetically.

Chapter Twelve

Everyone had seemed stunned by her decision to go away to school.

No, it's not too soon. *Yes*, she's ready.

Yet, no one said much about her decision to study Psychology, which really pissed her off.

She had spent hours memorizing what she would say. She had practiced what she would say for weeks before. In front of a mirror, so she could match the applicable facial expressions to their appropriate words. They had to be right. Their timing had to be perfect.

Megan had told Aunt Linda that she wanted 'to make herself a better person.' The matching facial expression she had adopted was one she'd recently seen on television. A well-known celebrity was visiting a third-world country and during an interview had said she was doing this to bring attention to the crisis in that country, because she wanted to make a difference in the world and she wanted to 'become a better person.'

She remembers the expression on the celebrity's face at that exact moment. That was obviously the applicable expression, so that was the expression she chose. The expression she used.

While her expression was pretend, her reason was true. Very true. She did want to make herself better.

Well, the real truth was, that was only part of the whole truth. What she really wanted was to make Jessica better.

Not better as in feeling better. *Fuck.* She felt great, stronger, and healthier. She looked pretty great, too. Fit, firm, blonde hair even longer and fuller. Eyes just as blue, but maybe a bit rounder from some of life's surprises she'd encountered along the way. All in all, a stunning package, a gorgeous package. A package all the guys wanted to inspect, unwrap, and paw over. A package all the girls envied, but never, ever felt threatened by. There was something definitely 'off about that girl.'

No, no. When she said 'better' she meant 'smarter.' Always-a-step-ahead-of-everyone-else kind of smarter. She had to become more resourceful, more skillful, shrewder, and more calculating.

To do that, she had to understand how the mind worked. How it processed information. How it could become so fragile that it was easily manipulated by others or how it could become so adept at using that knowledge to effortlessly control others.

Everything was going fairly smoothly. Had been going more or less okay since she'd arrived at the university.

She kept to herself most of the time, except when a course required her to participate in a group paper. That meant being around people. Even worse, strangers. People strangers. She still had trouble with that.

In her first semester, she had only been required to participate in two group papers. She always made sure she was the first to volunteer to be the group's official note taker. This justified her not having to speak much, look at anyone much or give a shit much. It was working for her. Apparently, it was working just fine for everyone else, too.

But it was also those times she found the most challenging, because they were unpredictable times and unpredictable situations. Full of unpredictable people.

It was those times. Those times that jammed her head with chaotic noises and disorderly voices. It was too much, all at once.

It was those times when she found it hardest to control the twitches undulating just beneath the surface of her skin like ripples on water, only these didn't make her feel warm and fuzzy.

Those were the times when her brain couldn't quite concentrate, because her mind was being distracted by tiny shards of random images. Flipping by, one after the other, like sepia-toned bits and pieces of old, silent movie films…jerky, spastic, and incomplete.

She senses there's a mystery within the bits. A story within the pieces. But she's only getting fragments, edited fragments for now.

She is, if nothing else, patient. Unbelievably, remarkably, mind-bogglingly patient. She'd had to be. She'd needed to be. She still must be.

It was in her third year at university that things began to change. Her classes required that she do more group papers. Not coincidentally, it was around this same time that her silent movie images began to unspool more often in her mind.

Started to turn from sepia-toned to color. Come to life as the shards turned into pieces. The pieces into tiles. And the tiles, working collectively, slowly forcing themselves together to try to make whole the shattered mosaics littering her psyche.

She closes her eyes at these moments and breathes deep, slow, and steady. She mustn't react. Mustn't lose control.

'Jessica,' a voice reaches her. 'Jessica, are you alright?'

She opens her eyes to find *him* standing there. Looking gorgeous, and he knows it. He has no doubts about it.

Zach Augustus. Popular, tall, dark, muscular, and lean. So fucking hot and talking to her. He's actually talking to *her*.

'Yes, I'm fine, thanks,' she can barely speak. 'I was just taking a few deep breaths of fresh air. Sleepy. Late night studying,' she lies through a pretend yawn.

He smiles at her. That smile, that body. The body and the smile that make females willingly cast aside their reputations for a one-night tumble in the 'Zach Sack.'

They knew his game, they recognized his agenda, but it didn't matter. He was a prize. He was *the* prize on campus.

'Want to get a coffee?' he suggests. 'Might help you wake up or at least stay awake for your next class.' He laughs. It's a confident laugh. But she recognizes a hint of insincerity there. She should know. She had reinvented insincerity when she invented Jessica. She categorizes her feelings at that exact moment. '*Uneasy.*'

'No thanks,' she decides. 'I'm almost late for my next class as it is. I really should get going,' she adds and turns to flee.

'How about a raincheck, then,' he tries to persuade her. 'Please.' To sway her. 'Pretty please.' She thinks his pleas are genuine and lets her guard down.

She didn't know that Zach would have done anything or said anything. After all, he had a lot of reasons riding on her answer. Two hundred and forty, to be exact.

Chapter Thirteen

Zach was persistent, almost relentless. A man on a mission. In the end, he proved irresistible, and he really did seem to like her.

Liked to be around her, wanted to be around her, even. Seeking her out, calling her. Leaving funny little notes for her in the most unexpected places. She'd never had anyone pay her this kind of attention before—caring, protective and patient— the kind of attention that didn't expect something, anything, in return. *Is that possible*, she wondered.

They went out for coffee a few times. Nothing serious. Nothing romantic. Nothing, at first.

Then one night, as he was dropping her off at her apartment, something changed. He came around, opened her car door, and helped her out. Always the gentleman.

Only this time he didn't let go of her hand. He held on to it, keeping it warm and safe within his own large, strong hand. He didn't just simply wish her good night and slowly drive off, but rather wrapped his burly arms around her and drew her into him.

What changed is that he looked right into her eyes, captured her gaze, and held it. For what seemed like forever to her. He didn't say a word. She was glad for that, because she was busy. Actually, her mind was busy, listening for her feelings, to her feelings. But there were too many. They were confusing her. Nearly overwhelming her. *Fuck, not now.*

What changed is that he unexpectedly lifted her chin with one cupped hand. Never taking his eyes from hers, he leaned in, slightly parted his moist lips and barely, ever so gently, grazed them across hers.

What changed is that he asked if she'd like to go to an off-campus party with him that coming weekend.

Nothing special. No big deal. Just a few friends getting together, hanging out, enjoying a few drinks. Spend some 'alone' time together. Get to know each other 'better.' What does she think?

She thinks she'd like that. Thank you. Should she bring anything? Would he be able to give her a ride? Great. Thanks, again. What time should she be ready?

She had been readying herself for days by the time he pulled up outside her apartment on that night. It was a beautiful evening. Balmy. Breezy. It should have been perfect.

She hadn't slept much. Hadn't eaten much. Hadn't been to classes at all since Zach's invitation. She had spent the past few days trying to repair the lacerations in her mind caused by the many serrated thoughts that sliced through it. Spent the better part of the past few days trying to tame the twitches that had begun to intensify.

She's got to get control. She has to take control. Especially now.

Zach would never understand. She'd only scare him away. He'd leave her, just like everyone else had ever done. She decided she'd never give him a reason to ever want to leave her. Then she decided she'd never, ever allow him to leave her.

She's wearing a new top that shamelessly molds itself to the shapely contours of her body. Its color complimenting the deep blue of her eyes. Her white skirt, sheer and sexy, made with just enough material to suggest a better view of everything might be possible, if one were so inclined. Old habits die hard.

She's chosen a pair of sandals that accentuate the length and leanness of her legs. The kind with long, flowing ribbons for laces. Ribbons that twist and twine their way in a sensual reptilian, crisscross pattern around her slim ankles, slithering their way up to coil in a knot at the top of her tanned calves.

Her hair, freshly washed and blown downy dry, flows over her shoulders like a shimmering, gold-infused stream of silk. Along the entire length of her back, finally coming to rest against the small hallow at the top of her perfectly formed ass.

A pair of gold hoop earrings bounce gently against the slender sides of her graceful neck with each step she takes. A matching gold chain around one delicate ankle jingles in tempo to her accomplished gait.

He's outside his car by the time she reaches him. He's leaning up against the passenger door, so she has nowhere to go. No time for her to take a moment to recover from the look he's giving her. Had been giving her from the moment she opened the front door of her building to this very second, standing just a foot away from him.

'What?' she asks, looking at him uneasily. 'What's wrong? Why are you looking at me like that?'

'Nothing's wrong, believe me,' he answers immediately. 'You look amazing,' he insincerely professes. He learned very early on in life that even the weakest attempt at flattery would get him everywhere…and anything. He leans in and kisses her tenderly on the lips. 'Incredible,' he whispers in her ear. He steps back and opens the car door for her. 'Let's go, baby doll. I've got a special night planned for us.' *Tic.*

He closes the door, walks around the car, slides into the driver's seat, and reaches his hand up to start the engine. Suddenly, an arm strikes out and a hand wraps around his, holding it there in mid-air. Gentle, but firm.

'Zach,' Jessica says quietly, 'I'd really appreciate it if you wouldn't call me that. Someone else used to call me that. But that was a long time ago, a lifetime ago. So, don't call me that. Don't ever call me baby doll again, okay? Please.'

'Sure, sorry,' he dismissively apologizes, knowing that's what she wants to hear. 'I didn't know. If I had, I would never have said it.' He smiles at her, leans over, and kisses her gently. 'Forgive me?'

She wonders if this is what love is like, is supposed to feel like. She doesn't honestly know. She's never been in love before. Never really been loved before either. Mama always told her...constantly reminded her...that she'd better love herself, because nobody else ever would. But Mama had been wrong about so many other things, so many other times. Maybe she was wrong about that too?

'Here,' he hands her a bottle of iced tea from a cooler he had behind her seat and gets one for himself, before pulling away from the curb.

'Thanks,' she accepts the bottle, untwists the cap, and takes a sip. It's cool. Refreshing. She takes a few more sips and uses the time to think about him. Think about how he makes her feel. How special he makes her feel. She lets the feeling slowly sneak its way in. No one's ever made her feel this kind of special before. She wants it. She deserves it. Surely, she's earned it.

They cruise along a twisty road as it hugs the side of a hill, then weave their way past the city limits, beyond the city lights, out through the countryside.

Past mustard fields that have faded from vibrant yellow to a royal gold in the setting sun.

Past bulky black shadows of the odd farmhouse, all dark save for a single light that glows eternal from a nearby barn.

Past well-lit, paved roads to a dark, dirt-packed trail. Past wide-open spaces and into a claustrophobic, wooded jungle. Past the point of no return.

Chapter Fourteen

Zach's friend Cory was left behind with specific instructions that he was to wait an hour after Zach and another friend Bruce left, then wake Jessica and drive her back to her apartment in the city.

She slowly comes awake and finds herself lying on a sofa, fully clothed, a warm blanket tucked around her and a small pillow under her head. How sweet. Zach must have done that, because she doesn't remember lying down, doesn't remember falling asleep, can't remember most of the previous night, actually.

She hears the distinctive 'snap, snap' of someone's fingers trying not so gently to rouse her from her mind's fuzziness. *Tic.* A voice she doesn't recognize is telling her she has to go, has to leave, has to get out. Tells her Zach and Bruce left earlier and says he is supposed to give her a ride back to her apartment. He'll be waiting for her outside. *So, get up. Hurry up.*

Her head is fuzzy. Her thoughts hazy. Her memory in splinters. She rubs her forehead, trying to appease the voices.

She makes it to a nearby bathroom just in time to vomit into the toilet. It's a while before she can come out. Feels steady enough to want to come out. When she finally does, she goes in search of her ride. She needs a ride in order to get to where she needs to go, and right now she needs to go to where the answers are. She needs to go to where Zach is.

Why had Zach left without her? What was so important that he would just take off and leave her here? That he even could take off and fucking leave her? *Tic.*

And who the fuck is Bruce?

She finds Cory sitting impatiently in his car at the front of an old cabin she has no memory of, in the middle of a nowhere she has no memory of. He never looks at her, never acknowledges her existence.

'Is something wrong with Zach?' she asks as she gets in and he starts the car, quickly pulling away. 'Why did he leave without me?' she wants to know.

'How the fuck should I know' is the only response she gets, before he turns the volume up on the stereo. Up to a level that left no room for conversation.

She spends the entire drive battling for self-control. Struggling to at least appear in control. 'There has to be a perfectly good explanation,' she assures herself. 'Or if not a perfectly good explanation, then an acceptably logical explanation. There just has to be something.' *Tic.*

She doesn't remember a lot about the long drive. Doesn't know how much second-hand smoke she was forced to inhale along the way. Thankfully couldn't recall which songs he sang off-key to.

She focuses her attention on where they are going and where they have just come from. She's stuffing every turn, every road sign, every notable landmark they pass into her head so it's so full she won't be able to think of anything else. Anyone else, especially Zach.

When the car finally pulls up in front of her apartment building, she can't get out fast enough. She can't get into her apartment soon enough.

She has to wash herself thoroughly, so that she can make a clean start with Zach. She needs to wash the bad thoughts from her mind and cleanse her whole body, so she can purge whatever it was that made Zach want to go away, to get away from her.

The first thing she does is strip off her clothes. The first thing she notices is a strange, opalescent blotch on her underwear. The second is bruises on both of her wrists, then faint ligature marks on her ankles. A small scratch on the inside of one thigh and a deep bite mark above one nipple. *Tic. Toc.*

* * * * *

She called Zach. After the first day of calling him once in the morning and once in the afternoon and him not picking up and her not leaving a message, she had called him every hour on the hour the second day. He didn't answer any of those. And she didn't leave a message with any of those either.

On the third day, she began to leave messages on his voicemail: calm messages, concerned messages, caring messages, rehearsed messages. 'Hi, Zach. This is Jessica. I just wanted to call and thank you for taking me to the party the other night. But I really want to talk to you. I want to make sure you're okay…that we're okay, actually…because I haven't seen you or talked to you since the party. Please call me. Thanks. I guess that's it for now. Okay. Well then. Talk to you soon. Bye.'

By day four, her messages for Zach were fractured. 'It's Jessica again, Zach. I…look, I'd really… Can you please… I just need to talk to you. Please just call me, okay?'

By the fifth day, her messages to Zach were desperate. 'What's going on? Why won't you return any of my calls, Zach? Can you please call me back? No, no, you *have* to call me back, Zach.'

By the sixth day, her messages to Zach were demanding. 'If you don't call me back by the end of today, I swear I'll find another way to talk to you, Zach. Either on the phone or in person, one way or another, you are going to talk to me. Got it,

Zach? Don't make me come looking for you, okay? I think you understand me now, Zach. Don't you?' Yet again, no response.

Under the cover of darkness on the evening of the seventh day, Jessica decided to make her way to Zach's fraternity house. She'd never been inside before, because Zach had never invited her. But she had been to the house itself. On a number of occasions, such as when she had followed Zach home after they first met and later when she knew the way to his house so well by herself. Found herself there so often. Where she sat outside the old, stately home watching him through first one window, then another and another. So many windows. So many possibilities.

That night, there were a lot of lights on in the house, as usual. It took her less than a minute to find him. Sitting in his favorite chair, in his favorite room. The large screened-in porch at the back of the house, usually the quietest part of the house. Only this night, it wasn't so quiet.

There was laughter. So much laughter, but only one voice speaking. Only one voice was responsible for summoning all that laughter. She'd recognize that voice anywhere. It was Zach's voice.

It was his voice that was addressing an audience. Zach's voice thanking his followers for the honor they had apparently just bestowed upon him. How he gratefully accepts on behalf of 'frat brothers everywhere.'

It was his voice she heard mildly protest when someone asked him to 'start at the beginning' and another pleaded 'don't leave out any details.'

She edges a little closer, yet still hidden beside the dense row of cedars sheltering one side of the porch. She can't help but smile. She senses an air of excitement. Everyone is chanting 'spill it' encouragement to Zach.

She's caught up in the moment, then just as caught up in guilt, her own guilt. Something wonderful had obviously happened to Zach this past week, which certainly explains why he hadn't returned her calls. Because he hadn't been able to return her calls all week. He'd been busy.

But, why didn't she know what had happened? Why hadn't she heard anything about it?

If only she hadn't decided to sit in the dark that night. Outside his house. If only she hadn't decided to listen in the dark outside his house that night.

Chapter Fifteen

It's been a hushed tradition for most of the fraternity's existence. At the end of just the second week of each semester, every member in the house had to write down on a piece of paper the name of a girl in one of his classes who he believes would never, ever agree to go on a date with him. Not in a million fucking years. Someone who was way out of his league.

Twelve pieces of the paper are put into a hat this semester, each containing a name. Attached to each piece of paper is a twenty-dollar bill. The amount of each member's entry fee.

What's at stake? Whether or not this semester's 'Designated Humper' can ultimately score with the girl whose name he draws.

The 'DH' had the entire semester to secure a win, but in order to claim the prize, he had to have proof. Irrefutable evidence that he had, indeed, done 'the deed' and had done so with the 'chosen one.'

If he did, then the whole purse would go to him. All two-hundred-and-forty dollars' worth this semester. If not, then the money would be split between the others. They'd get their money back, plus a little. No harm? No foul?

On the other hand, should the necessary proof of the DH's victory be forthcoming, the results were usually well worth the money sacrificed. It's viewed as a win-win.

This semester's 'Designated Humper' had already been decided by way of a vote. His name was Zach Augustus.

As part of the ritual, the 'DH' is the one who then randomly draws just one girl's name from the hat. The name Zach drew was not the one he had personally submitted, thankfully. In fact, he had no idea who she was. *Who's Jessica McCallum?*

He's told that she's a third-year Psych student who lives by herself off campus. Keeps to herself mostly, quiet, definitely bright, and drop-dead gorgeous.

'So, what's the catch? Why is her name even in the hat?' He's quickly reminded that, as the 'DH,' he doesn't need to know why her name is in the hat. He just needs to know that her name was in the hat and that her name was the one he drew out of the hat. She was the target. She was his target.

Zach had no doubts as to whether or not he could win. He'd never met a girl he couldn't charm. Often right out of her pants, usually on the first date.

His dark, European looks always drew at least a second glance from others, male and female alike. His relaxed manner, easy smile, and premeditated charm made him an attractive package. An irresistible turn-on to most.

Victims already littered his just-getting-started past. Emotional casualties. Each one a personal conquest. Each one memorable. Memorable because of the rush he got when the girl finally figured it out. Figured out that she had been just another notch in his belt. Another hump to his headboard. She didn't mean a thing. It didn't mean a thing. *Next*!

It had taken him a few days to track down this Jessica McCallum. He saw her for the first time across the campus courtyard, loaded down with books and sitting on a bench under a big oak tree.

His fraternity brothers hadn't been wrong. She was gorgeous; tall, blonde, and beautiful. He couldn't help the smile that spread across his face. Not only was he going to make some easy money, but it looked like he might actually enjoy this one, too. *Hello, baby doll!*

He watched her from a distance for another few days, before finally approaching her one afternoon and asking if she would like to join him for a coffee. He was surprised when she turned him down right away, saying that she was already late for a class as it was and had to get going.

The very next morning, he easily coaxed Jessica's telephone number out a frumpy secretary who worked in the college's administration office with the promise of a 'night out' and started leaving messages for Jessica; funny little messages, endearing little messages.

Next, he solicited a copy of her class schedule and began leaving little post-it notes everywhere for her; funny little notes, endearing little notes.

And so, it began…slowly, carefully, methodically.

After several months, his persistence paid off and they got together for coffee at Pete's Cafe a few times. He insisted on treating her. She thought it was sweet. He thought it a prudent investment.

He was attentive toward her. Gentlemanly, relaxed and easy to be with. But it wasn't long before he took his talents to the next level. It was time to ask her out. Get her out, away from people. It was time for him to earn his money.

Zach had arranged to meet his fraternity brother, Bruce Marshall, at a predetermined location. A location so out of the way, so off the beaten path, that no one would 'accidently' find it.

It was an old hunt cabin that had once belonged to Bruce's grandfather. Even though it was still in his family, it was rarely used by anyone. It was the perfect place. It was exactly the kind of place he needed to ensure tonight's victory and to guarantee his win.

* * * * *

Jessica had moved into her poky, off-campus studio apartment well ahead of her first semester. She had wanted enough time to get her bearings. She needed to get her bearings, because she had to make a plan. No matter where she went, she made a plan. She always planned two ways in and two ways out. One never knows. One shouldn't get too comfortable.

It was a surprise when someone knocked on her door one morning near the end of her third year. She rarely had anyone come to her door. She was in the middle of painting one wall in her apartment and the interruption was most unwelcome.

It was even more of a surprise when she looked through the peep hole and saw two official looking men in dark trench coats, sunglasses masking their eyes, and detective badges held up for her scrutiny. *Fuck.* She opened the door and greeted them with a dripping paintbrush and her best pretend smile.

The smell of fresh paint awakened the first of their senses, immediately activating eyes that dart about in an attempt to pinpoint the source. Quickly identified, they come right to the point.

Did she know someone by the name of Zachary Augustus?

Of course, she knew Zach. They had been on a few dates together. 'Why? Has he been a bad boy, Officer?' She was relaxed, teasing.

The officer tells her that Zach may well have been a bad boy, because Zach was now a missing boy.

'No, no, that can't be,' she insists. She had just seen him a few days ago. They had gone out for coffee together. They talked about what they were going to do this weekend. There's been a mistake. They've made a mistake.

'Been re-decorating, Ms. McCallum?' one of the detectives nonchalantly asks her. The good thing about professional curiosity is that it can easily be disguised within an innocent enough civilian question.

'Excuse me?' Jessica's brows come together ever so slightly. This is her play, now. She's the scriptwriter, the producer, the demanding director but, above all, she's the star.

She sees the same detective's eyes scan toward one particular wall as he gestures with a jut from his sturdy chin. Her eyes follow his. 'No,' she replies just as nonchalantly. 'I simply painted an accent wall…this place really needed some color.' But the truth is hiding in plain sight, veiled behind meticulously applied and prepped wall putty all sheathed beneath a soon-to-be-empty gallon of Home Depot's 'Crazy for You' pink interior paint. *Is irony still considered irony if it's lost on others?* she wonders.

They want to take her to their office and ask her a few questions.

Just 'routine,' mind you. Perhaps she knows something. They'd sure appreciate it. So would Zach's distraught family. Anything that might help.

It's a quiet ride, just the three of them. The only sound comes from muffled, disjointed voices being exchanged over the police scanner. Bodiless voices. She wishes they'd stop. Wait. Are they coming from inside the car? Or inside her head? Sometimes, it's just so hard to tell.

At the office, she is led to an interview room and offered a seat. She's left alone for a few minutes. She reminds herself that she's not alone, though. They are out there, watching her. There's always someone watching, listening, and plotting against her. But, she's ready, she's prepared, she's been preparing for so long.

A few minutes later, the door opens and the same two detectives enter. No pleasantries. No niceties. No loitering. They both pull up a chair across from her.

'We record all conversations that take place in these rooms—as a matter of routine, as I mentioned. So, for the record, would you please state your name,' Detective Logan asks.

'Jessica McCallum,' she answers calmly.

'Then, who is Megan McCallum?' the other one wants to know. She doesn't flinch. 'I was Megan McCallum,' she explains calmly. Quietly. 'But I haven't used that name for almost three years now.'

'And why is that, exactly?' the other one now wants to know.

She closes her eyes for a moment, not because she's stalling for a little time, but rather she's buying a little time to access the emotions that will make tears come. She feels the occasion calls for just a few.

Finally, one tiny drop manages to squeeze its way through dense lashes and slides, slowly, down a cheek. 'I didn't want to be Megan any more. I didn't want to be reminded of Megan, because Megan was having a tough time forgetting about the night her mother tried to kill her before committing suicide.' Another tear. Just like she'd practiced. Flawless. 'So, I moved away from the memories. But, mostly, I was moving as far away as I could from being Megan.' *Fuck*, if they only knew how true that was.

The detectives didn't react. They knew all this already. They too, had come prepared. They had done some homework of their own.

'Yes, we're sorry about your loss,' one of them offers in a voice that holds absolutely no trace of empathy, while the other nods in rehearsed, composed agreement.

Everything is hushed. Everyone is quiet. The silence in the room looms large and hungry. Who will be first to feed the monster in the room? She knows it won't be her. It will never be her.

She had studied hard, then applied what she had learned in order to master her patience. Not smug patience, like the kind that says 'told you I was fucking good.' No, no. She means the 'I'm just a dumb blonde with all the time in the world and nowhere to go' kind of patience. She sits tight and waits.

They break first, as she knew they would. 'When was the last time you saw Zach?' they want to know.

'I told you, I saw him a few days ago. We arranged to meet after one of my classes and had coffee together,' she explains.

'Where did you go for coffee?' one asks.

'We went to Pete's over on Main Street,' she answers confidently. 'That's where we always go.'

He makes a note on a pad of paper. 'Do you remember what time it was when you got there?'

'I think it was around 1:30 or 2 o'clock.' The detective adds this information to his notes.

'Did Zach seem upset about anything? Did you notice anything out of the ordinary about his behavior?' the other asks.

'No,' she replies. 'He seemed fine. We were making plans for the weekend. Maybe go to a movie or something.'

The detectives look at each other. They're getting nothing. This is going nowhere. They can read the frustration on each other's face. 'Can you think of any reason why Zach would just suddenly disappear? Without a trace? Without a word to anyone?'

She shakes her head a few times. 'No, I'm sorry I can't. I wish I could help, but I haven't seen him since we left the coffee shop.'

'Do you know where Zach planned on going after he left you?'

Again, she shakes her head. 'No, I don't know that either. I just assumed he was heading back for a class.'

'Did you see Zach get into his car and drive away?' he wants to know.

'No,' she says. 'When we came out of the coffee shop, I went left to go to my place and he turned right. So, I never actually saw where he was going or if his car was even there. I'm sorry.' She squeezes out one last tear.

One detective runs an impatient hand through his hair as both he and his partner simultaneously get up out of their chairs. 'We'll be back in a few minutes. Sit tight.' The door closes behind them, followed by the distinctive click of a manual lock on the outside. Her body reacts. *Tic.* She breathes deep. She recovers her thoughts. Quickly regains control.

She knows they've gone to check out her story. She knows they'll call Pete's. She knows they'll find out that she had been there. At the time she said she had been there. She knows they'll find out she had been with Zach and had met Zach there.

She knows they could, if they wanted to, verify her story by reviewing the coffee shop's video surveillance. Just as she had planned.

It's all good. Jessica's good.

Chapter Sixteen

She's sitting in the protective shadows of the cedar hedges alongside the sun porch at the back of the fraternity house, listening to Zach. She can hear a tone of pride in his voice. She can hear the excitement in others' voices. Finally, someone calls for quiet and the housemates settle down.

She slowly, cautiously takes a quick peek around the cedars and sees that the voice belongs to the guy who had driven her home from the party...Cory. Whatever. *Asshole.*

Cory is standing in front of Zach. 'Before I can officially declare you a true DH, Zach, you must first produce the mandatory proof.'

Zach smiles. This is the moment he'd been waiting for. That they'd all been waiting for: the proof. All two and a half raunchy hours of it. He picks up a remote control, aims it at a CD player in a nearby cabinet, and hits 'Play.' 'Here's all the proof you'll need, plus a little something extra for your viewing pleasure, boys.'

The smile on Jessica's face disappears in an instant. Her hand reaches up and just manages to choke off a sound that threatens to give her away. She can't believe what she is seeing.

On the frat house's big-screen TV, she sees herself lying naked, her wrists and ankles bound to a bed, while Zach fucks her hard. Again, then again. She sees Zach climb off of her image and another frat brother take his place. She recognizes him now standing among the Zach worshipers.

She watches as Zach's frat brothers gather around him. Congratulate him. Pat him on the back with what amounts to pride.

She sees Cory step before Zach and begin to count. *Twenty. Forty. Sixty.* He's counting money into Zach's palms. The others quickly join in. *Eighty. One hundred.* They finally stop at two hundred and forty, but not before one final ear-splitting cheer in recognition of Zach's efforts and his ultimate victory. Most of all, they appreciate the 'best DH evidence ever provided in the history of the fraternity.' Cory declares 'this semester's game officially over' and shakes Zach's hand in one final congratulations.

No, no. The game isn't over. It won't be over until she says it is. And she hasn't had her turn...yet. But she will. She'll make sure of it.

She can't recall how she got home that night or letting herself into her apartment. Nor does she remember going to the kitchen, taking a knife out of a drawer and using it to impulsively and viciously scratch and gouge at one wall.

* * * * *

'Can you please state your name for the record,' Blair Scott began his next witness.

'Cory Banks,' the young man now sitting at the front of the courtroom answered.

'And how is it, Mr. Banks, you came to know the defendant, Ms. McCallum?'

'I met her through a fraternity brother, Zach Augustus,' he admitted.

'When did you first meet Megan, or should I say Jessica, since that is the name you know her by?' the attorney questioned him.

'It was the night Zach took her to Bruce's grandfather's old hunt cabin,' he replied.

'Was there a party planned at the hunt cabin that night?' the attorney asked.

The witness was clearly nervous. He had no intention of ratting out a friend, but he was given no choice. Either he tells what he knows or he would face felony charges himself. It was his decision. So, here he was.

'No,' Cory answered.

'But isn't that where Jessica thought she was going that night? To a party?' he pushed. 'Isn't that what she was told?'

'I guess,' the witness answered quietly.

'Yes or no, Mr. Banks,' the attorney pushed harder. 'I guess' is not a sufficient answer in this court.'

'Then yes, yes that's what Jessica was told. Zach told her that he was going to a party with some friends and asked her if she'd like to go with him,' he finally relented.

'What was the plan that night, Mr. Banks? What had Zach arranged specifically for that night?'

He can't seem to sit still. 'Zach had spiked some iced tea he had packed in the car. He put in about a quarter gram of GHB and gave it to Jessica on the drive to the hunt cabin,' he stated.

'GHB. Isn't that what is more commonly known by your generation as *the date rate drug*?' the attorney asked.

'Yes,' the witness admitted. 'Zach did some research on the internet and found out that GHB was invisible when it was dissolved in liquid and that it wouldn't give off any smell. He was worried about the taste, though, because it's supposed to be salty. So, that's why Zach mixed it with the iced tea. He thought the sweetness of the iced tea would help mask any of the saltiness.'

Apparently, it had. Jessica had consumed the entire bottle of iced tea by the time she and Zach were within a half hour of their final destination. They were just seven minutes away when Jessica passed out completely.

'What happened when Zach and Jessica arrived at the hunt cabin?' Scott asked.

'I was already there, with Bruce. We were waiting for Zach and Jessica,' he continued. 'When Zach showed up, we gave him a hand and carried Jessica into the cabin.'

'What happened then, Mr. Banks?'

He would give anything at this very moment to be anywhere else in the world but here. 'We took her into one of the bedrooms and laid her down on the bed,' he added.

'Isn't it true that Bruce and Zach then stripped Jessica naked while you stood and watched?' he asked.

'Yes,' Cory answered. No shame was apparent. No regrets were obvious. No signs of guilt forthcoming.

'What then?' the attorney continued.

'We tied her wrists and ankles to the bed posts, then Zach had sex with her.'

'And what were you and Bruce doing while Zach was, in the eyes of the law, raping Jessica,' Scott pressed.

'I went to another room, but Bruce stayed behind because he was supposed to videotape the whole thing,' he added coldly.

'And what was the purpose of videotaping these rapes, Mr. Banks?' he asked.

'In order to win the bet, Zach had to prove that he had had sex with Jessica. He decided the best way was to videotape it, then no one would ever be able to question whether he had or not.'

'How many times did Zach have sex with the defendant, Ms. McCallum, that night?' the attorney asked.

'Three times,' Cory reluctantly admitted.

'Did you have sex with Jessica also, Mr. Banks? Did Mr. Marshall? Was that part of your deal with Zach?' he wanted to know.

He'll answer the question. He'll answer all of the questions, because he had nothing to lose. He had made sure he was given full immunity in exchange for his testimony against his friends.

'No,' he answered.

'And what about Bruce Marshall?'

'He had sex with her twice,' he admitted. Scott paced calmly, back and forth.

'So, in total, Ms. McCallum had been raped no less than five times that night, is that correct?'

'Yes.' *Just get it over with*, he told himself.

'And she was unconscious the entire time, is that also correct?'

'Yes, I think so, because she never made a sound. Never moved.' It would all be over. Soon.

'Who was it who left the deep bite mark on one of Ms. McCallum's breasts?' He knew the answer, because he had already endured the unfortunate experience of having to review the contents of the video prior to Jessica's trial.

'Zach,' Cory admitted.

Blair Scott took his time and walked back to refer to some notes. 'What time did you wake Ms. McCallum the next morning and tell her that Zach and Bruce had already left and that you were to drive her back to her apartment?'

'It was around 7:00 or 7:30 in the morning. I remember, because the sun had just started to come up as we were leaving,' he stated.

'How was Ms. McCallum on the drive back? Did she appear to be upset? Was she crying?'

'I don't know, because I had turned the radio up real loud so I wouldn't have to talk to her. I just wanted to get back and drop her off as fast as I could, so I didn't really notice what she was doing.'

'Did she say anything to you when she got out of the car at her apartment?' he asked.

'Yea,' he nodded. 'She told me that if I saw Zach, I was to ask him to call her right away.'

'And did you ever pass that message along to Zach?'

'No.'

'Why not, Mr. Banks?'

'Because I knew Zach wouldn't want to have anything more to do with her,' he finally admitted. 'He got what he wanted from her. He won.'

Chapter Seventeen

At first, the gouged-out wall in her apartment had puzzled Jessica. Then it began to frustrate her. Just what was the significance of the knife marks and slices that had been engraved into the wall, if there even was any significance? She doesn't remember putting them there, but they obviously had to have been made by her. No one else would have done it, could have done it. She was positive no one had crept past her in the night. She had been so vigilant, watchful and on guard in a corner the entire time.

Over the past ten hours, she had come to stand at least eight times, mesmerized, in front of that wall. Running her hands slowly, gently, up and over the knife-slashed veins that zigzagged their way in what appeared to be just a careless configuration. Nothing. Not a hint. Not even a telltale tic.

But, on her ninth visit to the wall, an underdeveloped pebble of possibility suddenly splashed into her brain, creating just the tiniest ripple of recollection.

She reached up and began, once again, to trace each line. This time, though, she closed her eyes and allowed her head to gently turn and twist as she followed along with her mind's eye, her fingertips guiding her as they felt their way.

On her third braille attempt over the wall, her memory suddenly identified an elusive acquaintance with the pattern lying under her touch and she froze; her body perfectly still and absolutely silent.

Not her mind, though. It was in hurried pursuit of images that now raced, unrestrained, in and out, back and forth.

Suddenly, her eyes flew open. She knew what the strange marks meant. What they represented, she remembered.

It was a crude map that led right to the front door of a little known, well-hidden, and rarely used cabin. She had apparently memorized every detail during the dreadful car ride back that morning. But why bother to scratch it into the wall? It's not as though she planned to go back there, ever again.

But, as the minutes passed by, turning into hours, she found herself increasingly drawn to it and drawing inspiration from it. Snatching up a blank piece of paper and a pen, she meticulously copied every detail of the wall, then studied it and memorized it. She memorized it until she felt certain she could find her way there again, especially in the dark.

* * * * *

For a few days, Jessica never left her apartment. She didn't eat much and didn't see the point in taking a shower. What for? She had no plans of seeing anyone and certainly no intention of letting anyone see her. She had more important things to put her energy toward.

She spent most of the time sitting with her back tucked tightly into a corner of her living room. As long as she sat like that, nothing could sneak up behind her and certainly nothing could get by her.

She had to concentrate and couldn't afford any distractions. Distractions led to mistakes. Stupid mistakes that could cost her everything. She wasn't about to let that happen. Jessica had come so far. Too far to give up now, to give in now.

Most of this time, she kept her mind busy. Busy figuring out how to take care of this problem… *What to do about Zach?*

All around her are papers…scrunched up balls of paper. Full sheets of paper with slash marks through them. Hundreds of torn bits of paper. To another person, it might look as though a corporate-sized shredder had been hard at work, but to Jessica, this was how she had taught herself to reconcile the thoughts flying in, out and around her cramped mind.

She writes all her thoughts down on paper, in whatever order they pop into her mind. She writes furiously for several hours at a time, then stops and begins the painstaking process of tearing the thoughts so that each word occupies its own miniature piece of paper.

Next, she arranges the slips of paper into groups, each sorted according to the categories she had made up so long ago: *happy, uneasy, terrified.* She had come to realize over the years that she didn't need any more than those three, couldn't waste time on any more than those three. Everything that happened in life had to be quickly sorted into one of those categories. It was that easy. It had to be that easy, because time was always critical. In order for her to deal with any situation, her mind had to first quickly assess which category it went into, belonged to.

Once the first cluster of sorting is done, she returns to writing down more thoughts and then, after another few hours, tears them into separate pieces. She does this over and over and over, until the voices have hushed. Until there are no more thoughts left. Until her mind is finally empty enough to sleep.

Jessica woke some time the following day, or perhaps it was the day after that. It didn't matter. There was no one in her life who gave a shit about what day it was, so why should she?

She looked at the rows upon rows of scraps of paper lying all around her, but didn't react. She already knew there was some sort of order to it all. There always was. The sight no longer startled her.

All she had to do was look at the pieces of paper. The solution would reveal itself just by the very nature of the way they were categorized.

If there were more pieces of paper in the '*happy*' category, she knew she had nothing to worry about. If there were more pieces in the '*uneasy*' category, she knew she'd best lay low for a while and let whatever it was that was making her feel that way pass.

However, she now knew and recognized that if there were more pieces of paper in the '*terrified*' category, something was going to have to happen. More specifically, something was going to have to happen to someone, someone who represented a threat.

Overnight, the pieces of paper had spoken and left no doubt in her mind. Zach was that 'someone.' As for the 'something'? That was the next task on her have-to list.

At the age of 21, she had moved way beyond must-do. She had learned that she had no commitment to a must-do list. No devotion to it. No faith in it.

A have-to list was just the opposite…it was a personal promise, a responsibility. It was a commitment to herself. Unlike most others in her life, she would never let herself down.

The next few days were spent cleaning up her apartment and preparing for a very special road trip. Removing every last shred of paper. Destroying every possible physical link between her and Zach. She had even filled in the knife gashes in the wall with putty and was now waiting for it to dry before sanding and painting it. Although she doubted whether anyone else would ever be able to decipher the true meaning of the mess on the wall, she wasn't about to test the potential or provoke the possibility.

While waiting for the putty to dry, she headed to the campus library. It wouldn't matter if everyone in the library remembered seeing her, because she had been a regular visitor over the years, like most other students at one time or another.

From her very first day on campus, Jessica had spent a great deal of time in the library, but her interests there were not something she wanted an electronic trail of. She only ever did research in the library where removing a book or two from its shelf and quietly putting her back to a wall in a corner to read it, hour upon hour, would not seem unusual at all. Nor particularly memorable.

There would be no trace of what she read. No trace of where her interests lay. No hint as to where her thoughts were headed. No warning to others.

Chapter Eighteen

It was several days before Jessica felt strong enough and put back together enough to call Zach. This time, she was well-prepared.

She knew she'd probably get his voicemail, but she had prepared for that as well. Hoped for that possibility, actually. She had spent a few hours writing down exactly what she was going to say and then practiced it over and over and over until she felt she had the inflection in her voice just right. The charm, just perfect.

'Hi, Zach, it's Jessica. Look, I know I've been a bit crazy lately and I just wanted to apologize. I was hoping we could get together for one last coffee and then I promise I'll never bother you again, ever,' she assures the machine, followed by a playful giggle. 'Besides, I have something of yours I found in my purse. I guess it must have fallen in when I was in your car the night we went to that party,' she says casually. 'Anyway, let me know if you want to get together at Pete's. Maybe tomorrow afternoon, around 1:30 if that works for you. That would be great. Let me know.'

Of course, she knew there was nothing that had fallen into her purse, but she suspected Zach would either be too curious or just panicked enough to want to find out if there was. She was pretty sure she would be hearing from him…soon…and she did.

Zach agreed to meet her the following day at Pete's for a coffee. He had no intention of ever seeing her again, let alone speaking to her. But the mention of something of his she found from their night together proved too compelling for him to pass up. He just had to find out what it was. He didn't need any loose ends.

Just past 1:30 the next afternoon, Zach arrived at Pete's Cafe. Jessica was already there. Had intentionally arrived a good 15 minutes before him.

Zach walked through the door and casually sauntered over to where he saw Jessica sitting, waiting for him, holding a cup of coffee up in the air to let him know that she had already bought him one.

Before he could say a word, whether it was to reject or thank her for the gesture, Jessica spoke up. 'I'm sorry I've been such a pain in your ass lately,' she offered, all the while forcing herself to look into his eyes, to look directly into his eyes. Not a blink. Not a waiver. 'Consider it a peace offering,' she smiled sweetly at him. 'Please.' She knew the best way to get to someone like Zach. She went straight for his ego, loading him with a false sense of superiority. 'I'm so sorry, Zach. At least let me buy you a cup of coffee.'

She held her breath, waiting. Her entire plan hinged on this very moment. It would all be up to him now. She mustn't force him, couldn't force him. Zach had to be seen voluntarily sitting down at the table with her. Witnesses had to remember the two of them enjoying a cup of coffee and each other's company.

Zach unzips his coat and sits down. No hesitation. No second thoughts. No worries, because he knows there's no way Jessica could remember what happened to her that night. *Fuck, it's a free coffee. Why not?*

'Thanks,' he says half-heartedly as he reaches for the cup, pops the lid and enjoys a long sip. Besides, Pete's always has great coffee brewing.

'So, how have you been, Zach?' Jessica asks, but doesn't actually care what his answer is. She's simply buying time and biding her time.

Time to establish their presence in the cafe. Together, as a couple. Time to create an opportunity for at least one of them to laugh, just loudly enough for others around them to hear and remember. Remember the girl reaching out every so often to touch the arm of the good-looking young man sitting across from her, tenderly, maybe even amorously. An attractive couple. A couple in love?

'I've been good,' Zach answers indifferently. He doesn't bother to ask her the same question. He doesn't care. He takes another gulp of his coffee. He's eager to suck down the contents and get out of there. While Jessica may be stunning to look at and great for the ego to be seen with on campus, there was definitely something different about her. He'd just never quite been able to put his finger on what it was. Nor had anyone else on campus who ever came into contact with her.

'No new adventures?' she teases. She's playing with him like a cunning cat with premeditated claws plays with a vulnerable mouse. It's amusing, for a while. 'Been to any parties? Seen any good videos lately?' she asks.

He shifts uncomfortably in his seat. 'No,' he finally answers. 'Been too busy with classes…and stuff.'

Jessica nods. 'Yeah,' she agrees, 'I know all about stuff. Life's full of stuff…good stuff…bad stuff.' She smiles vacantly at him and laughs loudly, purposefully. It draws the necessary attention from the patrons sitting closest to them.

She's toying with his mind. Trying her best to oh-so-subtly insert just the tiniest shred of uncertainty. She wants to force his emotions to the threshold of an uneasy precipice of possibility. Does she know? Does she? No.

She wants him to experience, even if it's just in the slightest, what's it's like to live almost every moment of every day of your life on edge.

Anxiety begins to fester in his mind, then gnaws at the depths of his belly. It's a feeling he's not familiar with. Doesn't know. He's always confident. Forever sure. Permanently in control.

'So, you said you have something of mine?' he finally asks, trying his best to sound indifferent.

'Oh, that,' she replies easily, 'turns out it wasn't yours after all,' she smiles. 'Belonged to someone else.' Inside, Zach is relieved, but doesn't show any reaction whatsoever.

'Then no need to hang around,' he decides as he quickly finishes his coffee and stands up to leave. But first, Jessica has a few more things to take care of before she can allow him to go.

She asks him for help putting her coat on, feigning a painful shoulder. Next, he's forced to lay one of his large hands on the small of her back when, for no apparent reason, she abruptly stops between two tables, forcing him to bump up against her then come into contact with one of the tables beside them. 'Sorry,' he offers quietly to a couple sitting at the table who look up at him…at them…at that very moment.

He only opens the front door of the cafe and holds it for her, because he's trying his best to move her along. He's anxious to get out of there. To get away from her.

Before he knows it, Jessica turns to him, stands up on tippy toes and plants a quick, soft kiss on one of Zach's cheeks, then wraps her arms around him. To others, it appears to be a hug, but pretend hugs are so hard to spot, to recognize, from a distance.

Each then turns in the opposite direction on the sidewalk in front of the cafe and seemingly walks out of the other's day.

All this in full view of everyone and anyone who is watching. Every detail, expression, and touch captured neatly on surveillance cameras positioned both inside and out front of the cafe. All unfolding as intended. As so diligently calculated.

Now it was time to make sure Zach understood that the game wasn't over. It wasn't going to be over until she had taken her turn.

But, not yet. Not quite. Patience, Jessica.

* * * * *

She walks away from Zach, forcing herself not to look back. She silently counts each step she takes, not because she cares how many there are or that a certain number holds a particular significance. Well, not this time, anyway.

No, this time, counting strides simply keeps her mind focused on the task. Keeps her on track. Appearing casual, yet focused, to others around her. Just another sleep-deprived student out for a breath of fresh air.

One, two…I'm coming for you.

Three, four…better lock your door.

She casually makes her way along the block before taking an abrupt turn to the left, through a shadow-less alleyway that runs between the old buildings and left again at the end. She's now heading in the same direction she knows Zach is going. Doubling back behind him.

Five, six…men are pricks.

Seven, eight…I can hardly wait.

She can't see him at the moment, but knows he's somewhere up ahead. Not too far up ahead either. He has a favorite, out-of-the-way spot where he always parks his car when he goes to Pete's Cafe. The sleek, white Corvette is 'his one true love'; protects her at all times. Shelters her everywhere, from everything. *He cares more about his fucking car than he does about anything or anyone else,* Jessica reminds herself.

But she's confident that Zach will soon come to realize the error of his ways. To understand just what an unfortunate choice he had made. Accept responsibility and express his remorse. She's just as confident that she can help Zach effectively express his feelings.

For Jessica, pain and agony are partners in life. Because without pain, there can be no sound…and without sound, there can be no manifestation of authentic agony. Soul mates.

And she was more than willing to keep trying until she found the perfect approach. The 'best line of attack.' She represses the sudden urge to giggle. She mustn't draw attention to herself. She has to blend in. No one must remember her being in this place at this time.

She rounds a familiar corner and immediately spots Zach, sitting in the driver's seat of his car, one hand draped out the open window, music faintly coming from the stereo.

She approaches Zach's car and its open window. 'Hey, Zach.'

He doesn't answer her right away, but is surprised to suddenly find her standing there. 'Jess,' he forces a less-than-genuine smile at her.

'Didn't I just see you a few minutes ago?' he asks, his tone delivering a fusion of uncomfortable playfulness and panic.

'Yes, you did, Zach,' Jessica teases seductively. 'We just had coffee together at Pete's, remember?'

Zach ponders her response for a second or two, before nodding in agreement. 'That's right,' he confirms. 'So, then what are you doing here?' he asks through an irritated look on his face. 'What do you want?'

Jessica slowly leans down and rests an elbow on the edge of the driver's door, exposing the ample, rounded tops of her breasts with their perfectly rose-colored nipples noticeably taut and teasing. Just out of sight and barely out of reach behind the sheer white gauze of her blouse.

Jessica knows exactly how to respond. Knows precisely what to say and how to say it. Has rehearsed it for a few days. 'I've heard so many things about you on campus,' she teases, 'I finally decided it was time I found out for myself if any of them were true or if they're all just a lot of hot air as I suspect they really are,' she smiles at him and leans in a little closer. 'I really, really want to find out,' she whispers slowly, deliberately, allowing her hot breath to reach out and excite the sensitive, erogenous inner canal of his ear. 'I want you to fuck me,' she whispers, '*now*.' Her words, delivered on the crests of her warm, moist breaths produce the desired effect. Zach visibly shivers from her testicle-tingling taunts.

'I've been having the most lifelike, erotic dreams about you lately...about me...about the two of us together. Fucking. Our bodies grinding away. Sweat glistening on my pussy,' she licks her lips seductively then raises a hand to ever so slowly and deliberately wipe away the trace of saliva suggestively and knowingly left behind in one corner of her mouth. It's a skill she had learned long, long ago and remembers it as perhaps the best in Mama's repertoire at the very height of her horniness. It proves as equally effective today.

Zach can't believe his good fortune. She'd been a passable fuck before, in spite of the fact that she hadn't been awake to actually participate in nor subsequently appreciate his skills, he recalls smugly. Now she was practically begging him to do it.

'Hop in, baby doll,' he instructs her as he leans over and opens the passenger door from the inside. *Tic.*

Jessica manages to tame the twitch in her left eye as she races around the car and jumps in. Zach starts the car and throws it into reverse, scattering gravel and dust into the air. 'Hang on,' he warns her while shifting into low drive and stepping into the accelerator, launching the nose of the car forward with enough power to pin her to her seat and force her head back. She had to admit it was a definite body rush, but they were also drawing way too much attention to themselves.

She discretely removes one of her earrings and drops it on the floor in front of her feet, giving her the perfect excuse to lean down and search for it, taking her out of the picture altogether should anyone happen to look up as the car thundered past. Someone might remember the car. No one would remember her. No one could say with absolute certainty that they had seen them together after leaving the cafe.

When she's sure they've driven a good number of blocks away, out of the busiest part of town and far enough from the campus, she sits up clutching the errant earring in one hand and returns it to her ear. 'Time to move this play along to the second act,' Jessica decides quietly to herself.

'I've got a special place we can go, Zach,' she says as she places a hand over his growing cock and leaves it there. Allowing the warmth of her hand to radiate through the denim and into the meaty density that lay trapped and unmistakably struggling beneath.

Her touch is driving him crazy. Making him crazy. It's all he can do to maintain control over the powerful vehicle in his haste to find a place, any place, where he can finally release the pressure that's building in his groin.

'Why don't you pull over and let me drive,' Jessica says as she skillfully kneads Zach's crotch. 'You can relax and enjoy the entertainment, while I take you somewhere very special. I promise, you won't regret it,' she smiles at him. 'Because you won't have time to regret it,' is what she maybe should have said, but somehow those words never do make it out of her mouth.

'What about your place?' he asks Jessica. It isn't far from where they are and he doesn't know how much longer he can control himself.

'Sorry, we can't,' Jessica lies easily, 'the landlord's doing some work in my apartment today.' But it wasn't the landlord who was repairing and painting her wall…it was Jessica. It was safer to do it herself than have to explain to the landlord how her wall got that way in the first place. For sure there would have been 'restraint vest' written all over that explanation.

Zach suddenly brings the car to a stop on the soft shoulder of the road and throws the gear into neutral. 'Where's this special place you know?' he asks her impatiently.

'It's not far, trust me,' she assures him as she continues to manipulate his manhood. His slight hesitation is all she needs to take full control of the situation.

She grabs Zach's face between her determined fingers and draws him to her, lips slightly parted and wet…tongue searching eagerly for his. Prodding. Penetrating. Provoking.

'Now, move over,' she demands when she finally decides to release her hold on him.

Before he knows what's happening, Jessica jumps out of the passenger's seat, runs around to the other side of the car and flings open Zach's door. He's reluctant. He's never allowed anyone to drive his car before, especially a female. But the ache in his testicles had taken over. Taken over any sense of awareness. Taken away his better judgment.

He quickly climbs over the car's center console and into the now vacant passenger's seat, ready to get to wherever it is they're going.

Jessica slides easily into the driver's seat, her short skirt riding up, up to reveal a shapely set of tight, tanned thighs. Up to that perfectly perfected position. The one suggesting, implying, almost guaranteeing that a more worthwhile view was doable, if one were so inclined.

Jessica places one foot on the accelerator and taunts the engine's enthusiasm. The erotic vibrations oozing up through her seat from the car's barely restrained power rumbling beneath her make her insides purr. The sensual growl emitting from the carefully chrome-tipped dual exhausts triggers a familiar dampness between her legs. Is it the car that's exciting her? The anticipation of reaching their final destination? Well, not so much her final destination as it was to be Zach's final destination. The thought brings a deceptively sweet smile to her face.

But, before Jessica pulls the car back onto the road, she quickly reaches behind her and grabs a bottle out of a large purse she had packed and brought along. Another object suddenly rolls out after it and comes to a stop, exposed and endangered. Her right hand lashes out, wrapping its fingers tightly around her target, like a falcon capturing its prey, finally succumbing to barbed talons. That was too close for comfort. How would she have explained the peculiar appearance of the red teddy bear candle to Zach?

She takes a long, slow breath to calm her mind as she slips the object back into her purse. She then returns to her original train of thought and hands the bottle to Zach. 'Here,' she offers, 'I know how much you like iced tea.' She reaches behind and retrieves another for herself.

'Here's to a memorable afternoon,' he winks at her and easily downs a third of the bottle's contents in one gulp. Perhaps if Zach hadn't been so preoccupied with thoughts of relieving his aching genitals, he might have grasped the irony of the situation. Or, at the very least, acknowledged tiny twinges of apprehension that were trying to get his body's attention.

'You have no idea, baby doll.' Jessica smirks as she eases the car out onto the road and past the city limits. Out through the cheerful countryside.

Past mustard fields, vibrant yellow in the warm, high, afternoon sun.

Past picture-perfect farmhouses that look nothing like their threatening, twilight-touched twins.

Past paved roads to a dirt-packed trail. Past wide open spaces into a claustrophobic tangle of trees.

'To grandfather's cabin we go,' she whispers to herself. The afternoon sun, the warm breeze, the comforting rumble of the car's engine and the triple helping of crushed Valium she had added to his iced tea had all worked in harmony, rendering Zach completely helpless just a few miles into their journey.

Poor little Zach. Such an unfortunate boy.

Chapter Nineteen

A breeze crosses Zach's face, like a gentle stroke, waking him. He finds himself sitting in the passenger seat of his car. No one in the driver's seat. Both doors wide open. A pitch-black night now surrounding him, laying siege to him.

What the fuck? His car was parked in front of his friend's grandfather's hunt cabin. *What were they doing here? Better yet, how had they gotten here?* 'Jessica,' he whispers her name. *How had Jessica found her way here?*

Something tells him not to hang around to hear the answer, though. Zach jumps out of the passenger seat, quietly closes the door, and runs around, hopping into the driver's seat. He feels the urge to leave, an overwhelming need to run. To get as far away from here as he possibly could. To get as far away from her as he probably should.

No keys. *Where the fuck were the keys?* He frantically gropes every inch of the car's interior, but finds no keys. *Fuck.* He closes his eyes and lets his head fall back onto the headrest, allowing himself a deep, calming breath. He has to get a grip. *Everything's fine. Nothing to worry about. There's no way she knows about that night. No way,* he reassures himself.

When he feels his nerves steady just a little, he slowly gets out of the car and makes his way up the handmade stone steps to the wraparound veranda that now shrouds the main entrance. The cabin's front door stands wide open, like a yawning black hole. Inviting someone to care, anyone to dare.

'Hello?' he calls in through the open door. 'Jessica?' No response. 'Jess, are you in here?' he asks in a weak voice. No answer. No movement. No sign of life. The house reeks of things that go bump in the night.

Zach looks back at his car as though expecting to discover a sudden solution to the situation he now found himself in. Nothing. He would have to go in. He would have to go in search of Jessica. He looks back inside and begins feeling his way along the long, narrow hallway that lies ahead.

Cautiously, Zach makes his way along the corridor until he abruptly bumps into something, making him shout out in surprise. Whatever it is, it isn't moving. It's not moving toward him, but it's not moving away from him either. It's just standing there, frightfully silent. Slowly reaching into the darkness, Zach feels around and begins to manually define what it could be. What it is.

Fuck, it was just the slide-down ladder in the trapdoor that led up to the attic. But what is it doing down? Strange, he's never seen it just left down like this. 'Jessica,' his voice calls up, simulating full confidence when really it was just the sudden infusion of fear adrenaline that misguidedly emboldened him. 'Jess, are you up there?'

No response from above, but a sudden noise somewhere behind him diverts his hearing. Was that a clicking noise or a snapping noise, he can't tell. And where had it come from? 'Must be my imagination,' Zach hopes. Prays.

After a cleansing breath, he takes a lighter out of his pocket and flicks it to life in an attempt to get his bearings. There's a door on the right, closed and quiet. He knocks tentatively, but again no response. He's going to have to open the door. The door to the room where he, Bruce, and Cory had taken Jessica. Where Bruce had videotaped what they did to Jessica.

His lighter flickers out, but he lights it again before turning the door's handle and timidly peering into the black beyond. Nothing. No one. *Wait. What was that on the bed?* Something shiny had momentarily seduced him through the emaciated glow of his lighter.

Zach walks over to the bed and leans down, his lighter revealing a picture of a little girl, lying on her stomach on top of a white rug in front of a fire. Strange, he doesn't remember the picture being in this room before, although there is something familiar about it. Has he seen the girl before? Should he know her? He returns the picture to the bed.

Another noise somewhere behind him and back down the hallway toward the front door gets his attention once again. A click? A snap? 'Keep moving,' he forces himself, making his way back into the hallway and closing the bedroom door behind him, softly.

Just ahead and to his left is another door. He remembers it's another bedroom, with the old kitchen beyond that.

In an effort to conserve the lighter fluid and his only source of light at the moment, because power to the cabin was routinely shut off when it wasn't in use for long periods of time, he takes a few steps then flicks the lighter. Once he's sure there's nothing and no one near him, he kills the light again. Another few steps, followed by another flick of the lighter.

He does this over and over, creeping further and deeper into the old cabin. His heart's racing; his breathing's irregular; his eyes alert; his hearing's intensified.

There it is again…that noise. A snapping sound? Difficult to define. It was far off and faint.

After Zach searches the entire first floor of the cabin and finds nothing and no one, he knows he'll have to make his way up into the attic. It's not a place he wants to go, but staying here all night is not an option for him either. The attic seemed to be the lesser of the two evils at this point, he decides.

He retraces his steps back down the hallway in complete darkness, this time somewhat confident without the help of his lighter. He can't afford to waste a drop of the lighter's fluid, because he had to have enough left for when he reached the attic. He has to find Jessica so he can find his keys. In order to find Jessica, he has to be able to first see her.

He feels his way along, until he comes to stand once again alongside the ladder suspended from the trapdoor above his head. She had to be up there. That's the one place he hadn't looked. Yet. A lop-sided leer slowly spreads across his face as he realizes an end to his predicament was near. Perhaps not the end he expected, but, yes, an end was coming.

Zach takes a deep breath, flicks the lighter to life and jumps on the first step of the ladder, yelling Jessica's name at the top of his lungs as he charges up into the attic, hoping that his loud actions and harsh sounds would either make her freeze on the spot or scream out in fright. Either way, she would be revealed. That was the plan.

But it's Zach who finds himself taken by surprise. He feels a sudden draft behind him. Turns to see the trapdoor closing. Hears the raspy, nails-on-a-chalkboard screech of a deadbolt lock as it slides into place on the other side. Smells the fear radiating from his own body. Comes face to face with overwhelming darkness when the lighter in his hand begins to flicker…at first. 'No, not now,' he begs, but it quickly morphs into a convulsive sputter, before it goes out, for good.

It is also at this exact same moment when he realizes he left his cell phone in the car. *Fuck!*

* * * * *

The darkness would be overwhelming for most, but not for Jessica. The black of night had become her sanctuary, a reliable refuge from the majority of the living who mysteriously thrive in the light of day. It is time to put the darkness to work. To exercise its terror.

Her thumb and go-fuck-yourself finger work in harmony, breeding an unnatural sound that strays off into the darkness. *Snap. Snap.*

Jessica and her large purse have taken up shelter and temporary residence behind an eight-foot-high pile of deserted firewood, around the corner from the front veranda, waiting for their cue.

She hears a slight rustling noise coming from Zach's Corvette, which she had left parked in the driveway. 'Let the show begin,' she whispers to herself.

She can barely make out Zach as he unfurls himself from inside the low-slung vehicle, a trail of profanities wafting behind as he carefully makes his way up the handmade stone steps, across the veranda, stopping at the threshold of the front door, which now stands wide open. Is it welcoming or forewarning?

Through the darkness, Jessica hears Zach call out her name, once, twice, through the open doorway. 'Hello, Jessica,' his voice somewhat tremulous, despite his attempt at authority. 'Jess, are you in here?'

As Zach begins to make his way inside the cabin and down the hallway, she and her purse slowly slip out from behind the woodpile and make their way around the corner, along the veranda until they reach the outside edge of the front door's frame. '*Snap, snap*,' go her finger and thumb after she hears Zach once again call out her name, only this time it was up, into the attic. She smiles. Zach had stumbled into the ladder she pulled down from the attic's trapdoor earlier as he slept outside. She needs him to go up into the attic.

'*Snap, snap*,' again. It has always astounded her how that one sound, a rather innocuous sound when you think about it, could make anyone stop dead in his or her tracks. Most people don't seem to recognize nor appreciate its power, but she does. Zach was proof, because it makes him stop every time. Unfortunately, he was not dead in his tracks. Not yet.

She waits just outside the front door patiently for Zach to complete his search of the cabin. She knows he'll soon figure out that he has to go up into the attic, because that's the one place he hadn't yet looked. But would he? He must. It was so important to the evening's outcome. To the grand finale that still lay a few hours into the future.

She hears Zach inch his way back along the hallway, but can see no evidence of the shaky amber blush being cast from his lighter as it had earlier. Perhaps he was saving it for the attic. *It won't do him any good, though*, she thinks to herself.

Jessica hears Zach take a deep breath, flick his lighter back to life again, and rush headlong up the attic's ladder, shrieking her name as he went.

She counts the number of steps he takes. She knows how many he should take to get up into the attic itself, because she had counted them earlier...*five, six*. There it was, her cue.

Jessica immediately steps across the threshold, quietly runs to the ladder, slides it up into place, swings the trapdoor back into place, and rams the deadbolt into place. Four seconds was all it took. She knew it would not be enough time for Zach to react. Not enough time for Zach to even begin to comprehend what lay in wait for him.

Satisfied, Jessica slips outside, across the veranda and back to her woodpile shelter. She has a few hours to kill, but no time to waste. She has a final task to complete, but this was an easy one. The hard work had already been done and it would soon be time to reap her rewards...to own her revenge.

She can hear Zach's faint pleas coming from the attic. Somewhat urgent and desperate at the same time. 'Jessica, what are you doing? Come on, let me out. What's wrong?'

The fucking nerve. His fucking nerve, she thinks. 'What's wrong? Are you fucking kidding me?' She's not about to waste any more conversation on this guy. But she was about to have a very important chat with one of Zach's friends…Bruce. He was the next actor to enter her play. Too bad he didn't know it.

Jessica had taken Zach's cell phone out of the car with her when they had first arrived at the cabin, while he was sleeping. She had quickly found Bruce's cell number in Zach's contacts. Now it was time to type out that text message she had already fabricated.

CAR DIED. AT YOUR GRANDFATHER'S CABIN. SORRY I DIDN'T TELL YOU. HAVE A HOT DATE. WANT TO PLAY WITH US? COME GET ME. NOW!

She hit 'SEND,' put the phone down on the stack of firewood in front of her and waited…waited for his response. Knew it would come. The message's inference would be much too tantalizing for him to pass up.

So, it wasn't long, nor was it a surprise, when she received a reply from Bruce.

YOU BET, I'M IN, BUDDY. NO PROBLEM. BE THERE IN AN HOUR OR SO.

The male species, so fucking predictable.

Chapter Twenty

Half an hour later, she turns her attention back to Zach, still calling out to her from the attic, although by the sounds of it, he was running out of steam. 'Time to reconnect with dear Zach,' she decides, although she makes no attempt to take herself from behind the woodpile.

She doesn't need to. She has everything she needs right here, in her purse.

Jessica pulls the purse's strap over her head from where it has rested on her shoulder this whole time and gently lays the manageable bundle at her feet. From within its depths, she retrieves only one-half of a pair of walkie-talkies. The other she had already placed up in the attic, atop the crossbeam of a truss. Not at all visible to the eye, just on the off chance that Zach had enough light that would allow him more time to evaluate his surroundings. Shame about his lighter.

'Hello, Zach,' a clear as day female voice calls out to him from somewhere overhead. He holds his breath, not fully comprehending what was happening, where the voice was coming from, whose body it belonged to. But there was no other body up here in the attic with him. Just a voice. A female voice giving him instructions to follow, before continuing.

'Do you know who this is?' the voice asks.

It must be Jessica, he thinks to himself, *because there's no one else at the cabin but us.* They had come together.

Unfortunately, they're now alone together. *What is she playing at?* He walks toward the area where he thought the voice was coming from and, groping his way overhead, finds a walkie-talkie exactly where she instructs him it would be. He puts it up to his mouth and pushes the 'talk' button to respond.

'Yes,' Zach finally answers. 'I know it's you, Jessica. Let me out now or else…'

What are you going to do, Zach, she ponders quietly to herself, *drug me, tie me to a bed, and rape me, again and again and again?* But she can't say the words…yet. For the moment, she must keep herself calm and completely in control. There's one thing she needs his help with and if she pushes his fear factor too far now, she doubts she'll have any chance at all of getting him to cooperate with her.

'Zach,' she calls him again, 'I've contacted your friend, I think his name is Bruce, and he's coming to pick us up. I fucked up your car on the way here, so we need him to give us a ride back to the city.' The deceit comes so easily.

Despite what happened to his precious car, Zach is relieved by her words. 'Well,' he falters, but quickly regains his bravado, 'that's good news for you. Now, slide that fucking deadbolt back and let me down.'

But she isn't going to do that just now. 'Zach,' Jessica speaks gently into the walkie-talkie, 'there's a set of shiny new handcuffs on the floor in the far right corner of the attic, just a few steps from where you found the walkie-talkie. Please find them, put one cuff on one of your wrists and then throw the other cuff over the beam that's overhead in the same corner and attach that cuff to your other wrist,' she instructs him. She had specifically chosen that location to hide the handcuffs, because if all went as she had planned, it would trap Zach far, far away from the only access to and from the attic. It would also reduce any possible aggression on his part when it was time for her to come face to face with him in the attic to duct tape his mouth shut, but not his eyes. She wants him to see what's coming. She also needs him to let Bruce know where he is, but only with his feet, not his voice. She isn't about to let him tip Bruce off.

Zach was now her soon-to-be victim, just as she had been his. Whoever coined the phrase 'payback's a bitch' obviously didn't know what they were doing. God, the rush!

'What the fuck, Jess!' Zach screams back through the walkie-talkie. 'I'm not cuffing myself to anything, so cut out the bullshit demands, and let me out of here.'

'Oh, I'm so sorry, but I can't do that,' she says back in an automated tone. 'It will be at least an hour before your buddy shows up and I don't want to have to worry about what you might do in the meantime. I need you to sit quietly, there's a good boy, until he gets here and I'll send him up to remove your cuffs, so the three of us can have a wee chat. How does that sound?' she asks him, but has no interest whatsoever in what he has to say. He does not yet understand that it didn't matter what he had to say, just as it never mattered to Mama what Megan had to say either.

* * * * *

Bruce slowly rolls his car into the driveway and parks it just behind Zach's, which sits abandoned. He shuts the engine off, but decides to leave the headlights on, since they seem to be the only source of light for miles around. He opens his door and steps out, then leans back into the car, and honks the horn twice, in quick succession. After a minute, when he gets no response, he leans into the horn a little harder and longer. *Surely someone heard that?* But, still no response. Actually, no sign of life anywhere. Strange.

A smile crosses his face when he remembers Zach had texted that his date was 'hot,' which means they're probably still 'doing the dirty deed' and can't hear him honk over their moans and groans. *Fuck, she'd better have a few moans and groans left over for me. Only one way to find out. Got to go inside the cabin and listen for the 'sounds of love.'*

Problem is, there's no love there. If he knows anything about Zach it's that the word 'love' never, ever enters his mind and certainly never passes his lips.

He settles on listening for just 'any old sound' coming from somewhere inside, from someplace inside. It would help him pinpoint where they were. What bedroom they were bouncing around in. He's more than ready to have his turn, to take his turn.

He hadn't thought to bring a flashlight with him, confident in his presumption that Zach had one with him. Apparently not, since it wasn't just the cabin itself that was eerily dark, but everything around it as well, except for the odd star whose naïve twinkle danced high above the dense pine trees that were packed together as far as the eye could see. 'This must be what it feels like to be buried alive,' he whispers to what he believes is no one in particular. But, someone in particular does overhear him. Jessica, once again secreted behind the woodpile, is just a few yards from where Bruce now stands. Well within eavesdropping distance.

Well, well, she sarcastically thinks after digesting Bruce's rather foreboding comment. *'He's smarter than I gave him credit for, it would seem. I like this guy...he's thinking ahead too, like me. The big difference is, though, Brucey boy, I'm well-aware of what's coming, while you have absolutely no hope of even beginning to imagine what's waiting for you.'*

Despite the numerous black shapes that seemed to leap out at him from every direction, Bruce heads confidently up the handmade stone steps at the front of the cabin, buoyed by his car's aloof headlights behind him. He crosses the width of the veranda and stops just inside the open front door. Turning his head from side to side, he lets his ears scan the silence. Nothing. Not a sound. He decides to call Zach's name. 'Zach, where are you buddy?' Zilch. 'Come on, this is getting real old real fast,' he warns. 'I'm going to leave you here, I swear, if you don't answer me right now, Zach.'

Somewhere in the bowels of the cabin he hears a loud noise, like a stomp. He listens for it again. It's coming from overhead, up in the attic. 'Zach,' he calls out, 'are you up in the attic?' He gets another stomp as a response. 'What the fuck are you doing up there?' This time, his question elicits several urgent stomps in rapid succession. 'Okay, okay,' Bruce acknowledges, 'I'm coming, hold on.'

Bruce feels his way along the hall with one hand, having left what light there was on the doorstep now well behind him, while the other flails ahead in search of the attic's ladder. Instead, his hand comes into contact with a piece of rope with a handle on the dangling end of it. *This doesn't make sense. How had Zach managed to get into the attic if the trapdoor is closed?* Another loud stomp from overhead intrudes on his hesitation. 'Okay,' Bruce responds, 'hold your horses.' He pulls the rope's handle, but nothing happens. Stretching as far as he is able, Bruce feels around in the dark and discovers that the deadbolt had been slid into place. If only he had stopped to think about this, even if just for a few seconds, he might have been in less of a hurry. He might not have simply slid the deadbolt open with one hand, while pulling the rope's handle with the other. He may not have stumbled his way in such haste up the ladder only to lose his balance, falling face first into the attic's rough and dusty wooden floor.

He might have had time to prevent the trapdoor from slamming shut behind him, its deadbolt making a deafening screech as it was once again slid back into place.

Chapter Twenty-One

Blair Scott took a moment to review his notes, before resuming his questioning of the witness. 'Detective Logan,' he began, 'during your search for Zach Augustus, what led you to the old hunt cabin that once belonged to Bruce Marshall's grandfather?'

'We couldn't find any immediate leads to tell us what might have happened to Zach or where he might have gone, or if he had just decided to take a break due to the pressures of school,' the detective offered. 'It was like he had simply vanished into thin air,' he remembered. 'So, we decided to go back to the two weeks prior to his disappearance and retrace his movements. Find out if he had had any problems with anyone. If anything out of the ordinary had occurred in his life.'

'And what, if anything, did you find, Detective?' the attorney asked.

'Well, initially, everything seemed to be fairly routine. Zach had pretty regular attendance and managed to maintain a solid, though average, grade point despite his busy social schedule.'

'Was Zach Augustus well known on campus, Detective?' the attorney asked.

'Yes, by all accounts, he was well known, but apparently not for his academic or sports achievements,' the detective added.

'If not those, then what was he best known for?' the attorney continued.

'He had acquired quite a reputation as a 'player,' I guess that's what they say nowadays…a 'womanizer' is what we called it in my day,' he admitted before continuing his train of thought. 'Someone who apparently got less pleasure hunting the women as he did having sex with them, which was his ultimate goal,' the detective explained. 'His satisfaction was in the conquest and not the hunt or the relationship itself.'

Scott paused for a moment, again referring to his notes. 'I understand that Zach belonged to a fraternity on campus, is that correct, Detective?'

'Yes, that's right,' the detective confirmed.

'Did you have an opportunity to meet with and interview Zach's fraternity brothers over the course of your investigation?' he inquired.

'Yes,' the detective answered.

'Is it also true that, as a result of your investigation at the fraternity, you became aware of an alleged rape of a female student who attended the same campus as the boys in the fraternity?' he questioned.

'Yes, that's true,' the detective confirmed. He knew where this line of questioning was going. He was prepared. He was ready.

'Is it also true that, based on this information, you immediately obtained a warrant to conduct a search of the fraternity house?' the attorney continued.

'Yes.'

'And did you discover anything out of the ordinary, Detective, during that search?' the attorney paced slowly in front of the witness, his voice calm, deliberate. 'Anything that set off alarm bells in your head?'

The detective quietly cleared his throat before answering. 'Yes, we found a CD hidden behind books along the top row of a large bookcase in the fraternity's common lounge area.'

'And what was on that CD, Detective Logan?'

The detective did his best to remain composed. He had been a witness many times before, so he knew the routine. How the system worked. How the process unfolded. But this one felt different. This one had unsettled him. Had equally disturbed everyone and anyone who came into contact with it, however frequent or isolated that might have been.

'It showed Zach Augustus and Bruce Marshall having sex with a young female,' he said.

'And did the female appear to be a willing participant, Detective?' he asked.

'No,' he responded calmly, 'she appeared to be an unconscious participant.'

Scott clasped his hands together behind his back, head slightly down, and walked over to stand in front of the jury. 'Unconscious,' he said slowly. 'Unconscious,' he repeated as though to himself, but it was really meant to manipulate the jury's collective mind. 'In other words, Detective Logan, the contents of that CD clearly showed the rape of a young female, isn't that right?'

'Yes,' confirmed the detective.

'The repeated rape of a young female, isn't that correct?'

'Yes, that's correct.'

'Just how many times is she raped, that you know of, Detective? How many rapes were actually captured on that one particular CD?'

'Five,' the detective answered. 'There was a total of five rapes on this one CD.'

'Do you know over what period of time these rapes occurred? In other words, how many hours are recorded on the CD, Detective?'

'We believe that the rapes themselves took place over four hours, but only a few hours' worth of footage were actually burned onto the CD itself,' the detective replied.

Scott then confidently walked to the clerk's desk, retrieved a small item, and turned back to the witness, a CD now clearly held in his hand, raised above his head for all to see. 'Let the record reflect that I am holding Prosecution Exhibit

B4. Is this the CD, Detective?' Scott asked while placing the object in front of the witness.

After an impromptu, physical inspection, the detective placed the object back on the ledge of the witness' box in front of him, desperate to finish his testimony and quickly seek out a sink where he could wash his forever-contaminated hands, yet again. 'Yes,' he confirmed.

Now was the time for planting and nurturing a tiny seed of doubt in the jury's mind. Scott turned back to his witness.

'And did you also come to learn the identity of the female on the CD?' he asked. 'Find out who she was? Locate her and tell her she had been raped and it had all been captured on video?' the attorney continued, his voice intentionally rising with each damning question. 'Then tell her it wasn't just the one time? That she had been raped five times, and those are just the ones you know about. And that each one had been captured on video?!' he practically yelled, pounding each sordid detail into the jury's mind. If not completely visible, then loudly lurking. Not willing to go silently.

'We did,' the detective answered.

'And who was that female, Detective? Can you identify her for this court, please,' the attorney asked, barely able to contain himself and so ready to savor this moment.

Detective Logan lifted one arm up, slowly, a finger outstretched and pointing directly in front of him. 'Yes,' he confirmed. 'It was the defendant, Jessica McCallum.'

Scott took his time, allowing the jury to absorb this latest information. To try to comprehend that the hour after hour of physical abuse was deliberately inflicted on this victim. Intentionally imposed on this prey.

'And could you identify from the CD where these brutal attacks had taken place,' Scott asked.

'Not initially. We were still chasing down a few leads we had, when we were suddenly called to a suspicious fire,' he remembered. Recalled the long drive out to the middle of nowhere, past mustard fields turned from vibrant yellow to a sickly brown tinge in the cool, pre-dawn mist. Past nondescript farmhouses and barns. Past paved roads to a dirt-packed trail. Past wide open spaces into a charred tangle of trees. Finally, to the smoldering remains of an old structure, its overcooked, but still standing handmade stone steps now leading up to nowhere, instead funneling the way to something horrible beyond its once threshold.

'We found Zach Augustus' white Corvette there in the driveway.'

'And did you find Mr. Augustus himself?' Scott struggled to keep his excitement, his tenor, in check.

Detective Logan shifted slightly in his seat, quietly cleared his throat and leaned in to the microphone perched in front of him. 'Yes,' he stated, 'sort of.'

'Sort of...what do you mean by that, Detective?' Scott inquired.

Leaning even closer to the microphone, Detective Logan provided his answer. 'We found what was left of Mr. Augustus within the burned structure itself.' Horrified breaths exploded in the courtroom's public gallery, but were quickly silenced by the judge's gavel. 'Order.'

'So, you discovered a burned body inside what was left of the structure and determined it to be that of Zach Augustus?' Scott asked once the room had quieted down.

'After some initial forensic tests, yes that's correct,' the detective explained. *One. Two. Three.*

'Was there anything else of interest that was immediately discovered in the ashes, Detective?' *Four.*

'Yes, there was a second body.'

* * * * *

She stands quietly in the hallway, just under the trapdoor she had bolted, and listens to the turmoil of Zach and Bruce overhead.

She knows one of them won't get out and the other can't get out. Perfect.

She turns and slowly makes her way back toward the front door, walkie-talkie still in hand. Taking refuge once again behind the woodpile, Jessica puts her mouth up to the transmitter.

'Hello, Bruce,' she says politely. 'So nice of you to join us.' She actually meant it, too.

She takes a breath and continues. 'I've scheduled this meeting tonight, because there are some things we need to clear up...well, specifically things I need to clean up.'

She reaches into her deep purse and digs out a plastic container of raw vegetables she had brought with her. One needs to keep one's strength up.

After a few savory crunches, she puts the lid back on and returns the container to its nest in the bottom of her purse. 'Time for the grand finale, boys,' she whispers to herself.

Once again, she activates the walkie-talkie and calmly speaks into it as she makes her way back to the cabin's front door.

'I know what you did,' her voice whispers slowly at them. 'You've been very bad boys,' she continues, 'and I've appointed myself your jury and your judge.'

She can faintly hear the distinct sounds of harried footsteps coming from the attic. 'It won't do you any good, boys,' she whispers into the walkie-talkie. 'There's no way out until I say you can come out, so you might as well settle in for a bit and listen carefully to what I have to say.' Almost immediately the attic goes quiet.

'Bruce,' she continues, 'first I need you to find your way over to Zach, reach around in the rafters above him and find the key that will unlock the handcuffs he's got on, there's a good lad.' It was imperative that Bruce removed the cuffs from Zach, because when the authorities arrive, and they most certainly will, it would raise some serious questions if they were still attached, especially to a dead body. It wouldn't matter if they found a pair of empty handcuffs just casually laying around, though. Boys will be boys.

She hears feet shuffling slowly across the attic's floor, toward where Zach was once again stomping the floor in an effort to quickly guide his friend to him. He wants to get out of there. He has to get out of there. This girl is one sick puppy; he thinks he now grasps what she's capable of. *Foolish boy, it was too late.*

Jessica again reaches into her purse and retrieves the small, red teddy bear candle, its wide eyes staring at her, its tiny, familiar smile soothing her. She lovingly kisses the top of its head, just to the side of the wick that now beckons to her.

She ignores the noises from overhead and goes in search of the perfect place to set the candle down. She thinks she knows just the one.

Jessica slowly enters the first bedroom…the one where she had been raped. She leaves the walkie-talkie on the bed. She won't be needing it anymore.

She next takes a lighter from her purse, lights the wick on the teddy bear's head and places it on the nearby window ledge. Right beneath a set of curtains. A very old, highly flammable set of curtains. 'A teddy bear is a furry friend,' she recites from memory as she heads for the front door, 'whose love and support never end,' she whispers in perfect rhythm to her gate. 'Keeps your secrets, never lies,' she walks calmly across the veranda and down the handmade stone steps, 'friendly, fuzzy, cozy, wise.' She slips on a pair of blue vinyl gloves she pulls from her purse as she heads down the driveway to Bruce's car, its headlights still poking at the dark. 'Tell it your secrets, it'll keep them well,' she slides into the driver's seat, turns the key and puts the car in reverse. 'You don't have to worry, it won't ever tell.'

She spins the car around, shifts into drive, but waits, her eyes fixated on the scene in the rearview mirror. She sees the first wafts of smoke, then the timid lick of an initial flame before it eagerly begins to consume everything in its path.

There, somewhere in the heat, she hears a noise she recognizes. It is one of pure agony.

Jessica smiles to herself, pleased that Zach had finally been able to express his emotions.

Chapter Twenty-Two

It is the second time someone has knocked on her door in the past two weeks. *Fuck.* But, if this were any other day or just another circumstance, she wouldn't have bothered to answer it. Today is going to be different, though. Today is going to be special.

She knows who will be standing behind the door before she even opens it. Knows they will come, eventually. Knows why they are here, but do they?

She opens the door and recognizes the two detectives she had originally spoken to, but offers no reaction whatsoever.

'Ms. McCallum,' Detective Logan begins, 'I wonder if we might come in for a minute. We have a few more questions we'd like to ask you about Zach Augustus.'

'You mean, you haven't found him yet?' she asks in her best pretend surprised voice.

'If we could just come in for a few minutes, Ms. McCallum, we'd rather discuss this in private,' he nudges his foot into the doorway. 'Or we can take this back to the office. Your choice.'

'No, it's okay,' Jessica immediately opens the front door wider, inviting them inside, 'come in.' Her mind functions at its best when in familiar surroundings. These walls defend her. Protect her. She needs them now. She can rely on them now.

The two detectives step inside, their eyes quickly scanning the space around them, each one of their senses hunting, seeking. It's a habit, or perhaps at this point in their careers, it's an addiction.

'So,' Detective Logan says, deciding not to yet reveal to Jessica any of the gruesome events that had unfolded over the past several hours, 'have you seen or heard from Zach since we last spoke a few days ago? Or maybe there's something else, some small detail you might have remembered that would help us.'

'No, of course not, or I would have been in touch with one of you,' she stresses through insincere sincerity. In the meantime, she can't help but notice the other detective again assessing everything in her apartment through the measured, panoramic rotation of his eyes. Did he faintly falter when, for just a fraction of a second, his eyes passed over a few, small, red teddy bear candles that stood mutely on a nearby shelf? Her tiny sentries of secrets. *Tic.*

Detective Logan takes out his notepad, casually flips through the pages until he comes to the first available blank space, his writing hand holding a pen that's poised for an imminent attack on the paper.

'Ms. McCallum, perhaps you'd like to take a seat,' he indicates a ratty, oversized chair shoved deep into one dark corner of Jessica's living room, just to his left.

Jessica follows his glance to the chair, then turns back, defiance written across her face. 'Thanks, but I'm good right here. Look, I'm busy working on a school paper that's due next week, so what is it that you want?'

Detective Logan looks at his partner and subtly shrugs his shoulders, as if to say 'If that's the way she wants to play this.'

'Fine,' he agrees, a hint of irritation staining his tone. He can see he's going to have to take another approach to this. Something with a little more meat to it.

'Ms. McCallum, during the course of our search for Mr. Augustus, we paid a visit to his fraternity and discovered a video tape we'd like to talk to you about,' he states.

Tic. Tic.

'Oh?' is all Jessica can manage. She can't think of what else to say, or what she is willing to say. She's wasn't about to volunteer any further conversation without a specific ask from either one of these idiots. Nor was she going to take the bait of silence that was really meant to ensnare her emotions and trap her tongue.

'I'm sorry to have to tell you this, but on the video, we found evidence that you have been raped,' he reveals. 'Now can we talk?'

Jessica's facial expression never wavers. She stares directly at Detective Logan for what seems an eternity, then collapses in a small heap at his feet. Just as she had practiced.

* * * * *

The prosecutor, Aaron Burgess, approached his witness. 'You are a Forensic Fire Investigator, correct?' he asked.

'Yes, that's correct,' Fire Chief Dan Wolchuck replied confidently.

'As an expert in your field, can you please explain for this Court what a Forensic Fire Investigator does?'

'Certainly,' the inspector began. 'Forensic fire experts rely on what their eyes show them, but also and much more importantly on what the science says. The first thing is to find out the origin of the fire. In other words, where the fire started. The point of origin is the smallest area you can identify, which can be as small as a book of matches or as large as an entire room.'

Burgess disliked these types of witnesses, because while they provided crucial facts, that was the problem in itself. The 'facts' were often dry and the scientific details tedious. He felt it was the easiest way to lose a jury's focus. Perhaps not this time, though.

'After determining the origin of the fire, I look for things that could have served as an ignition source, such as a burning cigarette or a frayed electrical wire on an old household appliance, for example,' the Fire Chief explained. 'I test each possible source to determine if it's a capable ignition for the fuels I have. To put it simply, you can light a piece of paper with a match, but you can't light a two-by-four with a match.'

'Great analogy, Inspector Wolchuck.' Burgess was beginning to warm up to this witness. 'And did you determine the point of origin of this particular fire, Inspector?' he asked.

'Yes,' he stated. 'We discovered the melted waxy remnants of a candle, a red one to be more specific. I believe that someone lit the candle, the 'ignition source,' and placed it somewhere dangerously close to a combustion source, the 'fuel.' Because the structure itself was built in the early 1900s and made completely from the trees surrounding the cabin, it not only would have ignited quickly, but spread even faster, engulfing everything in a matter of seconds.'

'So, this was an unfortunate accident then, Inspector?' Burgess asked.

'At first, that's what we all thought, but then a few unusual items were discovered among the ashes, once the fire had been completely extinguished and we were able to take a closer look,' the inspector stated.

'And what were those items, Inspector?'

'We found a charred pair of handcuffs.'

The prosecutor let that little tidbit of information sink in before he resumed his questioning.

Tic.

'And the other item?' Burgess continued.

After a quick glance at his notes, the inspector answered, 'A deadbolt that appeared to still be in a locked position.'

'Why did you consider that to be unusual, Investigator?' Burgess asked.

'According to the information we were given by family members, there was an attic space that was only accessible by way of a ladder that dropped down when a trapdoor in the ceiling near the front entrance of the cabin was released by way of a sliding deadbolt lock. But, based on the position and conditions of the bodies when we did our initial walk-through of the scene, my colleagues and I believe that both men were in the attic when the fire started.'

'And what, if anything, did this information suggest to you?'

'It didn't suggest anything, Mr. Burgess. It told me without a doubt that someone else was in the cabin and slid the deadbolt into place, basically trapping the two men in the attic. This was no accident. The fire was deliberately started. It was immediately deemed a double homicide,' the investigator concluded.

Chapter Twenty-Three

'Good afternoon, Detective McMahon,' Blair Scott welcomed his next 'guest.' 'You are Detective Logan's partner, correct?'

'Yes,' the rookie detective leaned forward and put his lips right up to the microphone in front of him, sending his overly enhanced voice ricocheting around the courtroom. Embarrassed and flustered, the rookie quickly backed away and tried to take a more relaxed posture, yet barely managed to strike a controlled pose.

'And you were his partner at the beginning of what initially began as the Zach Augustus missing person's case?'

Keeping a safe distance from the microphone this time, Detective McMahon continued. 'Yes, Detective Logan was the lead Detective. He handled all of the personal interviews and I did background checks into the people he interviewed, as well as any additional research that was needed.'

'And when did you first come across the name "Jessica McCallum"? Scott asked, his pulse quickening, the excitement building.

'When Detective Logan interviewed Zach Augustus' fraternity brothers,' he remembered. 'Logan took each one into a side room to speak to them individually. To see how consistent their stories would be. During those interviews, the guys said that Zach did not have one specific girlfriend at the time, all except for one guy who said Zach did have a girlfriend until very recently and gave us Jessica's name.'

'And did you and Detective Logan subsequently go to speak with Ms. McCallum?'

'We did. The very next morning.'

Scott again referred to his notes. 'Was there anything unusual or suspicious about Ms. McCallum?'

'No,' he answered, 'but we had interrupted her in the middle of painting an 'accent wall' in her apartment, so it was a relatively quick interview.'

'And did you have an occasion to subsequently return to Ms. McCallum's apartment a little over a week later?'

'Yes,' he checked his notes. 'It was the morning after the fire that killed Zach Augustus and Bruce Marshall.'

'What was the purpose of that visit, Detective?' Scott plowed ahead confidently.

'At first, we were going to inform Ms. McCallum that we had located Zach Augustus,' he explained. 'But then Detective Logan suggested we don't tell her about the fire just yet. Instead he wanted to tell her about the CD found at the fraternity house and what was on it. He wanted to gauge her reaction.'

'And what was Ms. McCallum's reaction, Detective?'

'She just stood there for a bit, then passed out cold on the floor.'

Scott returned to his notes, allowing the jury time to absorb the witness's words. 'If she was the young female on the CD who was repeatedly raped, over and over and over and over and over, Detective,' a fist repeatedly slamming down on the dais he stood before, one for each of the five horrific assaults, 'then why was it that Ms. McCallum was moved to the top of your person of interest list?' His voice was firm. On the edge of accusatory.

The rookie detective squirmed in his seat. 'There were too many 'coincidences,' he stood his ground. 'Detectives don't believe in coincidences, Mr. Scott. We work from and with the facts we're presented with.'

'In this case, Detective McMahon, what were the 'facts' that ultimately led you to arrest my client, Ms. McCallum, for the murders of both Zach Augustus and Bruce McCallum?'

The detective flipped through a folder in front of him, and pulled out a single piece of paper on which he had hurriedly scribbled some notes, and once again, spoke into the microphone.

'Jessica McCallum knew Zach Augustus.' He continued on down the list. 'She admitted dating Mr. Augustus for a very short period of time. She also acknowledged going to a party outside the city limits with Mr. Augustus.'

Scott jumped in. 'And did Ms. McCallum admit to knowing that the cabin, where this 'party' was held, belonged to Bruce Marshall's grandfather?'

'She says she didn't know until we told her,' he answered.

'Please continue, Detective,' Scott indicated.

'She had been raped by both Zach and Bruce while at the cabin.'

Once again, the defense attorney interrupted. 'Was Ms. McCallum even aware that she had been raped?'

'She denied knowing she had been raped,' he recalled, 'but she finally admitted that she had noticed some bruising on the insides of her thighs after being dropped off back at her apartment, only with no recollection of how they got there.'

'And what did all of these, when put together, suggest to you, Detective?'

'Motive.'

Scott paced back and forth in front of the jury box. 'The case against my client sounds as though it is based solely on circumstantial evidence,' he commented. 'When did you have an opportunity to speak with Ms. McCallum again after she collapsed in front of you, Detective?'

'It was a few months later,' he indicated.

Scott took a little time, intentionally of course, getting to his next question, slowly circling in front of the jury. 'And where did that conversation take place, Detective McMahon?'

'In a local mental health facility.'

* * * * *

She remembered how she had survived after Mama's first 'friend' had hurt her. By playing dumb and mute, despite the fact that there was nothing wrong with her hearing nor her speech. It had simply been the means to the end. The end of her true self. She felt it was best that way. Then she'd never be hurt again. No one could ever hurt her again. It had become her psychological suit of armor. It was time to suit up again.

And so it was that, no matter how hard the detectives, or anyone else tried, Jessica never uttered a single word, other than to her court-appointed psychiatrist, Dr. Fitzgerald. In spite of patient confidentiality, Jessica was careful to reveal only things about her childhood. Some true, some not. A good imagination was so incredibly useful at times.

The memories she eventually shared with Dr. Fitzgerald were meant to horrify him, sicken him, stir him to outrage…and ultimately lure him to her, to want to rescue her, to protect her.

In the end, she never admitted guilt, at least not out loud. She never acknowledged knowing anything about a red candle, at least not out loud. She never adopted the truth. And she never accepted defeat.

'Dr. Fitzgerald, it was my intention to put my client, Megan McCallum, or Jessica if you prefer, on the stand,' Blair Scott said to the witness. 'However, you convinced me not to do so, since you feel that her mental state is currently fragile at best, is that correct?'

'Yes, I strongly believe that to be the case, Mr. Scott,' the doctor confirmed.

'And why is that, Doctor?'

'Throughout my extensive career, I have never come across a more appalling example of abuse—emotional, physical and sexual—and over such an extended period of time, which amounts to most of her life, as I have in this case.' He paused, subtly shaking his head from side to side.

'She never stood a chance in the environment in which she was raised, I'm afraid.'

Another thoughtful pause. 'I'm surprised Ms. McCallum functions at all after everything she's been through,' he offered, then looked directly at the jury. 'What she doesn't need is more punishment.' He then moved his determined gaze toward the defense attorney. 'What she does need, Mr. Scott, is help,' he stressed. 'Society surely owes her that much.'

Scott let the doctor's words settle on the courtroom. Were the doctor's comments inducing guilt? Hopefully. Were they meant to stir up strong emotions? Absolutely.

'If the decision were yours to make, Doctor Fitzgerald, what would your recommendation be with respect to what should now happen to Ms. McCallum,' Scott pointedly asked the psychologist.

Dr. Fitzgerald knew through advanced notice from Mr. Scott that he was to be given an opportunity to offer his professional opinion. What he didn't know, though, was whether or not his pleas would have any impact whatsoever on this jury. He truly hoped so. For a number of reasons, some personal.

He was more than willing to try. He felt compelled to help Jessica. She had become such a big part of his life during the time they spent together over these past months. He found himself being protective toward her. Becoming a mentor to her. Perhaps even a father figure for her.

Strangely enough, what began as a professional relationship slowly evolved into more of a romantic fancy, but only on his part. Jessica eventually began to warm up to him. To offer the odd, woeful smile to him. Even reach out on occasion and touch him, ever so gently…seductively? His hand, his shoulder, nothing that would be considered outside of his profession's ethics, surely.

'I would recommend she continue treatment under my direct supervision,' the doctor explained. 'Over the past several months, my team and I have been working with Ms. McCallum to identify which drug will give her the stability and ability to, first and foremost, slow her mind down. Give her, literally, just a little peace of mind in order to allow her the chance to understand what it takes to make suitable choices in life. How to formulate good decisions. Learn how to live a relatively normal life at the very least.'

'And do you feel you have made some headway, Doctor?'

'Most definitely,' Dr. Fitzgerald asserted. 'Ms. McCallum acknowledged that there was something not working properly inside her mind and agreed to try some medication. Now, she is grateful, because the medication I prescribed has helped her significantly. My team encourages her to make several innocuous decisions throughout each day, then asks her to verbalize her reasoning for the choices she makes before gently role-playing with her to provide immediate direction and feedback, all the while helping boost her confidence. She's made remarkable strides, in my opinion as well as the opinion of her entire medical team,' Dr. Fitzgerald added.

'So, what you're saying Doctor, is that you would return her to the mental health facility where she is currently being housed? The very same facility where you are the Chief of Patient Care, overseeing every aspect of her treatment?'

'Yes, Mr. Scott. At the moment, that is the best place for her, and the best course of treatment for her. She's assimilated nicely with the facility's environment. The more comfortable she is with and in her surroundings, the more effective her overall treatment will be.'

Scott pondered these comments, 'Dr. Fitzgerald, how long do you believe Ms. McCallum's treatment could last?'

The doctor referred to his notes in a folder in front of him, but no one other than him knew that he was simply staring at a blank piece of paper, perusing its empty ruled lines. 'Based on our most recent re-assessment of Ms. McCallum, which took place just prior to this court hearing, we devised a schedule for her recovery that will require her to be our guest for the next several years, Mr. Scott.'

Tic.

Chapter Twenty-Four

Several raps from Judge Hanson's gavel suddenly cracked through the busy, overlapping noises of those milling impatiently around the courtroom.

'This Court will now come to order.' Crack.

'Would the defendant please rise,' the court clerk ordered.

'I am here to deliver my ruling on this case,' said the judge, 'but by no means is this final, as you will soon understand,' he cleared his throat before continuing.

'Ms. McCallum, I have taken into consideration all of the horrific events that led you here, to this Court. While I can't begin to understand the emotional and physical abuse you suffered throughout most of your young life, I have tried my utmost to take those into consideration when deliberating your future.'

The silence in the courtroom was deafening, the anticipation building, emotions stirring.

'As it was the jury's decision to find you, Ms. McCallum, not guilty of murder in the deaths of Mr. Zach Augustus and Mr. Bruce Marshall by reason of mental deficiencies, this Court hereby commits you to a minimum of 48 months in the mental health facility where you currently reside, under the direct care and guidance of Dr. Fitzgerald.'

He again silenced the room's verbal rumble with a light tap of his gavel. 'However, there are to be regular evaluations of your progress conducted by Dr. Fitzgerald only and those evaluations shared with me in writing twice a year. At the end of the 48 months, all parties here are to reconvene in my courtroom at a date and time you will be notified of, to ascertain what, if anything, should happen to you, Ms. McCallum, after that time. In other words, should you remain at the facility for further treatment or should you be released to face the world on your own?'

Bang. 'This proceeding is now adjourned.'

* * * * *

The detectives are shocked, not only by the jury's decision, but more so by the judge's ruling. 'What the fuck just happened? Forty-eight months for a double homicide?'

Dr. Fitzgerald, on the other hand, is quietly delighted. He is ready to take his protégé back, to get her back.

Blair Scott is wallowing in the notoriety of this case. The number of substantial monetary offers he's received to date are impressive, certainly lucrative. The world, it would seem, is fascinated by this case, his case.

As for Jessica? She sits quietly in the back seat of a police cruiser, not really looking forward to going back to the Mental Health Facility. 'But it's better than going to jail,' her inside voice reminds her.

She knows she can make the situation work for her. Make Dr. Fitzgerald bend to her wishes, her needs.

Dr. Fitzgerald is waiting for Jessica at the top of the circular driveway that leads to the entrance of the Mental Health Facility as the police car pulls up to deliver her once again into his care.

'Welcome back, Ms. McCallum,' he opens the car door and greets her professionally. 'Come inside and get settled first, but then we have much to talk about.' Jessica hesitantly exits the car, keeping her eyes down. He puts one hand very gently on the small of her back and guides her up the stairs to the imposing front doors. He removes an electronic access card from the inside pocket of his impeccably tailored suit jacket and swipes it past a code reader that stands guard over the doors. It recognizes him with the blink of a green light and an audible 'beep,' signaling his approved entry into a secret world that lay beyond.

Both are greeted inside by a gentle-faced nurse. 'Hello, Jessica,' she says. 'It's nice to have you back with us.'

'Nurse Anderson, would you kindly escort Ms. McCallum to her room and help put her things away, then bring her to my office,' Dr. Fitzgerald instructs.

'Of course, Dr. Fitzgerald,' the nurse says as she tenderly takes Jessica by the elbow and leads her away.

As she turns to go, Jessica glances back in the doctor's direction and unexpectedly winks at him. Uncertain of Jessica's intent, let alone the gesture itself, Dr. Fitzgerald glances around quickly, and relieved that no one had been around to witness the brief but rather intriguing exchange, turns away and retreats to the solitude of his office halfway down the long hallway.

The nurse takes Jessica up a flight of stairs, turns left at a small landing at the top, only to be met by yet one more electronically surveilled and guarded door. Another green blink of a light, a now familiar audible 'beep' and through they go to a well-lit, soulless corridor beyond.

After a few more steps, they stop in front of a closed door with the number 9 over it. 'We saved your room for you, Jessica,' the nurse smiles as she opens the door and takes Jessica through.

Jessica doesn't bother to look around. There's nothing that suggests this room belongs to any one in particular. It is sterile, also without a soul.

Nurse Anderson places Jessica's suitcase on the foot of a small bed, opens it, and begins to pull items out. 'Don't touch my things.' Jessica grits her teeth and barely whispers. 'Please,' she adds in an attempt to sound much more gracious than she feels. *Tic.*

'Oh, uh, sure,' the nurse gently puts the few things back in the suitcase and closes the lid. 'You can take care of these things later, when you feel up to it. In the meantime, let's go see Dr. Fitzgerald in his office, shall we? That's a good girl.' *Patronizing cow.*

Jessica already knows the way to Dr. Fitzgerald's office—could have found it with her eyes closed, if she was being honest—and most definitely would have preferred not to have an escort. 'I'm not a fucking child.' Jessica wants to scream at Nurse Anderson, but doesn't. Won't. Mustn't.

Down the stairs, along the hallway to another closed door with the name 'Dr. D. Fitzgerald' on it. After a light tap on the door, a lock on the other side is heard disengaging. It was an electronic safety feature Dr. Fitzgerald had discreetly installed some years ago after a particular nasty confrontation with a very disturbed, but thankfully now former patient.

Without his authorization and the press of a well-hidden button, whose location under his desk only he and the man who installed it know about, no one can gain entry to or, perhaps more relevantly, escape his office. 'Come in,' a male voice calls out from the other side of the door.

Nurse Anderson opens the door and ushers Jessica inside Dr. Fitzgerald's office. The interior is richly, warmly dark with floor-to-ceiling panels of mahogany on three walls, while the fourth is one massive bookcase filled with encyclopedias, an impressive collection of medical journals and an assortment of odd looking medical devices. She doesn't bother to take in the view from the office windows, because there are none. Dr. Fitzgerald says it's to safeguard the privacy of his patients and to prevent outside distractions from filtering in. Jessica suspects it's to protect prying eyes on the outside from discovering what was really going on in the inside.

Subtle tones of classical music fill the large space, but where it comes from, she doesn't know. She does know she's never been in this room when the music hasn't been playing. Its purpose she is convinced is to emit waves of tranquility that are meant to calm her, soothe her, lull her senses into accepting this as a truly safe space where she can express her emotions and verbalize her thoughts. Most times, though, the sounds simply annoy her, to the point where she shuts down completely and Dr. Fitzgerald is forced to end their session. If he would only figure out that she would react better to something that had more of a beat to it. Something that would keep tempo with her wildly animated thoughts. A beat that would pulsate in unison with her frenzied psyche. If only he understood.

In one corner of the room stands an ornate antique wood desk, behind which Dr. Fitzgerald now sits, with another chair on the opposite side of the desk facing him. It is used on those occasions when more formal chats with a patient are called for.

In another corner of the room, a beautifully upholstered chaise lounge strewn with matching pillows and a cashmere throw peeks out from behind a long, sheer white Chiffon panel that's suspended from a rod attached to the ceiling above it— a modern take on the 'psychiatrist's couch' and the one Dr. Fitzgerald prefers for his more 'intimate' sessions.

For now, though, he indicates to Jessica that she should sit in the chair opposite him at the desk. It had been a while since they'd had a moment to themselves, spent a moment by themselves, and he wanted to assess whether or not he'd be forced to start all over again with her 'treatment' or if he could pick up from where they had left off. He hoped it was the latter.

'So,' Dr. Fitzgerald begins, 'how do you feel being back here, Jessica? Are you happy to see me?'

She lifts her eyes and stares across the desk at him with absolutely no hint of any emotion. She's going to make him work for this, work for her. She's going to bring him crawling to her, but on her terms, not his. She knows she now has exactly 48 months to make that happen.

If Jessica has any chance whatsoever of walking out of here, she knows Dr. Fitzgerald is her key. He is the means to her end. He was also going to become her source of financial freedom. 'But, first things first,' she reminds herself.

Unfortunately for Dr. Fitzgerald, he wouldn't come to the awful realization that he was only ever meant to be her exit strategy until it was far too late.

The Finest Years

Once upon a time
in a mind so far adrift
There lived a little girl
who believed she had a gift.

She grew from no one's ugly duckling
into someone's beautiful swan
All the while encouraged
by the voices not yet gone!

Chapter One

'All rise. This Court is now in session,' the clerk called out.

Judge Hanson took his place at the bench and got right to the point. 'Dr. Fitzgerald, if you would kindly speak into the microphone before you.' Dr. Fitzgerald pulled the microphone closer, arranged it in front of him, turned it on, then opened a folder and nodded politely to the judge, 'Good morning, Your Honor.'

'Dr. Fitzgerald,' the judge acknowledged him with a return nod. 'I have thoroughly reviewed each and every one of the reports you submitted to me over the past 48 months regarding the progress of Ms. McCallum's treatment, and naturally, Ms. McCallum herself,' the judge nodded to the defendant who now sat before him looking alert, understandably a little apprehensive, and perhaps on the periphery of what, at first glance, could be misconstrued as timidity. *Tic.*

'I must say, I was encouraged by what I read,' the judge stated. 'Without getting into too much psychological jargon please, Dr. Fitzgerald, would you kindly provide this Court with a summary of Ms. McCallum's overall treatment and your personal recommendation as to the direction of her future.'

'Certainly, Your Honor,' the doctor said as he quickly referred to his notes.

'Ms. McCallum was initially reluctant to participate in treatment. However, I came to understand that this was not an act of defiance on her part, but rather an attempt at diversion because she was afraid of finding out who she truly was,' he said, then paused thoughtfully for a moment before continuing. 'You must understand that she had been so many different things to so many different people up to that point in her life that she'd never had the opportunity to know who she truly was. To know the real person trapped inside her.'

Tic.

'For the first few months, Jessica and I simply sat in my office and talked. Admittedly, I did most of the talking, but the objective was to slowly, carefully regain her trust and get her to open up more...to know that it was a safe environment where she could share her thoughts, her dreams, and her hopes, if she had any at that point,' he explained. 'I asked her what she hoped for her future. And, perhaps more to the point, what might her future hold for her? It is my professional opinion that if a person has no hope, then he or she believes there's no reason whatsoever to even think about a future. For these individuals, it's a fruitless and cruel cycle, and it's not long before they simply give up engaging altogether in life.'

Dr. Fitzgerald once again scanned his notes, then continued, 'Jessica had been studying Psychology prior to her incarceration, so I asked if she'd like to continue with her education, which to my delight she said she would. Psychology was of great interest to her throughout her teenage years and very early twenties, and she had passionately pursued what she had hoped would be a fulfilling career in the field and did so with impressive academic results, I might add.

'I arranged for Ms. McCallum to continue her studies online through our facility, though on a somewhat limited basis as my team's main focus was on Jessica's overall recovery. Certainly, her continuing education was an important part of the process, but it was not the priority in this situation.

'I also gave her limited access to the extensive library in my office for research purposes, should she wish to. And she did, often. I also made myself available, should she have any questions with respect to her studies. As I'm sure you can appreciate, Your Honor, I never did find as much time as I would have liked— outside of our professional contact, that is—to spend with Ms. McCallum.' Dr. Fitzgerald stopped for a moment to clear his throat. Was it meant to calm his conscience or was it intended to prevent an involuntary exorcism of the now too many lies that had begun to possess him?

'Ms. McCallum has an exceptionally gifted mind, Your Honor,' he noted in what he hoped was a most professional tone, despite the more personal truth.

What he failed to disclose to the Court, however, was his complete fascination with her, his emergent obsession over her.

Jessica was an enigma to him. A smart, beautiful, and complex paradox who seemed genuinely eager to learn about life as it is meant to be and not as it was for her. He was just as eager to show her that life, to provide her with that life. *My very own Eliza Doolittle,* he often thought to himself, *to my Professor Henry Higgins*, he often thought of himself.

'Dr. Fitzgerald,' the judge disrupted his thoughts, 'what if anything would Ms. McCallum like to do with herself, should she be granted the opportunity to rejoin society? Has she set herself any goals?'

Turning to another page in his binder, Dr. Fitzgerald nodded. 'She has, Your Honor,' his smile resembling that of a very proud parent.

'With the credits she had already attained prior to her incarceration, together with the additional credits she earned through the courses we arranged, Ms. McCallum is proud to advise this Court that she has just graduated with an Honor's Degree in Social Work,' Dr. Fitzgerald noted. 'While it is not the Psychology Degree she had hoped for, Ms. McCallum understands that although her felonious past does not prohibit her from pursuing that option, the reality is that it would, in all likelihood, preclude her from securing any doctorate position.'

Dr. Fitzgerald continued, 'Based on that, Ms. McCallum has instead chosen to hopefully pursue a Master's Degree in Social Work. That will still give her the opportunity to counsel others who may find themselves in the same abusive type of relationship as she did. After all, who better to truly understand and relate to them than someone who has survived those same experiences, in spite of the unfortunate, and hopefully temporary, outcome in Ms. McCallum's case?

'Ms. McCallum believes that this entire experience has made her stronger physically and emotionally, while at the same time preparing her for living on her own with the necessary and socially appropriate coping skills she will need,' Dr. Fitzgerald added, 'and I certainly support her eagerness to learn.'

The judge made a few notes on the paper in front of him and continued his questioning. 'There's one final concern this Court has, Dr. Fitzgerald, with respect to whether or not Ms. McCallum should be released, and that is where she will reside. Do you feel she is ready to live on her own?'

'No, Your Honor,' the doctor didn't hesitate to reply. 'I don't believe she's quite at that point,' he admitted. 'All in good time,' his ego quietly reminded him. Jessica and he had already spoken privately prior to this proceeding. Dr. Fitzgerald wanted her to know what he was going to say beforehand, so as not to catch her off-guard at the last minute. He wasn't sure how she would have reacted had he not forewarned her and he didn't want to take any chances, not when he was this close. Now that they were this close to being together.

It was also during that very same discussion with Dr. Fitzgerald that Jessica's mind recognized a familiar voice. Just a whisper, really. One that had been hiding, waiting, for some time now. It was struggling to get her attention. *Tic.*

'However, I do believe it would help her assimilate better to the world around her if she were to be placed in a more natural setting, such as a home where she can be somewhat monitored and supervised, especially with respect to the medication she must take on a daily basis.

'Ms. McCallum now understands that the medication she has been prescribed is vital to not just her overall recovery, but it's something she'll have to take for the rest of her life. Something she'll have to rely on for the rest of her life if she is to have any chance whatsoever of a life.'

'And is there such a place, Doctor, where she can continue her recovery?' the judge asked.

'There is,' Dr. Fitzgerald said as he removed a sheet of paper from the binder in front of him, then handed it to the bailiff who, in turn, walked it to the judge. 'It is called 'Hope's Home.' Not named after anyone specifically Your Honor, but rather a welcome sign that says there's hope inside…'hope is home.'

'It's a manor house that's located on the outskirts of Six-Mile Pond, a small town approximately 150 kilometers away. It is managed by a highly skilled psychiatric nurse, along with a small household staff,' he added. 'I visit the home once or twice a week, during which time I allocate at least one hour with each patient in order to monitor and assess progress,' Dr. Fitzgerald explained.

'The home's environment offers more one-on-one time between residents and their caregivers, which is why accommodations are limited to just four patients, or 'guests' as we refer to them, at any one time. And this facility is for female guests only, Your Honor,' he added. 'As you can imagine, the fewer distractions and/or temptations there are for our guests in their recovery pursuits, the better for all involved.'

The judge nodded in understanding. 'And what of her plans to continue her education?' the judge inquired.

'Coincidentally, Hope's Home is within short walking distance of a university Ms. McCallum is considering for her master's degree, but of course has not yet applied to pending Your Honor's final decision,' Dr. Fitzgerald added humbly, hopefully.

Yet, there was nothing coincidental about it. He had initially purchased the manor house and its vast grounds several years ago, well before he ever met Jessica, as an investment, with the idea of turning it into student housing due of its proximity to the nearby university.

As fate would have it, he never had found the time, nor quite frankly the inclination, to do anything about it or with it. And so, there it sat, forlorn, empty, abandoned. *Much like Jessica,* he recently thought to himself.

And so his passion to restore the manor house to its former splendor had been reignited when he met Jessica. At first, he fought the seeds of unethical thoughts that began to germinate their way into his daily life, both professionally and personally.

He couldn't stop himself, though. Nor had he been able to help himself. Something in him wanted to shape her life. To share her life. To be the only one in her life, if truth be told.

So, about ten months prior to this court proceeding, he began the complete renovation of the old manor house, including designing a special, private apartment just for Jessica on the second floor. He personally saw to it that only those who knew the value of discretion were hired as part of the staff.

All that was left to do was to figure out how to make all of it happen without raising anyone's suspicions, particularly his wife's.

* * * * *

Jessica sat calmly in her chair behind the big desk at the front of the courtroom, beside her lawyer, listening to the conversations taking place around her, about her. Why is it no one ever felt she could speak for herself? Such bullshit! In this instance, however, she was more than pleased with Dr. Fitzgerald's performance up to that point. He was doing an excellent job of pleading her case to the judge on her behalf, just as she knew he could, had planned that he would.

Yet, Jessica had come to realize early on in their relationship that dear Dr. Fitzgerald wasn't going to be so easy to influence, let alone control.

Several times when she had not so inadvertently touched his hand with hers or edged a knee closer to his, Dr. Fitzgerald had made it clear that he would never, ever risk his professional career and hard-earned reputation by crossing ethical boundaries with any of his patients.

We'll see about that, Jessica remembered thinking to herself at the time. As it so happened, she had plenty of time on her hands. 'Good things come to those who wait,' she reminded herself of one of Mama's favorite expressions.

However, it hadn't been Jessica who ultimately decided to test the peripheries, to push those boundaries. It had been the charming Dr. Fitzgerald, or had he? Who was pursuing whom?

Over time, Jessica began sharing memories from her past with the doctor, admittedly some containing a few not-so-factual truths. She hoped her words would create just a tiny crack in the doctor's outer shell. After all, everyone knew that if you constantly poked at a small crack, it more often than not led to more cracks, bigger cracks. Until finally the object shattered completely, exposing what was on the inside to what was waiting outside. Weakened. Susceptible.

First and foremost, she would immerse herself in her studies. She needed to learn more, to discover more, to solve problems better. Because next time, and oh how she craved a next time, she had no intention of making the same mistakes she had in the past, or any mistake, for that matter.

She knew exactly where things had gone so wrong on her last adventure—that fucking sliding lock in the trapdoor. The wooden door itself had naturally burned quickly, causing the lock to drop to the first floor due to its heavier weight, burying itself under other debris. As a result, it had been somewhat protected from the more extreme heat of the flames as the cabin burned to the ground. It was salvageable enough for forensics to recover a single fingerprint…her fingerprint. It had been the one piece that had led to her undoing. It would never happen again.

'Ms. McCallum,' her thoughts were interrupted when the judge suddenly spoke directly to her, 'would you kindly move the microphone in front of you, so you and I can have a quick conversation?'

Dr. Fitzgerald slid the microphone toward Jessica, but not up to her lips, afraid he might inadvertently touch her in the way he desperately wanted to at that moment. He could feel her anxiety, could sense her trepidation. He wanted to lay a comforting hand on her shoulder. He longed to turn her toward him and hug her, infusing her with confidence. He wanted to gently lay his lips on her forehead and reassuringly whisper 'there, there, my little one.' Instead, he did nothing.

Jessica inched the microphone toward her mouth and, in a barely audible voice, acknowledged the judge. 'Good morning, sir...I mean, Your Honor,' she corrected herself.

'Ms. McCallum,' Judge Hanson briefly acknowledged her before he continued, 'I am going to, once again, release you into Dr. Fitzgerald's capable hands.'

If you only knew, Jessica thought to herself while offering a rehearsed submissive smile to the judge. 'Thank you, Your Honor.'

'I am pleased with your determination and efforts to date, Ms. McCallum,' the judge began. 'However, as Dr. Fitzgerald points out, he feels you require further support with respect to your treatment, and also believes you would greatly benefit from practical, day-to-day experiences you would be exposed to in a more relaxed setting.'

Judge Hanson paused to shuffle some papers in front of him, finally coming to rest on a specific piece of information Dr. Fitzgerald had provided to him. 'It is this Court's decision that Ms. McCallum be transferred to Hope's Home under the continuing care of Dr. Fitzgerald for a minimum of two more years, at which time we will, once again, reconvene to access Ms. McCallum's progress, or lack thereof,' the judge so ordered with a firm tap of his gavel.

Jessica felt herself relax, but only a little. Nothing anyone else in the courtroom would have noticed. *It's time for this swan to spread her wings just a little further,* Jessica thought to herself. *Tic.*

Dr. Fitzgerald smiled humbly at Judge Hanson and nodded his head slightly. 'Thank you, Your Honor.' But inside he was doing his best to control his relief, his overwhelming excitement.

Admittedly, he had taken an oath when he graduated that, under no circumstances, would he ever compromise his professional ethics. And so far, he had not, nor did he plan to. But there was nothing in the ethics oath that precluded him from preparing for a future when Jessica would no longer be his patient. He was hoping for that day, planning for that day. Working toward that day. And with one final swing of the judge's gavel, that day was now much closer.

Jessica was well-aware that Dr. Fitzgerald thought he had his own designs when it came to her. What he hadn't yet figured out was that his naïve blueprint was the very foundation on which she was building her own future. This was going to be her opportunity to shape it, sharpen it, then execute it.

Chapter Two

Jessica had been given carte blanche by Dr. Fitzgerald when it came to decorating her apartment. He had provided her with a generous budget to create her 'personal space.' A collection of colors, furnishings, and odds and ends that would reflect who she is, who she was struggling to become.

Dr. Fitzgerald had also set aside additional monies for the possibility and potential that the apartment's interior would evolve over time as Jessica herself evolved, and if he were completely honest with himself, as their own relationship hopefully evolved.

He was encouraged by Jessica's enthusiasm for the decorating project and for her future. Watching her was like watching a child discovering bits and pieces of the world for the first time. For him, it was smile-inducing, heart-fluttering. For Jessica, it was envy-provoking, greed-stimulating.

As for Jessica's apartment, there was never any doubt about her choice in colors. She intentionally selected soft pastels throughout. There was only one bold accent color she planned to add to the décor…but, not just yet.

She wanted nothing gaudy. Nothing cheap. Nothing like Mama. She was nothing like Mama. Was she?

Her favorite purchase by far was the four-poster bed she had finally settled on. It was soft, romantic, warm…perhaps on the verge of inviting.

Jessica had fashioned panels of sheer, peach-colored chiffon into a seductive canopy that flowed above the bed then fell gracefully from each of the four posters, suggesting the peek-a-boo possibility that something wonderful awaited within, if one were so inclined.

Her apartment had a small galley-style kitchen where she could store and prepare a few basics such as tea or coffee, toast and snacks, if she wished to. Guests' formal meals were served in the dining room on the main floor of the house where everyone was expected for breakfast and lunch, should their schedules permit. Jessica made sure hers did not. Guests were, however, encouraged to attend dinner together in the dining room each evening.

Most of the time, though, Jessica preferred to eat alone in her apartment under the guise of 'I'm studying.' She did on occasion put in the 'mandatory' show-and-tell moments for others. She knew she was being monitored. Her habits measured. Her interactions with others noted.

Surprisingly, she's okay with all of that. Even tolerant. She could and would 'tolerate' the situation, because her mind reasoned that it was for a short period of time in relation to what awaited the rest of her life. Small sacrifices, big rewards.

There was, however, one tiny issue she had with respect to this entire arrangement. Well, not so much a 'tiny issue' as one 'super-sized matron' who went by the name of Fraulein Hildreth Müller, Head Psychiatric Nurse and humorless gatekeeper of Hope's Home.

She had been personally interviewed and subsequently hired by Dr. Fitzgerald, selected from among the few elite resumes that had been couriered directly to him from a reputable, highly discerning agency. Dr. Fitzgerald believed that Ms. Müller was the perfect fit.

She had worked in Europe for most of her career, discreetly caring for a number of very wealthy, very secretive, and apparently, very disturbed families and their hidden 'troubles.' She obviously understood the meaning of discretion, so Dr. Fitzgerald felt confident in his choice.

What her resume neglected to reveal to the good doctor was that, along the way, she had perfected a new skill...the art of 'negotiation.' After all, some 'troubles' were worth more than others, especially when brought to the attention of the right family member.

But, when opportunities in Europe began to wither as a result of a criminal investigation into her alleged professional misconduct, she arranged a hasty departure to North America. She knew there was so much 'new money' on that side of the world and she was after her share. Yet, she wasn't sure if the position under Dr. Fitzgerald held that level of potential. Only time would tell. Oh, and it would. Unfortunately for her, not in the way she had hoped, but rather in a way she could not have expected nor anticipated.

Fraulein Müller settled into her adequately appointed apartment on the ground floor of the manor house in a location Dr. Fitzgerald felt was the most suitable 'vantage point' from where she could keep a subtle eye on the 'comings and goings of the house.' What Fraulein Müller appreciated more, however, was the view it offered her into guests' habits and routines, their behaviors, their truths, specifically their ugly truths, for that's where the real value lay.

Next to Ms. Müller's apartment was a small room that kept the pulse of the house's state-of-the-art technology, security, and surveillance capabilities beating. Also, within this room were a number of unimpeachable witnesses. A dozen cameras that recorded everything and anything that occurred between nine at night and seven in the morning, the time guests were expected to be in and remain in their rooms. While their individual suites were not subjected to cameras, everything else, both inside and outside the house, was.

At nine sharp each night, as the house rules stated, no one should be going anywhere nor coming from somewhere. The house's interior cameras and other security features were automatically activated and remained on until the next morning at precisely seven. All of the exterior cameras remained on 24 hours a day, seven days a week. A precaution or a premonition?

Other than Dr. Fitzgerald, only Ms. Müller was given the keypad code to access the communication's room, though with sternly delivered instructions that it was only to be used in case of an emergency, such as if she believed there was something not right within the house or there was imminent danger to any of the 'guests' inside the house.

She was expected to have the presence of mind, if there were a situation during the daytime, to activate all of the house's cameras with the flick of a single switch, then all would be recorded and preserved for Dr. Fitzgerald to personally review the next day, or worst case scenario, as evidence to be passed along to the appropriate authorities.

He wanted…no, *needed*…to ensure the home was safeguarded. Jessica's home…and perhaps someday, in the not-too-distant future, it may be *their* home. A discreet hideaway for just the two of them. That's why he had chosen the name Hope's Home. *Come in…there's hope in this home.* Jessica was in this home and Jessica was all that he hoped for.

* * * * *

From the very beginning of their co-existence, under the same roof but not under the same privileges, Jessica began what she referred to as 'the courting phase' of her relationship with Fraulein Hildreth Müller. A yet-to-be-determined span that would give her the necessary time to befriend and bemuse Frankenstein Müller, as Jessica liked to silently refer to her. Ironically, there was just something about the old woman that Jessica felt uncomfortable with.

It was also shortly after Ms. Müller's arrival that Jessica made the decision to stop taking her medication. She continued to dutifully line up each morning to receive her pills, which were strictly meted out by Ms. Müller, but she never actually took them. Instead, she palmed them from one hand to the other while accepting a glass of water to wash the pills down. She made of show of popping something into her mouth, although her hand was empty, while taking a sip of water using the other hand that actually held the pills that were scrunched and held between the folds of her palm. She would smile sweetly at Ms. Müller then carry on with her day. Once out of Ms. Müller's sight, she pocketed the pills, went to her apartment, and flushed them down the toilet.

She didn't need the medication. She was fine. She actually believed she was better without the pills. Her mind was sharper and faster. More eager and determined to accomplish whatever needed to be done.

She needed to rely on all these strengths now particularly, because on more than one occasion recently, Jessica had observed Ms. Müller either entering or exiting the small communications room prior to Dr. Fitzgerald's expected arrival at 7:30 am. There was no reason for her to be in that room then, because the cameras were shut off at exactly 7 am. Was she curious as to what the cameras might reveal from the previous night? What they could possibly expose in the dark, where the naked eye might not?

True to his word, Dr. Fitzgerald visited the house once a week, at first. And also true to his word, he allocated one hour's time with each guest, but always with Jessica scheduled as his last appointment of the day. He wanted her to be last so he had something to look forward to at the beginning of the day, rather than her being first and he then suffering her absence for what was left of the day.

He also knew that if he went over his allotted time with Jessica, there wouldn't be anyone waiting in line, anxious for their appointment. He could take his time with her. He could simply be with her.

Late one afternoon, after just six months in these new surroundings, Jessica felt it was time to further her relationship with Dr. Fitzgerald. And so, at the start of her session that day with Dr. Fitzgerald, she extended an invitation to him to join her for dinner in her apartment, should their session run over, which she made sure happened more often than not lately.

Up to this point, she had patiently waited for Dr. Fitzgerald to come to her. To seek her out. And he had. He never missed an appointment with her, never brushed her off when she asked for his advice with respect to her studies. He had never refused her anything, come to think of it. But Jessica's focus remained on the end result she was ultimately seeking. That she was determined to accomplish.

As she expected, Dr. Fitzgerald graciously and eagerly accepted her dinner invitation. Jessica smiled sweetly at him across the small living room of her apartment where they now sat, facing each other, gauging each other. One chasing a fairytale ending, the other pursuing a lucrative new beginning.

'Excuse me for a moment, please.' She rose gracefully from the overstuffed soft pink chair in which she sat, slowly removed her sweater, undid the button at the top of her blouse, and seductively walked toward a phone that hung on the wall near her front door. Her left hand reached up and removed the hair clip that suppressed her long, blonde curls. Her right hand came up to join its partner, and together, they arranged the curls over each shoulder, being careful to leave one solitary strand of golden coils cascading freely down her back to where the little hollow at the top of her buttocks lay concealed beneath her clothes.

Jessica instinctively giggled softly to herself as she picked up the phone's handset and selected only two numbers, indicating she was calling someone inside the house. Almost immediately she was connected to the party on the other end.

'Ms. Müller, this is Jessica,' she said as she turned around so she could lock eyes with the doctor. 'Dr. Fitzgerald will be joining me for dinner this evening, so if you would be so kind as to bring two meals up to my apartment later, but make sure you call beforehand...in case we're in the middle of something.' She then smiled innocently at the doctor, yet her eyes suggested something altogether different.

'Thank you,' Jessica said into the mouthpiece after a few moments, then returned the phone to its perch. 'Ms. Müller doesn't seem to be too happy about us having dinner together...up here...alone,' she said as she returned to the overstuffed chair, but didn't sit down. 'I'm sorry if my invitation was inappropriate, Dr. Fitzgerald. It's just that I see how hard you work. Lately, it's been well past dinner time when we finish our sessions,' she said quietly, as she lowered her eyes and moved toward him. She came to stand directly in front of him, her stance wide, her waist narrow. She looked down at him, then bent over and placed a warm hand atop one of his. 'I wanted to do something special, so I thought by having our session over dinner, it would be a nice way for you to relax, even if that's just for a half hour or so.' She lingered over him just a little longer, before returning to her chair.

Dr. Fitzgerald sat quietly, unable to say anything until he could salvage some self-control. 'Don't worry about Ms. Müller, Jessica,' Dr. Fitzgerald eventually assured her. 'I'll speak to her personally and advise her of the sincerity of your intentions.'

Jessica's smile indicated she was happy with his decision, but not for the reason Dr. Fitzgerald believed. Jessica was happy because it would send a clear message to Fraulein Müller that Jessica's status in Dr. Fitzgerald's eyes was much greater and more important than hers. *Frumpy old bitch.*

'But, let's not dwell on that,' Dr. Fitzgerald said as he took a small box out of his pants' pocket, 'I have a little something for you.'

He rose from the couch and handed the box to Jessica who took it from him and slowly opened the red velvet-covered lid. Inside was a beautiful gold necklace with a tiny gold teddy bear figurine suspended from a delicate loop. *Tic.*

'I saw this the other day and immediately thought of you,' said Dr. Fitzgerald as he retrieved the necklace from the box and adoringly fastened it around Jessica's neck. 'I know from our conversations over the years that you have a particular fondness for teddy bears,' he smiled at her.

Jessica smiled at him in return. Yes, she does have a fondness for teddy bears, especially little *red* teddy bears. This one was gold, but it would do...for now. It was the sign of weakness she had been waiting for from Dr. Fitzgerald. The opening she needed in order to advance her plan.

'It's beautiful,' she said. 'Thank you, Doctor.' Yet, her expression didn't reflect gratitude.

'What's wrong, Jessica,' he asked, 'don't you like it?'

'No, no…it's not that,' she gently assured him. 'I love it, really I do, but…'

'But, what Jessica? Surely by now, you know that you can say anything to me and I'll never judge nor criticize you,' he assured her. 'Please, tell me what's on your mind.'

Jessica assumed a submissive pose, all the while looking at the floor beneath her. 'When I was a child, someone gave me a small red teddy bear candle with a little wick sticking out of the top of its head. Mama wouldn't let me light it, though. She said she would save it for me and wait for just the perfect occasion to light it for the first time.' She remembers that first time, that first man. It's what has kept her going, kept her hunting.

Jessica had been thinking of her words, practicing her words. What she would say at this very moment to achieve the results she wanted, the outcome she simply had to have.

'It would mean so much to me, Dr. Fitzgerald, if you could find one or two and buy them for me,' she appealed to him. 'It's been so long since I've had one. Your staff at the other facility didn't allow anyone to have a candle in their possession, let alone their room. I understand why,' she added quickly, 'but here, in this beautiful house and in this amazing apartment, I was hoping I might be permitted to have just one. It would be nice to put it on the table when you come for dinner…again,' she added suggestively.

Chapter Three

Dr. Fitzgerald did speak with Ms. Müller that same evening, after having left Jessica's apartment just prior to nine o'clock. Had he left a minute or two sooner, he wouldn't have had to go in search of Ms. Müller, because he would have found her standing right outside Jessica's apartment, one ear up close and personal with the door.

It wasn't unusual for Ms. Müller to be up on the second floor, though no one else was ever aware of it, or so she believed.

She moved stealthily from one door to the next most evenings between 8:45 and 8:57 pm, just before the cameras were activated, guaranteeing no witness to her nocturnal nosiness.

She sensed there was more to the doctor-patient relationship between Dr. Fitzgerald and Jessica McCallum. But she needed to be sure. She needed to see with her own eyes and know in her own mind that there was something definitely going on between them. This may be the opportunity she had been looking for, but she had to have solid proof in order to negotiate a worthwhile 'raise' with Dr. Fitzgerald.

A few days following Dr. Fitzgerald's visit, Ms. Müller and Jessica passed each other in the downstairs hallway. As Jessica went by, she deliberately reached up and played with the gold teddy bear pendant that still hung around her neck. She held the tiny figure between her fingers in a way that caught the overhead light and Ms. Müller's eye.

Ms. Müller stopped and commented to Jessica in an attempt to be friendlier to her following her 'little chat' with Dr. Fitzgerald. 'Well, now, isn't that a pretty little necklace. Is that new, Jessica?' she asked. 'I don't recall seeing it on you before?' Jessica also stopped, then slowly turned and walked back toward Ms. Müller. 'Why yes, it is new, Ms. Müller. How very observant of you. But I guess that's your job, isn't it? Watching over us, watching out for us.' Jessica inched a little closer and whispered into one of Ms. Müller's ears, 'Or just watching us,' then smiled, turned, and walked away, leaving a flustered Ms. Müller in her wake. Did she know? Did she? No.

It was several months following this verbal exchange before Ms. Müller felt composed enough to resume her subversive reconnaissance of the house and all of its inner workings…its internal secrets. She felt sure there were some…or at the very least one.

A few months later, she entered the communications room early one morning, before Dr. Fitzgerald was due to arrive. She was positive she'd heard footsteps quietly shuffling down the stairs earlier, but well past the previous evening's 9 pm curfew.

At the time, she hadn't been sure of what she heard, and after listening for a few moments and hearing nothing again, had drifted back to sleep…temporarily.

Her mind just wouldn't allow her body to settle, though. It tossed and turned the sound she had heard over and over again, her body rebelliously following.

After numerous failed attempts to find a comfortable position, Ms. Müller got up, wrapped herself in a bathrobe that was resting at the foot of her bed, and retrieved a small flashlight she kept in the nightstand beside her bed.

She checked to make sure the batteries in the flashlight were working, and satisfied with the amount and scope of light it projected, albeit weak, switched it off and headed to her door, out her door. Through another door and into the little room next to hers, all without a sound.

She still had about half an hour before Dr. Fitzgerald's morning arrival. Plenty of time, more than she needed, she suspected.

She remembered approximately what time it was when she had heard the strange sound, because she had looked at the clock on her bedside table, 12:30 in the morning or thereabouts. So, all she needed to do was rewind the recording to that time and see if any of the cameras captured something that may be of interest to her…or even better, of interest to Dr. Fitzgerald.

* * * * *

Ms. Müller knew which machine and which buttons to push to find what she was hunting for. She had been well-trained in these types of electronics while in Europe. There were times when she would be asked by 'clients' to discreetly erase surveillance footage of a specific day or timeframe. They didn't want whatever was on the tape to 'fall into the wrong hands,' so a few had, regrettably in hindsight, assigned the task to Ms. Müller.

At first, she had dutifully done as she was requested without thinking twice about it. Over time, though, curiosity got the best of her, and one day when she was asked to erase a recording, she decided to look at it first. Why not? It's not as though anyone else was ever going to see it. Anyway, it was probably something mundane or inane. Oh, but it was neither.

The footage showed a young man, her client's emotionally disturbed grown son whom Ms. Müller had been hired to care for, standing over a young female who was lying on her back in the tiny hallway that led to the staff's quarters.

He was slapping her, beating her, attempting to take her clothes off. She was fighting back, kicking him, struggling to keep her clothes on.

The scuffle lasted less than 15 seconds before the girl was simply overpowered by his obvious strength over her, his hands now clasping her tiny neck between them.

Just before the girl's hands, now scratching at the man's face, slipped to the floor as the life was being squeezed out of her, two figures race into the picture, one dragging the man off of the girl as the other pulled the girl out of harm's way and out of view of the camera's lens. She recognized the two individuals as her clients themselves, Monsieur Bertrand Benoit and his wife Micheline. But who was the girl?

Ms. Müller couldn't make out the identity of the girl, because she was in the shadows most of the time, with him on top of her. But it didn't matter—she had seen enough—enough to know that this was worth bringing to the family's attention. She did as she was told and erased the entire contents of that specific tape, but not before making a copy for herself. It was now the only witness.

Ms. Müller hid the CD with the copy on it in her room, which she kept locked whether she was inside or not, and went in search of her patient, Lucien Benoit. She climbed the carpeted stairs to the second floor and on up to the third floor, where Lucien was 'kept' in a beautiful suite of rooms to which only a few people had access.

She selected a key from the heavy ring that always hung from a loop on her skirt's waistband and used it to unlock Lucien's door. She entered a dark environment, despite the day's vast sunshine, made her way to a row of large brocade curtains that shrouded an equal number of large leaded glass windows and pulled them aside, one by one.

Behind her, she heard a pained moan and turned to see Lucien cocoon himself deeper within a very expensive duvet. 'Shut the fucking curtains!' he screamed.

Ms. Müller, undeterred by these familiar morning greetings, stepped to the side of his bed and tried to gently pull the covers back, but her efforts were met with resistance.

'Lucien,' Ms. Müller insisted, 'please let me see you for just a minute, so I can assure myself that you're alright, and then I'll order a nice, big breakfast for you. How does that sound?'

Cautiously, the covers released their hold on Lucien and revealed a head encased in unruly hair, a face covered in deep scratches and eyes plagued by heavy sedation.

'Oh my, Lucien,' Ms. Müller smoothed the hair back from his face to study the damage that had been done. 'What happened?' she asked, although she already knew the answer. She was hoping he would reveal the girl's name. She simply must learn the name of the girl in the surveillance footage if she was to make this work to her best financial advantage. She was sure the Benoits would negotiate a little something extra to keep her from taking the evidence to the poor girl's family, thus opening up a whole new can of worms, legal and otherwise. But she had to know the girl's name first. This was too important for her to try to bluff her way through.

'I don't know,' Lucien cried, a child trapped in a man's body. 'I don't remember.' She'd heard the excuse before…many times before. It was the way Lucien chose not to recognize nor deal with his 'troubles.' He didn't ever want to talk about them. He didn't ever admit to them, because he knew his parents would make everything go away, just as they always did. He knew it would only be a matter of a few days before this latest 'trouble' would be hidden, silenced forever, and life would carry on as though evil didn't reside in this house.

Ms. Müller knew she'd never get a straight answer about the girl's identity from Lucien, so she decided to try a different approach to discovering who she was. She headed for the kitchen…the hub of the mansion's activity…and the source of all gossip, some true, some not. Surprisingly, mostly true.

As she entered the kitchen, Ms. Müller quickly scanned the large room and took note that one of the cook's assistants, Lizbeth, was absent. At that hour, all kitchen staff should be busy preparing the morning meal for the household.

'Mrs. Tierney,' Ms. Müller asked the cook, 'are you missing a member of your kitchen staff this morning?'

The cook, although she kept an eye on the delicate eggs she was preparing, did answer. 'Damned right I am,' she snapped. 'Appears Lizbeth got an offer from another family who live closer to where she was born and so she decided to move back home. At least that's what Monsieur Benoit told me earlier this morning,' she added.

'I'm sure he did,' Ms. Müller responded under her breath.

Coincidentally, Ms. Müller also left the Benoit's employ soon afterward. She received a very healthy severance package. The Benoits received a signed Non-Disclosure Agreement.

While the arrangement may not have been mutually agreeable, it was nonetheless mutually beneficial.

Chapter Four

Ms. Müller rewound the recording to roughly the time she remembered hearing the sounds coming from the stairs at the front of the house and pushed 'play.' Nothing but an empty staircase, an empty foyer, a seemingly empty house. Perhaps it had been her imagination after all.

Suddenly, the barely distinguishable figure of Dr. Fitzgerald could be seen moving down the stairs, crossing the foyer to the security alarm pad, entering a code, looking at the illuminated dial on his wristwatch and waiting. Waiting for the necessary amount of time between deactivation and reactivation, otherwise the alarm would sound. *A scenario he would prefer to avoid, I'm sure*, Ms. Müller thought to herself as she continued to watch. Little did she know that Dr. Fitzgerald had a ready, and certainly plausible, explanation as to why he would be here at that hour of the morning, should he find himself in a position where one was required. Simply put, Jessica had reached out to him for help, and as her primary caregiver, he had responded in a manner consistent with his professional obligations. End of story. He didn't know that it didn't matter whether he had an explanation, plausible or not.

The camera next showed him taking his eyes off his wristwatch and reactivating the system. From this point, Ms. Müller knew he had only ten seconds to get out the front door and close it behind him before the alarm sounded. Which he obviously did successfully, because she knew without a doubt that no alarm sounded in the house last night.

'Now that's interesting,' she said in a barely audible voice. 'But, if he left the house at 12:30, what time did he get here?' she quietly asked herself before pushing the 'rewind' button and stopping at 12 o'clock midnight...no sign of Dr. Fitzgerald. *Perhaps she had gone too far back,* she thought at first. She pushed fast forward to 12:15 am, but again, no Dr. Fitzgerald. The hint of a smile appeared on her face as she pushed 'rewind' once again. Eleven-thirty...nothing. Eleven...still nothing.

Ms. Müller's smile grew even wider. Her future was looking more rewarding with each rewound minute.

Ten-thirty and there he was. Dr. Fitzgerald entering the darkened house, deactivating the alarm system, then making his way cautiously up the staircase to the second floor, Jessica's floor.

Ms. Müller knew it wasn't yet enough to confront Dr. Fitzgerald. But it was enough for her to enthusiastically and greedily pursue her suspicions.

'Dr. Fitzgerald arrived at 10:30 and left at 12:30. Just what did the good doctor do over the course of those two hours? And just what kind of 'treatment' did Jessica receive over the course of those same two hours?'

Ms. Müller was satisfied, for the moment, with what she had learned and once again fast-forwarded the video to 7 am, the time it would have automatically deactivated. Dr. Fitzgerald would never know she had already watched it, should he decide to review it himself and subsequently erase all evidence of the previous night.

Less than an hour after Ms. Müller's hasty exit from the communications room, Dr. Fitzgerald arrived at the manor for his usual rounds. Ms. Müller was sitting at a small table just inside the foyer waiting for him, but made it appear as though she was studying a few patient charts.

'Good morning, Ms. Müller,' Dr. Fitzgerald greeted her as usual. 'I take it all was quiet last night?' A typically innocent remark.

Ms. Müller slowly removed her reading glasses, took a handkerchief from one of her skirt's pockets, and began to clean each lens. 'Good morning, Dr. Fitzgerald,' she smiled at him. 'Oh yes,' she said as she continued cleaning her glasses, 'as quiet as a mouse.'

'That's always good to hear,' Dr. Fitzgerald responded. 'Well, I shall excuse myself and let you get back to your charts, while I begin my rounds, Ms. Müller.' He nodded to her, turned, and headed to a large, double pocket door protected office where he conducted all of his business, except when it came to Jessica.

He felt she was more at ease and much more open when they met privately in her apartment. There, together, they talked about how people behave differently in certain situations. Quite often, though, they talked about how she was worth being in love and being loved. Professionally speaking, of course.

'Come to think of it, Dr. Fitzgerald,' Ms. Müller suddenly called to him just as he was about to slide the doors closed behind him, 'there was one strange thing last night, actually.'

'And what was that?' Dr. Fitzgerald asked, never imagining that it was anything other than perhaps an irritatingly drippy tap or a sensitive water pipe.

Ms. Müller returned her glasses to her face and looked directly at the doctor. 'The thing is, I thought I heard footsteps on the stairs well after curfew.'

Dr. Fitzgerald hesitated for just a split second before replying. 'Did you get up to see what it was?'

'No, no…I didn't get up. I did listen for a while, but heard nothing else. It was probably just my imagination, right Dr. Fitzgerald?' she smiled at him.

'Yes, of course, Ms. Müller,' his tongue faltered as it tried to form the words. 'Now, I really must get to it,' he said while quickly slamming the pocket doors shut behind him.

Now alone, Dr. Fitzgerald leaned his forehead against the doors, inhaled, exhaled, then slowly walked to his desk and sat down, his mind racing. Had she seen him?

He had planned first thing this morning to erase the surveillance tapes from the night before, but now it would have to wait. It would look too suspicious if he suddenly ran to the communications room. Besides, no one else had any reason to look at the footage, so he felt it would be safe to wait until he could compose himself. Maybe in an hour or so, or lunchtime at the very latest.

Yes, he had been to see Jessica after-hours. She had called him on his personal cell phone that only she had the number to and asked if he could...if he *please would*...come and see her. She had been startled awake when her mind finally understood that it was wedged inside a horrifying nightmare. She'd really like to talk to him, she needed him, please.

None of it was true, of course. Jessica was just testing him. Testing the strength of his weakness when it came to her. She had to be sure he would come to her when she summoned him...and he had.

Dr. Fitzgerald arrived at approximately 10:30 pm, quietly let himself in the front foyer, immediately deactivated the security alarm and then re-activated the system. He stopped and listened for any signs of life from within the house, but heard nothing. He then made his way cautiously up the stairs to the second floor, crossed the landing and tread lightly along the hallway to the only doorway in this wing of the house...to Jessica's apartment.

No need to knock. He simply used his key to let himself in.

Chapter Five

Ms. Müller went about her usual routine, day in and day out, all the while keeping a particularly keen eye on Jessica. Looking for anything, really. A new piece of jewelry, a new outfit, a new attitude, something.

As for Dr. Fitzgerald, initially he wasn't so easy to keep in her sights, since he only visited the manor twice a week. Or so he wanted everyone to believe. He didn't know that Ms. Müller had recently added a new task to her daily rounds, despite the fact that it also added at least an extra hour to her already long day. But she saw it as a necessary inconvenience.

It involved spending just a brief amount of time in the communications room early each morning and a considerable amount of time logging each day's personal and electronic surveillance secrets each evening.

One particular night, just a few minutes before curfew, Ms. Müller skulked up the stairs to the second floor to begin her stealthy patrol outside Jessica's door.

Leaning one ear as close to the door as she possibly could without actually touching it, Ms. Müller heard Jessica's muffled voice inside. Ms. Müller knew she wasn't speaking to Dr. Fitzgerald, because he had not been at the house today, or was she?

Ms. Müller continued to listen and realized she was hearing just bits and pieces of a one-sided telephone conversation.

'Yes, I missed seeing you today, too,' she clearly heard Jessica say. Ms. Müller glanced down at her watch and saw that she had just a little over a minute to get back to her room before the internal surveillance cameras were activated.

She thought about her two choices—stay or go—for just a split second before heading for the stairs, blundering down the stairs, and to her own room.

These days, she had to be extra careful, because Dr. Fitzgerald seemed to have taken quite an interest in the communications room as of late and she couldn't risk getting caught.

As a result of Dr. Fitzgerald's interest, Ms. Müller had also developed just as much, if not slightly more, interest in the same communications room.

* * * * *

It was true. Lately, Dr. Fitzgerald had been spending more time in the communications room. Only because he had been spending more time with Jessica, after-hours when everyone had long gone to their rooms for the night. So, the only witness to his indiscretions resided in the communications room.

Following those late nights, he would arrive, as was usual on those days he was working at the home, no later than 7:30 in the morning, walk straight to the communications room, quickly erase all traces of his existence from the night before, then calmly begin his rounds. No one was the wiser.

His relationship with Jessica was, in his opinion, coming along quite nicely. They now had dinner together two nights a week and then simply spent time together, alone, two other nights a week. The former everyone knew about, the latter no one knew about. It was her secret, it was his fantasy.

He so looked forward to those clandestine evenings with Jessica. There was nothing intimate about their time together. Not yet. He now had less than a year left before he and Jessica were due back in court again. *How time has flown. How things have changed,* he thought to himself.

It was his hope that the judge would see how far Jessica had come and grant the one thing he wanted most in life…and that was for her to have a life. Only then could he truly be with Jessica, because she would no longer be his patient and his strained ethics could finally be placated.

He planned to close 'Hope's Home' and make it into a beautiful private residence…for Jessica, for them. A place where they would finally be free to express their love for each other, for he was convinced that underneath her often-vague demeanor, lay a woman eager to love and be loved.

As for him, he was no longer in love with his wife, Lara. Hadn't been for some time. Over the thirty some years they have been married, they had drifted apart, no longer content with each other, yet unable to break away from each other. Lara because she knew no other life than the current one, which was fulfilled through expensive toys, gala events and glamorous people. She rubbed elbows with the rich and famous on a daily basis and was not about to walk away from any of it, which she knew she would have to do if her husband no longer supported her in the lifestyle to which she had become more than just a little accustomed.

As for Dr. Fitzgerald, he sat on numerous hospital and university boards, and any one or all of them might force him to resign in order to avoid any negative publicity from what would certainly be a high-profile divorce between him and Lara.

In the end, the two decided to remain together, in name only. They both agreed to attend a few of the year's most prominent events as a couple, but otherwise they would lead separate lives. He knew she was delighted to keep her lifestyle. She didn't know he was thrilled to keep his 'Eliza.'

Of course, he had discussed none of this with Jessica. He hadn't felt the need, since nothing much would change in their relationship. She knew very little about his wife, because it was a topic Dr. Fitzgerald preferred not to discuss and Jessica had agreed, for now.

What he did hope to discuss with Jessica was how they could and would spend more time together. Finally, be together, in the most intimate of ways. But only ever behind closed doors. There would be no going out in public together, ever.

He was convinced Jessica would be excited by this new arrangement, since it gave her the freedom to pursue her career without the added hardship of financial pressures. It would also allow her to continue to live in this beautiful home and enjoy the extravagant attentions he hoped...*wished*...to shower upon her. He would see to it that she would want for nothing. Oh, and he would, although it would not be the result of his own doing.

As for Ms. Müller, he would have to ask her to either resign or help her find another position if Jessica were to be released and he could begin the manor home's renovations. At that point, neither he nor Jessica would be requiring her services any longer. It was a simple business decision, or so he assumed it would be.

Any guests still in the home when renovations began would be transferred to a suitable, but alternative, treatment facility, under the supervision of Dr. Fitzgerald.

As for household staff, he would like to keep the housekeeper, Mrs. Powers, in his employ. She knew her place and would not interfere in his personal life nor Jessica's. Whether she agreed with their arrangement or not didn't matter.

* * * * *

Ms. Müller sat by the light of a single lamp atop the small writing desk in her equally small living room, a small notepad in front of her and pen in hand. When the two connect, it results in a strange and seemingly jumbled combination of letters and numbers. Clearly, she has something of importance to document, to tell, that only she could decipher if the notes were ever discovered.

Perhaps she was making reference to the time she had observed Jessica and Dr. Fitzgerald together late one afternoon as they were heading up the stairs to Jessica's apartment for her 'session.' Ms. Müller was positive she had seen Dr. Fitzgerald's right hand gently brush up against Jessica's left hand as they walked side by side. What's more, Jessica's hand responded with a slight squeeze to his hand. While Dr. Fitzgerald's gesture could have easily been dismissed as a chance encounter, Jessica's could not. It had been deliberate.

On that occasion, Jessica had been quite aware that Ms. Müller was secreted behind the heavy swag curtain that hung gracefully between the entryway and the foyer where the stairs began. She had suspected her there before, seen her there before. Hoped she'd be there today…and she was.

Or perhaps Ms. Müller was strangling the pen in her hand in an attempt to recount one night less than a week ago when she stood outside Jessica's door, listening intently. She knew Dr. Fitzgerald had been in Jessica's apartment for the better part of three and a half hours by then.

She had just a few minutes to keep her ear to the door before the evening's curfew was enforced. Turns out, it was just enough time to hear the tail end of a conversation that was taking place on the other side between Dr. Fitzgerald and Jessica.

How she had called him 'darling' and he had responded in kind with 'my love.' How she had asked about their future. How he had told her not to worry—he was taking care of everything, including the relocation of the other guests and the termination of all household staff, with the exception of the housekeeper Mrs. Powers.

Or maybe Ms. Müller was detailing an incident that had occurred early this morning. She had entered the communications room, as usual before Dr. Fitzgerald's arrival, which she knew would be shortly after 7:30 because he was scheduled to hold sessions today.

She pushed the 'rewind' button to 10:30 the night before, since she already knew that that hour of night was Dr. Fitzgerald's preferred visiting time with Jessica. Back and forth she went until she found the footage of Dr. Fitzgerald's arrival, precisely 10:30.

Next, she went hunting for Dr. Fitzgerald's departure, which she believed she'd find by stopping the machine around the 12:30 am time indicator. She knew he liked to keep an exacting schedule, both professionally and personally, and that was his typical departure time as evidenced by previous footage.

But he didn't appear on the video at that time, so she hit the 'fast forward' button, pausing at every 30-minute interval to scrutinize the image. By the time she got to 5 am, she was hitting 'pause' in 5-minute increments.

By the end of the video, Ms. Müller had come to the very valuable realization that Dr. Fitzgerald had not yet left the house.

Chapter Six

Dr. Fitzgerald had, indeed, been to see Jessica that night. Precisely at 10:30 pm as the video verified. And he was well aware that he was not shown as ever having left, because he hadn't.

They had enjoyed a wonderful dinner together, followed by a respectful snuggle on the couch afterward. He toyed with her hair, she toyed with his emotions.

She had plied him with a little more wine than usual, although he was by no means an excessive drinker. And it wasn't long before Dr. Fitzgerald simply nodded off, his head coming to rest on the arm of the sofa. Jessica went off to bed with a smile on her face and absolutely no intention of waking the dear doctor.

When he finally did wake, the next morning just before 7:30 am, he panicked. He was still in Jessica's apartment. He'd spent the night inside Jessica's apartment. *Shit*, he'd seriously screwed up.

He knew the alarm system would be off by now, but the daily activities within the house would be on. How was he going to explain himself if someone saw him coming down the stairs at that hour?

He needn't have worried, because he encountered no one on the stairs, no one in the foyer, no one near the communications room, which is where he went first. He must erase all of last night's footage, then go to his office, clean himself up and begin his day like any other.

Unfortunately, today would turn out to be anything but like any other.

It started with a phone call from Judge Hanson's law clerk to ask if Dr. Fitzgerald, Ms. McCallum, and her lawyer might be able to meet with the Judge in his Chambers just before noon. It seemed that Judge Hanson had a trial rescheduled due to a last-minute request from a defense attorney, which the judge had granted. Which meant that the judge had some time to reallocate and, since the case involving Ms. McCallum was scheduled to reconvene in less than a week's time anyway and there were so few involved in this case, would all parties concerned be interested in settling this matter today?

Dr. Fitzgerald was taken aback by this unexpected request, but managed to advise the Judge's Law Clerk that he would call her back immediately to confirm, once he made sure he cleared his own schedule and notified both Jessica and her attorney, Blair Scott.

But he didn't immediately move after hanging up the phone. He needed time to fully digest what had just occurred and what was about to happen.

He was confident Jessica would be released by the judge, since she had come such a long way, accomplished so much.

This meant that he and Jessica could now build a future together. Could have a life together, starting this very afternoon. Could it be true? Will it be true?

He collected himself enough to get in touch with Blair Scott who agreed to meet at the courthouse at 11:30 that morning. Next, he raced up the stairs to Jessica's apartment, so intent on telling her this exciting news that he forgot to stop, knock, and wait for her to answer. Instead, he pulled his key from his pant pocket and opened the door, letting himself in.

And so, it was at that very moment Ms. Müller exited the suite down the hall from Jessica's, having just administered a sedative to an anxious guest. She was just in time to see Dr. Fitzgerald put the key back in his pocket and simply walk into Jessica's apartment.

Should she add this little tidbit to her notes this evening, or had she seen and heard enough already? Ms. Müller decided it was more than enough and began to plan her own very special evening with Dr. Fitzgerald.

* * * * *

They had a lot to celebrate that night. Judge Hanson had finally granted Jessica her freedom, confident that she would adapt well to being out among the general population.

He wished her well on her upcoming exams for her Master's Degree in Social Work. From what he had been told by Dr. Fitzgerald, she had progressed through the advanced two-year program with impressive grades.

The Judge also offered her some advice. 'Ms. McCallum, I hope you take the opportunity that is being given to you today, and everything you have learned over the past six years, and put them to good use by setting an example for others that it's possible to achieve something in their lives...to do something with their lives...if they want it badly enough,' he stated.

Oh, yes, Judge, I do want it badly enough, Jessica thought to herself as she did her best to feign interest in what he was saying. 'Yes, Your Honor,' she smiled at him. *Tic.* 'Thank you.'

And so, the judge's gavel came down on this case for the final time. Jessica would have her freedom. Dr. Fitzgerald would have her.

Together, they arrived back at Hope's Home where they were greeted by Ms. Müller, anxious to know how things had gone in court. Anxious only because if Jessica had been granted release today, it meant that Ms. Müller would have to have that conversation with Dr. Fitzgerald about his 'troubles' much sooner than she had anticipated.

For Ms. Müller, this latest ruling put her entire plan in jeopardy. She knew Jessica would soon no longer be considered Dr. Fitzgerald's patient, and therefore, could do what she wished and go where she wanted. It would also mean that Ms. Müller would lose a certain amount of negotiating leverage if that happened. So, tonight had to be the night.

In the meantime, Jessica and Dr. Fitzgerald made their way upstairs to Jessica's apartment, eager to be alone. Impatient to be together, but not yet as man and woman. They had one more hurdle to pass before the judge would sign the final papers and that was for Jessica to not only take her final exams, but also pass them. She must first earn her degree.

After an hour of just holding each other and quietly talking to each other on Jessica's sofa, it struck them that neither had eaten anything since breakfast that morning. It was no surprise, then, that the few celebratory drinks they shared had an immediate effect on them both.

Jessica made her way on slightly unsteady legs to the phone and pressed two numbers. 'Ms. Müller, this is Jessica,' she giggled, turned to Dr. Fitzgerald, and put her right index finger up to her lips, indicating he shouldn't say a word. He readily obliged, because all he really wanted to do was look at her, appreciate her, to love her.

'Dr. Fitzgerald and I would like to have a private dinner in my apartment this evening. He's helping me prepare for my final exams and we need a quiet place to work,' Jessica said into the phone. 'Please bring our meals to us when they are ready.' She didn't wait for a response. She simply hung up the phone. As of today, she no longer cared what Ms. Müller thought.

'Darling,' Dr. Fitzgerald called across the room to her, 'I believe the time has come for you to no longer refer to me in private as Dr. Fitzgerald,' he smiled at her. 'When we're alone, it would be so wonderful to hear you call me by my name.'

Jessica hesitated for a moment while she thought about his offer. 'What would you like me to call you…when we're alone, of course?' she teased him, in spite of the anger she felt building inside of her. He was suggesting that their relationship continue to remain a secret, despite the judge's ruling today.

'Declan, naturally,' Dr. Fitzgerald responded with a smile, very aware that she knew perfectly well what his first name was. She was teasing him. Playing with him.

'Well, Declan,' Jessica said with a smile, 'it's nice to finally meet you.'

Jessica returned to the sofa and found that her spot beside Dr. Fitzgerald was now occupied by a small, beautifully designed gift box. 'What's this?' she asked.

Dr. Fitzgerald picked the box up and patted his hand down on the sofa beside him, indicating Jessica should take her original seat. 'I had a feeling that today was going to be special, so I thought what better way to celebrate than with a special gift for a special someone,' he said as he held the box out to Jessica. 'Go ahead, open it,' he insisted.

Jessica took the box from his outstretched hand and laid it in her lap. With delicate fingers, she untied the big white bow that embraced the box and slowly lifted the lid.

Inside, she discovered several layers of silver tissue paper that were hiding something beneath. She reached in, removed the paper, and found another smaller box. This time, it was a beautiful, rectangular black box. Not overly long. Not overly tall. What could it possibly be? Another necklace? That new diamond bracelet she had hinted at?

She took the box out, rested the base in one hand while she removed the lid with the other. Her heart immediately beat harder, then faster.

Inside was a set of three red teddy bear candles, laying side by side, their eyes looking directly into hers, their smiles directed only at her. *Tic. Toc.*

'You remembered,' Jessica whispered as she gently put the box back in her lap and turned to Dr. Fitzgerald. She threw her arms around him and kissed him slowly first on one cheek, then the other, before intentionally coming to rest on his lips. This time, he didn't object, wouldn't object. This was what he had been hoping for.

A few moments later, they were interrupted by a knock on Jessica's apartment door. Dr. Fitzgerald himself went to the door and opened it to find Ms. Müller holding a tray on which two meals had been placed. 'As requested, Dr. Fitzgerald, I come bearing sustenance,' Ms. Müller said through a forced smile.

'Come in, Ms. Müller. If you would kindly leave the tray on the kitchen table and then see that we are not disturbed for the remainder of my session with Ms. McCallum, thank you,' Dr. Fitzgerald instructed. 'Please tell Mrs. Powers that one of us will return the tray and its contents to the kitchen later on.'

'Certainly, Dr. Fitzgerald,' Ms. Müller said as she walked over to the kitchen table and gently slid the tray onto the surface. She then turned and headed for the door with Dr. Fitzgerald right behind her, he anxious to not only close the door, but lock it as well.

Before he had a chance to completely shut the door on Ms. Müller's retreating back, she turned to face Dr. Fitzgerald. 'I wonder if I might have a quick word with you please, Dr. Fitzgerald,' she began. 'I'm sorry to have to take you away from Ms. McCallum...and her studies of course...but we had a situation with one of the guests while you were at the courthouse today and I would very much appreciate your input and approval to change her medication as soon as possible.'

Dr. Fitzgerald was not at all happy with Ms. Müller's timing, but knew he couldn't simply ignore a situation involving one of his patients until tomorrow morning. 'Give me a minute, Ms. Müller, and then we'll go down to my office where we can talk about this in private,' he impatiently muttered as he pushed the door closed, leaving Ms. Müller on the other side. She was more than happy to wait for him. She knew it would be well worth it in the end…at least for her.

Dr. Fitzgerald returned to the door a few minutes later and left Jessica's apartment, with Ms. Müller following in his wake. Once settled in his office, Dr. Fitzgerald turned and faced her. 'Now Ms. Müller, if you would kindly get right to the point.'

'It would be my pleasure, Dr. Fitzgerald,' she smiled at him as she placed her well-used notepad in front of her. 'Let's see now, where shall we begin?'

* * * * *

Jessica left both dinners on the kitchen table where Ms. Müller had left them and waited for Dr. Fitzgerald…'Declan,' she had tried out the name…to return, which he told her shouldn't be more than 15 minutes. She assured him it wasn't a problem.

And it wasn't. Ms. Müller's interruption gave her time to privately revisit Dr. Fitzgerald's latest gift, which she was desperate to do.

She returned to the sofa and picked up the small black box before sitting down. She delicately removed the lid and smiled down at the three, red teddy bear candles staring up at her. She lifted the box to just below her nose, closed her eyes, and deeply inhaled the scent of the candles. 'Long time no see,' she whispered. 'I've missed you.'

She lovingly replaced the lid, put the box in the crook of one arm, and gently began to rock it, back and forth, back and forth. 'Hush little babies, don't make a sound,' she softly sang to the tune of the classic nursery rhyme, 'Mama's so happy to have you around.'

Jessica opened the drawer in the bottom of the coffee table in front of the couch, placed the black box at the very back left corner of the drawer and covered it with the shawl she kept there. Before closing it, she blew a kiss down into the drawer. 'Now, be good little baby dolls and Mama will be back soon. The next time you see me, it'll be time to put on our own special play.' She slid the drawer closed just as Dr. Fitzgerald returned to her apartment.

'You've been gone a while, darling,' she quickly recovered herself. 'Is everything alright?' she asked when she saw him leaning heavily against one wall just inside the front door, all color drained from his face, one hand held up to his chest. But he was unable to speak, couldn't speak. It's still too soon for him to find the right words, to figure out the right words. His mind had not yet processed what had just happened in his office between him and Ms. Müller.

Jessica could see he was in distress and came to his aid. She took him to the sofa and sat him down, then went to the kitchen and returned with a glass of water, placing it on the coffee table in front of him.

'What's wrong, darling? Should I call 911?' she asked him out of concern. That is, concern for herself, because if Dr. Fitzgerald suddenly died as a result of the heart attack he appeared to be having at that very moment, where would that leave her? Fuck! *Tic. Fuuuucccckkkk!*

Dr. Fitzgerald picked up the glass of water and swallowed half of it before speaking. 'No, no,' he insisted. 'No need to call anyone. Please, I just need a moment to compose myself.'

'But, if there's something I can do...' she began, before being abruptly interrupted.

'Jessica,' Dr. Fitzgerald barked at her impatiently, 'please. Stop.'

It was obvious that Jessica was wounded by his terseness. Her eyes widened in shock and her body involuntarily pulled itself slightly back from him.

Dr. Fitzgerald reached out and pulled her into him. 'I'm sorry, Jessica,' he apologized. 'You're the last person in the world I'd ever want to hurt,' he confessed. 'Please forgive me?'

Under different circumstances, Jessica would have made him work a little harder for her forgiveness. Perhaps something in 14k gold with a few sparkly bits thrown in might help to pacify her.

But this circumstance felt different. It felt awkward. It felt *uneasy.*

Chapter Seven

Declan had finally relented and told Jessica the unsettling conversation he had just had with Ms. Müller. He hadn't intended to tell Jessica, because he wanted to handle the situation himself and not worry her, or perhaps it was more to protect himself. But the enormity of Ms. Müller's demands had seriously shaken him and he had broken down in front of Jessica.

'What am I going to do?' he whispered, his head down, eyes closed, shoulders slumped. 'She knows about us, Jessica,' he finally admitted. 'Ms. Müller knows about our plans for this house and our future,' he continued to confess. 'I don't know how, but she knows all of it.'

Jessica is momentarily confused, unsure why Ms. Müller's discovery should be so devastating for Declan. 'But, Declan,' Jessica began, 'I don't understand why you're so upset. Isn't that why I spent all these years, and why we put in all this effort and work, so that we could finally be together?' Declan couldn't bring himself to look at her.

'Declan,' Jessica reached out and placed a gentle hand over his, 'answer me. What's going on?'

It was all Declan could do to force himself to finally look up. 'Well, yes,' he began, 'this home will be a place where we can share time together, spend time together, and finally just be together,' he said.

'And it will…soon darling,' Jessica added. 'So, what if Ms. Müller says she knows about us. Now that I'm so close to no longer being your patient, our relationship doesn't have to be kept a secret any longer?'

Declan's eyes immediately dropped. 'You don't understand, Jessica,' he said. 'Ms. Müller said she'll tell my wife everything, then go on to destroy my reputation and career unless I pay her money to keep the whole thing quiet. A lot of money.'

Jessica slowly removed her hand from atop his when the realization of what his words really meant to her…for her…finally hit. *Tic.*

Declan never did have any intention of ever leaving his wife nor did he have any intention whatsoever of marrying her.

'Jessica,' Declan interrupted her thoughts, 'did you hear what I said? She's going to destroy me…destroy my life…if I don't pay her.'

'Yes, I heard you Declan,' she answered calmly, but 'fuck' she screamed internally. She was only ever meant to be his 'piece on the side.' His 'dirty little secret.' Nothing more.

But Jessica wanted more, so much more. She wanted to become Mrs. Declan Fitzgerald. She needed to be her. She was determined to be her.

Jessica had been so certain that once she was no longer his patient, Declan would divorce his wife and marry her. After all, hadn't she toyed with him for years now? Hadn't she played with him for years now? Fuck, she had earned this. She deserved this.

And as her final hearing had approached, Jessica had ridden Declan to the brink of physical ecstasy so many times in the privacy of her apartment, but just as many times she intentionally never allowed him to cross that final threshold.

She had to become Mrs. Fitzgerald first. She promised herself that she would only grant him his final reward once her demands had been fully satisfied, and not one minute before.

For now, though, she had to put her energies into Ms. Müller. What should she do about this situation? Was there a situation?

Declan told her that Ms. Müller had given him a week to come up with the money or she would make his life a living hell. He hated her, but he believed her. He would make arrangements to raise the $1 million Ms. Müller had demanded, then send her on her way and put all of this behind him. That was the end of that discussion, at least as far as he was concerned.

Long after Declan left, which that night was well before the 9 pm curfew, Jessica made sure her apartment door was locked and all the curtains closed.

Next, she went to her bedroom where she backed herself into a corner and sat down. She leaned her head back, closed her eyes, and allowed her mind to fly freely into the winds of trepidation that gusted through her psyche. She never made a sound. She never moved…for hours.

Until, suddenly, Jessica's eyes flew open. Wide, clear, determined. She knew what she had to do.

She got up off the floor and made her way into her kitchen where she took a pad of paper and a pen from a drawer, then returned to wedge herself into the corner once again.

She spent the next few hours writing her thoughts on paper, tearing them into little pieces and then arranging them around her in the oh-so-familiar pattern her mind instantly recognized, but hadn't seen in such a long time. It was incredibly comforting.

In the end, it was her old *terrified* category that spoke to her. That meant something was going to have to happen. More specifically, *something* was going to have to happen to *someone*. But who? Ms. Müller? Declan? Lately, both had begun to piss her off. To get under her skin. She knew she would have to change the dynamics in the house, whatever form that took.

Fortunately for Declan, he, now more than ever, held the final piece to her freedom and financial future, despite the existence of Mrs. Fitzgerald. Perhaps that particular problem could be her next project. But for now, Jessica had to focus all of her attention on Ms. Müller.

Jessica suddenly smiled. 'I hear you're leaving us soon, Ms. Müller,' she whispered to herself, 'so, I got you a little going-away gift.' She got up and walked to the living room and over to the coffee table. She pulled open the drawer, lifted the shawl, and retrieved the little black box that was hiding beneath. She removed the lid and looked down at the three, red teddy bear candles lying side by side, all smiling up at her.

'See, I told you I'd be back soon,' she smiled at them. 'Now, which one of you wants to be in Mama's special play?'

* * * * *

Standing in the dark foyer of the house a few days later, Ms. Müller checked her watch and saw that it was still 45 minutes before this evening's curfew. Tonight, however, she decided that there was no point in continuing her 'rounds,' since Dr. Fitzgerald had assured her, that very afternoon in fact, that she would get what she had asked for, *insisted on* actually…money…and plenty of it.

She didn't doubt Dr. Fitzgerald's word. Just as she didn't doubt the panic in his eyes when she went over her thoroughly detailed notes with him, point by painful point.

In the end, things had gone quite smoothly really, at least from Ms. Müller's perspective. She knew Dr. Fitzgerald had little choice but to pay her, if he had any hope at all of salvaging his entire life. Without his reputation and his esteemed standing in his field, there would be nothing left for him. His reputation would wither, then his business would dry up. Even his wife would eventually leave him as soon as she realized there was to be no more of the fabulous lifestyle she currently enjoyed.

Not even his precious Jessica would be left, Ms. Müller thought to herself. She was convinced that Jessica wouldn't want anything to do with a ruined old man who no longer had a career, no prospects, no money. No nothing.

Very pleased with herself, Ms. Müller decided to retire early. She felt she had earned a well-deserved rest that evening.

She entered her room and began to undress. Perhaps she should run herself a nice hot bath and allow herself to think about what to do with all that money. She could retire quite comfortably now. Somewhere with a beach, lots of sunshine and fabulous food. Her own little piece of paradise.

Ms. Müller went to her bathroom and began to draw herself a hot, bubbly bath. As she waited for the tub to fill, she returned to her bedroom and finished undressing. She grabbed the housecoat from the foot of her bed, put it on, fastened the tie around her waist, and went back into the bathroom.

'I'm going to enjoy this,' Ms. Müller said aloud once she had tested the temperature of the water with one hand. She then dropped the housecoat where she stood and carefully climbed into the inviting tub, her body slowly disappearing beneath the steaming, aromatic foam.

Several minutes later, the phone in her apartment came to life, tearing her away from the extravagant daydream she had been savoring.

She knew it was an internal call, because of the two short rings it emitted. Strange. *Who could be calling her at this hour,* she wondered. 'I'd better get it,' she decided, then rose from the tub, stepped out, re-wrapped herself in her housecoat and headed for the phone. 'Hello,' she said into the receiver.

There was no answer. 'Hello,' she inquired again. Still no response. 'Who is it?' she asked firmly. She then heard the distinct click of the line's disconnect, followed by dead air.

Ms. Müller shrugged and lowered the phone into its cradle, then went back to the solace of her bath.

No sooner had she lowered herself into the water when she heard two short rings once again coming from the phone. 'For heaven's sake,' Ms. Müller ranted as she hauled herself from the depths of the tub and retraced her steps into the other room, this time without her housecoat.

Just as she reached for the phone, it ceased ringing, but Ms. Müller picked it up anyway and simply listened. Again, there was nothing, no one, on the other end.

Ms. Müller returned the phone to its cradle, a puzzled look on her face. She simply stood there, beside the phone, for a few seconds before deciding she probably should put something on and have a look around the house.

It's a shame she didn't have the presence of mind to activate the internal cameras, just in case. While it would not have changed the outcome for poor Ms. Müller, it most definitely would have changed the initial course of the subsequent investigation.

Chapter Eight

In an effort to determine Ms. Müller's exact whereabouts, Jessica had quietly descended the stairs from her apartment and secreted herself behind one of the sliding pocket doors to Declan's office.

Jessica was very aware of Ms. Müller's nightly prowls around the house, had been from the very beginning. But tonight was going to be different. Tonight, Jessica was going to surprise Ms. Müller by adding a little something special to her otherwise mundane routine.

She heard the sound of a door closing at the far end of the hallway that ran the length of the house on the other side of the staircase. Curious, Jessica returned to the staircase and peeked around the bannister to see if anyone was there. At the end of the hallway, she saw the faint hint of light coming from under Ms. Müller's door.

Jessica knew it was a while before curfew, so thought it odd that Ms. Müller would have gone to her room already. *Shit,* Jessica thought to herself, *why isn't she snooping around tonight?* Apparently, things were not going to go according to her original plan for this evening. She would have to improvise quickly. No problem.

Jessica hugged the paneled wall of the hallway as she made her way to Ms. Müller's door. She put her ear up to it and recognized the faint but telltale sound of running water inside. It appeared that Ms. Müller was running herself a bath. Perfect.

Jessica stood there for a moment, thinking, before she crept back down the hallway, across the foyer and into Declan's office. She crossed to the desk, lifted the phone from its cradle, and dialed the familiar two-digit extension for Ms. Müller's room.

When Ms. Müller finally answered, Jessica listened for a few seconds, but said nothing. Finally, Jessica gently hung the phone up and began to count.

When she reached one hundred, she lifted the phone and once again dialed Ms. Müller's room. She thought it would be just enough time for Ms. Müller's ample body to have again submerged itself beneath the water.

This time, she hung up after just the third set of double rings. Enough time for Ms. Müller to hoist herself out of the tub and head for the phone, but not enough time for her to actually get there to answer it.

Jessica was prepared to do this for as long as it took in order to get Ms. Müller to leave her room. She knew Ms. Müller wouldn't be able to contain her curiosity as to what was going on, because the calls were obviously coming from somewhere inside the house.

It was another five minutes before Jessica heard the door to Ms. Müller's room open and close quietly. Another minute before she recognized the familiar groans of the steps protesting under the weight of Ms. Müller's generous body as she slowly ascended to the second floor.

Jessica waited another thirty seconds before she slid out from behind the pocket door of Declan's office and glanced up the staircase, just in time to see the shadowy figure of a bathrobe-clad Ms. Müller turn down the long corridor toward Jessica's apartment, a weak, tiny flashlight trying unsuccessfully to identify the darkness that waited ahead of her.

Jessica tiptoed up the stairs until she was just five steps from the top. Retrieving a small box-cutter knife she had secretly taken from the kitchen this morning from her sweater's pocket, she knelt down and began to gently cut away at the outer edge of the carpet runner that graced the entire length of the long staircase. Just enough to expose one strand of the thick pile that, when pulled on, began to disfigure the once perfect pattern, leaving a small gash in its wake. She continued to pull until the strand unraveled to the other side, where it was held firmly in place by a stronger edge-finishing seam. There was a chance it might not hold, but Jessica was willing to take that chance. She wondered if Ms. Müller would take the same chance if she knew.

Jessica then looped the carpet strand around the base of the closest spindle before quietly shuffling across the step to the other side where she hurriedly tied the end of the strand to the opposite spindle.

Barely an inch above the height of the step itself, no one would ever know the strand was suspended there, especially at night, in the dark. A perfectly silent predator.

Satisfied with the carpet strand's discreet, horizontal position, Jessica headed back down until she reached the foyer's ornately black-and-white tiled floor at the base of the stairs. She reached into another pocket and pulled out a small object before taking a few steps away from the bottom of the stairs and once again coming to a stop.

She bent down, placed the object on the floor in front of her, and reached into the same pocket. The spark from a small lighter in her hand had barely enough life in it to illuminate the object now sitting in front of her, but just enough to bring the object itself to life.

'Now, my dear friend,' Jessica whispered as she ignited the tiny wick emerging from the top of its head, 'it's your turn to play.' She smiled down at the glowing red teddy bear candle on the floor before retreating again behind one of Declan's office doors, waiting, wanting, wishing.

Wishing Ms. Müller would hurry up and find her way back through the near darkness to the top of the stairs. She had just a few minutes left before curfew when the cameras would once again be activated and there had to be no onlookers. There must be no witnesses.

Just then, Jessica heard the swish of material from Ms. Müller's bathrobe as she made her way back along the upstairs hallway to the landing and toward the stairs, coming to stop at the very top. She made no sound…at first.

'What on earth,' Ms. Müller finally wondered aloud as she peered down the stairs at the small candle sitting on the floor at the very bottom, its lit wick barely charring the darkness around it.

Curious yet cautious at the same time, Ms. Müller hiked up an edge of her long bathrobe with one hand while working the anemic flashlight in the other and began to descend, one foot at a time, one step at a time, toward the object below.

'I can't imagine how that got there,' she muttered as her foot found the first step. 'Who would have done such a thing?' she asked the stillness that surrounded her as her foot found the second step. 'Why, it could so easily start a fire and burn the whole place down,' she complained on the third step. 'I can only imagine what might have happened had I not been here,' she speculated as her foot touched the fourth step.

Her foot felt down for the fifth step, but instead came into contact with something else. Something different. Something not right.

Something she couldn't stop herself from tripping over. Something that catapulted her headfirst into the darkness below her. Something that caused her to meet a fatal ending at the foot of the stairs.

It's a shame Ms. Müller never got the chance to appreciate the little red teddy bear candle that glowed just a few feet away from her face, smiling at her, its image forever burned into her now lifeless eyes.

* * * * *

Dr. Fitzgerald received a phone call early the next morning from the housekeeper, Mrs. Powers. Something terrible had happened at the manor house and he was to come as soon as possible. No further explanation was provided, just a dead phone line.

Jessica was all he could think about as he drove from the home he begrudgingly shared with his wife Lara to the manor house he lovingly shared with Jessica. She was the only thing he had been thinking about since he got that call.

It was just a few minutes after eight in the morning when he finally arrived at the manor house and the sight that greeted him only served to drive his anxiety level even higher.

There were police cars everywhere, their lights flashing. Yellow crime scene tape cordoned off the main entrance to the grounds, preventing Dr. Fitzgerald from driving through the gated entry and up to the front door. Without thinking, he left his car right in the middle of the chaos, the driver's door wide open, and rushed toward the house, only to be stopped by several officers. 'Sir, you can't go in,' one officer said.

'My name is Dr. Declan Fitzgerald and I am the owner of this house,' he said in what he hoped was an authoritative voice. 'What's all this about? What happened?'

The officer immediately lifted another band of yellow tape overhead, allowing Declan to cross the boundary. He was going from unknowing spectator to willing participant in whatever had happened. There was now no turning back on this truth.

'Wait here while I get the detective in charge,' the young officer instructed before heading into the house. Declan impatiently scanned the grounds, looking for any sign of Jessica among the professionally diverse who now littered the grounds like discarded lawn ornaments.

A hand was suddenly placed on his right shoulder, 'Dr. Fitzgerald,' a voice behind him said, 'I'm Detective Lubovik, I'm the guy in charge,' he offered his other hand as Declan turned to face him.

'In charge of what?' Declan asked. 'What exactly happened here?'

'Seems there's been an accident involving one of your staff, Dr. Fitzgerald,' the detective began. Before Declan could stop himself, he raised a hand to his mouth and let out an audible sigh, for all he had heard was 'one of your staff' and knew immediately that whatever had happened didn't involve Jessica. She was safe. She was okay.

'Are you okay, Dr. Fitzgerald?' the detective asked Declan, having noticed the abrupt change in his demeanor. His facial expression had transformed from one of pure anxiety to one of complete relief. 'You don't seem to be troubled by whatever happened here, even though you don't yet know exactly what did,' the detective pointed out. 'Why is that, Dr. Fitzgerald?'

Despite his momentary lapse in emotions, Declan recovered his composure quickly. 'I apologize, but when I heard you say something happened to one of my staff, I knew right away that it didn't involve any of my patients...our guests,' Declan explained. 'As you can imagine, that was a great relief to me, as they are my responsibility and I take their care and well-being very seriously, Detective.'

Detective Lubovik didn't respond, but rather locked his eyes on Declan's for several seconds before continuing. 'Should I take that to mean you don't care so much about your staff, Dr. Fitzgerald?' the detective smiled quietly. He's poking, provoking. It's a tactic he acquired early on in his career and one that typically ruffled the guilty but only annoyed the innocent. He had a knack and reputation for quickly separating the good from the bad. And yet, he wasn't convinced there was anything bad here, but he also felt there was something not so good either.

'Certainly not,' Declan responded angrily. 'Now, will you please just tell me what has happened?'

Detective Lubovik pulled out his note pad and flipped through a few pages before finding what he's looking for. 'It would seem that one of your nurses, a Ms. Hildreth Müller, had a rather nasty fall down the stairs sometime last night,' he said matter-of-factly, then quickly looked at Declan to gauge his reaction.

Declan was taken aback for a second. 'Ms. Müller,' he responded with no emotion, 'yes, she's actually our Head Psychiatric Nurse. Is she okay?' Declan asked with what seemed to be sincere concern in his voice and expression on his face.

Detective Lubovik eyed Declan again, trying to quickly assess his body language, to read his facial expression, to dissect his verbal response.

'Unfortunately, no Dr. Fitzgerald,' the detective answered, 'she was found lying at the bottom of the main staircase, in the foyer, early this morning by the housekeeper, Mrs. Powers,' he flatly stated. 'Ms. Müller was subsequently pronounced dead on the scene by first responders.'

'Dead?' Declan said in disbelief. 'My God, but how? What happened?'

Detective Lubovik ran a hand through the thinning hair on the top of his head before answering. 'Initially, it looks to be an accident,' he stated. 'We'll have to wait for the medical examiner's report on the official cause of death, of course, but at first glance, it appears as though she was on the stairs and either slipped on or tripped over a piece of carpet runner that we found had come unraveled on one of the steps near the top.'

Declan looked puzzled. 'That can't be, Detective, since the house is extremely well maintained,' he offered. 'We take the safety of our guests very seriously, which is why, if there was a problem with the runner, I'm sure the housekeeper, Mrs. Powers, would have either advised me or done something about it herself.'

'Well, we thought about that too, so I asked Mrs. Powers and she said that when she cleaned the staircase yesterday, the runner was just fine,' Detective Lubovik responded. 'And Ms. Müller was wearing slippers with no heels, so there's no way her footwear would have caught the carpet and caused it to unravel. Bit of a puzzler, that one. We'll have to wait and see.'

Declan was beginning to grow impatient with the detective. At that moment, all he wanted to do was to find Jessica, to speak to Jessica, to know she was okay. 'And what of my patients, Detective, are they alright? Where are they?' Declan asked.

'They're just fine, Doc,' the detective answered casually. 'We asked them to stay in their rooms until one of the officers can take a formal statement from each of them. Procedure,' he shrugged, 'you know how it is.'

'Well, can I at least see...see them?' Declan inquired carefully. He was so close to saying Jessica's name only, but managed to salvage his near mistake. 'I'm just concerned about how they are coping with all of this.'

'I'm afraid not, Doc,' the detective answered, 'but it shouldn't be much longer. I have officers with them right now.'

Both men were suddenly distracted by a commotion behind them. They turned in unison to see the white plastic-shrouded body of Ms. Müller being wheeled out of the house and down the front steps on a gurney by two employees wearing jackets that identified them as being from the medical examiner's office. They were rough, unfeeling, uncaring.

They had no connection to this body or any other body they picked up. It was just a job.

'In the meantime, if you want to wait in your office, Doc,' the detective spoke to Declan, but his eyes followed the gurney for some distance, 'that's fine. We'll be done soon.'

Declan also watched the gurney as it bumped its way toward a dark van, its back doors open, ready to ingest yet another unfortunate soul. 'Thank you,' he nodded briefly to the detective before tentatively making his way to the front door.

He stepped inside and his eyes were immediately drawn to the pool of deep red blood that had dared to deface the perfection of the crisp black-and-white tiles at the foot of the staircase. Declan did his best to avert his eyes from anything else and everyone else as he headed to his office just to the right of the staircase.

He didn't slide the pocket doors completely closed, but left them open just enough so that he could easily peer up to the second floor in the hopes that he might see Jessica. Back and forth he paced behind the pocket doors, stopping occasionally to look up at the landing at the top of the stairs. He checked his watch, again. Then again.

Several times, he lifted the handset of the phone on top of his desk, desperate to call Jessica's number. If he could just hear her voice, talk to her for a second, he would be able to settle himself.

A light rap on the outside of his office door broke his thoughts, but before he had a chance to answer it, the pocket door was rolled back to reveal Detective Lubovik on the other side. 'We're all done here, Doc,' he explained. 'The forensics team has finished up and we have statements from all of the people in the house, so we'll be leaving.'

Declan nodded. 'Thank you, Detective,' he began. 'Please let me know what you find out and if there's anything I can do to help.'

The detective turned toward the front door and spoke as he made his way. 'Will do, Doc,' he called back over his shoulder before disappearing out the front door.

It was all Declan could do not to run across the foyer and up the stairs, all the while calling Jessica's name. But first, he went in search of Mrs. Powers and asked her to kindly clean the foyer and remove all traces of blood, any discarded wrappings from forensic tests that were performed on the scene, the odd dirt-smudged footprint from the night's insensitive traffic, and any remnants that may be reminders of what had occurred there. It was imperative that everyone in the house overcome and move on from the myriad of emotions that go hand in hand with any tragedy.

He left Mrs. Powers, wringing an old tea towel in her hands, in the kitchen at the back of the house and finally went in search of Jessica. He had just placed a hand on the bannister at the bottom of the stairs and looked up, only to see Jessica standing there, at the top, steadying herself against the railing.

'Jessica,' he called up to her, 'Jessica,' this time he whispered her name as he raced up the stairs to her, but didn't dare hug her as he so wanted to. Instead, he placed a warm hand on one of her shoulders and asked, 'are you alright?'

She looked up at him, her eyes wide and strangely excited. 'Of course, I'm fine,' she smiled at him. 'Poor Ms. Müller, though,' she said as she looked back down the stairs to the bottom. And had Declan's eyes not followed Jessica's gaze down, he might have noticed the Machiavellian sneer that possessed her face as she stood mesmerized by the sight of the dark pool of blood.

Declan took her by one arm and pulled her away from the stairs and the horrible sight below, down the hall and to her apartment, gently closing the door behind them. 'Oh my God, Jessica,' he hugged her close, 'I was so worried. Thank goodness you're alright,' he said as he pulled back from her and simply stared at her expressionless face.

'Jessica, do you know what happened to Ms. Müller?' he began. 'Did you see anything…hear anything last night?' he wanted to know.

Jessica raised her big blue eyes to Declan's. 'No, I'm sorry Declan, I don't know what happened,' she replied. 'I didn't hear anything last night.' Her eyes never blinked, never faltered in the least.

She didn't feel the need to tell him about hearing the pure silence that followed Ms. Müller's timely tumble down the stairs. Jessica had waited a moment to make sure no one had heard the commotion and would come to see what it was. She was sure no one would. The other 'guests' were, by that time of night, well under the spell of their prescribed sedatives.

She had emerged from behind the office door, walked with confidence across the foyer's floor and picked up the flickering candle, the wax on the top of its head beginning to melt and sending just the tiniest trickle of wax down, over its forehead, over one eye, then over one cheek as a teardrop might.

'Good baby doll,' Jessica whispered to the still smiling candle, before she licked two fingertips and quickly put out its flame between them. She slipped the candle into a pocket before heading up the stairs to her room, intentionally and impassively stepping over Ms. Müller's contorted body in the process.

Before retreating to her apartment, though, Jessica untied the strand near the top of the stairs and undid the loop from the opposing spindle before casting the strand in a downward direction.

She entered her room, locked the door, and checked the time. It is exactly 8:58 pm. Just two minutes before the security system would begin recording and, therefore, no witness.

As for Ms. Müller, her body laid there, at the foot of the stairs, all night, but not quite alone. It had the silent companionship of the security camera that had automatically activated at its specified time, which coincidentally was just a few minutes after Ms. Müller's body came to rest with a thud at the bottom of the stairs. The camera had dutifully watched over her body until its electronic shift ended at the designated time the following morning.

It was then, and only then, that the entire house was awoken by screams coming from Mrs. Powers.

In the police report, it was noted that Mrs. Powers was the first person to find the body. Unfortunately, no one thought to consider who the first person might have been to *see* the body.

Chapter Nine

Dr. Fitzgerald spent the better part of the next two weeks at the manor house. The treatment plans he had originally and painstakingly created for each individual client had been disrupted following Ms. Müller's unfortunate death, and rightly so. But he was determined to get the house and its occupants back on track as soon as possible. Even more so determined to get his plans with Jessica back on track.

He spent time with his patients each day, listening to them, talking to them, reassuring them that 'it was simply an unfortunate accident.'

He had also temporarily transferred a psychiatric nurse from his larger facility to the manor house to help out, but she didn't reside there as Ms. Müller had. Instead, she arrived each day to dispense the necessary medications, took the time to interact with each patient, and updated patient files.

As for Declan, Ms. Müller's death turned out to be both a blessing and a curse. A blessing because it meant he no longer had to pay her the one million dollars she had demanded to keep her mouth shut about him and Jessica; a curse, because he couldn't go ahead and make the necessary arrangements to move the patients to another facility so soon after 'the accident' without risking their already delicate mental states. It seemed he was having to remind himself on more than one occasion lately that he must, simply had to, put his professional reasons ahead of his personal ones. Which meant that having Jessica all to himself would have to wait just a little longer. Yet another just a little longer.

In the meantime, Detective Lubovik had become a familiar face at the house. There hadn't been a day since Ms. Müller's death that he had not dropped by, unannounced but never unprepared.

He always had just one more question; just one more thought; just one more thing he needed to understand. This morning, his ring of the doorbell was answered by Mrs. Powers wearing her usual clean white apron and recently acquired ashen-white complexion. 'It's just you again then, is it, Detective Lubovik,' she offered tersely. She didn't like him, because he reminded her of that awful day and the awful accident. How was she supposed to 'move forward,' as Dr. Fitzgerald liked to say, if the detective kept coming around?

'Sorry to bother you, Mrs. Powers,' he responded, though he was not one bit sorry. If nothing else, he had learned that at least pretending to be civil got him a lot further than actually being an asshole.

'I wonder if Dr. Fitzgerald is here yet this morning?' he asked, 'only I have a few questions I'd like to ask him. Shouldn't take more than a couple of minutes,' he added. 'I know how busy he is, so I won't take up too much of his time, I promise.'

'No, I'm sorry Detective, Dr. Fitzgerald isn't here yet, but we do expect him in an hour or so,' she stated and began to close the door, hoping he would simply go away and leave her alone. Leave everyone alone.

'Well, I've got nothing else to do, so I'm sure you wouldn't mind if I came in and waited for him in his office,' he said as he stepped into the entrance, preventing the door from coming to a complete close.

Mrs. Powers sighed in resignation and fully opened the door to him. 'Fine, but don't touch anything in Dr. Fitzgerald's office,' she scolded him. 'He's very particular about his things.'

Detective Lubovik had no intention of *touching* the good doctor's things. On the other hand, if something of interest were, say, lying out in full view, he had every intention of *looking*.

He entered the office and scanned the paneled walls, the rows of books, the ornate fixtures, the imposing desk behind which Doctor Fitzgerald always sat. Except the doctor wasn't here at the moment, which meant that the files on top of his desk were unprotected, unguarded.

Detective Lubovik looked over his shoulder to ensure no one was around then nonchalantly began to walk around the room, stopping every so often to feign interest in a particular book or object, until he finally came to stand behind the desk.

There, he took another look toward the door and out into the foyer beyond. Assured that no one was out there, he leaned over the files that were lying neatly in single file on top of the doctor's desk and saw that each had a tab on the side with the name of a specific patient. The first file he looked at just happened to have the name Jessica McCallum on it. He noticed that it also had a few hastily scribbled, handwritten words, almost what some might describe as 'doodles,' randomly scattered across the face of the folder. Words like 'Eliza,' 'Müller,' and something that looked to be the number 1 followed by the letter *M*.

'Well now, that is curious,' he said out loud, though quietly. 'I wonder what's on the inside of the file.' He looked up at the door, before resting an elbow on top of the file and not so subtly swiping it off the desk and onto the floor. 'Oh now, would you look at that,' he said out loud for the benefit of anyone who may come upon the scene. 'Sorry, my bad,' he said as he bent down to pick up the now loose contents of the file, taking his time to visually scan as many pages as he possibly could.

'What are you doing?' a voice at the door startled him and he immediately stuffed the papers back into the file folder and returned it to the top of the desk.

Detective Lubovik looked up to find Jessica standing in the doorway, a defiant air about her. 'I'm waiting for Doctor Fitzgerald,' he answered her, despite the fact that he didn't have to. 'Mrs. Powers said I should wait in here.'

'I'm sure she didn't say you should look through Doctor Fitzgerald's files,' Jessica said as she moved into the room and slowly, perhaps a little seductively, walked toward the detective, a smug, caught-you-with-your-hand-in-the-cookie-jar expression on her face.

Detective Lubovik simply shrugged. 'It slipped off the desk. What could I do but pick it up, right?'

Jessica reached the desk and lowered herself into one of the plush chairs that complemented the desk, where she assumed a familiar position. A hand draped delicately just there. One leg tucked under her. The other bent at the knee, tipped slightly to the right. Just enough to suggest a better view might be possible, if one were so inclined. Detective Lubovik's immediate reaction signaled he was definitely declining.

He came around from behind Doctor Fitzgerald's desk and took a seat in the other plush chair beside Jessica's. 'I'd like to ask you a few questions while I wait for the doctor,' he casually stated.

Jessica reached her hands up over her head, released the clip that restrained her hair and let the curls loose to fall over her shoulders. She selected an unruly tress from the many that surrounded her and began to wind it slowly around one index finger.

'Of course, Detective,' Jessica answered. 'I'll help any way I can,' she added as she reached up and seductively put the tip of her ring finger to her tongue, then provocatively wiped the corner of her mouth.

He didn't respond. He just simply stared at her, hard and long.

Jessica knew from the look he was giving her that he wasn't amused, let alone aroused, by her words or her body language. He was pissed. She was confused.

No man had ever not wanted her. No man had ever dismissed her the way he just had. She was humiliated, then angry. *How dare he?*

Jessica pulled herself together and sat up a little straighter, telling herself that he was too old and too fat for her to waste her talents on anyway. As far as she was concerned, he was insignificant. A nothing. A nobody.

'Ms. McCallum,' the detective interrupted her thoughts, 'tell me about Ms. Müller.'

Jessica's eyes immediately darted to the detective's eyes. 'What about Ms. Müller?' she asked.

'Oh, nothing specific,' he began, 'I just wondered how well you knew her. Did everyone here like her? Is there anyone you can think of who might have wanted to hurt her?' his questions flooded out, much too fast for her brain to process at the same speed. *Tic.*

154

'I thought you said last week that it was an accident,' she finally managed to calmly say, yet her mind was racing. Her thoughts running wild.

'Whether or not it was an accident doesn't matter so much to me right now,' he stated. 'What does matter is that I get to ask all the hard questions I want to ask, and as many times as I want to ask them, before I make a final determination on what actually happened here.' In other words, he was calling the shots. She needed to know that. She needed to remember that.

The two just sat there, staring at each other for what seemed the longest time. It was the detective who finally broke the silence, just as Jessica knew he would because she knew she never would. Never did.

'So, what can you tell me?' he asked.

Jessica continued to twist the curl around her finger, although the detective thought he now recognized just a hint of tension in the motion. The curl around her finger just a little tighter. The gesture itself moving just a little faster.

'Nothing much,' she replied matter-of-factly. 'Ms. Müller was okay, although she was a little nosey, if you ask me.'

The detective nodded, as though he could relate to what she was saying, despite the fact he really couldn't give a shit. 'What do you mean by nosey exactly?' he asked her.

Jessica hesitated, as though she were thinking. 'I saw her sneaking around the house at night on a few occasions,' she said. 'Maybe that's what she was doing the other night when she…fell,' Jessica speculated.

The detective sighed. 'I already told you that we don't yet know for sure what happened, Ms. McCallum.'

'Sure,' she replied, 'so you said.' Jessica calmly put a hand in one of her sweater's pockets and pulled out a stick of gum, which she proceeded to ever so slowly unwrap and place in her mouth. She took her time savoring the flavor, rolling it around and over her tongue a few times before finally biting into it. She chewed the piece until it was soft enough to pull long strands from her mouth, which she then seductively wound around her tongue before sliding her tongue back into her mouth.

The detective didn't react whatsoever to Jessica's suggestive behavior. 'Did you like Ms. Müller?' he continued to press her.

Jessica abruptly rose from her chair. 'I have nothing more to tell you, because I didn't know her well and I was asleep in my apartment the night she…the night of the accident,' Jessica said. 'I didn't know what had happened until the next morning when I heard Mrs. Powers' screams. That's it. Now if you'll excuse me, Detective, I have final exams to prepare for.' She didn't want to be around him anymore. He was making her uneasy. *Tic.*

She made it as far as the doorway, before the detective called out to her. 'There is just one more thing, Ms. McCallum, if I could.'

Doctor Fitzgerald arrived at the manor house a few minutes later and was greeted by the sight of Jessica running up the stairs. 'Jessica,' he called to her with a smile on his face.

But Jessica never responded. Never looked down. Never looked back.

'Jessica,' Declan called again, this time with a look of concern on his face.

It was then that the detective made his presence known to Declan. 'Good morning, Doc,' he greeted him from the office doorway.

'Did you do something...say something...to upset Ms. McCallum, Detective?' he insisted, for it was obvious that Jessica was distressed.

'I didn't think so, Doc,' he answered. 'We were just talking about Ms. Müller is all.'

'You must understand, Detective, that Ms. McCallum...all of my patients, of course...are naturally upset about what happened to Ms. Müller, so I must insist that you do not interview any of them further without me being present,' the doctor instructed. 'They are all here due to fragile mental conditions, and Ms. Müller's death only added to their fragility. You simply can't approach them in the same manner as you might under normal circumstances,' he tried to explain.

The Detective stood quietly, listening to Doctor Fitzgerald's words, every once in a while nodding as though he not only understood but agreed, neither of which was true of course. 'I hear you, Doc,' he said. 'Sorry, won't happen again.'

'Well, thank you for that,' Doctor Fitzgerald relaxed a little. 'Now, I assume you are here for a specific reason,' he commented, anxious to get rid of the detective because he was anxious to get to Jessica. *What had the detective said that had rattled her so?*

'Oh, ya,' the detective finally said, 'I almost forgot what I came here for,' he chuckled to himself. 'It's like I told Ms. McCallum before she took off,' he began, 'the lab found something unusual and I thought maybe she might be able to help me figure it out.'

'Is that right, Detective,' he responded. 'Well, if you would care to explain to me what it was the lab found, I'll do what I can to help,' Declan offered.

Detective Lubovik removed his notepad from an inside pocket of his coat and shuffled through a few pages. 'Here it is,' he stopped. 'Seems there was a drop of something strange found right next to Ms. Müller's head,' he read.

'At first, the crime scene tech thought it was blood, you know, because it was right there beside all the other blood and it was also red,' he stopped and looked at the doctor. 'So, he collected it and sent it to the lab, along with all the other samples he collected.'

'I take it that it wasn't blood,' Declan commented, not sharing the detective's apparent enthusiasm for suspense.

The detective nodded for a few seconds before replying, 'You're right, Doc, it wasn't blood at all. It was a very small drop of wax…red wax to be more specific,' he said.

Declan appeared puzzled by this information. 'Red wax?' he asked the detective. 'Is the lab certain?'

'Absolutely certain, Doc,' replied the detective. 'What's so strange about it, is that it doesn't fit the scene at all. It's like a misfit. It sticks out like a sore thumb. What's it doing there? How did it get there?'

'Well, I'm sure I don't know,' Declan offered. 'Did you ask the housekeeper, Mrs. Powers? Perhaps it's something she used to clean the floor.'

'No, not yet. I was going to ask her on my way out,' the detective indicated.

The two continued to stand there, each looking at the other. The silence was uncomfortable for Doctor Fitzgerald, who decided it was time to end the conversation. 'Well, if there's nothing else at the moment, Detective, I must see to my patients,' he walked to his desk and proceeded to sit in the large chair behind it. 'I'm sure you'll find Mrs. Powers in the kitchen,' Declan added.

'Okay, Doc, well you have a nice day,' Detective Lubovik said over his shoulder as he walked out of the office and headed in the direction of the kitchen.

Chapter Ten

Detective Lubovik walked past the staircase, his thoughts understandably flashing back to the night of Ms. Müller's death and the scene that awaited everyone, right there, at that very spot.

He walked on, continuing down the long hallway that met a t-intersection with another hallway right at Ms. Müller's room, which still had yellow tape crisscrossed on the door with the message 'DO NOT ENTER' in bold black letters stuck to it. He decided the housekeeper would have to wait a little longer.

He stood in front of the door for a short time, before pulling the tape off and placing a hand on the knob. Not only had he already been through the room several times himself, but the entire forensics team had as well. No one had found anything of significance. Nothing nefarious to suggest that Ms. Müller's death was anything but an accident.

And yet, something continued to pull him back here. Something just didn't feel right to him. And until that feeling was either pacified or proven, he would keep looking, keep thinking, keep wondering.

Detective Lubovik slowly opened the door to Ms. Müller's room and let it swing wide while he simply stood in the doorway, absorbing, processing.

He finally entered and began a slow perimeter walk of the main living area, but still nothing stood out to him. Still nothing called out to him. Everything was as it was yesterday and the day before, and the day before that.

Next, he went into the bathroom, turned on the light and stood there. Again, nothing. He moved on to Ms. Müller's bedroom. He entered, switched on the overhead light, and walked to one side of the bed, then the other. He wasn't sure what he was looking for but knew for sure that he was looking for anything. Shit! Shit!

His gut kept telling him there was something here. Has been telling him since he first entered this house nearly two weeks ago now. *Shit!*

He was beyond frustrated, he admitted to himself. He placed his hands on either hip, took a deep breath, stood up straight, and quickly checked himself in a mirror that hung over the only dresser in the starkly furnished room.

Jesus, he looked like shit, he thought to himself. He rubbed his face between both hands and then smoothed down the unruly hairs that were sparsely sprouting every which way from his head.

'Fuck!' he quietly reprimanded himself. There was just something about this case that bothered him…a lot.

With one final glance in the mirror, he decided he looked slightly less disheveled than before. That was good enough for him.

Before reaching to turn the light switch off, he took a second to straighten the mirror, which was slightly off-kilter. He didn't know whether he had accidently done it or if it had been like that, but thought the least he could do was straighten it. And so he did. Respect for the dead and all that.

He stood back a little and judged what he thought should be the middle of the mirror, then eased the mirror a little to the right, making sure the wire on the back of it maintained its perch on the hook that was anchored to the wall behind it. It appeared perfect. He let go.

Only the mirror leisurely returned to its original position, slightly lopsided. Once again, Detective Lubovik nudged it back, but then chastised himself for being overly anal.

He stopped for a second to consider whether or not he was developing OCD, but quickly dismissed the idea, since there was nothing else in his life that would suggest he was even remotely OCD. If anything, people who knew him, and these days they were fewer and farther between, might consider him to be the complete opposite.

The detective reached up and fiddled with the mirror in an attempt to center it, which he managed to do. The problem was, the position that was needed to perfectly balance the mirror was not the center itself, but rather just left of center, maybe not even half an inch or so. Something was throwing it out of balance, but on the surface the detective couldn't see what that might be. So, he reached up, removed the mirror from the wall, and turned it over.

'Well, well, what do we have here?' he quietly muttered to himself. He laid the mirror face down on top of the dresser and stared at the small Manila envelope that had been taped to the backside of the mirror. Whoever had taped the envelope to the mirror must have done so in a hurry, because it wasn't centered on the back, and as a result, the weight of the envelope and its contents was causing the mirror to tilt down and to the left, but only slightly, barely noticeably.

He hadn't thought he would need latex gloves today, so he hadn't brought any, but he didn't want to contaminate anything just in case. He took a pen from his shirt pocket and used the tip of it to gently lift the flap of the envelope, revealing what appeared to be several small pieces of paper containing handwritten notes that had been neatly folded and placed inside.

He picked up the mirror, and holding it over the bed, began shaking it up and down in an effort to dislodge the notes from the envelope. He was afraid if he used his pen to extract the notes from the envelope that he may rip them or damage them somehow. Not a good idea. The guys back in the lab would have his ass for that.

While he couldn't be sure that whatever was in the envelope was never meant to be found, he was absolutely certain there was a good reason why it had been concealed there in the first place.

After a few good shakes, the notes slipped from the envelope and fell on top of Ms. Müller's bed. Using the tip of his pen again, he managed to extract a single sheet from the small bundle of notes and splayed it open.

The handwriting on the paper was so fine, he had to bend right down to see it. Was it a note from a secret admirer of Ms. Müller? Perhaps a vestige of unrequited love?

He was pretty sure it was neither one of those. Whoever had written the notes had done so in some sort of shorthand. Cryptic to say the least. There were no complete sentences, no punctuation, no rhythm at all to the letters *and* numbers that filled both sides of the paper. Very odd.

Whatever it was, he knew he needed to take it back to the lab for analysis, but first he had to find something to put it in, preferably something unused. A freezer baggie you'd typically find in a kitchen, like Mrs. Powers' kitchen, would be ideal. He'd been headed that way anyway.

The detective left the notes as they had fallen on the bed and exited Ms. Müller's apartment, making sure to close the door behind him and re-attach the yellow crisscross tape. He turned left in the hallway outside Ms. Müller's room and headed toward the rear of the house where the kitchen was located, and hopefully, where Mrs. Powers would also be found.

He was in luck. The housekeeper was busy making bread. 'Morning, Mrs. Powers,' the detective interrupted her, 'you wouldn't happen to have one of those plastic freezer baggies, would you?'

Mrs. Powers stopped what she was doing. She didn't answer him, but rather reached behind her, opened a drawer, extracted a new, clear plastic baggie and placed it on the counter beside her. She had enough to do, so she wasn't about to use her valuable time walking the baggie over to the detective. If he wanted it so badly, let him come and get it, she decided.

Detective Lubovik wasn't the least taken aback by Mrs. Powers' attitude. He had been doing this job for nearly 30 years now and had seen and dealt with every kind of attitude mankind could throw at him.

'Just one more thing, Mrs. Powers,' he added as he scooped up the baggie, 'you wouldn't also happen to have a sample of Ms. Müller's handwriting, would you?'

Mrs. Powers looked at the detective, a curious expression on her face.

'A what?' she couldn't help herself from asking, unsure that she had heard him correctly. 'A sample of Ms. Müller's handwriting?'

'Yes, that's what I asked for,' the detective confirmed. 'A sample of Ms. Müller's handwriting, if you have one.'

'Well, I'm sure I don't,' Mrs. Powers answered, angrily wiping her hands on her apron. 'You'll have to ask Doctor Fitzgerald about that,' she indicated. 'Ms. Müller made notes in the patients' files all the time, so I'm sure he'd have a sample.'

'Thank you,' the detective responded. He turned as though to leave the kitchen, when he remembered there was one more thing he needed to ask the housekeeper. 'Sorry, Mrs. Powers, but I also need to know if you use any kind of cleaner or polishing wax on the tile floor at the front of the house that has red in it?' he asked.

'You mean the tiles in the foyer?' she responded.

'Yes,' the detective confirmed.

Mrs. Powers frowned. 'Certainly not,' she replied, obviously offended by the detective's inquiry. 'Now, what kind of a housekeeper would I be if I used anything red on a black-and-white floor?'

The detective feigned a smile at her. 'That's what I thought, Mrs. Powers,' he placated her before leaving the kitchen and heading back to Ms. Müller's room to bag the notes he'd found.

Using a clean tissue he had taken from a box he found in Ms. Müller's room, he carefully and successfully transferred the notes from Ms. Müller's bed to the baggie, sealed it, made a few notes on the outside of the baggie, and slipped it into an inside pocket of his coat. He then went, once again, in search of Doctor Fitzgerald. Things just got a little more interesting.

He retraced his earlier steps back to the doctor's office. As he was crossing the foyer, he could see that the pocket doors to Dr. Fitzgerald's office weren't quite closed all the way, which he thought odd since the doctor had seemed to be in such a rush earlier to get to his patients. Surely, he would have closed the doors if he had a patient with him, privacy issues and all.

As he got closer, he glimpsed just the shape of Doctor Fitzgerald's figure pass by. There he was again, then gone. Again, and gone. It suggested that the doctor was not simply sauntering but rather pacing behind the doors. An agitated back and forth, back and forth.

The detective pulled one pocket door back, startling Doctor Fitzgerald on the other side. 'Detective,' he was annoyed, 'you're still here? I thought you left a while ago.'

'Sorry to interrupt, Doc, but there's just one more thing I need from you before I leave,' he began 'and that's a sample of Ms. Müller's handwriting. Mrs. Powers said Ms. Müller made notes in client files all the time and that I could get a sample of her handwriting from you,' he explained.

Declan was surprised by the detective's request. 'May I ask why, Detective?'

'It's just that I found some handwritten notes in Ms. Müller's apartment and want to verify whether or not she wrote them by comparing them to a known sample of her handwriting,' he explained.

Declan froze. In the turmoil that followed Ms. Müller's death, he had completely forgotten all about the notes Ms. Müller had meticulous kept. The ones she used and referred to, *often*, the night she met with him. Notes that detailed his relationship with Jessica, his plans for Jessica, for the two of them. Details that could still destroy him.

Declan had to think fast. 'If you'd care to show me the notes, I am certainly qualified to vouch for Ms. Müller's handwriting,' Declan offered casually, but inside he was desperate. Were the notes the Detective was referring to one and the same notes that Ms. Müller had used to blackmail him?

'Well, unfortunately I already sent them off to the lab to be analyzed,' he lied. He wasn't about to share his findings until he was sure what they were. For all he knew, they might not have anything to do with Ms. Müller.

'So,' the detective asked Declan again, 'can I get a sample of Ms. Müller's handwriting please, Doc?'

At that very moment, Declan couldn't come up with a valid reason not to give the detective a sample of Ms. Müller's handwriting, at least not without appearing uncooperative, or even worse, suspicious.

'Certainly, Detective,' Declan relinquished and went to his desk where he looked through a stack of papers that were sitting in his 'in' box. 'Here you are,' he pulled a sheet that didn't contain any personal patient information from the bottom of the pile and handed it to the detective. 'It's from a list Ms. Müller had prepared with respect to some supplies she was requesting,' Declan explained as he handed the sheet to the detective. He had purposefully picked that sample because Ms. Müller had printed most of the list instead of writing it, and had also used short forms for many of the words. He hoped it might prove less than helpful, if not completely useless.

Detective Lubovik scanned it quickly, then folded it in half and placed it in the same inside coat pocket as the baggie of notes. 'Thanks, appreciate it,' he said. 'I'll let you know what I find out,' he called over his shoulder as he headed for the front door.

It was all Declan could do to remain calm, let alone perfectly still, as he watched the detective leisurely walk across the foyer and out the big front door.

He was suddenly interrupted by the phone on his desk. He knew it was an inside call by its two short rings so he answered it without hesitation. 'Hello, darling,' he responded into the mouthpiece. 'I need to see you, please.'

He listened to Jessica's reply. 'I'm happy to help. Let me just finish up a few things in my office and then I'll come up.'

Declan returned the handset to the phone's cradle and sat down heavily in one of the big chairs. He needed a little time alone to think, to reason, to pacify the uneasy flutters that had started nesting in the pit of his stomach. The only problem was, he hadn't yet been able to identify their source.

Chapter Eleven

Jessica left Declan's office and quickly ascended the stairs. Detective Lubovik had seriously gotten under her skin and into her head. *Shit! The red wax. Fuck!*

Jessica let herself into her apartment and locked the door behind her. She crossed to the living room and went directly to the coffee table, which she lingered over, merely stared at.

Slowly she lowered herself on to the couch and gently pulled the coffee table's drawer open toward her. She reached into the back left corner, lifted the shawl, and looked down at the little black gift box that lay beneath. She smiled down at it. So ordinary on the outside, so extraordinary on the inside.

After a moment, Jessica reached in and retrieved the gift box and laid it gently in her lap. She slowly removed the lid to reveal the red teddy bear candles all neatly lying in a row. All three still smiling in harmony despite the fact that one had so obviously suffered an injury, its blackened wick protruding from the top of its head, which itself had been slightly disfigured by the just-starting-to-melt-from-the-heat wax.

She wasn't sure what to do. Should she throw just the used candle away? Or should she get rid of all three? Remove any trace of them altogether? The only other person who knew about them was Declan. *Tic.*

Jessica closed the drawer in the coffee table and lifted the gift box in her hand. She got up off the couch and went to her bedroom where she backed herself into a corner and sat down, the gift box now cradled in one arm.

She needed time. She needed to think. While she didn't see the red wax itself that was found in the foyer as a threat to her, the fact that she had three red candles in her apartment, one of which had obviously been used, was most certainly a direct connection to her, thus now a direct threat to her.

But Jessica just couldn't bring herself to get rid of the candles. She had waited years for them to come back into her life and she wasn't willing to part with them. She had only just begun to know them, had only just started to play with them. She simply had to figure out another way.

And so, it was that Doctor Fitzgerald would come to her rescue, once again unwittingly. Jessica rose from the floor in the corner of her bedroom, returned to the living room and the coffee table. Before placing the black gift box back in its corner, she took the lid off and gently removed the candle with the charred wick and slightly melted head.

She tucked the candle into a pocket in her sweater, put the lid back on the box, placed the gift box back in its corner, put the shawl back on top of the box, and closed the drawer.

Jessica then went to the phone on the wall by her door, picked up the handset and punched in the two-digit number for Declan's office, which was answered almost immediately.

'Hello, Doctor Fitzgerald,' she purred into the mouthpiece. A self-satisfied grin crossed her lips as she listened to his enthusiastic response on the other end.

'Yes, I would like to see you too,' she pretended. 'I thought maybe you could come up to my apartment,' she began. 'I have a few questions I was hoping to ask you about the social control aspect of human behavior,' she lied. She knew he wouldn't refuse her request if he thought it involved her studies, since the judge had insisted that getting her degree was a condition for her final release. Even more importantly, getting her degree meant she would no longer be considered Doctor Fitzgerald's patient. He *wanted* it to happen. She *needed* it to happen.

She always though it was probably for the best that most people never took the time to really consider and comprehend the difference between *want* and *need*, a perilous difference.

The first was driven only by desire. It may or may not happen, depending on the strength of one's desire. Not much of a commitment there.

But the second was driven to survive. There was no fight or flight. There was only a fight to the death. Jessica understood which one was stronger, which was more powerful, which was more capable of doing anything it took.

She listened for his response. 'Wonderful, I'll see you in a while then,' she answered in an almost whisper before replacing the handset. Jessica removed the red teddy bear candle from her pocket and smiled at it. 'We have company coming,' she whispered. 'Time to get ready.'

Jessica returned the candle to her pocket and went to the kitchen where she calmly retrieved two long-stemmed glasses from an overhead cupboard, a corkscrew from the closest drawer, and a bottle of red wine from a nearby shelf. She took her time opening the wine, maliciously twisting and burrowing the corkscrew, before leaving it on the countertop to breathe.

Next, she went back to the living room where she turned on the stereo and tuned it to an instrumental-only station. She couldn't risk outside voices filtering into her mind and contaminating her thoughts. Not tonight.

She then scattered several textbooks in a haphazard arrangement on the carpet to make it look as though she had been studying and simply tossed each one aside as she finished with it before going on to the next. She threw in a lined, yellow notepad of paper she had been doodling on the day before, a pen and various colored highlighters. The scene was almost set. She just needed Declan to arrive.

She was in no hurry. Good things came to those who waited. But she didn't have to wait long.

An hour later, a knock on Jessica's door drew her away from a mirror where she had been studying her appearance. Her now red lips, her now faint red polka dotted cheeks, her now fine black-lined eyes. She smiled seductively at her image, before crossing to the door and opening it. 'Come in,' she encouraged Declan, 'I'm so glad you came.'

Declan closed the door behind him and reached out to her, drawing her close to him. 'Jessica,' he began, 'it's all I could do to not run after you earlier when the detective was here. What did he say that sent you running up the stairs so fast?'

Jessica pulled back from him so she could see his face. She needed to be able to see his eyes, his expressions, if she were to continue to read him properly. She was constantly reassessing his readiness, persistently re-evaluating his willingness.

'I honestly don't remember now,' she intentionally dismissed his question. Instead, she reached up and stroked his cheek with the back of one of her hands. 'Listen, why don't we have a glass of wine, get comfortable and you can answer a few questions for me in preparation for my final exam tomorrow.'

'Sounds wonderful,' Declan easily succumbed to her invitation and followed her into the kitchen. 'Here, allow me,' he offered, taking the wine bottle and steadily filling each glass halfway. He handed one glass to Jessica, 'Here's to us,' he said as he lifted the other.

Jessica simply nodded as she raised her glass in response to his toast before taking just a sip. 'Come, let's sit in the living room,' she said as she led the way. 'My notes are in there,' her lies continued.

Declan lowered himself into a large, comfy chair opposite the couch, where Jessica now sat. 'You have makeup on tonight,' Declan observed. 'You look even more beautiful than usual, if that's at all possible,' he smiled fondly at her.

Jessica returned his smile. 'Thank you, Declan. I decided it was about time I looked more like a woman than a schoolgirl.'

'Well, you've certainly succeeded,' Declan commented quietly. He could sit there all evening and simply look at her, admire her, and yes, fantasize about her, too. He couldn't help himself.

He recently came to the harsh conclusion that somewhere along his life's path, he had stopped being a man and started being just a doctor. Someone who approached everyday life as he would approach a patient—clinical, sterile, unemotional.

But Jessica had unearthed emotions he had intentionally buried so long ago. Reawakened feelings he thought had died so long ago.

'Why are you looking at me like that, Declan?' Jessica smiled at him.

'I can't help it,' he responded genuinely. 'You truly bring out the best in me.' Declan leaned over and gently placed his wineglass on the coffee table in front of him and rose from the couch. He so wanted to hold her.

'Wait,' Jessica recognized the perfect opportunity, 'I have a surprise for you. Now close your eyes,' she insisted as she put her glass of wine down beside his. 'Keep them closed,' she instructed, 'or you'll spoil my surprise.'

Declan sighed, but gave in to her adorable request. He closed his eyes and just stood there, smiling, listening.

He heard the rustling sound of material, followed by the clicking noise of what he thought sounded like the flick of a lighter. Next, his nose picked up just a trace of something familiar. He recognized it as the distinct odor of a candle's wick, burning.

'Go ahead,' Jessica said, 'open your eyes.'

Declan was immediately drawn to the charming glow of a red teddy bear candle as it sat flickering on a small dish atop the coffee table that stood between them. 'It's the first time I've used one of the special candles you gave me, Declan,' she offered.

'Thank you, Jessica, but I thought you were saving it for a special occasion,' he said. 'What's the occasion?'

Jessica was prepared. 'Well, this isn't so much an occasion as it is a celebration,' she smiled seductively at him.

Declan was intrigued. 'Is that so,' he playfully responded. 'And just what is it that we're celebrating?' his mind wanted to know. His body hoped to find out.

Jessica took an index finger and slowly leaning over the coffee table, dipped her finger inside his wineglass, swirled it lazily around the blood red contents, then raised her finger to her mouth, inside her mouth. Then slowly extracted it from her mouth, her lips moist and plump. Her eyes never wavering from him the entire time.

'It's the night before my final exam,' she said, 'and one day closer to us being together.' Jessica was well aware that she had intentionally led Declan on by making him believe that perhaps tonight would be the night they finally consummated their relationship. But it was not to be.

For Declan, it could not be until Jessica earned her degree. For Jessica, it would never be until she owned him, *completely*. It never would be until she was legally acknowledged as Mrs. Declan Fitzgerald.

While Declan was frustrated that their celebration obviously wasn't going to involve something much more intimate between the two of them, he was nonetheless happy to raise his glass to her, to them.

'To our future.' Declan delicately touched the rim of his glass to the rim of her glass. Little did Declan know that she'd already decided his future was going to look a whole lot different than hers.

Jessica leaned slightly over the coffee table to offer him a kiss. Declan leaned toward her, looking down at the candle to make sure his tie wasn't floating too close to the flame, when he noticed something that momentarily distracted him.

'It looks like the candle has already been used,' he commented, so quietly that at first Jessica wasn't sure what he had actually said. 'See, you can tell there's a spot on the top of its head where it looks like the wax has already melted,' he pointed out.

Jessica remained calm but was strangely excited by the challenge Declan had unwittingly posed. It kept her on her toes. It kept her mind engaged. This was the mental stimulation she craved, had longed for, had missed for so long.

'No, silly,' she stepped around the coffee table, nestled up to his chest, slowly leaned in, and delicately ran the tip of her tongue up the length of his neck. 'I was waiting to share the first one with you,' her assurances untruthful. 'I wanted you to be the first,' her insinuation intentional.

Declan slipped an arm around her waist and held her tight against himself. His body melted into her warmth. His reasoning melted away under her control. 'Thank you, Jessica,' he whispered into her ear, 'that means a lot to me.' All thoughts of the red teddy bear candle's misshapen head now gone. But had they been forgotten?

'No, it's me who should be thanking you, Declan,' she whispered back, her head resting up against his chest. 'Thank you for all you've done for me.' She smiled to herself.

* * * * *

Rather than taking the handwritten notes he'd found hidden behind the mirror in Ms. Müller's room straight to the lab, Detective Lubovik decided to take a quick look first. He was curious more than anything but would claim he was working on a theory if caught.

He made his way to his desk where he now sat, the freezer baggie with the notes inside it laying on top near his left hand and the sample of Ms. Müller's handwriting he got from Dr. Fitzgerald near his right hand. Side by side.

Lubovik didn't need a handwriting expert to tell him that they were written by one and the same person, and that person was obviously Ms. Müller.

He got up from his desk, the baggie in his left hand, and went to the photocopier. Before handing the baggie and its contents over to the lab for processing, as well as a handwriting expert to verify what Lubovik himself suspected about Ms. Müller having written both, he wanted to get a copy of the first page of the notes inside the freezer baggie. He wasn't about to waste time sitting around for what could possibly be weeks waiting for the items to come back from the lab before he could get a closer look at the notes. At least if he had a copy of the first page, he could get a head start on trying to decipher the cryptic writings. He was sure there was a story hidden within the distressed symbols.

He made the copy, dropped it on his desk, before heading to the lab to have everything properly submitted and processed. He filled out the necessary paperwork, handed the items to the lab clerk and calmly returned to his desk, stopping along the way to grab a coffee from a pot that magically never seemed to empty. Apparently, the magician's name was Officer Penny Smithers, the only female on his shift. Hard to teach new tricks to a chauvinistic old dog.

He opened the top right hand drawer of his desk and withdrew a pad of paper, placing it neatly on the desk in front of him. He removed the pen that resided permanently in his shirt pocket and allowed his hand to hover over the paper as his eyes began to scan the photocopy.

What the fuck was this mess? Scribbled on the very first line were letters and numbers, some together, others orphaned.

Tma2 2230 D F X

He copied them onto the pad of paper. At first glance, he couldn't imagine what the jumble meant, but was resolved to work at it. Next time he goes to the manor house, he'd have to remember to ask the doctor if he had any idea as to what any of it meant. Could it be a drug code? Or possibly a patient's file number?

In addition to the mystery of the notes, he had other things to think about. First, just what was that spot of red wax the forensic tech had found in the foyer doing right in front of Ms. Müller's face? How did it get there? How long had it been there? Second, how had the stair's carpet runner come unraveled? And why only that one strand?

As for the wax, he was still waiting on another report from the lab. While they had identified the material as being wax, they were hoping to narrow down what type of wax it was and what most often it is used in, for example if it was floor wax, despite the harsh objection from Mrs. Powers, the housekeeper, that she *did not* nor *would not* use such a thing on the black-and-white tile floor.

The only other thing that immediately came to his mind when it was first discovered was that it was possibly candle wax. Could the wax have come from a candle? Yet, there had been no candle found near Ms. Müller's body nor in the foyer of the house itself. There was no sign of any candle in Ms. Müller's room either.

There were candles found on the main floor, which was the only part of the manor house covered under the current search warrant. So far, Detective Lubovik hadn't felt the need to apply for an amendment to the warrant to include the second floor, which he knew was solely for the purpose of guest accommodations. So far, everyone had been pretty cooperative. Maybe a few yellow flags along the way, but certainly no red ones at this point.

The candles that were found were in plain sight in the kitchen and were part of an emergency kit; they were not used, they were not red, they were not relevant.

He'd have to add that red candle question to his list for the next time he goes to the manor house, which looks like it will be tomorrow. He's got too many questions and not yet enough answers.

The next morning, the detective once again stood outside the manor house, an index finger working the doorbell. 'Come on,' he said impatiently under his breath.

After a minute or so, Mrs. Powers opened the door with more force than she looked capable of. 'Sorry to disturb you, Mrs. Powers,' he said insincerely. 'I'd like to have a word with the doctor please. I see his car is parked out front, so I know he's here.'

Mrs. Powers was at first visibly annoyed, but quickly progressed to verbally annoyed. 'Detective, if you would be so kind as to not ring the doorbell more than one time. I am not deaf,' she insisted, 'what I am is an old lady who has to come from the very back of the house every time you ring that damned thing.'

'Sure thing, Mrs. Powers,' he says offhandedly as he made his way through the door. 'I know where the doctor's office is, so I'll announce myself.'

The detective didn't wait for her to respond, but rather walked right past her and straight to Dr. Fitzgerald's office. The pocket doors were closed, but he didn't care. He knocked sharply, but only once, before pulling back one door.

Inside, he found Dr. Fitzgerald sitting behind his desk, alone, but apparently not hard at work. He appeared deep in thought. 'Morning, Doc,' the detective said. 'Thought I'd find you here.'

Declan sat up abruptly, taken aback by the detectives sudden and loud appearance. 'Detective Lubovik,' he acknowledged, 'what can I do for you today?' Declan was clearly annoyed.

'Well, you asked me to get back to you, if we found out anything more about those handwritten notes that were in Ms. Müller's room,' the detective explained. 'Turns out, we found something.'

Declan's demeanor briefly stalled, before he indicated to the detective that he was welcome to sit in the chair opposite his. 'Please, Detective,' he offered, his curiosity naturally piqued. His nerves unnaturally taut. 'And what did you find out, if I'm permitted to inquire?'

Detective Lubovik reached into his coat and pulled out his notepad and began flipping through it. He stopped at a blank page, 'Here it is,' he said, a look of great concentration on his face. 'Our Forensic Handwriting Expert confirmed that Ms. Müller did in fact write those notes,' he blatantly lied. There wasn't a hope in hell that anyone in forensics could get results of any kind back to him in just one day.

'Is that right,' Declan responded, his face an expression of puzzled panic. It kind of struck the detective that that's what a deer might look like in a car's headlights just before the two meet face to face. 'You alright, Doc?' the detective asked. 'Only you look a little surprised.'

Declan managed to recover himself. 'Not at all, Detective, please continue,' he quickly encouraged.

'Well, the only thing is,' the detective continued, 'we haven't quite figured out what the notes say. You see, they're written in some kind of shorthand. I thought maybe if you had a look, you might be able to figure out what's what.'

Declan didn't know what to think. Should he be relieved, because no one had yet figured out what the notes said? Or should he be reserved, because there was still yet a chance someone would eventually figure out what the notes said?

'Of course, Detective, I'd be happy to have a look and render an opinion, but I don't think I can solve something that even your experts haven't been able to,' he humbly added.

'Well, it's worth a try, right Doc, since you worked so closely with Ms. Müller,' the detective said as he slid a piece of paper that showed the first line he had transcribed from the cryptic notes across the desk to Declan.

Declan looked at the piece of paper with the odd collection of letters and numbers. At first, it made absolutely no sense to him either. He tried to recall the night Ms. Müller had gone over her notes with him and remembered that she had been very specific about the exact dates and precise times of his many ethical transgressions with Jessica. Then he knew. He knew what the letters and numbers were most likely trying to convey.

Tma2 2230 D F X

The first group he was sure represented a specific date, while the second group was written in what appeared to be military time. But what about the three letters at the end, each one on its own? The *D* and *F* could be his initials. Suddenly, it all began to make sense, at least to him.

Tuesday, May 2, 10:30 pm, Dr. Fitzgerald Exited. It was the exact date and time of night on but one occasion when he had left Jessica's apartment after hours. 'One night of many,' he recalled. And one night of many Ms. Müller had also recalled.

'No, I'm sorry, Detective,' Declan pushed the slip of paper back across the desk, 'I have no idea what it means.'

The detective was disappointed. 'Well, that's okay,' he began. 'I'll just leave this with you,' he said as he pushed the paper back toward Declan, 'in case something comes to mind.'

Declan didn't dare to touch the paper. He was afraid his unsteady hand might betray his anxiety; could suggest his lie.

Detective Lubovik remained seated, remained quiet. He often wondered if anyone else understood as well as he did just how loud silence can be. Just how telling no words can be.

'There's just one more thing, Doc,' he finally said. 'Are you aware if any of your patients has any candles in her room? Specifically, a red candle.'

Chapter Twelve

Declan sat in his office for a while after Detective Lubovik left, thinking about the conversation they just had. Recounting his words, recalling his convictions, reliving his objections.

'Well, yes, Detective,' he remembered freely offering, 'as a matter of fact, I recently gave Ms. McCallum a gift of a set of candles.'

The detective was interested, but remained indifferent. 'What was the gift for, Doc?' he asked, thinking it odd that a doctor would give any patient a gift, not to mention that he was pretty sure it was contrary to the physicians' code of conduct.

'If you must know, it was in recognition of all the hard work Jessica had put in over these past six years,' Declan explained.

The detective pondered this information for a bit before continuing. 'Kind of an unusual gift, don't you think?' he commented. 'I mean, that's a long time, six years. Must have been a lot of work. So why not flowers? Or at the very least a congratulations card and a box of chocolates?' He was curious. He was also puzzled.

'I'm sorry, Detective, but I'm afraid I can't share that information with you, since my answer would require me to divulge professional conversations I've had with Ms. McCallum,' he noted. 'Client confidentiality. Doctor-patient privilege. I'm sure you understand.'

Detective mulled Declan's explanation over before nodding his head. 'Sure, I understand, Doc,' he replied. 'It's just that it seemed to be a perfectly harmless question, if you ask me.'

Declan considered the detective's remarks and decided to relinquish, but only just a little. 'Suffice it to say, Detective, that I was present and personally saw Ms. McCallum light the first of the three candles I gave her. I can assure you that they were all new. None had been used until then.'

'Is that so,' the detective made a quick note in his pad. 'And that was before or after Ms. Müller's death?'

'After, of course,' Declan replied. Then it dawned on him what the detective had just said. 'Certainly, you're not suggesting that Ms. McCallum had anything to do with Ms. Müller's death, are you?' Declan demanded.

'Did I say that?' Detective Lubovik smiled quietly. 'Funny, but I don't recall saying that?' He loved this part of his job. Getting under people's skin and then waiting to see what crawled out.

'Not in so many words,' Declan answered, 'but you certainly implied as much.'

The detective shrugged. 'Your interpretation, not mine,' he threw back at Declan. 'By the way, there is just one more thing I've been meaning to run by you. Get your take on, so to speak.'

'And what might that be, Detective?' Declan asked impatiently.

'It's just that I'm still stumped by the whole frayed carpet runner on the stairs thing,' he began to explain. 'Mrs. Powers swears there was nothing wrong with the runner when she cleaned the entire staircase that very day, and we know that Ms. Müller wasn't wearing anything on her feet that night that had a heel of any kind, so it couldn't have caught the carpet, causing it to rip.'

Declan wasn't sure if the detective expected him to respond or not, so chose to remain silent.

'I got to thinking about all of that, so went back and looked at the photos the Forensics Team took of the carpet runner and the stray strand itself,' the detective continued, 'and it all looked too clean. Like it was maybe cut.' He waited for Declan's reaction. Nothing.

'On purpose,' the detective added, again waiting to see if Declan would react.

And he did. He was suddenly outraged. 'You think someone here intentionally cut the carpet runner and what, lured or pushed Ms. Müller to her death at the bottom of the stairs?' Declan raised his voice even more. 'That's preposterous!' he shouted. 'And what possible reason would anyone here have to want to harm Ms. Müller?'

Although Declan himself knew of one pretty convincing reason. And one that could possibly be enough of a convicting reason. She had tried to blackmail him and now she was dead. *Fuck.* He knew he had nothing to do with Ms. Müller's death, but would anyone else believe him if the truth were uncovered?

Detective Lubovik just looked at Declan and smiled. 'Well, Doc,' he finally answered, 'I'm sure I don't know. I still gotta ask the tough questions, though.'

Up on the second-floor landing, Jessica had been standing perfectly still behind a pillar listening to most of the conversation between the detective and Declan, doing her best to capture words that filtered up to her from below, but not having much success. She needed them to speak up, to talk louder.

She only managed to piece together the gist of their conversation when she heard Declan's voice explode. '…someone here intentionally cut the carpet…what possible reason would anyone here have to want to harm Ms. Müller?'

Jessica froze on the spot. *Fuck.* She forgot to return the box cutter she had used to cut the carpet with to the kitchen where she originally got it. *Fuck!*

She raced back to her apartment, let herself in, made sure she locked the door and went to the closet in her bedroom. There, she tore through all her sweaters, looking for the one she had been wearing that night.

'There you are,' she whispered aloud as she pulled the sweater from its hanger and threw it on her bed. She checked one pocket, then the other, where she found what she was looking for. The small box cutter knife. She knew she had to return it to the kitchen and quickly.

She held the knife in her hand for a few seconds, before slipping it into the front pocket of the jeans she was wearing, overtop of which she wore a tucked-in white shirt. The knife made a slight bulge in her pocket, so she untucked her shirt and let it loose to fall just about her thighs. No more visible bulge.

She went to her door again, and before exiting, took the time to inspect her image in the mirror: a pat to the hair, a fingertip dab to the corner of her mouth where the lipstick refused to hang on, a pretend smile that looked back at her. 'I won't be long, baby doll,' she whispered to her image.

* * * * *

He left Doctor Fitzgerald in his office, sitting in his chair. His mind apparently angry, his face obviously red. 'His problem, not mine,' the detective decided.

He wandered through the main floor of the house until he reached the kitchen. 'Sorry to trouble you again, Mrs. Powers,' the detective announced from just inside the kitchen's doorway where he now stood, 'but I'm wondering if you're missing a small knife of any kind.'

Mrs. Powers dropped the small dish she had been holding, which broke into tiny pieces the second it came into contact with the kitchen's slate floor. 'Good Lord,' she shrieked as her hand reached up to clutch the apron's material at her chest, 'you might try making a little noise instead of sneaking up on a person!' she yelled at him.

Lubovik had neither the time nor the inclination to apologize. 'Have you noticed if any of your knives have gone missing?' he asked again.

'Not that it's any of your business, but no, I haven't,' Mrs. Powers relinquished.

'What about any other type of cutting thing, like scissors, or a box cutter?' he persisted. 'Anything like that missing?'

'It's not as though I have an inventory of everything in the kitchen,' she protested. 'I can't be expected to keep track of everything.'

'Well,' Detective Lubovik continued on undaunted, 'if you wouldn't mind having a quick look around…a drawer or two…and just see if anything immediately jumps out at you. Or, in this case, doesn't jump out at you,' he smiled, appreciating his own humor even if no one else did.

Mrs. Powers sighed and closed her eyes. 'God give me strength' is what the detective thought he heard her say under her breath. She turned and pulled open one drawer, pushed a few things around, and apparently satisfied, closed it shut. The drawer beside it, same thing. Pulled it open, shuffled a few things around, and apparently unsatisfied, left it open.

'Well, I was sure…' she began, followed by a little more tactile mining of the drawer. 'I could have sworn…'

'Something missing, Mrs. Powers?' Detective Lubovik asked from behind her.

'Well,' she began, 'I usually keep a small box cutter knife in this drawer here. I get bulk deliveries of things like paper towel and so on, and I use it to open the boxes they come in.'

The detective was a little curious, but not overly optimistic about this panning out. 'When was the last time you remember seeing it, Mrs. Powers?' he wanted to know.

She thought for a moment before answering. 'I think it's been a few weeks now,' she admitted. 'Yes, that's right, because the last big delivery we had was…why it was the morning of Ms. Müller's accident.' Mrs. Powers' hands involuntarily began to choke her apron's material, scrunching it and twisting it. Unscrunching it and untwisting it.

'Could you have put it somewhere else by mistake?' the detective wondered aloud. 'Maybe misplaced it?'

'I'm sure anything is possible in your world, Detective,' she snapped, 'however, in my world, I am fastidious when it comes to things being put in their right places. I don't have time to waste looking for things all the time, so I'm very diligent about where everything goes,' she insisted. 'Therefore, if it isn't here, I'm sure I have no idea where it is.'

'So, what you're saying is, it's missing?' the detective wanted to confirm her words.

'What's missing?' a voice in the doorway behind them interrupted the verbal back and forth between Detective Lubovik and Mrs. Powers, who both turned at once.

'Ms. McCallum,' the detective was the first to acknowledge her. 'Mrs. Powers was just telling me that she thinks a knife has gone missing from the kitchen,' he explained. 'A small box cutter knife, to be more specific.'

Jessica offered no response, no reaction.

'Nothing to concern yourself with,' Mrs. Powers assured her. 'I'm sure I just misplaced it and it will turn up in a day or so.'

Jessica pushed her hands into her jean's pockets. 'I'm sure it will too, Mrs. Powers,' she offered with a smile on her face and a concealed hand wrapped around the small knife that temporarily lived in her pocket. 'Things like that have a habit of turning up when you least expect it, don't you find that to be true, Detective?' she teased him.

Detective Lubovik smiled at her, then turned to go. 'I'm sure it's nothing, but do me a favor, Mrs. Powers,' he called back over his shoulder, 'be sure and let me know if and when that box cutter turns up?'

'I'll do my best, Detective,' is all she would commit to, 'but I'm very busy. Now, if you're finally on your way, I'll see you to the door,' she insisted.

Detective Lubovik obligingly proceeded toward the front of the house and eventually out the front door, Mrs. Powers following behind, closing the front door on his back. 'About time,' Mrs. Powers muttered aloud as she headed back to her kitchen, eager to look for the misplaced knife, if the truth be told.

It wasn't like her to not put something back in its proper place, so this bothered her. More so than she would ever admit to the detective, or anyone else, for that matter. She had her pride.

Mrs. Powers returned to the kitchen and saw that Jessica was still there. As though she had been waiting there. 'Can I help you with something, Jessica?' she asked.

'No, not really, Mrs. Powers,' Jessica replied. 'I was just wondering if you'd like me to help you look for the knife the detective seemed so interested in.'

'Well, that's very thoughtful of you, I'm sure,' Mrs. Powers responded, 'but there's no need. It'll eventually show up. Now run along, you've got that last exam tomorrow.'

'If you're sure, Mrs. Powers,' Jessica smiled sweetly at her. 'You're right, I probably should get back to my books.' She turned and casually made her way out of the kitchen, back down the long hallway to the foyer and its central staircase, and straight to Declan's closed office door.

She knocked gently on the door, then deliberately shoved her hands once again into her jeans' pockets and was rewarded with a heartbeat of excitement from their emptiness.

She wondered how long it would take Mrs. Powers to find her precious box cutter.

Chapter Thirteen

'Come in, Detective!' Declan shouted from the other side of the door, but it was Jessica who slid the pocket door back. 'Sorry to disappoint you, Declan, it's only me,' she smiled.

'Jessica,' Declan began. 'I thought you were Detective Lubovik again. He can be rather annoying, can't he,' Declan stated, rather than asked. 'Although I'm sure there are those who admire his tenacity, but they've probably never been on the receiving end of one of his little visits.'

Jessica slid the office door closed behind her, smiled at Declan, and making her way around his desk, pushed his chair back and proceeded to straddle his lap. She was emotionally high at the moment, having successfully accomplished what she had set out to do in the kitchen, and was struggling to control the impulses she was feeling, wanting so much to express.

'Jessica,' Declan half-heartedly tried to push her off, 'we really shouldn't do this here. We still have to be careful, although not for much longer,' he reminded her. 'Besides, I think Detective Lubovik is still in the house. The last time I saw him, he was headed for the kitchen.'

Jessica leaned into Declan and kissed him hard, his face between her two hands. 'Don't worry, Doc,' Jessica finally let go of his face, 'the detective left about ten minutes ago, and while I would love to sit here all day,' she said as she encouraged her hips to settle even further into Declan's lap, teasing him, 'I just came to tell you that I am going upstairs to my apartment, locking the door behind me and studying for the rest of the day. Tomorrow's a big day for me…for us.'

Declan let out a frustrated moan as Jessica lifted herself from his lap. 'I know, darling,' Declan agreed, 'but even just one more day seems too long, not to mention too painful,' he smiled at her as he reached a hand down to the front of his pants in an attempt to manually discipline his awakening erection.

Jessica smiled at him, leaned over his chair, but instead of kissing him, ran one of her hands through his hair while the other hand reached down, between his legs, and gently kneaded his manhood through his dress pants, causing him to audibly gasp. 'Oh, God,' was all he could manage before Jessica just as suddenly removed her hand, stood up straight and walked to the door, a wicked smile on her face.

She slid open one pocket door, stepped across the threshold to the foyer beyond and turned back to slide the door closed behind her. 'By the way,' she said, 'you might consider putting some of that expensive therapy you learned to good use.'

'What do you mean?' Declan was curious.

'When I went to the kitchen, I found detective Lubovik in there. I think he upset Mrs. Powers, because she couldn't find some knife he asked her about.'

Declan was confused. 'You mean he asked her for a knife she had in the kitchen?'

'No,' Jessica explained, 'he asked her if there was a knife missing from the kitchen and apparently there was.'

Declan thought about Jessica's words for a moment, before it dawned on him what the detective had been after. 'I don't think it was a coincidence,' Declan commented.

'What do you mean, not a coincidence?' Jessica asked, her senses suddenly heightened.

'It's something he said this morning,' Declan began to explain, 'about the runner on the stairs and how he thought it might be possible that the carpet had been deliberately cut.'

Jessica showed no emotions. She had already heard Detective Lubovik's theory when she had been hiding on the second-floor landing earlier, so now Declan's words had no effect on her.

'Jessica,' Declan repeated, 'did you hear what I just said? That Ms. Müller's death may not have simply been an accident.'

'I heard you, but personally I doubt it,' Jessica dismissed the idea. 'Think about it. Ms. Müller was obese, old, was dressed in a floor-length housecoat that night, and was wearing slippers that didn't have any tread on them. Not to mention it was pitch dark, except for the flashlight she had, which I understand provided so little light that it was basically useless.' Declan considered Jessica's words.

'Put all those factors together and place them at the top of an imposing staircase,' Jessica was feeding Declan's mind, 'and tell me how it could be anything other than an unfortunate accident?'

Declan looked at her before slowly nodding his head once again. 'Those are all compelling reasons to suggest it was nothing more,' Declan agreed, 'and yet, how do explain the piece of frayed carpet on the staircase runner?' he wanted to know. He was desperate for a sound explanation, or a reasonable one at the very least. Anything to discourage the whole situation from evolving into something far more complicated, much more disturbing.

Jessica considered Declan's question for a moment before she replied. 'There are a number of possibilities that come to mind,' she began. 'For example, it's conceivable that Ms. Müller slipped first, and in an attempt to reach out to the nearest bannister to try to catch herself, her flashlight somehow got caught in the carpet and caused it to fray,' she offered.

Declan nodded. He was doing his best to keep an open mind. 'You said you had a number of possibilities, so what else do you think could have happened?' he asked her.

Declan assumed she was speaking spontaneously. Only Jessica knew she was speaking deliberately. This was not the first time she had voiced these same words. Nor was this the first time she had presented these same possibilities.

She had rehearsed by herself, performed for herself several times in front of the full-length mirror in her bedroom. She had worked hard to do it right, to get it right.

'Well,' she pretended to think about her next words, 'is it possible that Mrs. Powers was wrong? That the carpet was already frayed, and unfortunately for Ms. Müller, she didn't notice and either slipped on it or tripped over it?'

Declan continued to nod, his head slightly down in thought, one hand pulling on his bottom lip. 'Alright, go on,' he encouraged her.

She had one last hypothesis to pitch. 'It's also possible that the stair runner had absolutely nothing to do with Ms. Müller's death,' Jessica began. 'Perhaps she suffered a stroke or a heart attack at the top of the stairs and simply fell, or fainted and then fell. I'm sure you'd agree that she was not the healthiest person?' Jessica asked.

'I certainly agree with you about that,' Declan responded. The whole situation was unsettling, for everyone. 'Well, I think all any of us can do for now is carry on as best we can and wait for the medical examiner's findings.'

Jessica smiled as she began to slide the pocket door closed. 'Which I intend to do right now…carry on studying.'

She headed up the stairs, stopping for just a brief moment on the fifth stair from the top. 'Poor Ms. Müller, what an unfortunate bitch,' she whispered to no one then went on her way. There was also no one to appreciate the Cheshire cat grin on her face. And certainly no one to admire the adrenaline-stimulated spring in her step.

* * * * *

Detective Lubovik had, of course, also considered all of the possibilities. Had mentally acted out all sorts of scenarios and yet none of them fit. The pieces just didn't go together, no matter how hard he tried or how badly he wanted them to.

As for the cryptic notes, he was no further ahead on those either, despite the fact that he had enlisted the help of a few others on his team. He had provided each of them with a copy of that first page of the notes and asked them to wrap their heads around the mess and see what they could come up with. The following day, one of the young officers on his team approached him and said he thought that the numbers in each line were times, as in time of the day, but were noted in military time. As for the rest of it, he was stumped.

Detective Lubovik had already figured that out, but didn't say anything. The guy was a rookie and had only just transferred to his unit, so Lubovik didn't want to be the one to throw cold water on his enthusiasm. Give him a few more years and the job would probably do that on its own.

Lubovik would admit only to himself that he was discouraged by the notes. Without understanding what the rest of each line meant, the times on their own were worthless. He also had to consider the possibility that the notes were nothing at all. Had absolutely nothing to do with Ms. Müller's death. In which case, everyone, including himself, would be pissed because of the time they had spent on them. Wasted on them, really at that point. The thing was, in his line of work you never knew for sure what was going to waste your time until it had already been wasted. But it was a necessary part of the job and he had to keep trying, had to continue digging.

As for the carpet runner on the stairs, the lab had confirmed that the single, frayed strand hadn't come apart on its own. It hadn't disfigured itself. It had to have been cut.

While it still wasn't enough to definitively say that Ms. Müller's death was a homicide, it was enough for Lubovik to seriously consider that it may not have been an accident.

So, where to go from here? He still hadn't looked over the second lab report about the spot of red wax found at the foot of the staircase. So, he fanned through the reams of paper that littered his desk until his hand found what it had been looking for. Just as he thought all along, it was positively identified as simple candle wax. Only it wasn't turning out to be so simple.

A few days ago, he had been mulling over the conversation he and the doctor had had about the doctor's gift to Ms. McCallum…the set of candles. The doctor had sworn that Ms. McCallum lit the very first candle in the set for the first time right in front of him, which was *after* Ms. Müller's death. *How could he not take the word of such a well-respected man as Dr. Fitzgerald?*

Yet, no other red candles had been found in the house, and no other candles whatsoever were reported to be in any of the other guests' rooms, which occupied the entire second floor of the house.

Ms. McCallum was the only person in the house who had a red candle in her possession at the time of Ms. Müller's death, which could lead one to assume that she was somehow involved. And yet, none of the candles in her possession were used until *after* Ms. Müller's death, which could then lead one to presume that she was in no way involved.

As for the missing box cutter knife from Mrs. Powers' kitchen, he subsequently learned that, indeed, Mrs. Powers had simply misplaced the knife and it was safely in her possession once again. He was also advised that it had since been returned to its rightful place in her kitchen. How it wound up between the end of a cabinet and the refrigerator was still a mystery to her.

Also, the medical examiner had found nothing unusual during Ms. Müller's autopsy, nothing outside of what you'd expect to find when a body falls down a flight of stairs, such as a broken leg, some fractured ribs, various cuts and contusions, and blunt force trauma to the head, which was noted as probably being the final and fatal blow that ultimately caused her death. As for the manor of death, that was officially noted as 'UNDETERMINED.'

That didn't sit too well with Detective Lubovik. And it wouldn't sit well with him until he had that changed to read either 'HOMICIDE' or 'ACCIDENTAL.'

He just couldn't help feeling that there was something here. There was something he was missing in all of this. His gut repeatedly insisted, yet his mind continually resisted.

Chapter Fourteen

The manor house changed considerably within six months of Ms. Müller's death. The part-time psychiatric nurse who had filled in for Ms. Müller had returned to her former position at Dr. Fitzgerald's larger facility, her services no longer required as no 'guests' remained on the premises. Dr. Fitzgerald, as intended, had ensured the placement and transfer of the three other patients to equally suitable facilities.

Mrs. Powers retained her position as housekeeper, continuing to run the house as she had. She showed her appreciation to her employer, who generously offered to pay her the same salary despite the fact that there was a lot less work because the house now had a lot less people in it, by turning a blind eye to the comings and goings of the house. Specifically, Dr. Fitzgerald's comings and goings.

It seemed that the only person who had changed along the way was Detective Lubovik. Sure, he was just as obstinate. He was just as determined. But he was not just as composed as he had been.

The investigation into Ms. Müller's death had stalled. As a result, the Detective's trips to a local bar or two had taken off. He had become a frequent flyer. Some days were higher than others.

As for Jessica, she was no longer considered a guest. She had passed her final exams with honors and received a Master's Degree in Social Work.

The occasion should have been cause for celebration. Instead, it was the cause of the return of her extreme behaviors. But it wasn't her fault.

It was Declan's. His actions had forced her to accelerate her ideas, to expedite her plan. He was the one responsible, not her.

That day, Declan had called her second-floor apartment from his main floor office phone. He had asked her to please come down. He had something for her, something special.

Jessica remembers being so thrilled, so energized, so certain that Declan was going to propose to her, because she was no longer his patient. So convinced that he was going to tell her that he was finally divorcing his wife, Lara, and making her, Jessica, his new wife.

Everything she had done over these past six years had led her to this moment, had brought her to this moment. *This* was to be her moment.

She ran out her apartment door, along the second-floor hallway to the landing and the top of the stairs. She hesitated for just a split second, before an innocent smile crossed her lips as she began to descend slowly, gracefully, confidently.

Declan stepped out of his office and crossed to the bottom of the staircase, where he stopped to look up at her. *She was radiant, positively glowing,* he thought to himself.

'Come,' he offered her a hand as she reached the bottom step, 'I have something special for you in my office.' He gently took her now-outstretched hand in his and led her to his office, not bothering to close the door behind them. Other than Mrs. Powers, who rarely left the kitchen, there was now no one in the house who would interrupt them. No one who would question their relationship. And no one who would prevent this moment from happening.

Declan led Jessica over to one of the big chairs that stood in front of his desk and gently lowered her into it. 'Don't move,' he instructed her playfully, 'and close your eyes,' he insisted.

Jessica was absorbing every second. Memorizing every detail. This moment would define the remainder of her life. Give her what she deserved for the remainder of her life: money, status, and power. *Look at me, Mama,* Jessica thought to herself, *what do you think of your baby doll now?*

She heard Declan open a drawer in the credenza that took up a large portion of the wall behind his desk. She heard him take something out of the drawer, its noise the sound of paper reacting to a light touch. In Jessica's mind, she heard the sound of gift-wrapping.

She recognized the soft pad of Declan's footsteps as he retraced his path back across the carpeted office, where he sat down in the other big chair in front of her. In Jessica's mind, she heard the sound of Declan getting down on one knee in front of her.

'Go ahead,' Declan said, 'open your eyes, Jessica.'

She took a deep breath and slowly opened her eyes. But there was no little velvet box, no one knee, no 'will you marry me,' no ring. No. *Fuck!*

Instead, Declan sat forward in the chair and held out a beautiful gift bag, its handles tied together with a big lavender-colored satin ribbon. 'Open it,' he encouraged her.

This wasn't what she had expected. The gift bag was too big for a ring. It wasn't what she deserved. Jessica felt her face flush pink from the rush of blood as it began to angrily pulse throughout her body, recognized the irritated spasm that pulled at her left eyelid. *Tic.*

Jessica forced a smile to define her expression, before reaching out and taking the gift bag from Declan. She placed it gently on her lap, untied the satin ribbon, removed several delicately crumpled sheets of white tissue paper from the top of the bag, and reached inside. Her skin instantly experienced the richest, softest material it had ever known. It belonged to a gorgeous, floor-length aqua-blue silk dress exquisitely accented with hand-sewn floral embroidery, a high Mandarin collar with a heart-shaped opening below it that would showcase her ample cleavage, a very low-cut back and a sensual floor to thigh slit up the front of it.

'The color reminded me of your eyes,' Declan whispered. 'I just couldn't resist. Do you like it?'

'It's so beautiful, Declan,' Jessica answered sincerely, for it truly was the most beautiful thing she had ever seen, let alone owned. 'Thank you.'

Declan leaned over and kissed her softly on the lips. 'You're so welcome, darling,' he smiled at her. 'But, there's more. Look in the bottom of the bag,' he guided her.

'I had it specially made for you, and it also matches your eyes,' Declan beamed at her with pride. 'There won't be another woman on this planet as beautiful as you after tonight, darling.'

Jessica looked into the bottom of the bag and saw an oval-shaped, black velvet-covered box lying there. This was it. Declan had just been teasing her with the first gift. *This* was going to be her moment.

Jessica reached in and lifted the box from the bottom of the bag, lowered the bag to the floor in front of her and laid the box gently in her lap. She was savoring this moment. She was treasuring this time.

She closed her eyes, took a deep breath, and opened the gift box. While it would certainly have been a moment any woman would have loved to experience even once in her lifetime, it was not the moment Jessica had spent six years of her life working so hard for.

Inside the box lay a stunning diamond and turquoise necklace that encircled a matching and equally stunning pair of earrings.

Jessica could immediately see that the necklace was made up of mostly diamonds, with a perfectly placed turquoise set every sixth stone apart. Declan explained that it represented the six years they worked so hard, together, to get to where they were today, to be where they are today. It would be something that was just between the two of them. Something no one else would understand the significance of.

The showpiece of the necklace itself was a large diamond pendant suspended in the middle. Jessica thought it resembled a beautiful teardrop, but a teardrop nonetheless. How apropos.

Each earring boasted an identical diamond teardrop floating inside a gold ring that was adorned with slightly smaller diamonds and turquoise, its six-stone design perfectly replicating that of the necklace.

'They're beautiful,' Jessica couldn't help herself. The set was truly magnificent.

But the fact remained that it still wasn't what she wanted, what she had been after all along, what she had earned, what she felt she deserved. *Tic.*

'Why don't you go upstairs and put the dress on,' Declan encouraged her. 'I can't wait to see you in it, darling.'

Jessica thought about it for a moment before replying. 'Declan,' she began, 'thank you for the gifts. It was very sweet of you.'

Jessica decided it was once again time to test Declan, to find out just what he thought this relationship was about. Did it have a future? Or was it headed for a dead end. *Literally.*

'I'll make you a deal, Declan,' she pretended to tease him, 'if I put the dress on and the necklace and earrings, will you take me out for dinner tonight to celebrate?' It's what she wanted. It's what she would now demand.

Declan's head fell forward in frustration. 'Jessica,' he started to explain, 'we can't go out in public. We just can't risk being seen together. We've been over this already. I'm not going to change my mind, Jessica. You have to accept that.'

Jessica took her time before responding, her voice as flat as her demeanor. 'Fine,' she offered. But she wasn't fine. The situation wasn't fine. But it would be. She just needed to make a few adjustments. The first one being Declan's attitude.

'What if I put the dress on and the jewelry, and we enjoy a nice dinner here tonight, together. Our own private celebration,' she proposed. 'I'm sure Mrs. Powers would be thrilled to show off the French culinary skills we've all heard so much about but have never had the pleasure of sampling,' she was playful. She was disarming. She was defusing.

'And then later, you can come up to my apartment and help me take the dress off. The zipper looks a little complicated, so I think I'm going to need some help,' she nearly purred.

'I'm sorry, Jessica,' Declan unwisely began, 'and believe me when I say that nothing would give me greater pleasure, but I'm afraid I have a previous commitment this evening that I can't get out of. It's an annual charity gala that we…that I attend every year, and my presence is expected.'

Jessica knew there was more to Declan's claim than he was letting on, because he had not been able to look her in the eyes as he said it.

Instead, he had busied himself by pretending to brush imaginary lint from the front of his suit jacket as he spoke. 'You know I don't particularly enjoy going to these things,' he unwisely continued, 'but I must. I'm on the Board of Directors for the organization that is hosting this event.'

'Take me with you, then,' Jessica pushed him further. 'There's still plenty of time for me to get ready. We'll pretend we don't know each other, but at least we'll still be there together,' she pleaded.

'I'm sorry, Jessica,' Declan repeated, this time with a little more force behind his words, 'it's just not possible. You see, my wife…Lara…we're going together.

It's one of the few events we agreed to attend as a couple, for the sake of appearances. I told you about the arrangement Lara and I have.'

Jessica simply sat there, staring blankly at Declan. She knew it was unnerving to those who had to sit across from her, but that was the point of the exercise; to make the other person fidget, to make the other person uncomfortable, to make the other person anxious, and Declan appeared to be experiencing all of those at the moment.

'Jessica,' Declan attempted to soothe the uneasiness between them, 'I promise I'll make it up to you, but just not tonight. You understand, right?'

Jessica leaned over, picked up the gift bag that contained Declan's gifts and walked calmly to the doorway of his office. She stopped and slowly turned back to Declan. 'Oh yes, Declan, I understand,' was all she said, before she smiled sweetly, turned her back on him, and with all the sophistication she could summon, ascended the staircase to her apartment.

* * * * *

But Jessica had been furious, beyond enraged. How dare he? How dare Declan not give her what she wanted? How dare he think he could simply pacify her with a few shiny objects? *Tic.*

If Declan wasn't going to give her what she wanted, she would have to take what she deserved. And so it was at that very moment that Jessica shed her role as 'guest' once and for all and began to create a new identity for herself.

She would transform herself into mistress of the manor. She would see to it that only she reigned over this beautiful house and all within it, its people and its possessions, especially Declan.

His actions left her with no choice. She was going to take him firmly by his balls. How hard she squeezed would ultimately be up to him.

Jessica waited for Declan to leave the house before intentionally descending the stairs. She then deliberately headed to the kitchen in search of Mrs. Powers. She purposefully went through the ritual of making herself a mug of tea.

'Dr. Fitzgerald seemed pretty excited about tonight,' Jessica casually said to Mrs. Powers. 'I guess he was really looking forward to this event.'

'I know,' Mrs. Powers, who was her usual busy self, didn't look up from folding a mountain of tea towels that lay on top of the kitchen table. 'It's something he and Mrs. Fitzgerald look forward to every year,' Mrs. Powers stated innocently enough. *Tic.*

'I can't wait for tomorrow's newspaper, because there are always pictures on the front page showing a few important guests at the event and what they were wearing,' she smiled. 'Dr. and Mrs. Fitzgerald are usually one of the couples featured, and they make such an attractive couple, if I do say so myself,' Mrs. Powers smiled as though she had something to do with it. *Tic.*

Jessica continued to play with the tea bag in her mug, swirling it around and around and round in an effort to calm the tempo of her mind. 'So, it's a pretty fancy affair, then?' she wanted to know.

'Oh, yes,' Mrs. Powers answered as she carried on folding. 'The men all wear tuxedos and most of the women wear formal gowns with all the accessories. You know, like expensive jewelry and shoes. Not to mention those silly little designer evening bags,' she let out a snort of judgment.

'You know the ones I'm talking about. They're so small they look like they'd barely hold a tube of lipstick and, if you ask me, I think it would take a lot more than just lipstick to touch up some of those faces.'

Jessica was no longer listening. Her efforts were temporarily focused on pulling the tea bag out of her mug using the string it was attached to. She began to methodically wind the string around, around her spoon, tight…tighter. Until not one more drop could possibly be strangled from the bag.

'I've heard there are a few large charity balls every year,' Jessica was choosing her words very carefully now. 'Which one is it tonight again? I know Dr. Fitzgerald told me, but I can't remember?'

'Well, now let me think,' Mrs. Powers put down a tea towel mid-fold while she thought about it. 'I believe it's the big cancer fundraiser,' she finally decided. 'Yes, that's right,' she awarded herself, 'Dr. Fitzgerald said they were going to the Ritz-Carlton this evening and how much he liked going there, because everything was impeccable.'

'Of course,' Jessica pretended to agree with her, 'now I remember.' She trashed the now deceased tea bag and went to stand by Mrs. Powers. 'Are you heading home soon, Mrs. Powers?'

Mrs. Powers stopped to look at a clock that hung over the kitchen sink. 'Yes, I see it's almost that time,' she answered. 'I'll just finish folding these towels then I'll be on my way.'

'Nonsense, Mrs. Powers,' Jessica insisted as she playfully tugged a tea towel right out of Mrs. Powers' hand. 'Why don't you leave a little early today and I'll take care of the rest of the folding. It'll be our little secret.'

Mrs. Powers face offered a sincere smile in response. 'That's very kind of you, Jessica,' she said as she reached over and placed a warm hand on Jessica's arm. 'If you're sure?'

'Not only I am sure, Mrs. Powers,' Jessica turned and hugged her, 'but I insist.'

'You're a dear, Jessica, thank you,' Mrs. Powers began to remove her apron. 'I made a casserole for you for tonight's dinner,' she mentioned as she retrieved a sweater from a hook by the back door. 'It's in the refrigerator, so you'll have to warm it up first,' she added as she retrieved her purse from the same hook. 'Would you like me to write the heating instructions down for you before I go?' she stopped and offered.

'Not necessary,' Jessica was struggling to control her tone of voice. Doing her best to restrain the growing sense of urgency for Mrs. Powers to leave, to get out. 'I think I can handle it.'

'Well, then,' Mrs. Powers decided, 'that's it for me for today. I shall see you bright and early in the morning, Jessica. Have you got any plans yourself?'

Jessica answered as she followed Mrs. Powers to the back door. 'Not really, Mrs. Powers,' Jessica assured her. 'I thought I might take care of something I've been putting off for a while.'

Jessica held the door open for Mrs. Powers. 'Well, good for you, dear,' Mrs. Powers answered as she exited the house.

Jessica watched Mrs. Powers walk along the backyard's flagstone path to a side gate, where she quietly let herself out.

'Yes, Mrs. Powers,' Jessica whispered, 'it will be good for me.'

Chapter Fifteen

She stood in front of the full-length mirror. The silk of the dress molding itself to her body like a second skin. Underneath, she wore absolutely nothing. Pure silk against pure skin. The feeling was sensual. The knowledge erotic.

She created plump, soft pink lips. She added rose blush to her sculpted cheeks. The color of her eyes was complimented by the deep aqua blue color of the dress, while a pair of delicate false eyelashes added an exotic touch.

She slipped the diamond and turquoise necklace around her slender neck, making sure the large teardrop diamond pendant hung perfectly within her ample breasts. It would solicit the attention she intended, the gazes she desired.

She slipped on one earring, then the other. Light from the gallery lamp atop the mirror brought them to life, irradiating the entire length of her neck.

Next, her hands, whose nails she had newly finished in her favorite French style, reached up and freed the mass of blonde curls that had been temporarily clipped at the top of her head.

She carefully divided the long curls into three sections. She draped one over one shoulder, then the other. The third she left to cascade freely down her back, tickling the little hollow at the top of her buttocks where the dress seductively plunged. But her costume wasn't yet complete.

She sat on the edge of her bed and slipped on a pair of silver stilettoes. She collected the matching evening bag and made one final check in the mirror. It was time to introduce this beautiful swan to the world.

She arranged a taxi, gave the driver instructions on where she wanted to go, which was exactly a block from the Ritz-Carlton. From there, she walked calmly toward the hotel's entrance but didn't immediately approach it. She waited.

Waited until she saw a tuxedo-clad gentleman walking toward the hotel from the opposite direction. He was alone. He was perfect.

She started walking again, toward him, pacing herself so they would come together at the foot of the stairs at the main entrance to the hotel at almost the same time.

She was one step ahead of him and intentionally stopped and bent down to attend to an imaginary problem with one of her high heels, exposing a very shapely leg that peeked out from the dress's seemingly endless slit. Its design suggested a better view might be possible, if one were so inclined. He was single. He was most assuredly inclined.

'May I be of any assistance?' the man graciously inquired.

She smiled at him. 'As a matter of fact, you can, if you would be so kind,' she began. 'I'm afraid I'm late and my husband texted me that he was already inside,' she continued. 'I'm worried about getting my dress caught in these heels. Would you be a gentleman and allow me to borrow your arm on the stairs?' she asked sweetly.

'It would be my pleasure,' he offered her an elbow, which she accepted, then lifted the hem of her dress with the other hand and together they went, up the stairs, through the ornate main entrance, across the chandeliered foyer, right to the ballroom's massive double mahogany doors. He had an invitation, she did not.

The star-struck young hostess at the door welcomed them as a couple. Neither one corrected her because he was flattered to be entering any room with such a gorgeous woman on his arm. She simply because…she didn't have to.

The ballroom was magnificent. She thought it must look exactly like what the inside of a palace would look like…regal. Everything on a grand scale. She didn't suit it, it suited her.

So taken with these first impressions that she forgot she was still holding onto the arm of the man who had so innocently escorted her in. He wasn't quite sure what to think, what to say, what to do now.

'Do you know which table you and your husband are seated at?' he finally inquired. 'I'd be happy to see you there.'

She squeezed his arm gently. 'No, thank you,' she caught herself, 'I'm sure I can find my way, but thank you again for your gallantry. I hope you enjoy a wonderful evening,' she added before turning and quickly heading into the crowd. He watched her walk away and told himself if he had a wife that looked like that, he'd never leave her on her own.

She wove her way around the room's periphery, hunting the entire time, seeking her prey.

Her journey did not go unnoticed. Her dress did not go unenvied. Her jewelry did not go uncommented upon. Eyes followed, heads turned.

'Excuse me,' a rather overstated woman in an equally overstated gown suddenly appeared in front of her, 'but I couldn't help noticing your stunning necklace and earrings. Where did you find such treasures?' she wanted to know. 'And they match perfectly with your gorgeous dress.'

'They were a gift from my husband,' Jessica lied politely. 'And before you say anything, yes I realize I'm a very lucky woman,' she added.

'Is your husband here this evening?' the woman inquired.

She pretended not to have heard the woman's question. Instead, she posed one of her own. 'Have you seen Dr. Declan Fitzgerald and his wife, Lara, this evening?'

'You know the Fitzgeralds?' the woman asked, her curiosity getting the better of her. She was familiar with most people in society's best circles these days, but the aqua marine goddess who now stood in front of her was not among them. She would have remembered her. Anyone who had seen her would have remembered her.

'Yes,' Jessica answered easily, 'we're very close.'

The woman had always promoted herself as being a real lady, despite the fact that she sometimes had to work hard at maintaining that pretense. No matter how much she wanted to, she would never stoop to blatant curiosity, especially while in the presence of so many of society's most distinguished. She decided it was best to follow protocol in this situation. 'I saw Dr. and Mrs. Fitzgerald just a few moments ago,' the woman provided. 'I believe they are seated at table number one.'

Jessica smiled. 'Thank you. If you'll excuse me, I shall make my way there now. I promised to stop by and say hello.' With that, she turned and disappeared once again into the crowd.

She didn't rush. She couldn't rush. Her next move had to be deliberate. It must be precise. She would only get one shot at this.

She stood still and began to scan over the heads of the guests. There, in the distance, she found what she had been looking for. What she had been hunting.

Declan was standing behind a chair, a drink in one hand. His other hand resting on the bare shoulder of a woman seated in the chair, his wife…Lara.

Declan looked so handsome, so very virile. It was all she could do to keep herself from walking right up to him. But she couldn't, she wouldn't, at least not yet.

She watched him. She watched her. She watched them together. Smiling not just for others, but for themselves as well. Occasionally touching each other on an arm or a hand. *Tic.*

A few minutes later, she saw Declan help his wife up from the chair and they began to move among the other guests, stopping occasionally to chat briefly with one then another.

She waited, some distance away, hiding in plain sight among the forest of people, their arms animated like branches answering the call of the wind.

She was struggling through the overwhelming noise of the room, the bodies who pushed in upon her, and the smells that surrounded her.

Her mind wanted to obey the demands of her internal voices, yet the temptation to shadow the many external voices was proving difficult.

She froze, unable now to form a complete thought of her own. Without a clear internal voice, her body didn't know what to do with itself, what its next move should be.

Intuitively, she looked down, seeking out the safety and emptiness of the floor beneath her...her childhood place. Floors have no eyes. Floors never pass judgment.

She inhaled, exhaled, then again. She needed to refuel her soul.

She slowly raised her eyes. Her body followed, her stance once again tall and controlled. Her internal voices once again strong and clear.

Her eyes sought out Declan and his wife. She locked eyes on them and slowly moved toward them, but not so close that she might risk being seen by Declan. Not yet.

She saw Declan lean into his wife's ear and say something. His wife nodded politely in response. Declan then took the empty wineglass his wife held out to him, turned and began a seemingly impassable route to the bar. She estimated that it would take him at least ten minutes to get there and back. It was enough time.

It was Declan's choice to leave his wife alone at that very moment. Had he not done so, even if it was just for those few minutes, his life would not have changed so drastically nor abruptly as it was about to.

She moved toward Declan's wife, her chin high, her body poised, her attitude determined, a disarming smile on her face.

She was now a second or two away from her prey. Just a few more steps from her final destination.

'I'm so sorry,' she offered politely as she intentionally bumped into Declan's wife, who immediately turned around.

'Please, no need to apologize,' Lara assured the woman, 'it would be almost impossible not to bump into someone in this crowd.' She extended a jeweled hand to the woman. 'I don't believe we've had the pleasure of meeting,' she began, an accomplished society smile on her face, 'I'm Lara Fitzgerald.'

Jessica graciously accepted the woman's hand. 'Megan Foster,' Jessica easily lied, although the name did hold a certain amount of significance for her from much earlier days. It was strangely comforting. 'A pleasure to meet you as well.'

Jessica gave no indication she was prepared to move along. 'Are you enjoying the evening so far?' Lara felt compelled to continue the polite dialogue. After all, it was expected of a lady in a social situation such as this.

'Yes, very much so,' Jessica answered, but didn't return the pleasantry. She didn't care.

Lara's eyes were suddenly drawn to the jeweled pieces Jessica was wearing. 'I can't help but admire your necklace and earrings,' she commented. 'They are exquisite.'

Jessica's hand reached up and played with the diamond teardrop in her necklace, now warm to the touch from having been nestled between her barely contained breasts.

'Thank you,' Jessica acknowledged the compliment, 'they were a gift from my husband.'

'You simply must introduce him to my husband,' Lara's society charm carried her. 'Perhaps your husband's impeccable taste will inspire mine,' the laughter that accompanied her words was society appropriate as well.

'Your husband is here, then, tonight?' Jessica asked innocently.

'Oh yes,' Lara responded. 'We both so look forward to this event every year,' she explained. 'It's one of the highlights of the season for us. We wouldn't miss it for anything.'

At that moment, Jessica realized Lara's eyes had traveled from her face to somewhere over her shoulder. 'Speaking of husbands,' Lara said, 'here comes mine now.'

Declan appeared with a glass of wine in each hand, the crowd having parted to let him through to stand less than a foot away from his wife and the woman she was speaking with who stood with her back to him.

'Darling,' Lara said as she reached out to accept her glass, 'I'd like you to meet Mrs. Megan Foster. Mrs. Foster, this is my husband, Dr. Declan Fitzgerald.'

Jessica turned and extended a steady hand to Declan, 'It's my pleasure, Dr. Fitzgerald,' she smiled sweetly at him. 'I've heard so many wonderful things about you from others this evening. It's finally nice to meet you.'

The hand Declan offered was not so steady. 'Mrs. Foster,' the words almost stuck in his throat.

'I was just telling Mrs. Foster that she simply must introduce you to her husband,' Lara jumped in, politely covering for Declan who seemed to have forgotten even the most basic social grace of polite, but idle, conversation, 'because you might learn a thing or two from him about buying your wife the perfect gift,' she teased him. 'It seems that he is responsible for not only Mrs. Foster's gorgeous gown this evening, but her stunning necklace and earrings as well.'

Declan struggled to gain some sense of composure. 'Your husband is with you?' his voice nearly cracked under the pressure.

Jessica casually pretended to look out over the sea of heads that bobbed around them before turning back. 'Yes, he is,' she answered, looking directly into Declan's eyes as the words left her mouth.

'Well, if you find him in this maze of people, please bring him over. We'd love to meet him,' Lara insisted before Declan could plausibly object as he so wanted to in an effort to extricate himself from the terrible situation he now found himself in. 'Isn't that right, Declan?' she looked at him.

Fuck. Why wouldn't she just stop talking? Why couldn't she just shut her fucking mouth? 'Of course,' Declan replied through a forced smile.

Jessica stood perfectly still, the only movement coming from her eyes as they looked from Lara to Declan, stayed on Declan, stared at Declan. He flinched, she didn't.

'In case we don't find each other again this evening, it has been a pleasure meeting you, Mrs. Fitzgerald,' Jessica reached out and offered a hand to the woman. 'I'm sure our paths will cross again, soon,' Jessica said, then turned and made her way back through the crowd, but not before one final look over her shoulder.

She saw Declan's eyes following her, but Lara's eyes had already moved on to a potential social advancement opportunity nearby, so unfortunately, she didn't see Jessica trace her lips with the tip of her tongue nor did she notice the kiss Jessica blew in Declan's direction. And she certainly missed her husband's reaction, which was probably a blessing, because there was no mistaking the look in his eyes.

Suffice it to say, it was not one of love, as it might have been at one time for Jessica. Nor was it one of lust, as it had been numerous times for Jessica. It was one he had never used at any time toward Jessica. It was one of pure rage.

Chapter Sixteen

Jessica confidently made her way across the ballroom floor, past the double mahogany doors, through the foyer and out the main entrance of the hotel. She then made her way home, alone as she intended, to the big manor house and all its splendor.

Still in her gown and jewels, she sat in Declan's office, in his big chair behind his big desk, and re-evaluated her position within the household. Re-appraised her status within the household.

There was no question in her mind that the balance of power had shifted tonight. All in her favor. All to her favor. She would soon be in complete control.

She didn't know if Declan had figured that out yet or not. Based on the expression on his face when they parted tonight, she didn't think so.

But she was more than happy to sit down with him when he arrived in the morning and explain it all to him. She was confident she could make him understand and accept that any other option would prove far too messy, for all parties concerned.

The next morning, she awoke early, eager to begin the day. It was going be a good day for her, a prosperous day for her, she would make sure of it.

She left the warmth of her bed, wrapped her white terry cloth robe around her, and exited her apartment. She knew it was far too early for Mrs. Powers to have arrived, but she needed a little time to take care of some housekeeping chores she hadn't gotten to last night.

She made her way to the kitchen, opened the refrigerator, and took out the casserole Mrs. Powers had prepared and left for her. She removed the foil that covered the casserole, retrieved a spoon from the cutlery drawer beside the sink, then turned the tap and garburator on before sacrificing half of the casserole to the churning god. The remainder she recovered with the foil and placed the dish back in the refrigerator.

Next, she turned her attention to the tea towels she had not folded last night, as she had promised Mrs. Powers she would do. She put the kettle on to boil while she folded the remaining tea towels and put them away in a pantry cupboard.

By the time Mrs. Powers arrived, Jessica was sitting quietly at the kitchen table, a steaming mug of tea in front of her and not a tea towel in sight.

'Good morning, Mrs. Powers,' Jessica looked up and smiled, 'did you have a good night last night?'

'Yes, thank you, it was delightfully quiet,' Mrs. Powers answered as she hung her purse and coat up on the hook near the kitchen's back door. 'And how about you?' she asked in kind. 'Did you get done what you said you wanted to do?'

'Almost, Mrs. Powers,' Jessica continued to smile. 'I just have a few loose ends to tie up this morning.' Jessica rose from the kitchen chair and walked to the refrigerator with her mug, to which she added a little more milk. 'I also wanted to thank you for the casserole,' Jessica added, 'it was delicious. I'm sorry I couldn't finish all of it, but I covered the rest up and put it back in the refrigerator.'

'Well,' Mrs. Powers said as she tied on an apron she had retrieved from another hook, 'you're welcome, Jessica, I'm glad you enjoyed it. And don't worry about leftovers,' she assured Jessica. 'I suspected I may have made too much.'

Jessica took her mug and went to stand by Mrs. Powers. 'Busy day today, Mrs. Powers?' she asked innocently enough.

'I should say so,' she answered. 'I've got baking to do, but will have to go to the grocery store first to get a few things I need before I even get to the baking. But, before I do that, I'll go and put a load of laundry in,' she continued. 'My dear, once you leave this kitchen, I doubt you'll see me again until well into this afternoon,' Mrs. Powers stated matter-of-factly.

'Funny you should say that, Mrs. Powers,' Jessica said as she headed toward the kitchen door that led to the hallway beyond, 'because you won't be seeing me...or Dr. Fitzgerald, for that matter...until well into this afternoon either.'

'Is that so?' Mrs. Powers asked as she began to prepare a list for that trip to the grocery store. 'And why is that?'

Jessica, who by now had reached the doorway, turned and leaned up against the doorframe. 'Dr. Fitzgerald and I have a meeting this morning, as soon as he gets here,' Jessica calmly lied.

'A meeting now is it?' Mrs. Powers teased. 'And what's all that about?'

Jessica smiled at her as she left the kitchen, calling over her shoulder as she went. 'It's all about my future, Mrs. Powers.'

'Well,' Mrs. Powers called after her, 'I'm sure Dr. Fitzgerald will do whatever he can to help you.'

'Yes,' Jessica's voice could be heard coming from down the hallway, 'I'm sure he will too, Mrs. Powers.'

Jessica carried her mug up to her apartment and went straight to her large walk-in closet. There, she sat down on a padded stool and began to look around her. She had to be sure of her choice. What she wore today would be important. How did she want to feel? How did she want to look? How did she want to be perceived?

In the end, she decided to put the beautiful aqua blue gown back on, the one she had worn the night before, and all the jewelry that went with it.

She remembered how incredibly empowered the silky sheath dress had made her feel. How very cool the jewels felt against her skin, soothing her.

She stood in front of the full-length mirror and looked at herself. The reflected image was beautiful, confident, and serious. She wanted Declan to know just by looking at her that she didn't, for one second, regret her actions last night. He was the one responsible for what happened, not her. And now he was going to pay for it.

She exited her apartment, walked the long second-floor landing to the top of the stairs. She picked the hem of her dress up in one hand while the other hand took hold of the bannister. She began a slow descent delighting in every step she took, in command of every step she took, owning every step she took. Just as she would soon own Declan.

When she reached the foot of the stairs, she dropped the hem of her dress and walked to Declan's office. She entered and silently slid the pocket doors closed behind her. When Declan arrived, which she knew he would, she didn't want him to see her right away. She wanted him to find her. She wanted him to seek her out.

She crossed Declan's office to his desk and intentionally sat in his chair. There, she automatically arranged herself; an elbow perched like so, here; a hand draped delicately just there; one shapely exposed leg crossed over the other, the long slit in the front of her dress suggesting a better view might be possible, if one were so inclined.

To pass the time while she waited for Declan, she decided to look through his credenza. He usually kept it locked, but apparently in his haste to get home and change for the charity event last night, he had forgotten to lock it. The key, however, was still in the lock.

She opened a few drawers, but found nothing of interest. Mostly medical journals. Next, she opened the two large center doors and discovered an ornate wooden humidor. She pulled the humidor out and placed it on top of the desk, where she lifted the lid. Inside were a number of cigars, each in its own fancy wrapper.

'*Eenie meenie miney mo*,' Jessica began to chant the classic nursery rhyme as she ran a fingertip back and forth across the cigars. She finally chose one and removed the wrapper. '*This is what happens when you tell me no*,' she laughed as she took the cigar cutter she also found in the humidor and symbolically and brutally snipped the end off, before putting the cigar up to her mouth and slowly wetting its entire surface gently, suggestively, into her mouth, out of her mouth.

She then lit the cigar with the lighter she also found in the humidor and leaned back in Declan's chair. She began to blow smoke rings, trying her best to get each inside the one before it, like links in a chain.

By the time she heard Declan slam the front door of the house, she had tired of both the smoke rings and the cigar and had snubbed the cigar out in a plant pot on top of the credenza, but a blue, smoky haze still hung in the air. It added a slightly ominous presence to the room. She liked it.

She heard Declan cross the foyer and stop at the bottom of the staircase, calling her name out loud. 'Jessica!' he shouted up the stairs, 'Jessica!' No response.

She knew he'd head to his office next. She sat quietly, prepared, poised.

She heard Declan close the remainder of the distance between the stairs and his office with just a few foot-pounding strides.

He slid one of the pocket doors back with such force that it slammed against the frame, the resulting noise echoing loudly out through the foyer and beyond. He blinked in reaction, she did not.

'How could you?' was all Declan managed to ask. Was all he wanted to know.

Jessica was not the least bit intimidated by Declan's physical nor verbal presence. She knew she was now in control of the situation. Unfortunately, Declan had not yet reached that same conclusion. But he would.

'How could I what, Declan?' she began. 'If you mean how could I go out and enjoy myself for an evening, I don't see how that is any of your business.'

'You made it my business when you decided to introduce yourself to my wife!' Declan screamed at her.

Jessica smiled at him. 'Ah, yes,' she nodded, 'Lara. I have to be honest, Declan, she's not at all what I expected. Don't get me wrong, darling,' Jessica began, 'I'm sure she's a fabulous hostess and knows all the right things to say at the right times, but honestly Declan, she is rather a plain Jane, wouldn't you agree? And I don't imagine she's any more exciting in bed.'

Declan was not at all amused. 'That's enough, Jessica,' Declan demanded angrily.

Jessica calmly sat up in the chair, rested her elbows on top of Declan's desk, and folded her hands under her chin, never once taking her eyes off of his. 'No, Declan,' she began, her voice deliberate and controlled, 'that's not enough. I suggest you take a seat. There are a few things you and I need to discuss. Well,' she decided to correct herself, 'if I'm being completely honest darling, which I assure you I am, you only need to listen. I'll be the one doing all the talking.'

Declan unconsciously flexed his fists in an attempt to control any sense of civility he had left. 'I'm warning you, Jessica,' he said through a clenched jaw, 'I'm not in the mood for any of this.'

Declan's bravado only served to amuse Jessica. 'Don't be so dramatic, Declan,' she suggested to him. 'Now, be a good boy,' she half-heartedly chastised him as a mother might, 'and sit down.'

Declan simply stood there for several seconds, his face red with anger, his body taut with indignation, until he reminded himself that he was the professional here. He was the one who was supposed to maintain his composure. To make sure cooler heads prevailed. He was the one who was meant to be rational.

With this rejuvenated sense of professionalism, Declan forced himself to relax. He audibly exhaled, then sat down in a chair on the opposite side of the desk, and looked directly at Jessica.

'What is this all about, Jessica?' he wanted to know. He needed to know. Jessica's behavior was just as confusing to him now as it had been last night.

Jessica smiled across the desk at Declan. 'What this is about, Declan, is my future,' she began. 'I decided it was about time I took a more active approach with respect to what is and what is not in my best interests.'

Declan remained quiet, still at a complete loss as to where this conversation was headed, never mind where it would end.

'It's important for you to understand that what I'm proposing really is a compromise on my part,' she continued, 'and it would be very wise on your part to keep that in mind as you listen to and think about what I'm saying. Do we understand each other?' she rhetorically asked and Declan chose not to respond to.

Jessica inhaled slowly, exhaled just as slowly, then rose from the chair. She leisurely walked around the desk until she stood directly in front of Declan. She lifted herself and sat down on the desk's edge, crossed one leg over the other and leaned back, placing the palms of her hands slightly behind and to the sides of her. She was well aware that where the slit at the front of her dress ended was the exact same place where Declan's most sought-after desires began. What he most wanted…wanted even now. She could see it in his eyes, right next to the anger. She considered taking advantage of that lustful anger, right here, on the edge of the desk, but it just wasn't the right time, not yet.

'I have come to realize and accept that you will never leave your wife, Declan,' she began, 'not even for me.'

Declan couldn't help being caught off guard by this sudden assurance. He breathed a sigh of relief, 'I am pleased to hear you say that, Jessica,' Declan sincerely offered. 'As you can imagine, after last night I wasn't sure what you were going to do.'

'Well, after last night, I now know exactly what I'm going to do,' she smiled at Declan as she slowly slid off the desk, her feet coming to rest again on the plush carpet beneath them. She circled back around the desk and sat down in the big chair. 'I'm going to give you what you want most, darling,' she assured him. 'Me.'

She waited for Declan to fully absorb that one single word, before she continued. 'As well as my promise that I'll never go near your wife again. In exchange, you're going to give me what I want most.'

It was several hours later when Declan finally left the house, much less well-off than he had been when he entered the house that very morning.

As for Jessica, it did, indeed, turn out to be a good day for her, a very good day. While it was still not the outcome she ultimately had her sights set on and had put her mind to, she was so close now.

There was but one final matter left for Jessica to take care of. She knew it was going to be her biggest challenge, if done right. She also understood it would have the biggest consequences, if done wrong. But all in good time. For the moment, she was going to savor her most recent rewards.

Declan was on his way to his attorney's office to take care of a few legal documents. The first was the transfer of title for the entire manor house and its contents from Dr. Declan Fitzgerald to Ms. Jessica McCallum. This document also detailed the monthly operating expenses for the house, including Mrs. Powers' wages, the sum of which would also be taken care of by Dr. Declan Fitzgerald, until his death.

The second document guaranteed Ms. Jessica McCallum a monthly allowance of $10,000, compliments of Dr. Declan Fitzgerald. He also agreed to a $3M life insurance policy, the beneficiary being one Ms. Jessica McCallum. She wasn't about to risk losing anything, should the dear doctor meet his demise, especially before she was ready.

The third, and final document was the one Jessica had been the most excited about. While the first two documents certainly gave her what she needed, it was the third document that gave her what she wanted. At least for now.

It stipulated that Dr. Declan Fitzgerald would not only cover the costs associated with redecorating his office in the manor house into an office for Ms. Jessica McCallum, but that Ms. Jessica McCallum was to become a full partner in a new business venture Dr. Declan Fitzgerald would set up. As part of this agreement, Dr. Declan Fitzgerald would refer clients to Ms. Jessica McCallum for counselling. And, yes, the cost of creating a beautiful, brass plaque to hang on the outside of the manor house, right beside the front door, would also be covered by Dr. Declan Fitzgerald. It was to read:

MS. JESSICA MCCALLUM, MSW THERAPIST/COUNSELLOR

She had no intentions of working, but she did have every intention of seeing a few clients, or more if necessary. She knew she couldn't publicly discriminate against female clients without drawing attention to herself, but privately she was only seeking male clients. More specifically, one male client.

She would give herself a year to find the one. That one whose psyche was so fragile and so susceptible. That one who would worship her. That one who would obey her. That one who would ultimately *kill* for her.

Declan had been adamant that he would never leave his wife. But what if his wife left him? For good. *Forever.*

Jessica had gone to her apartment after Declan left, eager to finally take off the silk dress and all that went with it. She put on her white terry cloth robe, tied it around her waist, and went to her kitchen where she poured herself a celebratory glass of wine.

She took her wineglass and went to the living room, where she placed the wineglass on the coffee table, before sitting on the couch. She gently opened the drawer in the coffee table, reached into the back left hand corner, lifted the shawl, and removed the black gift box that was still lying beneath it. She placed the box in her lap, took the lid off, and smiled down at the red teddy bear candles, the first-used candle still part of the original set.

She reached in and removed one of the two still-new candles, which she lovingly cupped in the palm of her hand. 'Hello, my friend,' she smiled at the candle, 'there's someone I'd like you to meet,' she whispered, 'her name is Lara.'

The Final Years

Teddy bear, teddy bear, touch the ground.
Teddy bear, teddy bear, turn around.
Teddy bear, teddy bear, run upstairs.
Teddy bear, teddy bear, say your prayers.
Teddy bear, teddy bear, blow out the light.
Teddy bear, teddy bear, say good night.
Author Unknown

Chapter One

'How's that look, Ma'am?' asked the installer, having just hung a new brass plaque to the stone façade outside the front door of the manor house.

'Let me just give it one final wipe down,' he said as he buffed vigorously. 'There you go,' he stood back to admire his work. 'It's ready for your very first client. Congratulations, by the way.'

She wouldn't stoop to acknowledge his compliment. She stood proud, arms folded across her chest and finally let it all sink it. She'd done it. She'd succeeded at everything she had put her mind to up to this point...to what her mind wanted...to what her mind had to have. Mrs. Jessica Fitzgerald, MSW (Master of Social Work). That's right, she's now that Mrs. Fitzgerald, as in Dr. and *Mrs.* Declan Fitzgerald.

But, what's next? Where would she go from here? Without another hunt on her horizon, her mind would soon get trapped in tedium. It would begin to hunger for more, because it hadn't been fed in some time.

She loved to relive that last hunt. It had been her most challenging to date, but it had also proven to be her most exhilarating. She loved every minute of it. Thrived on every successful second of it.

She remembers her passion for the pursuit. How she actively searched for an 'unknown.' Someone to play the lead while she took the lead. And she had found one...found him...Garrett Armstrong. But had she? Or had he found her?

He was her client, referred to her by Declan himself. The irony of that alone proved immensely rewarding to Jessica.

True to his commitments to Jessica, Declan had not only relinquished his office in the manor house for her to set up as her own office, but also began referring a few clients to her for basic counselling and therapy. As for Declan, he took on the more psychologically challenging clients. While their business partnership was acknowledged, their personal relationship was still not.

And true to her commitment to Declan, Jessica had not so much as verbally acknowledged the existence of his wife, Lara. Hadn't mentioned her name. Hadn't even objected to those occasions when she knew Declan and Lara were out at some event or another, together. *Tic.*

She had decided to leave the consequences of Lara's existence to the others, to the voices, the ones that lived inside her head. But they were no longer transient, no longer coming and going as uninvited guests might. Talking over each other, no longer.

They were constant, consistent. Each strong in its own right. Collectively loud, much louder, more persistent, much more demanding.

She remembers the first time she met Garrett, he was just 17. He had shown up at her office with a chip on his shoulder and defiance in his attitude. She understood where he was coming from. She could empathize, because he wasn't here by his own choice. The courts had mandated him to undergo counselling to get his anger under control following a particularly brutal street brawl.

It seems he took offense one night when someone passing him on the street may or may not have verbally insulted him. Garrett, convinced the man had done so, persuaded him to apologize after a relatively short period of fist-inflicted pain. The victim had been taken to the emergency room, while Garrett had been taken to juvenile detention.

Garrett came from not just a broke home, but a badly shattered home. A place where love didn't exist, let alone like. His mother did her best to absorb the abuse of his alcoholic father who, in turn, did his best to prove to Garrett and his younger sister that they were nothing more than an inconvenience to him and the rest of humanity.

When Garrett was just 12 years old, he and his sister replaced their mother in the boxing ring of this life. She had had enough and decided to end the relationship with Garrett's father, one way or another. She had tried so many times before. Each time, she would take the children and hide, but only as far as what little money she had stashed away could get her. It wasn't far. It was never far enough. Each time, he would find her. Each time, he would take her back home. Every time, he would beat her.

One day, after a particularly brutal beating the night before, she made a decision. She would give it one more try. Just once more to finally rid herself of this monster in her life.

It was this last time that ended successfully for her. It was this final try that proved permanent. She chose to take her own life. Her final thoughts were for her children. She hoped that God would show them some mercy. She would never know that her pleas would be answered, unfortunately only for one of them.

It wasn't long after his mother's death that Garrett's father started to teach him to fight. Not because he wanted him to know how to defend himself, but as a punching bag for his own drunken anger. An outlet for his father's personal frustrations over his own miserable existence.

At first, Garrett simply stood there, taking blow after blow from his father's closed fist, never uttering a sound, never allowing himself to shed one tear. He simply took it, for a few years, until finally one night at the age of 14, he decided he could no longer stand still, would no longer be still.

His father had come at him in an alcohol-fueled rage, both fists raised and intent on inflicting their usual damage. Garrett had been ready, was prepared. He picked up the baseball bat he had hidden behind the door near where he stood and started swinging, continued swinging, didn't stop swinging until his father collapsed on the floor at his feet, blood seeping from his mouth, his ears, his head.

It was this final, though surprisingly not fatal, incident that resulted in Garrett and his sister being justly removed from the home by Child Protective Services and unjustly placed in separate homes within the foster care system.

Over the next two years, Garrett bounced from one foster home to another due to his unwillingness to 'follow the rules' or his inability to 'control his anger.'

Jessica knew that Garrett had already undergone many months of serious counselling under Declan's direct supervision before he came to see her. Declan and she had discussed the case over the phone several weeks ago. Declan felt Garrett was progressing well and might now benefit from Jessica's unique perspectives on life. Declan felt that because Garrett and Jessica were closer in age, perhaps he might relate better to her. Declan also felt that Jessica was the perfect therapist for Garrett, because she could identify with his appalling past. The irony of it all amused her.

Despite Declan's still simmering anger toward Jessica for having nearly exposed their relationship to his wife, and thereby ruining everything for everyone, he was impressed by her understanding of the human psyche. Her grasp of how and why the mind works as it does. If nothing else, at the moment Declan believed they had professional respect for each other.

Declan knew better than anyone how hard Jessica had worked to earn her degree and was immensely proud of her. Which is why he never hesitated, not for one second, to recommend that Garrett continue his treatment under Jessica's care. Declan was confident that he was putting him in good hands. Most people don't stop to consider the possibility that even good hands are capable of doing bad things.

Garrett spent his first session with Jessica sitting in the chair across the desk from her, his head hanging down the entire time. He didn't bother to look up. He wouldn't bother to look up. It was the same old bullshit. 'Let's talk about how you're feeling' is how these sessions usually started. 'Can you share your thoughts' is how they typically progressed. A silent 'fuck you' is how they definitely ended, for him, anyway.

But not this time. Jessica simply sat in her chair, looking at him, a barely noticeable smile on her face. For nearly 15 minutes, neither of them said a word.

For Jessica, this stalemate was not uncomfortable in the least. It was something she'd being doing for most of her life. Something she'd perfected over most of her life.

'I'm going to fucking walk out in a minute, if you don't say something,' Garrett finally threatened. He wasn't used to silence. There had never been any room for silence in his life. It had always been loud...loud words, loud punches, loud living.

Jessica smiled at him. Good. He had reacted first. He had taken the first bite.

Is this bitch serious? Garrett wondered to himself. *What the fuck? Was she just going to sit there?* This whole thing was going to be a waste of time. She was going to waste his time. 'Fuck off,' he spit out.

'Sorry, not going to happen,' Jessica finally spoke, calmly. She could almost physically see the anger that lived inside of this young man. It was palpable and blatant. It was also one of the must-have attributes she was searching for: serious anger issues. Box number one ticked.

'Listen, Garrett,' Jessica finally said as she rose from her chair and came around the desk to sit in the chair opposite him. 'I'm not your enemy,' she assured him. 'In fact, I think if you just gave it a chance, you and I could become friends. Good friends.'

'I don't need any friends,' he threw back at her.

Jessica remained seated, stayed in control. 'Well,' she chuckled quietly, 'you may not, but I sure as hell could use a friend or two.'

Garrett wasn't buying it. 'You're just like all the others,' he accused her. 'You just want to make yourself feel better. You don't give a fuck about me.'

Smart kid. He's right. She didn't give a fuck about him. Which is why he was so perfect. He was expendable to her, completely disposable to her. And the rest of the world too, she suspected. There was no one left to care. No one left to notice.

'What if you're wrong, Garrett?' Jessica asked him. 'What if I am that one person who finally takes the time to really get to know you? To understand what it is you're dealing with? What if I am that one person who can actually make a difference in your life?'

She could see that he was thinking about her words. Was perhaps even a little confused by her words. No one had ever spoken to him like that before. They were always too busy telling him what they think he should do with his life. What they think he needs in his life.

'Are you willing to take that chance? Are you willing to risk going back to juvenile detention all because you don't think you want to be my friend?' she continued.

Still he chose not to respond, so she pushed a little harder. 'Well,' she got up from the chair and walked back to the other side of the desk, sat down in her chair and rested her hands on top of the desk, 'that's pretty juvenile, don't you think? So maybe juvenile detention is where you really do belong.'

She could see him tense up, but only slightly. She had hit a nerve. A tiny one, but a nerve nonetheless. That told her she was on the right track.

'I took you for more of a man, really,' she goaded him. 'Guess I was wrong,' she shrugged indifferently, before she picked up a pen that lay on top of her desk and pretended to write in the file folder in front of her. 'Doesn't play nice in the sandbox with others,' she said aloud. 'Doesn't like to share his toys with others,' she continued.

She looked up at Garrett, quickly examined his facial expression, then looked back down and continued the writing pretense. 'Keeps his head down most of the time, which is a shame because he has the nicest eyes.'

Again, she quickly looked up at him. Was that a hint of a smile on his face or was it simply a face that now appeared a little less angry? Either way suggested progress.

'As for his smile, no one has ever seen it, so we don't know if the patient is even capable of smiling,' she continued the ruse, 'which is a shame, because he has such a beautiful mouth.'

She was slowly baiting him. Carefully luring him into something his young age could not resist. Something his inexperience would want to run toward as opposed to run away from.

There it was. The flicker of his eyes, up, then down just as quickly. He had looked at her, even if it was for a fraction of a second. That fraction of a second was all it took for her to identify his sexual vulnerability. Box number two ticked. Just one more and it would be a perfect score. He'd be the perfect score. He would be that one she had been hunting for.

But, ticking off the third box was going to require a little more time, if it could even be done. Could he do it? Would Garrett do what she wanted him to do? And would he do it without asking why?

She dropped the pen and closed the file folder. 'That's enough for today,' she suddenly told him. 'See you next week,' she intentionally dismissed him. She wanted their first meeting to end in uncertainty for Garrett, and for the most part, it did.

He left the manor house uncertain as to what had just happened. Uncertain just what it was he was feeling. But absolutely certain he would return. Jessica was just as certain, too.

Chapter Two

Declan hadn't been back to the manor house since the day of that last awful argument with Jessica, nearly nine months ago now. Yes, he had been angry with her. But he had also been just as angry with himself. Had he expected too much of her? What exactly had he expected of their relationship? Maybe he was to blame for how awkward things were between them at the moment?

During this time, the only contact they had with each other was over the phone and only then on a professional basis. Admittedly, most of those calls were initiated by Jessica, as she intended.

In the first call, she had a question about a patient's medication and would Dr. Fitzgerald please confirm what the patient had been prescribed and the dose. She wanted to ensure that the information was noted accurately in the file.

In her fifteenth call, she accidently on purpose called him by his first name. 'Declan,' she had started the conversation, 'I'm sorry, I meant to say Dr. Fitzgerald of course.' Her tone of voice certainly came across as sincere.

In her thirty-ninth call, she asked if he would kindly recommend a reference journal for specific case studies she wished to review. Not one of those calls was anything other than a pretext.

With each call, Declan found himself thinking more and more about the manor house, missing the manor house. And with each call, Declan also found himself thinking more and more about Jessica. He missed her more.

For Jessica's part, she made sure her voice became softer with each call, smoother with each call, slower with each call. Who knew the subject of psychology could be made to sound so sensual?

In her fifty-first call, she decided it was time to test Declan's resolve. Just a little. 'Dr. Fitzgerald, I wonder if you could find time over the next day or two to go over Garrett Armstrong's file with me?'

'Well, certainly,' Declan responded without hesitation, his first thoughts turning to the troubled young man who had been sent to him by the court system for treatment. 'Is there something wrong?' he asked with concern, fearing Garrett had gotten himself into trouble. Again.

'No, no,' Jessica easily assured him, 'he's fine. It's just that we seem to have reached a bit of an impasse in his treatment,' she lied.

'What do you mean by impasse?' Declan asked.

'Well, I was hoping we could speak about this in person,' she said. 'You see, I've put together a report that outlines a long-term treatment program for Mr. Armstrong. I would like you to review it and provide feedback.'

Declan thought about Jessica's request. 'Can you send me an electronic copy and I'll have a look at it in the next day or so?' he asked, unsure whether or not he was yet prepared to see her in person.

'I could, yes,' she answered with a rehearsed response. 'However, I based my findings on several theoretical examples I found, but I didn't include those in my original notes. I simply put sticky notes on the pages where the case studies appeared in the reference materials I used,' she lied. 'Without those, I'm afraid that my recommendations may lack credibility. Honestly, I feel my proposal would be incomplete without them,' she added, then waited. Waited for Declan to consider her words, to believe her words.

'I see,' Declan finally relented. 'Yes, well, do you want to meet at my office? I'm available on Wednesday afternoon if that works with your schedule,' he suggested.

Tic. He had to come to her. She had to make him come to her. 'Would you mind coming to the house?' she asked innocently. 'Only there are a number of books I would have to bring along with me and I'm not sure I can carry them all.' She threw in a soft laugh.

Then waited, again. 'Unless you're afraid to see me,' she provoked him.

She heard Declan's audible sigh. It was enough to put a smirk on Jessica's face. Her words had pushed his thoughts off the path they had been taking. He was briefly disoriented.

She knew then that she had him. Right where she wanted him, for now.

'I'm kidding, of course,' she laughed quietly into the phone. 'But I was serious about all the material I've put together to support why I believe this new treatment plan for Mr. Armstrong would be beneficial to him,' she explained. 'I'd have to hire a moving company to help me box up all these books, take them to your office, and then lug them all the way back again.' A quiet laugh, again. It was effective.

'You're right,' Declan finally conceded, his voice gentler. 'When you put it like that, it doesn't make sense to meet at my office. Very well, I'll come to the house. Is Wednesday afternoon still a good time for you?'

'Yes, that would be perfect. And Declan,' she added softly, but quickly, 'thank you. I look forward to seeing you.' She didn't wait for a response. She didn't care if he had a response. In the overall scheme of things, it didn't matter. The only thing that mattered was that he was coming to her. In two days. She had two days to prepare.

She looked at her watch, 4:15. Garrett should arrive any minute for his bi-weekly appointment. So far, he had never been late and he had never missed an appointment. She was sure he never would either. Not because of the threat of being returned to juvenile detention if he did not, but because his hormones were now in charge of his decisions. There was only one head making most of the decisions, and it wasn't the one on his shoulders. Jessica had made sure of that.

Following their first session, the one in which Jessica had planted that original seed of sinful possibilities in Garrett's psyche, she began the deliberate and methodical nurturing of his soul. His entire being. He would soon belong to her.

She started with the odd light touch from her hand to his shoulder. One arm, his hand. Eventually a knee, then slightly higher. Moving closer and closer to the one thing that would seal the deal and ultimately seal his fate.

Four weeks ago, Jessica stepped up her physical contact with Garrett. She made a point of hugging him at the end of each session. At first, their bodies came together for a few brief seconds, not unlike a sister and brother might hug each other.

Three weeks ago, Jessica began to hold the hug just a little longer. Started to press herself into him a little harder. Allowed one hand to slide gently down the length of his back, coming to rest at his waist, not unlike a girlfriend and boyfriend might touch each other.

Two weeks ago, her hug came with lips that ever so lightly brushed up against his neck and a hand that ever so slowly slid down, coming to rest on the genital-generated warmth of denim that covered his crotch, not unlike a couple of horny teenagers might grope each other.

A few nights later, Jessica suggested they go out to dinner together, not unlike a couple might do. A week after that, they went to a movie together. Another afternoon, they went shopping together.

All along, she encouraged him to open doors for her, to slide chairs out for her, to help her on with her coat.

And so it was, over a relatively short period of time, Garrett came to believe that he and Jessica really were a couple. Just as she had intended.

She had brought him to the point where he wouldn't do anything without first discussing it with her. He couldn't go anywhere without first checking in with her. But would he obey her? Would he do what she asked of him? It was time to find out. She had to know for sure before her meeting with Declan in just two days.

She had intentionally given Mrs. Powers that afternoon off so when Garrett arrived for his session, rather than close themselves off in her office, she led him to the big kitchen at the back of the manor house.

There, she selected a bottle of red wine and asked Garrett to open it. She knew he was only 17, but she knew she didn't care. She didn't have to care because there was no one around to make her care. This was her house. This was her wine. This was her show.

Garrett poured them each a glass of wine, then held his up to Jessica. 'To us,' he toasted their togetherness. 'You have no idea how much you mean to me, Jessica,' he said as he looked her in the eyes.

Fuck. Whatever. 'Me, too, Garrett,' she sweetly patronized him, then leaned in and kissed him lightly on the lips. 'Listen, there's something I really need you to do for me,' she said as she slipped an arm around his waist.

'Sure,' he responded eagerly. Wholeheartedly. 'What is it?'

'Well,' Jessica began, 'I bought a Budgie this morning, as a gift for Mrs. Powers because I know how much she loves them. I thought it would be nice for her to keep it here, since she spends so much time here,' her voice now suggested sadness. 'I thought it would be good company for her.'

Her head now hung in sadness. Her eyes were down in sadness.

'What's wrong, Jessica?' Garrett reached a hand out to her. 'What is it?'

A single teardrop left a wet, sad trail down one of Jessica's cheeks. 'I don't know how it happened, but by the time I got the Budgie home in the box the pet store had put him in, one of its legs was broken,' she explained. 'I feel awful. What if it was something I did that caused the leg to break?' she looked at Garrett. She knew he would reject her confession, poor boy. He never considered, not even for a second, that she might be telling the truth. She was.

She had gone out the evening before, after Mrs. Powers had left for the day, and bought the beautiful teal-colored Budgie at a local pet shop. It was perfect when it left the store.

It was wonderful on the ride home. It was happily chirping for the first few minutes it was in the house.

By the time of Mrs. Powers' arrival the next morning, all it could do was flounder in the bottom of the box, one leg horribly twisted beneath it.

'Of course you didn't do anything,' he hugged her to him and stroked the long curls that hung down her back. 'I'm sure it was just an accident. Maybe he was already like that when you got him? Why don't I take you back to where you bought it and you can get another one for Mrs. Powers?' he gently suggested.

Jessica reached out and pulled a tissue from a box that lay next to her on the countertop. She dabbed at her teary eyes. 'I don't want another one,' she began. 'It hurts too much. Garrett, I think the bird is suffering,' she said. 'I left it in the box and hid the box outside. I didn't want Mrs. Powers to see it. You need to put the bird out of its misery,' she pleaded with him. 'It's the only humane thing to do, please, Garrett. I tried to do it myself, but I just couldn't,' she was now pretend-sobbing.

Garrett hesitated, unsure exactly what Jessica was suggesting. 'You mean, you want me to kill it?' he finally asked.

'Well, yes, you have to, Garrett,' she insisted. 'Please, for me?' she persisted.

Shortly after Garrett left that evening, Jessica locked all the doors and slowly ascended the stairs to her apartment. There, she poured herself another glass of wine and settled into the couch. She leaned over and pulled the coffee table drawer open, reached into the back left corner, lifted the shawl and retrieved the black gift box beneath it.

She placed the box in her lap, gently removed the lid, and looked inside. 'I have some exciting news, baby dolls,' she whispered to the three red teddy bear candles that lay neatly in a row at the bottom of the black silk-lined gift box. 'I think I've found him,' she smiled. 'I think I've found the one.'

Mrs. Powers never did receive a Budgie. She was never meant to.

* * * * *

Declan arrived at the manor house two days later, as he and Jessica had arranged. Even though he still had a key to the front door, he rang the doorbell. It wasn't his home any longer. He could no longer just walk in any time he wanted. It was a strange feeling. It was also a sad feeling.

Mrs. Powers answered the door, still in a clean white apron, but no longer pale and anxious. Whatever had happened in the house lately was none of her business. She just knew the house ran smoother, was now quieter, calmer.

'Dr. Fitzgerald,' she greeted him, 'how nice to see you. It has been some time.'

Declan stepped into the foyer as he spoke. 'Yes, it has been a while,' he agreed. 'We've all been so busy lately,' he said to disguise the truth, 'I just haven't found the time.'

'Between you and Jessica,' Mrs. Powers continued, 'it's a wonder you two aren't constantly sick. You know the old saying? All work and no play makes Dr. Fitzgerald a dull boy,' she smiled at him, almost maternally.

Declan decided it was time to move the conversation along. He didn't know if he could stay in the house any longer than was absolutely necessary. 'Speaking of Jessica,' he began, 'is she in her office? We have a meeting arranged for this afternoon.'

'Yes,' Mrs. Powers answered. 'But she's not in her office. She's in the dining room. She asked that you join her there please, Dr. Fitzgerald,' Mrs. Powers instructed and began to lead the way, taking his overcoat in the process.

Mrs. Powers hung Dr. Fitzgerald's coat on the hall tree they passed on their way to the pocket doors to the left that, when pulled back, revealed a beautifully set dining table, complete with a vase of fresh cut flowers in the center. On the side table lay a feast of fresh-steamed asparagus, a Caesar salad with grilled and sliced chicken breasts on top, a selection of fruit, croissants with churned butter, homemade lemonade, and coffee.

Jessica was seated at the far end of the table. At the head of the table. A position that suggested authority. A posture that implied power. The place she specifically chose.

'Dr. Fitzgerald,' Jessica welcomed him, 'Mrs. Powers prepared an early but light supper for us and you're just in time. Please, won't you join me?'

Declan wasn't sure what to do. If he said no, he ran the risk of insulting Mrs. Powers. On the other hand, if he said yes, he ran the risk of forgiving Jessica. The first he certainly didn't want to do. The second he wasn't sure he was ready to do.

Jessica had turned not only his life upside down, but his world as well, and he didn't know if he was ready to move past it all. Just being around her was difficult. Chitchatting over a casual meal might prove more so.

Jessica could sense his reluctance. 'We can discuss Mr. Armstrong's case while we enjoy this beautiful food Mrs. Powers made,' Jessica offered. 'Kill two birds with one stone, so to speak.' Well, one bird at least. She recalled the Budgie and smiled for herself. Declan believed the smile was meant for him.

'Well,' Declan finally relented, 'if you're sure you don't mind making this a working meal, then I'm happy to join you.'

Mrs. Powers had already set a place for him just to Jessica's left, as she had been instructed. 'Take a seat, Dr. Fitzgerald,' Mrs. Powers said. 'Would you like to start with a cold lemonade or would you prefer some coffee straight away?'

'We're fine, Mrs. Powers,' Jessica callously interrupted her. 'I know you have things to do, so please don't worry about us. I'm sure we can manage for ourselves.'

Mrs. Powers, feeling dismissed, as she was meant to, smiled awkwardly. 'Right then,' she responded, 'I'll just head back to the kitchen where I belong.' She quietly left the room, annoyed that Jessica hadn't given her the opportunity to visit a little longer with Dr. Fitzgerald. Jessica knew how fond she was of him. Surely a few more minutes wouldn't have made any difference? She'd have to have a word with that young lady after Dr. Fitzgerald left later, which turned out to be an inaccurate assumption on her part.

Declan poured himself a cup of steaming coffee from the silver urn on the sideboard and took his place at the table. 'Dr. Fitzgerald,' Jessica began. She needed to initiate the conversation itself. She wanted to control the direction of the conversation. 'I appreciate you taking the time to meet with me,' she continued. 'But, before we talk about Mr. Armstrong, there are a few things I would like to say. Things I need to get off my chest,' she admitted and hurried on. 'First, I want to apologize...sincerely apologize to you for my recent behavior. I know I was a complete bitch. The only explanation I have is that I couldn't help myself. I couldn't help myself because I realized that night how much I love you, Declan,' she looked him in the eyes.

'Jessica, I...' Declan tried to respond.

'Please, let me finish before I lose my nerve or, worse yet, cry like a girl,' she smiled sweetly at him. 'Then I promise we'll get right down to business.'

'Go on,' Declan softly relented.

'I know I love you, but I also know that I can't have you,' she explained. 'I have accepted that, truly I have. But there's no reason why I can't have at least a small piece of you. And, in return, you get a small piece of me,' she suggested, her eyes coy, her means cunning. 'I'd be happy with that,' she added. 'I'd be content with that.'

Declan was taken aback. This was not at all what he expected when he arrived today. Far from it. Very far from it. He had hoped that they would, at the very least, be civil and professional with each other. This was more than he was prepared for.

'I'm not asking you for an answer right now,' Jessica continued. 'I appreciate that it's a lot to process all at once. But what I am asking for, hoping for, is that you will at least consider what I've said,' she pleaded.

She pushed her chair back, came around the corner of the table to where Declan sat, placed one of her hands on either side of his face, then slowly leaned in and kissed him.

At first, she was tender. Her lips soft, her breath controlled, her actions measured. She was pleased that Declan didn't seem inclined to resist. He wasn't pushing her away nor was he turning his face away.

She took her tongue and used the moist tip of it to trace the outline of his lips. 'I've missed you,' she whispered as she continued to explore his mouth.

'Jessica,' Declan barely managed, 'Jessica, what is it that you want from me?' he asked. He had to know.

She stood back, took one of Declan's hands in hers, and pulled him out of his chair. 'Shhhhhhhhhhhhh,' she put an index finger up to his lips as she pulled on his hand to indicate he should follow her.

She gently led him out of the dining room, across the foyer, past the grand staircase to what was Declan's office. She was determined to mark what was now her territory. What better way.

She still held one of his hands in hers, but used her other to slide the pocket doors closed behind them. She guided Declan around the desk and pushed him down in the big, comfy chair that sat behind the desk.

'Jessica,' Declan said her name as she lifted the hem of her skirt and straddled him. He didn't know whether it was to object to her advances or whether it was to encourage them. His mind wanted the first, but his body chose the second.

It was the next morning, lying naked beside Jessica in her big four-poster bed, before Declan admitted to himself that his common sense had been superseded by his carnal sense.

He didn't care. He wanted her now more than ever.

Chapter Three

I think it's important that we agree on a treatment plan for Garrett going forward,' Jessica said to Declan as she buttered a piece of toast in the big kitchen at the manor house early the next morning. They sat across from each other at the large island that was the hub of the impressive room, both wrapped in white terrycloth robes.

Declan took a sip of his coffee before replying. 'Well, that would depend on what you feel is not working with his current treatment plan,' he stated.

Their conversation was easy this morning. It was comfortable. Whatever strains had been between them were now sexually exhausted. Left behind in the tangle of satin sheets that littered her bed upstairs.

'He's too angry these days,' Jessica explained. 'The least little thing seems to set him off and when I ask him what made him that angry, he can't answer me. He says he honestly doesn't know. It's just something inside of him, he says.'

'But, Jessica,' Declan countered, 'that's not new. That's how he's been since I started working with him, just varying degrees at varying times. I designed his current treatment plan specifically to address his anger, so why would you want to change it?' he questioned.

Jessica was following a script that only she had read. That only she had memorized. 'Because it's not working as well as I think it could,' she offered.

'And why is that?' Declan asked, interested to hear her thoughts.

Jessica took a bite of her toast before she replied. 'Garrett will be 18 in a few months.'

'Yes, so?' Declan wasn't sure where this was going.

'So, that means he'll no longer qualify for the foster care system. He'll be kicked out and forced to fend for himself,' she explained. 'He's not ready for that, Declan. I think that's why his anger has reared its ugly head again. He's scared and doesn't know what to do. Where to go,' she continued. 'He has no one to help him. No one who cares enough to help him, really.'

'I take it you have something in mind?' Declan smiled at her. She was obviously leading up to something.

'As a matter of fact, I do,' she returned the smile. 'But you have to promise to hear me out before you say anything,' she insisted of him.

'Fine, I promise,' Declan appeased her.

'Well, I thought he could move in here,' she said.

'Jessica, I don't think…' Declan began.

'You promised, Declan,' Jessica interrupted him. 'You promised me you'd hear what I have to say.'

Declan put his two hands up in mock surrender. 'Sorry, sorry,' he offered. 'Please continue.'

'It's either move in here, and I have plenty of room as you know, or he'll end up in some halfway house or boarding house, both of which will cause his anger to escalate even further and neither of which will give him the stability he so desperately needs in his life,' she explained.

Declan continued to look at her, but didn't interrupt. Jessica could read the uncertainty on his face. She jumped down off the breakfast stool she had been sitting on, walked around the island to where Declan sat, spread his knees apart, undid the tie on her bathrobe, and pressed herself firmly up against the front of his robe, draping her arms around his neck.

'Look, I know it's not a conventional approach, but there are exceptions to everything in life and I think Garrett is one of those exceptions. He needs to know there's a consistent place for him in his life. A place where he can express himself without fear of punishment.' Jessica pushed on. 'If he were to find some type of employment and begin to assimilate himself into the norms of life, I think that would be a great starting point for him. And knowing that at the end of each day there's a stable environment for him to go to, to feel safe in, I think he would stand a much better chance.'

Jessica took a second to read Declan's facial expressions before she continued. So far, so good. She deliberately undid the tie on Declan's robe before she continued. 'I would also be available on a more consistent basis to help him walk through and talk through situations he may encounter on a daily basis, but at the time didn't quite know how to handle,' she argued.

'By no means am I suggesting this as a permanent solution, Declan,' Jessica assured him as she gently nibbled on one of his earlobes. 'Maybe six months,' she proposed. 'Nine at the most,' she added. After that, she didn't anticipate she'd have any further need for Garrett. He would serve no further purpose to her.

'May I speak now?' Declan teased her.

Jessica leaned in and kissed him again. 'Yes, but be nice,' she teased back.

'I understand what you're trying to do here, Jessica,' Declan said, 'but you can't get that involved in a patient's life. It's not healthy, for either one of you,' he insisted.

Tic. 'I know that, Declan,' she answered him, 'I've given a great deal of thought to this, but I keep coming to the same conclusion. If someone doesn't reach out to him now, I think he'll be lost forever and that would be a shame,' she said. 'He's a good kid who had a bad start in life, but I truly believe he can turn himself around if he's given the chance.'

Declan was thinking. 'And how exactly would this arrangement work, Jessica?' he asked. 'There would have to be some serious ground rules.'

'Of course,' Jessica immediately assured him. 'He could start out working here, for me. There's a lot more to do around here than I initially thought and it's quickly become apparent that what this place needs is a good handyman,' she continued. 'Admittedly, Garrett doesn't have a skill or a trade of any kind, but he is eager to learn and I think he'd prove to be a dependable worker, under the right circumstances.' She was counting on it, actually.

Declan still wasn't convinced, but he did appear to be softening, at least in his heart. It was the rest of his body that was becoming harder. The warmth of Jessica's nakedness against his was making it difficult to fully absorb every word she was saying. That was the point.

'Once he becomes comfortable with the normal structure of life we put in place for him here, he can then progress to outside social interactions, whether that's through employment or joining a gym, or just going out to a movie,' she continued.

'Besides, I could use the company,' she teased him. 'I have a feeling that I'm going to be lonely a lot of the time.' She knew she couldn't have Declan all to herself. At least not yet.

Declan smiled at her. 'Got a crush on the young Mr. Armstrong, have you?' he teased in return.

'Certainly not,' Jessica protested jokingly. 'There's only one man I have my sights set on, and I can assure you that it's not Mr. Armstrong.' She smiled at him before leaning in and kissing him softly.

Declan returned the kiss. 'And who might that be?' he asked playfully.

Jessica took one of Declan's hands and pulled him off his stool. 'Come on, I'll introduce you to him,' she smiled at him seductively as she pulled him through the kitchen, down the long hallway, across the foyer to the grand staircase and up to her apartment, their cast-off terrycloth robes left somewhere behind.

There was never any doubt in Jessica's mind that by this time tomorrow, Garrett would be living in the house. It would also be in this house where Garrett would become someone he never imaged he could.

* * * * *

'What do you mean there'll be someone else living in the house now?'

Mrs. Powers stopped her ironing and looked questioningly at Jessica.

'Well,' Jessica began to explain, 'you remember that meeting that Dr. Fitzgerald and I had yesterday? And by the way, the food you prepared was delicious, thank you,' Jessica smiled sweetly at her.

219

'You're welcome,' Mrs. Powers answered, although she was now more interested in Jessica's statement than she was in Jessica's compliment. 'You were saying about your meeting with Dr. Fitzgerald?'

'Yes, well, you know that young man I've been counselling, Garrett Armstrong? He was originally a patient of Dr. Fitzgerald's?' she began.

'Yes,' Mrs. Powers answered.

'Well, Dr. Fitzgerald felt that Mr. Armstrong would do much better if he were living in a consistent environment as opposed to the foster home where he currently resides, so he suggested that he move into one of the apartments upstairs where I can keep a closer eye on him,' she easily explained. 'Work more closely with him on a regular basis.'

It was immediately obvious that Mrs. Powers didn't think much of the idea. 'What is Dr. Fitzgerald thinking?' Mrs. Powers blurted out. 'For heaven's sake, inviting a man into the house that no one else seems to want anything to do with,' she ranted. 'That should tell him something, I should think,' she continued on.

'Oh, now, Mrs. Powers,' Jessica pacified her, 'he's a good kid, deep down. He just needs a little structure in his life. And it won't be for too long. I'm sure everything will be fine.'

'Well, you've got a lot more faith in him than I do at the moment,' Mrs. Powers put in her two cents worth.

'Yes, I do,' Jessica smiled at Mrs. Powers. 'I have every confidence that things will work out as they are meant to.' And she meant to get what she wanted.

'Don't expect me to cook his meals or do his laundry,' Mrs. Powers protested. 'I'm not his mother.'

'Of course not, Mrs. Powers,' Jessica reassured her. 'He's a big boy. He can make his own meals and do his own laundry. You'll hardly even know he's here,' she teased.

'Why, I have a good mind to call Dr. Fitzgerald and give him a piece of my mind,' Mrs. Powers stated. 'Letting a young man, an unpredictable young man at that, stay here, with you, alone. It's not right.'

Fuck. She couldn't let Mrs. Powers call Declan. She might find out that it hadn't been Declan's idea at all and everything she was working toward would be ruined. She couldn't start all over again. She wouldn't.

'Please, Mrs. Powers,' Jessica asked her, 'can't we just give it a try? For a little while, please? It would mean an awful lot to Dr. Fitzgerald, I know.' Jessica hugged her.

They were interrupted by a knock at the kitchen's back door. 'That's probably Garrett now,' she said as she went to answer the door. 'He's bringing his things over this morning. Please try your best to make him feel welcome, Mrs. Powers,' Jessica asked. 'He's quite a lost soul at the moment.'

Jessica opened the door and smiled at Garrett. 'Welcome to my humble home, Mr. Armstrong. Please come in,' she said as she stepped aside to allow him in.

Garrett became a little flustered when he spotted Mrs. Powers in the background, but managed to cross the door's threshold. 'Um, thanks,' he acknowledged. 'I just have the one bag,' he indicated the badly soiled duffle that was slung over one shoulder. 'Where should I put it?'

'You have your own apartment upstairs,' Jessica explained. 'Let's put your things away there first, then I'll show you the rest of the house.'

Jessica passed by Mrs. Powers and gave her a quick peck on one cheek. 'Thank you, Mrs. Powers,' she winked as she continued on her way out of the kitchen with Garrett following closely behind. 'This way,' she said to him.

Garrett had only been in certain parts of the house before. The kitchen, of course, the foyer and Jessica's office. He had never been up on the second floor. He had never been invited, until now.

'Your apartment is at the front of the house,' Jessica explained as they ascended the grand staircase. 'You have your own key for the apartment, as well as a key for the back door. The only time we use the front door is when I have a client or when we have company,' both of which she knew were rare. In fact, one of them was now non-existent. She no longer had any other clients.

She had asked Declan to seriously consider not referring any clients to her for a while. She felt that the intense level of counselling Garrett currently required could only be accomplished if she didn't have to divide her time between Garrett and other clients. Again, it would only be for a short period of time. Declan had reluctantly agreed.

By now, they had reached the door to the apartment at the front of the house. The one Jessica had chosen for Garrett. The one furthest away from her own apartment.

She inserted the key she had in her hand into the lock and opened the door. 'The kitchen is small, but it has a microwave oven, a toaster, and electric kettle. You also have a small fridge. In the house's former life, most of the meals were served in the dining room downstairs. The kitchens in the apartments up here were only ever meant to prepare the basics. We'll work something out,' she smiled at him and continued.

'And over here is your bedroom,' she said as she walked into the room. 'You have everything you need, including extra linen, blankets, and towels,' she explained. 'And right beside it is a full bathroom.'

Garrett was no longer paying attention to her words. Instead, he was paying attention to her body, her movements, her lips. 'Jessica.' He moved toward her, unable to resist touching her, finally.

'Garrett.' Jessica repelled his advance with a hand against his chest. 'Garrett,' she repeated his name tenderly, then led him to the edge of the bed where they both sat down. 'I need you to listen to me,' she instructed, 'very carefully, okay?'

'Okay,' he answered.

'You know there's nothing in this world I want more than to be with you,' she looked at him, her eyes big, 'don't you?'

'Yes,' he answered.

'But we have to be careful when there are other people in the house,' she explained. 'If Dr. Fitzgerald ever finds out that we're in love, he'll send you away from me. You wouldn't want that to happen, would you?'

'No,' he quickly responded. 'I won't let that happen.'

'Well, then it's important that you're careful, that we're careful, whenever there is anyone else in the house. No one can know how we feel about each other, do you understand?'

'Sure, I understand Jessica,' Garrett answered. 'But when there's no one else in the house, can we be together then?' he wanted to know. He needed to know.

'Of course, my love,' Jessica leaned over and kissed him tenderly, but quickly. 'Now, why don't you unpack your things and come down to my office,' she said as she rose from the edge of the bed and headed out the door. 'We have a lot of work ahead of us, so I'd like to get started.'

Soon it would be time to introduce Garrett to Lara. But first, he had to learn a few things about her, all of which were completely untrue of course, but necessary. As for Lara's part in all of this, Jessica didn't feel she needed to know anything about Garrett. In fact, it was probably best that she didn't.

Chapter Four

Detective Lubovik finished off a third breakfast burrito and tossed the wrapper into the trashcan next to his desk. He had gotten an early start this morning, determined to take a fresh look at everything that had been collected so far surrounding the still undetermined death of Ms. Hildreth Müller. He had even gone to bed sober the night before, hoping that maybe one night without alcohol might result in a somewhat clearer mind today. It was time to find out, to decide if he was working on an accident investigation or if he was working on a homicide investigation. Actually, a potential premediated murder in the eyes of the law when it came right down to it.

He rose from his desk and headed for a small conference room, stopping along the way to replenish his coffee. He opened the door to the room and turned on the overhead fluorescent lights. At the center of the room were two cheap metal desks, pushed together to make one larger working surface on which lay a few laptop computers, a myriad of colorful file folders, pens, pencils, empty Styrofoam coffee cups, some upright, some not.

One wall of the room was entirely devoted to graphic pictures of the crime scene itself and the area immediately surrounding the scene. Another wall was entirely devoted to a list of people who had contact with Ms. Müller, direct or not, beginning a month prior to her death. Alongside each name was noted the relationship between that person and the deceased.

Of those people, there were six he identified as having had contact with Ms. Müller both the day before and the day of her death. Lubovik had started there.

He taped pictures of these six to another wall, with the name of each noted underneath. There was Dr. Fitzgerald, of course; Mrs. Powers the housekeeper; and four patients or 'guests' as they were referred to by Dr. Fitzgerald.

Beside each picture, Lubovik had added basic background information. He was looking for a connection, a reason, a possible motive, as to why any of these six individuals might want to harm Ms. Müller.

He started with Dr. Fitzgerald. While there was certainly nothing 'typical' about the world-renowned Dr. Declan Fitzgerald, there was nothing outwardly suspicious about him either. He had a wife, a thriving practice, international recognition, bags of money. He was the owner of a large, private teaching clinic, as well as a private treatment residence, which was the location where Ms. Müller was found dead.

He knew that Dr. Fitzgerald had personally hired Ms. Müller, so if things weren't working out, Lubovik felt he probably would have just fired her. He wouldn't have had to kill her. Dr. Fitzgerald's name went to the bottom of his 'person of interest' list, for now.

As for Mrs. Powers, he had crossed her off the list almost right from the start. She wasn't even in the house the night Ms. Müller died. Sure, she was feisty, but he didn't think she was capable of murder.

He had next turned his attention to the four patients who were in the house at the time of Ms. Müller's death. He had already done background checks on three of them and turned up nothing of note. Nothing of interest. Nothing suspicious to suggest that he dig a little deeper into any one of them. They were simply three spoiled and entitled young women who had been sent there by their rich parents who didn't know how to handle them. Lubovik suspected it wasn't the daughters who were the problem.

The fourth patient, Jessica McCallum, was the only one he hadn't yet checked out. He had intentionally left her to last, because there was just something about her that didn't sit right with him. Hadn't from the very beginning. He couldn't put his finger on it yet, but his gut was still giving him grief. He'd learned to listen to his gut over the years.

Now that he had all but eliminated the first five, he could concentrate on Ms. McCallum. He sat down at one of the desks in the middle of the room, opened the nearest laptop, and typed in a few instructions. Within a minute, a printer in one corner of the room came alive, spitting out several sheets of paper. Lubovik retrieved the pages and returned to sit at the desk. He took a sip of coffee and began scanning the pages.

'Well, well,' he said about halfway through the pages, suddenly sitting upright. 'What do we have here?' he asked aloud of no one. Something in the fine print had caught his eye, enough to send him back to the first page. He started to read every word, as opposed to just skimming the pages as he had been.

That first report had led to several more. By lunchtime, he had a pretty good pile. By the end of the day, he had a pretty good headache.

At 11:00 that night, he decided to call it quits for the day and head home. He needed to get some sleep. There was something pulling at him from inside those reports, but his mind had finally surrendered to his fatigue. It had all but given up. He'd make another early start tomorrow.

It was going to be a busy day. He had a lot to get done. First, he wanted to revisit all the reports and see if he could find any similarities between them. Anything that would tie everything together. Or at least give him a piece of string to grab on to that might lead him to the other end.

The highlight of the day he suspected was going to be his unannounced visit to Hope's Home. It had been several months since he'd last been there. He hadn't felt the need to, until now.

* * * * *

Garrett and Jessica had settled into a safe routine within the manor house. They agreed on what essentially amounted to a daytime set of rules and a nighttime set of rules.

During the day, they were simply two people living separately but under the same roof, one a therapist and the other her patient. There was never anything on the daytime façade of their relationship to suggest otherwise.

If anyone were to ever question the arrangement, Jessica would simply refer them to Dr. Fitzgerald. As Garrett's psychologist, she had made sure he signed off on her new treatment plan. She had casually asked him to sign it a few seconds after she deliberately asked him if he wanted a blowjob. She believes he would have signed just about anything at that point.

But it was the nighttime façade that Garrett and Jessica both looked forward to the most, although for completely different reasons.

For Garrett, when the sun went down, when the shades were drawn, when there was no one left in the house to care, that was when Jessica came to him. When Jessica seduced him far beyond his wildest dreams.

For Jessica, it was those nights when she appeased his inexperienced lust for her. It was a means to an end. The perfect storm in which to reinforce her control over him. His growing dependency on her.

'You're all I want, Garrett,' she would whisper in his ear. 'I don't want anyone else in my life,' she would assure him. 'We don't need anyone else in our lives, as long as we have each other.' But she always saved the best words, the important words, for her last words. The last words Garrett heard each time he rode the surging wave of a climax. 'I would die for you.'

The one concern Jessica did have was with Garrett's growing jealousy over the nights Declan came to the house, which was now once a week. Garrett knew he was not to leave his apartment when Dr. Fitzgerald was around, unless of course Dr. Fitzgerald specifically asked to see him, which he had not since Garrett moved into the house.

Jessica had assured Declan that Garrett's treatment was going well and was right on track. She didn't see the need for Declan to meet with Garrett just yet. She still had some work to do with him, but hoped it would be just a matter of a month or two. Declan accepted her explanation. He put Garrett out of his mind. It wouldn't stay that way for much longer.

Jessica had equally assured Garrett that her relationship with Dr. Fitzgerald was strictly professional. They were partners. Dr. Fitzgerald came over once a week to discuss business matters and nothing more.

'Why do you meet in your apartment instead of your office?' Garrett had tentatively questioned her on a morning following one of Dr. Fitzgerald's evening visits to the house.

'You know why, darling,' Jessica carefully responded. 'Dr. Fitzgerald is an extremely busy man, so I try to accommodate his schedule. We have a lot to discuss, so we choose to use our time wisely by working over a light meal,' she explained. Which was true. They did discuss a lot, like how his hardened penis felt inside her. How her nipples reacted to the slow circles his wet tongue drew around them. How his hands made her body come alive as they explored every inch of her. How they enjoyed a glass of wine with crackers and cheese afterward, still lying naked amid dampened sheets.

Overall, Jessica was excited by Garrett's progress. He had proven himself to be a good student, an attentive student, and a student dangerously in love with his teacher. Perfect.

And so, after dinner the following evening when there was just the two of them left in the house, Jessica told Garrett to go to his apartment and she would join him there in a few minutes. There was something she needed to get from her place first. Something special she wanted to share with him. Something no one else knew about.

Five minutes later, she let herself into Garrett's apartment and found him sitting on his couch, two glasses of wine on the coffee table in front of him. Jessica sat down beside him and placed an object in her lap.

'What's that?' Garrett asked her.

Jessica smiled at him before lifting the lid off the black velvet box in her lap, revealing three red teddy bear candles lying side by side. 'These were given to me by my mother,' Jessica began to explain, 'a very long time ago. They're very special to me.'

Garrett reached over and pointed to one of the candles. 'You've only slightly used one of them.'

'I know,' Jessica replied. 'I had been saving them all these years for just the right moment. For the perfect occasion. And I finally had that first one.' She smiled.

'You did?' Garrett wanted to know. 'What was it?'

Jessica picked up the one candle Garrett had pointed to, its wick charred, its head slightly dented in the top where the wax had melted. 'It was after the first time we made love,' she lied to him. 'I wanted to do something special to mark the occasion, so I went back to my apartment and lit the first candle. It made me think of my mother. She would have adored you.' *How disturbingly true,* Jessica thought to herself.

'Would have?' Garrett asked. 'You mean she's dead?'

'Yes,' Jessica responded with just the right amount of sadness in her voice. 'She died in a terrible accident many years ago. But I think about her all the time. I often wonder what she'd think of me today, if she were alive.'

Garrett put an arm around Jessica as they sat side by side on the couch. 'I think she'd be very proud of you, Jess,' Garrett offered. 'I know I am.'

But it was what Garrett said later that night, after they had made love again in the soft amber glow of a red teddy bear candle, that told Jessica he was ready…ready to take that next step. He finally told her that he would die for her, too.

Chapter Five

It was about four o'clock in the afternoon when Detective Lubovik rang the doorbell at the front of the manor house. He decided to give Mrs. Powers a break and not push it more than once.

But it wasn't Mrs. Powers who answered the door. It was a young man, a familiar young man. Detective Lubovik was sure he'd seen him before at the police station as he was being escorted in by two officers, one on either side of him, and roughly placed inside a holding cell. He rarely forgot a face. What the fuck was he doing here?

'I'm Detective Lubovik. I'd like to speak to Dr. Fitzgerald, please,' the Detective said as held his badge out in front of him.

Garrett flinched when he saw the badge. 'Wait,' was all he could manage before quickly closing the door.

Detective Lubovik just stood there, taken aback by having a door slammed in his face. It didn't happen often, unless there was something to hide inside. Or someone to hide inside. He reached up and rang the doorbell again, this time not giving a shit about how many times he pushed the damned thing.

It was a few minutes before the door opened again. This time, he was greeted by Jessica McCallum. 'Detective Lubovik,' Jessica looked at him calmly, 'Dr. Fitzgerald isn't here at the moment.'

'Actually, it's you I came to see,' the detective explained. 'It'll just take a few minutes, can I come in?'

Jessica hesitated, but eventually swung the door open. 'Of course, please,' she offered. 'Why don't we go to my office where we can talk privately,' she suggested, then turned and walked across the foyer toward what used to be Declan's office. She slid a pocket door open and invited him in. 'Please, have a seat,' she gestured toward one of the chairs before sliding the pocket door closed behind her.

She made her way around the desk, sat down in the big chair, and turned to face the detective. 'What is it you wanted to see me about, Detective?' she carefully ventured.

'So, this is your office now?' he asked as he looked around. 'Yes,' Jessica answered succinctly.

Detective Lubovik stirred slightly in his chair. Apparently, Jessica wasn't going to make this easy for him. 'So, where's Dr. Fitzgerald's office now?' he was curious.

Jessica crossed her arms in front of her and leaned back in her chair. 'Detective, I'm very busy today, so if you would kindly get to the point,' she insisted. She wanted to play it her way.

Lubovik looked at her before reaching into the inside pocket of his coat and removing a small notepad. 'Sure,' he began. 'Why don't we start with who the guy was who answered the door just now,' he asked her.

'Not that it's any of your business, Detective,' Jessica smiled sweetly at him, 'but he's a client of Dr. Fitzgerald's. He's receiving specialized treatment, so the doctor felt it would be best if he resided here on a temporary basis. Why do you want to know?'

'Just curious,' the detective offered nonchalantly. 'What's his name?'

Jessica was beginning to tire of the cat and mouse game taking place between them. 'His name is Garrett Armstrong. Now, can you please tell me what it is you want? I have a meeting in half an hour,' she lied.

Detective made a note before he spoke. 'Right, do you still have that set of candles Dr. Fitzgerald gave you as a gift a while back?' he asked.

Tic. 'Yes,' Jessica fought to remain calm. 'May I ask why?'

'Well, I'd like to have a look at them, so if you wouldn't mind getting them, I'd appreciate it,' he requested.

Fuck. 'Certainly, give me a minute,' she said as she rose from her chair and left the office. She made her way up the stairs and to her apartment, anxious to close the door behind her and catch her breath. Slow her now racing heartbeat. She leaned up against the door, closed her eyes, and took a deep, cleansing breath. She can do this. She *had* to do this.

She retrieved the boxed set of candles from the coffee table, removed the lid, and looked down. 'It's okay, baby dolls, Mama's here,' she whispered before replacing the lid.

She returned to her office and placed the gift box on top of her desk before once again removing the lid. 'Is this what you're looking for?' Jessica asked him.

Detective Lubovik looked into the box and saw three red candles, each in the shape of a teddy bear. Two were unused. One was not. That one Dr. Fitzgerald had assured him had been used for the first time in front of him. Its head had melted to the point where it was now just a warped smile above a chin. It gave him the creeps.

The detective made another quick note before continuing. 'Why didn't you tell me your name used to be Megan McCallum?' he unexpectedly threw out to her.

Tic. 'It wasn't relevant then,' Jessica insisted, 'and it's not relevant now.' The smile had left her face. 'If you have done your homework, Detective,' she looked at him, 'as I suspect you have, then you already know the answer to that.' She wasn't going to give him anything.

'It would seem that tragedy follows you around, Ms. McCallum,' he noted quietly. 'Terrible, don't you think? What happened to Ms. Müller?'

Jessica wasn't going to take the bait. 'Listen, Detective,' she sat up and stared at him across the desk, 'what happened was a long time ago and I have more than paid my dues. Megan McCallum no longer exists, so there's no point in talking about her.'

Lubovik simply nodded his head up and down as though he were in agreement. He was not. 'It's just that I can't help but wonder about something,' Lubovik continued to look directly into Jessica's eyes.

'And what's that, Detective?' Jessica feigned interest.

Lubovik stood up from his chair, tucked his notepad back in an inside pocket of his coat, walked to the pocket doors and slid them open. He turned and began to slide the doors back to their closed position, but not before one final thought. 'There was red candle wax found at the scene of the fire you set that killed those two college kids,' he calmly delivered. 'Then there was a spot of red candle wax found near Ms. Müller's body on the night she died.'

Tic. Jessica remained calm on the outside, but inside she could feel her anxiety creating knots in her stomach, in her back, in her thoughts.

'You're the only one in the house who has a red candle,' Lubovik nodded toward the gift box of red teddy bear candles still lying on top of Jessica's desk. 'I don't believe in coincidences, Ms. McCallum. I have a feeling we'll be seeing each other again, soon.' He never took his eyes off of hers as he slowly, deliberately slid the pocket doors closed, leaving Jessica behind. Alone.

It wasn't until she heard the large front door close that she knew the detective had left the house. Only then did she trust herself to look down at the candles, to touch the candles, to caress the candles. 'I was hoping we'd have a little more time, baby dolls,' she said aloud, 'but, we have to get ready sooner than I expected.' She smiled at each of them, replaced the lid, and climbed the stairs to her apartment. She returned the gift box to its corner in the drawer in the coffee table.

She picked up a pad of paper and a pen and went to her bedroom. There, she backed herself into one corner and slid down the wall until she came to rest on the floor.

It was going to be a long night, but she didn't care. She needed a good plan more than she needed a good sleep.

* * * * *

One night, a few weeks later, Garrett was awakened by several loud bangs on his apartment door. He looked at the clock and saw that it was just after midnight.

He quickly got out of bed and went to the door as more knocks sounded. 'Garrett,' he heard Jessica frantically call out to him from the other side, 'Garrett, please open the door,' she pleaded.

Garrett unlocked the door and pulled it toward him, revealing an emotionally shaken Jessica staring back at him. 'What is it, Jess?' he asked. 'What's going on?'

She didn't wait for an invitation, but instead pushed her way past him and inside where she began to pace. 'Garrett, I don't know what to do. I'm so scared. I think I'm being stalked,' she finally managed to tell him.

'What? Who?' he wanted more details.

'A woman, but she's no longer just following me,' Jessica insisted. 'She's also sending me threatening letters and now she's calling me too.'

Garrett could see how distressed she appeared to be, so he went to her, tucked her head under his chin, and enfolded his burly arms around her like a cocoon. 'What do you mean by threatening letters, Jess?' he asked. 'Why didn't you tell me about this before?'

'I wanted to, Garrett,' she looked up at him with her big, round, innocent blue eyes, 'I promise you I did. But...'

'But, what?' he looked back at her. 'Jess, tell me.'

'But I knew you'd want to do something about it. I don't want you to get into any trouble because of me,' she explained. 'I was hoping to take care of this myself.'

'Tell me who she is, Jessica,' Garrett sudden demanded. 'I want to know her name.'

'That's the problem, Garrett,' Jessica worked her word spin magic, 'I don't know who she is.'

'So, what happened tonight that made you so scared?' he looked at her.

'She called me,' Jessica continued to unravel the lie. 'I don't know how she got my number, Garrett, but she called me.'

'What did she want?' Garrett asked her.

'She said she was a friend of Dr. Fitzgerald and she knows what's going on between you and me,' Jessica played on. 'She said she saw us together one night when we went out for dinner.' She took a dramatic breath before continuing. 'She's going to tell Dr. Fitzgerald and he'll have no choice but to send one of us away. She's going to ruin everything I've worked so hard for. Everything we've worked so hard for, Garrett.'

Jessica buried her face in Garrett's chest and quietly sobbed. 'Garrett, what are we going to do? I love you. I don't want to live without you. I can't live without you. Please, we need to do something.' She had no intention of 'we' doing anything. It would only be Garrett. Poor lad. What an unfortunate boy.

'First, we have to find out who this woman is,' Garrett decided. 'Do you have any idea at all who she might be?'

'No, I know where she lives, but I don't know her name,' Jessica offered.

'How did you find out where she lived?' Garrett asked.

'Well, I saw a woman from an upstairs window very early one morning walk up the driveway and drop a small envelope through the mail slot in the front door. She had a scarf and dark sunglasses on, so I didn't get a good look at her face,' Jessica said.

'What was in the envelope?' Garrett wanted to know.

'It was the very first note she ever left,' Jessica answered.

'That doesn't explain how you figured out where she lived,' Garrett countered.

'I think it was the third time I saw her drop an envelope in the mail slot, just a few weeks ago now,' Jessica continued. 'I decided to follow her when she left. And I did. She led me straight back to her house.'

'Tell me what to do, Jess,' Garrett pleaded. 'Tell me what to do and I'll do it.'

Jessica raised her head from Garrett's chest, wiped the fake tears from her face, and smiled at him. 'I know you will, my love,' she touched a hand to his cheek. 'You're the one person I can always count on, aren't you?'

Garrett picked her up in his arms, carried her to his bedroom, and laid her gently on his bed. 'It's okay, Jess,' he soothed her through tender kisses, 'I'm here. I won't let anything happen to you, to us. I promise.'

She was counting on that promise. There was just one more thing she needed him to do for her. But, would he? Could he?

Chapter Six

Of course, there was no one following her. There was no one leaving her threatening notes. No one calling her late at night. But Garrett believed it. She made him believe it.

A few nights following Jessica's tall tale of a stalker, she waited until the house was dark before venturing down the hallway to Garrett's apartment. She knocked gently on the door.

'Garrett,' she called out, 'open the door. I need to talk to you.'

It was less than a minute before a sleepy Garrett answered the door. 'Jess, is everything alright?'

Jessica let herself into the apartment and sat down on the couch. 'Yes, darling, everything is great, or it will be very soon,' she smiled wide, her voice full of excitement. 'Sorry it's so late, but I just couldn't wait to share my news with you.'

Garrett sat down beside her. 'What is it?' his voice took on her excitement. 'Come on,' he insisted.

Jessica turned toward him and took his hands in hers. 'I know how we can make that woman stop harassing us,' she whispered to him. 'Stop her for good.'

Garrett smiled back at her. 'How?' he asked. 'What do we have to do?'

'Well,' Jessica leaned in and kissed him softly on the mouth, 'I think it's a good plan, but I'm not convinced that you can handle your part.'

'I can, Jess,' he insisted. 'Honest, just tell me what you want me to do and I'll do it. You'll see. Please.'

Fucking puppy dog, honestly. It was almost too easy. 'Okay,' she relented, 'if you're sure. But it's going to take a real man to do this,' she looked at him. 'Are you a real man, Garrett? Are you *my* real man?' She slid one hand up his knee until she found what she was looking for: his hardness. The place where he was most vulnerable. 'Oh my,' she felt his erection, 'you are a real man, aren't you?'

Garrett audibly moaned. 'Yes,' he managed to respond, 'yes, I am.'

Jessica had him just where she wanted him now. It was time to lay out her plan. 'Tomorrow, you and I are going for a little drive,' she explained. 'I'm going to show you the way to that woman's house, because you'll have to find your own way there when the time comes.'

'Why do I have to go by myself?' he asked hesitantly. 'I thought we were going to do this together?'

'We are, my love,' Jessica assured him. 'Absolutely we are. We're going to do it together. We just won't be doing the same thing at the same time. You will have your part and I'll have mine. We'll be a real team.'

Jessica continued to gently knead his crotch. 'But your part is so much more important than mine,' she falsely assured him. 'I can't do what I need to do until you take care of what you need to do. I can count on you, Garrett, can't I?'

He was struggling to keep his breath steady under Jessica's touch.

'Yes, Jess,' Garrett managed to exhale. 'I'll do whatever it is you need me to do.'

Jessica smiled at him. 'I want to believe you, Garrett, really I do,' she said. 'I want to trust you to do what needs to be done.'

'God, yes, you can, Jess,' he eagerly assured her. He was quickly losing his will to speak, let alone think. Her touches were driving him crazy. They were taking him to a place where the word 'no' simply couldn't exist for him. A place where he had been taken so many times before that he now went without question.

'I called her and pretended to be a telemarketer and asked her if I could set up a pre-arranged call to complete a survey over the phone and she said she'd be home next Thursday night,' Jessica began to weave her distorted magic. 'That's the perfect time for you to pay her a little visit, Garrett. There won't be anyone else around.'

'What do you want me to say to her?' Garrett asked. He still wasn't sure what Jessica wanted him to do.

'That's what's so great about this plan, Garrett, you don't have to say anything to her,' Jessica assured him. 'You just need to show her something. It's that simple, really.'

Garrett would have agreed to anything at that particular moment. What he ultimately did agree to was something he'd never done before. Something he never thought he could do, let alone would do.

'There's only one way we'll know for sure that she'll never tell Dr. Fitzgerald about us,' Jessica said as she began to not just remove her clothes, but tear them from her body. 'If you can't do it for me, Garrett, then you have to know that this will be the last time we can be together. This is the last time we will ever make love to each other, because that woman is going to tell Dr. Fitzgerald everything.'

Jessica left Garrett's room an hour or so later and returned to her apartment. She went to a kitchen cupboard, took down a wineglass, and filled it from a bottle of red wine she had sitting on the countertop.

She took the wine into the living room, made herself comfortable on the floor at one end of the coffee table, slid the drawer open, and removed the black gift box from the back left corner. She laid the box beside her on the floor, before gently taking the lid off.

There they were. Her three little baby dolls. She reached for the one used candle and held it up in front of her. 'You know how proud I am of you, don't you?' she smiled at it. 'But it's time to give one of the others a chance,' Jessica spoke to it as she returned the used candle to the box then picked up the candle right next to it. It was unused. It was pure. It was untainted. 'I have a surprise for you,' she smiled at it. 'You're invited to a very special dinner next week. Next Thursday night, to be precise.'

The next morning, Jessica and Garrett took her car and went for that drive she promised him. An hour later, she pulled the car up to a curb, just down the street from a beautiful antebellum-style home with its pillared façade, immaculately landscaped grounds and gated entrance.

'That's the house,' Jessica pointed with a finger. 'That's the house where the lady lives.'

She didn't feel the need to tell Garrett the woman's name. He didn't need to know that it was Lara Fitzgerald, wife of the noted psychologist, Dr. Fitzgerald. And hopefully the soon to be widower Declan Fitzgerald.

* * * * *

A few days later, Jessica went to her office, slid the pocket doors open, sat down at her desk, picked up the phone, and called Declan at his office. 'Good morning, Dr. Fitzgerald,' she purred into the phone. She hadn't thought to close the pocket doors behind her.

'Good morning to you, Ms. McCallum,' Declan responded in kind. 'To what do I owe the pleasure?'

'Well,' Jessica began, 'I wanted to invite you for dinner next Thursday. I have something special planned,' she teased him. 'Something very special.'

'Is that so?' Declan was interested. 'And just what might that be?'

'Uh, uh,' she replied, 'You wouldn't want to spoil the surprise now, would you?'

'A surprise, is it?' he laughed quietly into the phone. 'Well, how can I resist such an invitation? I have my schedule right here. Let me see what I've got going on that night,' he said as he began to flip forward in his calendar. 'Although, to be honest with you, if I do have anything, I'm inclined to either cancel it or re-schedule it now in light of your intriguing offer,' Declan stated.

'You won't be disappointed,' Jessica assured him, 'I promise you.' Disappointment would be the furthest thing from Declan's mind come next Thursday night. He might be shocked, certainly. Possibly upset. Perhaps even bewildered, but not disappointed. Disappointment is not an emotion typically experienced when one's spouse is brutally bludgeoned to death.

'Ah, here it is,' Declan commented. 'Lucky me,' he laughed suggestively, 'I have nothing scheduled for next Thursday night. I'd love to join you for dinner, my love,' he spoke softly to her.

'That's wonderful, darling,' Jessica responded. 'Can you spend the night?' She didn't care one way or another. Her question wasn't so much about him as it was a means to another end. Where would his wife be and what would she be doing that night?

'Sorry, Jessica,' Declan softly spoke into the phone, 'I can't. My…Lara has a presentation to one of the many charity Boards that she sits on the next morning and I promised I'd review her speech the night before, which is why I didn't have anything on my calendar to begin with. But we can have dinner and spend some time together afterward. Not a late night, but certainly a rewarding night, wouldn't you agree?'

'I'm sure it will be, darling,' she responded. 'A very rewarding night.'

'I can't wait to see you, Declan,' Jessica added. 'Can you be here for six o'clock?'

'Wild horses couldn't keep me away,' was Declan's affirmation before he hung up the phone.

Jessica sat there for a few moments. She couldn't help but smile. Her plan was coming together quite nicely. Just a few more details to tend to and everything would be set.

She left her office and went in search of Mrs. Powers. As she was crossing the foyer, heading in the direction of the kitchen, she saw Garrett up on the second story landing at the top of the staircase. 'Garrett,' she seemed surprised. 'How long have you been standing there?' *Had he heard her one-sided telephone conversation with Declan?*

'Who were you talking to just now, Jess?' he asked down at her. She could see the beginning signs of anger on his face. She had to think fast. If she couldn't pacify him at this very moment, everything she was working toward was in serious jeopardy. 'It was a client,' she managed to casually answer.

'I thought you didn't have any other clients but me,' he commented.

Jessica put her hands on her hips and smiled up at him. 'That's sweet,' she said, 'you're jealous.'

'So, what if I am?' he threw back at her. 'I heard you use the word 'darling.' Why would you say that if it was just a client?'

Jessica had a plausible explanation. 'I didn't use the word 'darling.' I said 'Darwin.' That's the client's name, which I shouldn't even be telling you because of confidentiality standards. He had a situation and needed some advice. Since I used to counsel him, I felt obligated to help him,' she smiled easily up at him. 'You know I wouldn't lie to you, Garrett.'

She could see him start to relax. 'Now, why don't you come down and wait for me in my office. I have a life skills exercise I'd like you to try, but I need to speak with Mrs. Powers first.'

Garrett, appearing momentarily appeased, relented. 'I guess maybe I did hear you wrong,' he said as he began walking down the stairs. 'I'm sorry.'

'I know,' Jessica answered him. 'Don't worry about it. Just wait for me in my office, okay.' With that, she turned and headed to the kitchen.

'Hello, Mrs. Powers,' she cheerfully greeted the housekeeper as she entered the kitchen.

'Hello, Jessica,' Mrs. Powers said as she looked up from a recipe she was reviewing. 'Is there something I can help you with?'

'Well, yes,' Jessica went and stood beside her. 'I need to ask you a huge favor.'

'A favor, now,' Mrs. Powers responded. 'What kind of favor?'

'I was hoping you could prepare a special dinner for next Thursday evening,' Jessica said as she crossed her fingers on both hands and held them up in front of Mrs. Powers. 'Pretty please.'

'And who would this special dinner be for?' the housekeeper inquired.

'It would be for Dr. Fitzgerald and myself,' Jessica began to explain. 'It's coming up to our one-year anniversary as business partners and I wanted to surprise Dr. Fitzgerald with a nice dinner. I just wanted him to know how much I appreciate everything he has done for me,' she continued. 'Besides, if I cooked the meal myself, it would definitely be a surprise, but not a good surprise, I'm afraid. I'm hopeless in the kitchen, Mrs. Powers,' Jessica playfully admitted.

'In that case,' Mrs. Powers responded enthusiastically, 'I'd be honored to make you both a really nice meal. Did you need me to stay and serve too?'

'Oh, no, Mrs. Powers,' Jessica insisted. 'That won't be necessary. I think I can manage that part of it surely. No, I just need you to prepare the food and get it all ready, then I'll take over from there. But thank you for your kind offer,' she added.

'And would you like me to set a nice table in the dining room?' Mrs. Powers further asked.

'Oh, yes, please,' Jessica gave Mrs. Powers a quick peck on the cheek, 'that would be lovely.'

'Well, then' Mrs. Powers concluded. 'Next Thursday it is. It'll give me something to look forward to.'

'Me, too, Mrs. Powers,' Jessica smiled at her. 'Me, too.'

Chapter Seven

'I don't quite understand what it is you want me to do,' Garrett admitted to Jessica who sat across her big desk from him in her office.

'I know it sounds a little unconventional,' Jessica explained, 'so let me go through it again with you, okay?'

Garrett nodded. 'I think that would help.'

'As I explained, I have been doing a lot of research lately into an experimental exercise that's had some really wonderful results in the field of Psychology,' Jessica began to weave her web. 'I think it might be of great benefit to you when it comes to your anger issues, Garrett, but it will take some courage and honesty on your part. Do you think you're ready for that?'

'I guess so,' Garrett agreed. 'I'd be willing to give it a try, if you think it will help me.'

'Oh, I do,' Jessica assured him. 'I think it will make all the difference.'

If he only knew how true that statement would turn out to be.

'Okay, so tell me again what it is you want me to do?' Garrett asked her.

'The purpose of this exercise is to begin with a totally hypothetical situation. A situation in which there is only you and one other person. We want to start small,' she continued.

Garrett nodded. 'Okay, then what?'

'The person you pick has to be someone you know and are comfortable being with and around, say like Dr. Fitzgerald, for example,' Jessica calmly but intentionally suggested. 'Would that be a good person for you to have a hypothetical but comfortable conversation with?'

'Sure, I think so,' Garrett answered. 'I like Dr. Fitzgerald. He's always been nice to me.'

'Perfect, then Dr. Fitzgerald it is,' Jessica confirmed. 'Now, we have to decide on a hypothetical situation, something that happened between you and Dr. Fitzgerald. Something that wasn't pleasant. Something that would be difficult to talk about.'

Garrett wasn't yet convinced. 'Why would I want to talk about something that happened between Dr. Fitzgerald and me that wasn't nice?'

Fuck. Fuck! 'It's simply an exercise, Garrett,' Jessica did her best to remain calm. 'It's like pretending. The benefit to this type of exercise is that if you can feel comfortable talking about an uncomfortable situation with someone you like, then you can develop the appropriate skills to handle a situation involving someone you either don't like or don't know. It's an exercise that's designed to prepare you for a situation you may encounter later on. Do you understand?'

'Sort of,' Garrett answered. 'But what type of uncomfortable situation should I talk about?'

'Well,' Jessica pretended to think about his question, 'what if, say, Dr. Fitzgerald found out about us and he was going to send you away? How would that make you feel, Garrett?'

'I'd be angry, very angry!' he reacted.

'Of course you would, and you would have every right to feel angry,' Jessica continued to feed his mind. 'Now, take a situation like that and write down your thoughts on a piece of paper first. Like you're writing him a note. What do you think you would say to Dr. Fitzgerald if such a thing were to happen?'

'I think I'd start by telling him that he wasn't going to break us up,' Garrett started.

'That's good, Garrett,' she encouraged him. 'You could also tell him how much you love me. That you believe we're meant to be together.'

Garrett picked up the pen that lay atop the pad of paper Jessica had put in front of him and began to write. 'Dear Dr. Fitzgerald,' he said aloud as his pen scribbled the words.

Jessica struggled to maintain her composure. 'Garrett, I don't think you would use the word 'Dear' when writing an angry letter. It sounds too nice, don't you think? Just Dr. Fitzgerald would do fine.'

'You're probably right,' Garrett conceded and stroked out the 'Dear' part of the salutation he had just written. 'Dr. Fitzgerald,' he read aloud.

'Perfect,' Jessica smiled at him. 'Garrett, listen, I have an idea,' she decided to offer, her frustrations with him mounting. 'Would it help if I were to give you a few examples of what you might want to say in your letter? Sort of like starting points that you can then build on. Put into your own words. In your own handwriting.'

'Would you, Jess?' Garrett looked at her, relief on his face. 'That would be great, thanks. I still don't quite understand yet what it is you want me to say.'

'I'd be more than happy to, Garrett,' Jessica assured him. 'I know the first time doing this can be a bit tricky, so whatever I can do to help, you know you can count on me.'

That evening, long after Jessica had fucked what was left of the poor boy's brains out, she returned to her office. She sat at her desk, opened a big drawer in the credenza that lined the wall behind her, pulled out a file folder, and placed it on her desk.

She opened the folder and removed the piece of paper that sat on the very top. The piece of paper that contained Garrett's handwritten note to Dr. Fitzgerald. The one she told Garrett she was placing in the file, so she could track his progress.

She folded the note and placed it in her pocket. It wouldn't matter if her fingerprints were found on the paper, because she and the soon-to-be guilty lived in the same house. Their fingerprints would naturally be found everywhere, on just about everything. No worries.

* * * * *

The following Thursday, just before six o'clock and Declan's arrival at the manor house but well after Mrs. Powers departure from the house, Garrett slung his ratty old duffle bag, in which he had packed the few necessary items Jessica had given him, over his shoulder and headed out in Jessica's car.

He was to drive to the house Jessica had shown him and park just down the street, preferably where there were no streetlights. Once there, he was to wait in his car until precisely nine o'clock, at which time he was to take the ski mask and gloves out of his duffle bag and put them on. He shoved his hand into the bottom of the bag and checked to make sure the pronged hammer Jessica had given him was still there. She had made him hold the hammer numerous times before now. She needed to be sure his finger prints were left behind, but she told him it was important for him to first get a real feel for the hammer without gloves on. That's what Jessica had suggested. He loved that she was so smart. She loved that he was not.

He had been instructed to go to a motel Jessica had found after he had done what he was supposed to, and wait for Jessica to contact him. She had given him enough cash, so that, should he have to, he could stay there for several days. Jessica was sure it wouldn't be that long. Probably a day at the most.

Once Garrett left the house, Jessica found the master set of keys and let herself into his apartment. There, she took the letter Garrett had written to Dr. Fitzgerald and placed it on top of Garrett's bed. It would be plainly visible to anyone who entered the room.

Next, she quickly changed into something sexy. Something black. Something with an exposed back and bare shoulders.

She checked her watch. Declan would be here any minute. She had just enough time to add that extra special touch to the evening. She walked across her living room to the coffee table. She gently pulled open the drawer and took out the black gift box. She removed the lid, reached in, and removed a candle. One of the two yet unused candles. She delicately placed it in the palm of her hand and smiled. 'I'm so glad you could make it, baby doll,' she whispered to the candle. 'It's going to be a very special night, Mama promises.'

240

Jessica carried the candle in her hand as she left her apartment. She descended the long staircase to the foyer, across the foyer and into the dining room Mrs. Powers had meticulously set for tonight's dinner.

She took a small dish from the sideboard, put the candle in the center of the dish, and placed the dish on the table between the two place settings. 'Perfect,' she whispered to no one.

She then headed to the back of the house and the kitchen. The smells wafting from Mrs. Powers' culinary creation that she left warming in the oven were making Jessica's mouth water. She was strangely surprised at how much of an appetite she had worked up today.

Her thoughts were suddenly interrupted by the sound of the doorbell. It was Declan. Right on time.

She casually walked to the front door and opened it. 'Darling,' she smiled at Declan standing on the other side, 'I've been waiting for you.'

Declan stood back and simply looked at her...her beauty, her near radiance tonight. 'Have I told you lately how stunning you are?' he asked.

'Stop it, Declan,' Jessica feigned shyness. 'You'd better come in before I change my mind.'

'Oh no, you don't,' Declan joked as he quickly entered the house and wrapped her in his arms. 'You're stuck with me for at least a few hours tonight,' he kidded her. 'Not only do you look fabulous, but something smells fabulous too. By the way, where is Garrett tonight?'

Jessica closed the big front door and took Declan by the hand. 'I let him borrow my car,' she stated. 'He's been doing so well lately that when he asked me this afternoon if he could use it to meet a friend at the movies, I told him it was okay. I was just happy to hear that he was making friends.'

'I'm not sure I would have loaned him my car, Jessica,' Declan admitted. 'But I see how hard you're working with him and how much you care about him, so if that works for you two, that's what matters. I won't interfere, unless you ask me to, okay?'

'Thank you, Declan,' Jessica stopped, stood on her tippy toes, and kissed him sweetly. 'Your support means a great deal to me. Now let's eat, I'm starving,' she teased as she pulled him toward the dining room.

'By the way, don't expect this all the time,' she chided him when she saw the look of delight on his face. 'I have to confess that Mrs. Powers made the dinner tonight. I wanted it to be a special night, so I asked Mrs. Powers if she would help. What you are smelling is Mrs. Powers' talents, not mine.'

'Ah, but you have talents that I can assure you Mrs. Powers does not,' he said as he kissed her longingly, passionately.

'Declan,' Jessica managed to say, 'we really should eat first. Mrs. Powers will be horribly insulted if we don't finish every last morsel of food.' She laughed. 'Come on, let's sit down.'

Jessica pulled him into the dining room and took him to the seat she had chosen for him. 'I'll be right back,' she blew him a kiss on her way to the kitchen, 'why don't you make yourself useful and open the wine and pour us a glass.'

'Aye, aye, Captain,' he teased her, but smiled and allowed his eyes to follow her out of the room. She returned a few minutes later carrying two steaming plates of roasted chicken breast with snow peas, garlic sautéed mushrooms, and roasted new potatoes.

'A feast fit for a king,' Jessica said as she placed the plates on the table. 'Or at least my king,' she leaned over and kissed Declan on the lips.

'Oh, wait,' Jessica sudden remembered something. 'I almost forgot to light the candle.'

Declan looked down at the red teddy bear candle in the dish between them. 'I see it's one of the candles you haven't used yet,' Declan commented. 'So, what's the special occasion tonight then?'

'It's special, because I wanted you to know that I'm always here for you,' she said as she held a lighter to the wick, 'forever, Declan.' She didn't feel the need to be the one to tell him that after tonight, they would be together forever. He'd find out before the sun had a chance to rise on another day.

She picked up her glass of wine and lifted it in the air. 'Here's to us, darling,' she toasted. She wanted to add a little something about their future, but realized that would be a tad premature. Their future wouldn't officially start until tomorrow.

Chapter Eight

Jessica hadn't slept since Declan left late last night. She had been far too excited to sleep. Now, all she had to do was wait. Wait for everything to unfold. Just as she had planned.

Shortly after nine o'clock in the morning, she heard the distant but persistent ringing of the doorbell at the front of the house. She had a pretty good idea who it was even before Mrs. Powers answered it. She had anticipated this visit, had waited for this visit.

A few minutes later, she heard persistent tapping on her apartment door. 'Jessica, it's Mrs. Powers. There's someone here to see you.' Mrs. Powers said, the tension in her voice obvious. 'It's urgent and you need to come down straight away, is what he said.'

Jessica got out of bed, tied her terrycloth robe around her waist, and went to open the door. 'Who is it, Mrs. Powers?' she asked innocently.

'It's Detective Lubovik, Jessica,' Mrs. Powers struggled to explain. She was almost breathless from anxiety. 'There's been a terrible accident and he needs to speak to you right away.'

Jessica tied her robe tighter and left her apartment. 'Alright, Mrs. Powers,' she said as she headed for the staircase where she stopped and looked over the railing to the tiled floor of the foyer directly below. Standing just inside the entry way was Detective Lubovik and a half dozen uniformed officers.

'Detective Lubovik,' she said as she began to descend, 'Mrs. Powers said there has been some sort of accident, is that right?'

By now, she had reached the bottom of the staircase. 'Why don't we take a seat in my office,' she directed him there. 'Mrs. Powers, if you would be so kind as to bring us some coffee. By the looks of it, Detective Lubovik could use one and I know I certainly could, please and thank you.'

'Certainly,' Mrs. Powers answered and hustled for the kitchen. If she came back as quickly as she could, she might not miss too much of what was being said. Whatever it was, she was sure it would definitely be worth eavesdropping on.

'Please, sit down, Detective,' Jessica gestured to one of the guest chairs in front of her desk, while she took the chair behind her desk. She had only ever allowed herself to imagine how much she was going to enjoy this moment. Now she could actually live it.

'Do you know where Garrett is, Ms. McCallum?' he asked her point blank.

'Why, yes,' Jessica answered, 'he's upstairs in his apartment. Probably fast asleep. I think he was out late last night,' she added. 'Why are you asking about Garrett?'

'Because we believe he's responsible for the brutal murder of Dr. Fitzgerald's wife, Lara, sometime last night.' Detective Lubovik wasn't one for small talk.

'Oh my God,' Jessica cried out, before putting a fist up to her mouth. 'Oh my God, no,' she repeated, only this time much quieter. 'I don't believe it, Detective,' Jessica insisted. 'I know Garrett is a troubled young man, but murder? Why? Poor Dr. Fitzgerald,' she managed to squeeze out a solitary tear, 'How is he? Where is he?'

'Unfortunately, he was the one who found his wife's body, so as you can imagine, he's pretty shaken up,' Lubovik commented. 'He's downtown at our office right now. He needs a little time to collect himself, then we'll talk to him and find out more, I hope.'

'Of course,' Jessica nodded.

'Do you have a key to Garrett's apartment?' the detective asked.

'I have a master key,' Jessica responded, 'why?'

'I'd like you to stay here while I take a few officers upstairs and pay Mr. Armstrong a visit.'

Jessica opened the center drawer in her desk and pulled out a ring with a few keys on it. She selected the correct key and handed it to the detective. 'It's that one,' she indicated.

'Thanks,' the detective took the key from her hand. 'Stay here until I tell you otherwise, got it?' he instructed her.

'Please, Detective,' Jessica called after him, 'don't hurt him.' She pulled the pocket doors closed after the detective left her office, returned to her seat and waited. Good things came to those who waited.

A few minutes later, she heard a number of footsteps pounding down the staircase. One set of footsteps came toward her office and one pocket door was wrenched open. It was Detective Lubovik holding a note in one latex blue-gloved hand. 'Garrett's not there,' the detective told her, 'but we found this.'

'What is it?' she asked.

'It's a note,' Lubovik answered.

'Garrett left a note?' she asked. 'What does it say?' Jessica asked.

'I'm afraid I can't get into the specifics,' he explained. 'For now, I just need you to confirm whether or not it's Garrett's handwriting,' he requested. 'If you could take a quick look,' he held the note up in front of her. 'Is this Garrett's handwriting?'

Jessica put her head down. 'Yes, Detective, it is,' she confessed. 'But why,' she looked at the detective, 'why would he do such a thing?'

Detective chose not to speculate. 'Do you have any idea where he might be right now?' he asked.

Jessica pretended to think about his question. 'No,' she offered. 'I'm sorry, I don't.'

'That's too bad,' the detective commented. 'In the meantime, I'd like you to stay inside. Don't go anywhere. I'm going to leave a few officers outside, just in case Garrett shows up,' he added.

'Thank you, Detective,' Jessica smiled weakly at him.

'Just one more thing. Do you own a car Ms. McCallum?'

'Yes, it's parked out front. It's a white Mazda CX-3,' she told him.

'It wasn't out there when we arrived just now,' he noted. 'Is it possible Garrett has it?'

'Well, yes,' she explained, 'I let him borrow it last night. He said he was going to meet a friend and they were going to go and see a movie. I was in my apartment most of the night, so I didn't hear him come in. I just assumed he came home at some point.'

'We'll need the license plate number,' the detective instructed.

Jessica removed a pad of paper from her desk, wrote the number on the top piece, ripped it off, and handed it to Lubovik.

The detective rose out of his chair. 'Thanks, I need to get this information out over the radios. But I'll be back,' he said as he went. He had just about reached the front door, before Jessica called him back.

'Detective Lubovik,' she called out, 'I just remembered a place where Garrett might have gone.' She was going to lead them right to Garrett.

The detective stopped and turned to face her. 'Where?' is all he wanted to know.

'It's possible that he went to a motel two towns over,' she told him. That was true. 'I believe it's called Shady Nook Inn or Pines or something like that.' Also true.

'Why would he go there?' the detective asked.

'It's a place where his family used to go on holiday,' Jessica added the first lie. 'Every once in a while, he just goes there and stays overnight in the room they used to stay in as a family. Kind of a nostalgia thing, I guess,' Jessica added her next lie. 'If he is there, you'll probably find him in room number nine. That's his favorite room,' she added the final lie. She was doing everything she could to not just point them in the right direction, but give them the exact location. She was doing everything she could, except taking them by the hand and personally leading them right to him. She didn't feel the need to. She had now given them enough to quickly hunt him down.

She hoped Garrett would stick to the script. If he didn't, he might survive. That wasn't part of her plan.

* * * * *

Garrett had arrived at the motel Jessica told him to go to just before midnight. He had a fresh set of clothes on when he checked in, as Jessica had instructed. He paid cash and signed his real name to the registry, also as Jessica had instructed.

All he had to do now was lay low in his motel room, room number nine, and wait for Jessica to call. She promised she would contact him no later than noon. He had some time to kill. He laughed at this humor.

He couldn't sleep, though. He was still pumped from the adrenaline rush. His body was restless, driven by a mind that was fixated on the exciting images of what he had just done. What he had done for Jessica, for the two of them, for love.

He had parked Jessica's car down the street from the woman's house and waited until nine o'clock. Just before nine, he removed the ski mask and gloves from his duffle bag and put them on. He slung the duffle bag over one shoulder and stepped out of the car, making sure not to slam the door behind him. He wasn't supposed to draw any attention to himself. In head-to-toe black, he zigzagged his way through the lush landscape of several yards before he came to a particular house. The one Jessica had pointed out to him.

He crept round to the back of the house where he jimmied a small bathroom window and slithered inside. This was not his first rodeo when it came to breaking and entering. While not a pro, he was well seasoned. This window was no challenge.

He waited a full 30 seconds to make sure no one had heard him and would come to check it out. Nothing. No one. Next, he gently placed the duffle on the floor in front of him, unzipped it, and reached inside. He took out the hammer and began tossing it back and forth from one hand to the other. Which one felt better? He stopped to consider which hand he should use. Should he use his dominant hand to swing the hammer, or should he use his other hand and leave his dominant hand free in case he needed it? He decided to use his dominant hand. It would most likely get the job done better and faster.

He opened the door and listened for any sound at all. In the distance, he could just make out faint noises. It was the familiar tap-tap-tap of a computer keyboard under attack. The woman was working at the computer somewhere in the house. He just needed to follow the sound and it would lead him right to her.

He raised the hammer slightly over his own head, his grip firm and steady, and began making his way through the house, the clicking of the keyboard emitting an acoustic trail for him to follow.

He silently made his way past the kitchen, through the large living room and down a long hallway. The only light he could make out was coming from a room at the end. It was the recognizable glare of a computer screen.

246

He carefully, slowly inched his way toward the room, hammer at the ready, its double prongs facing forward. Jessica had suggested using the prongs instead of the hammerhead. It made a lot of sense. Imbedding metal into a skull would be much more efficient than simply bashing the outside of it.

He stood outside the door for a few seconds, listening, waiting, breathing. When his heart rate had slowed somewhat, he tilted his head slightly, just enough for one eye to peek around the door frame and quickly scan the room. There she was, sitting at a computer, typing. Completely focused on the task. Her back to the door. No sense of foreboding. Nothing to suggest she might want to turn around. It wouldn't have made any difference if she had.

Garrett crept up behind her, his hand gripping the hammer he now held high above his head, ensuring he harnessed as much downward force as possible.

He was never supposed to say anything. Yet, he couldn't help himself. What came out of him was completely involuntary, but it did give him just that little bit of extra anger he needed to finally bring the prongs down, hard, right on the top of the woman's head. 'You fucking bitch!' he screamed.

Unfortunately, his words didn't drown out the grotesque sounds that resulted when the prongs came into contact with her head. Nor did they muffle the splattering sounds of blood and brain matter that flew about the room when he wrenched the prongs out, again and again and again.

He only stopped flailing when the woman's body fell out of the chair and onto the carpeted floor below. Jessica told him to make sure she was dead before he left. So, he knelt down beside the mangled remains and quickly checked for a wrist pulse. None.

Garrett left the hammer behind, its prongs fully embedded in what little remained of the woman's skull. Jessica told him not to worry about fingerprints, because he would be wearing gloves. He forgot all about the number of times before this when he had held the hammer in his hands with no gloves on. He does remember, though, how sweetly Jessica had smiled when she suggested to him that he try out the hammer beforehand.

He returned to the bathroom where he had initially entered the house, took all of his bloodied clothes off, wiped himself down with the towel he had in his duffle bag, then redressed himself in clean, all black clothes. He wrapped the cast-off bloodied clothes in a plastic bag he also had in the duffle, then repacked the bag.

He reached up to shove the bag out the bathroom window, but it caught on the frame on his first try. When his second attempt was successful, he crawled out after it. He retrieved the bag, slung it over his shoulder, and retraced his steps back to where he had left Jessica's car. He quietly opened the car door, threw his bag into the passenger seat, and climbed in. He checked his watch. It was just before ten o'clock. Not bad. He couldn't wait to tell Jessica that he had done everything exactly as she had told him to do. And he had done it all in under an hour. He thinks she'll be proud of him.

He didn't realize the identification tag that had been attached to his duffle bag snapped off when it caught on the window's ledge in his first attempt to throw it out. He hadn't seen it flutter down and land on the bathroom floor. It was just one of the many pieces of himself he left behind that night. But it was the one that left little doubt in anyone's mind at the crime scene as to who the person was who committed the heinous crime.

Chapter Nine

It was a beautiful fall day. *Far too nice for a funeral,* Jessica thought to herself, but then death was rarely a scheduled occasion. She'd have to remember to check weather forecasts the next time. Shame to waste a sunny day.

Hundreds of mourners had gathered at the cemetery, a sea of black as far as the eye could see. A gentle breeze carried the Minister's voice, his baritone tenor surprisingly comforting. His words were doing their best to convey the same, yet failed sorrowfully. Some stood with tears quietly falling, while others supplemented theirs with the suitable sounds of suffering.

Jessica stood on the periphery of the mourners, alongside Mrs. Powers who was also struggling to keep her emotions in check. But Jessica couldn't take her eyes off of Declan who stood stoically alongside his wife's casket, his head slightly bowed down. She so desperately wanted to go to him and hold him at that moment. To kiss him tenderly and tell him everything would be alright. She knew it would be, but he had not yet had enough time to come to that same conclusion. He would, though. She would help him.

Jessica's thoughts were suddenly interrupted by Mrs. Powers. 'Isn't it all so tragic,' Mrs. Powers was tugging at her coat sleeve. 'I can't bring myself to look at Dr. Fitzgerald, the poor thing,' she whispered as she dabbed a tissue to the corner of one eye. 'He looks absolutely devastated. Imagine finding your wife in such a state,' she continued. 'It'll be a long time before he's able to get that image out of his head, I'm sure.'

Jessica was growing increasingly annoyed. For fuck sakes, she didn't want to hear any more about Dr. Fitzgerald's *dearly departed wife.* She'd heard enough about her over the past week. Lara's picture and 'tragic' story had been splashed across every possible newspaper and tabloid. Her story had also been subjected to hours of graphic mutilation by televised forensics experts, legal analysts and criminologists, none of whom had any firsthand knowledge of the tragedy nor the individuals involved. Narcissistic assholes.

'Please, Mrs. Powers,' Jessica sternly whispered back, 'just be quiet. This isn't the time or the place.' 'Fuck off' is what she really wanted to say to her.

Mrs. Powers responded by blowing her noise, loudly, into the handkerchief she clutched in her hand.

As the casket was being lowered into the ground, Jessica saw Declan gently kiss a single pink rose before he cast it into the dirt pit below. How touching.

A final prayer was delivered before the crowd slowly began to disperse, with a few remaining behind in the hopes of offering an appropriate personal condolence to the bereaved. Jessica suspected those were the nose-rubbers. The suck-ups who were simply looking to advance their status in Declan's world.

As the crowd thinned, Jessica spotted Detective Lubovik standing well away from everyone, leaning up against a big oak tree. She knew he'd be here, of course. Not because of his heartstrings, but because it was his job.

He'd also been the only other person Jessica saw yesterday, sitting in his car quite a distance away from her, as she witnessed Garrett's casket being lowered into an anonymous plot of ground in an equally anonymous portion of a cemetery that had been earmarked for the insolvent and the occasional Jane or John Doe. The only reason she decided to go at all was because she felt that by not going, it would look suspicious. After all, she had been his therapist. She had every reason to be here. She was the person he was closest to. There really was no one else to care. Garrett hadn't seen or heard from his sister since they were separated years ago.

It was a shame Garrett had to die, but it had been necessary. It was a compulsory casualty of the cause. Admittedly, Jessica would miss the sex. The readiness and resilience of his young age had been exceptionally satisfying.

Like Lara, poor Garrett hadn't met a very nice ending either.

Detective Lubovik, along with several squad cars and a heavily armed and fortified tactical team, had descended on the motel where Jessica told them he 'might' be. They learned from the desk clerk that Garrett had, indeed, checked in late the night before. And yes, as it happens, he was staying in room number nine. He had specifically requested that room.

The tactical team had quickly, but surreptitiously, evacuated all other guests who were staying at the motel, which amounted to less than a handful. Once they were safely out of harm's way, the tactical team moved in. They used a handheld battering ram to smash the door nearly off its hinges, followed instantaneously by a powerful flashbang bomb that could be heard for miles around, according to numerous accounts.

The chaos had startled the deep sleeping Garrett awake so violently that his fight-or-flight instinct in that first split second was to run, to get out. Unfortunately for Garrett, he ran straight for the door, with his arms thrashing at his sides and his screams involuntary.

Detective Lubovik had been quoted in a recent article stating what had happened that day. "Instead of surrendering peacefully, Mr. Armstrong chose to attack the first officers who entered the motel room. As a result of Mr. Armstrong's aggressive actions, those officers felt they had no choice but to defend themselves.

Mr. Armstrong was pronounced dead at the scene as a result of multiple gunshot wounds." End of Garrett. End of story. Or was it?

Detective Lubovik had asked to meet with Jessica, back at the manor house, following Mrs. Fitzgerald funeral. Jessica arrived home with just enough time to change into something a little less formal before he arrived. She wanted her body to feel relaxed and not irritatingly encumbered as it had been in the depressing black skirt suit she wore to the funeral.

A half hour later, she answered the doorbell's ring and found the detective standing on the doorstep. 'Come in, Detective,' Jessica greeted him as any respectable hostess would. 'I can ask Mrs. Powers to bring you something to drink. Iced tea? Coffee?'

'No, I'm fine, thanks just the same,' Lubovik replied.

'Very well,' Jessica said. 'Shall we go to my office?' she asked.

'Sure,' Lubovik answered and followed her across the foyer. Jessica waited for him to take a seat before she closed the pocket doors, then made her way around the desk to her seat on the opposite side.

'So, what did you want to see me about today, Detective?' she casually inquired.

'Well, it's about the note that Mr. Armstrong wrote,' he began. 'The one we found in his apartment just after Mrs. Fitzgerald was murdered.'

'Yes, the one you asked me to verify whether or not it was his handwriting.'

'Had you ever seen that note before then, Ms. McCallum?' he asked.

'Unfortunately no, Detective,' she responded calmly. 'Perhaps if I had, I might have been able to do something to prevent all of this. Does the note give you any idea as to why Garrett did it?'

'Were you aware that Mr. Armstrong was in love with you?' the detective asked.

'What? No. Well, I mean I knew he had feelings for me, certainly,' Jessica lied, 'but I never imagined for a second that he was in love with me. Are you sure?'

'Yes, very sure,' he responded. 'He wrote the note to Dr. Fitzgerald personally, but in it, he says how in love he is with you. He also said that Dr. Fitzgerald had found out how he felt and that the doctor was going to send him away. Garrett apparently decided that he wasn't going to let that happen,' the detective paused.

'Well, that's just not true, I can assure you Detective,' Jessica stated. 'There was nothing going on between Garrett and me, and, therefore, there was nothing for Dr. Fitzgerald to find out about.'

'True or not, Ms. McCallum,' the detective responded, 'it's what Garrett believed and it's that belief that drove him to do what he did.'

'I don't quite understand,' Jessica began. 'If Garrett was so angry at Dr. Fitzgerald, why did he kill his wife?'

'He says in the note that he did it so Dr. Fitzgerald would know what it felt like to lose something he loves,' Lubovik shrugged. 'That was pretty much the gist of it all.'

Jessica looked at the detective. 'Well, if there's nothing else I can do for you today, Detective,' she rose from her chair, 'I've got loads of paperwork to get to. I'll see you to the door.'

Detective Lubovik remained in his chair, indicating he was in no hurry to go anywhere himself. 'I gotta be honest, Ms. McCallum,' the detective took a deep breath, let it out with great fanfare then continued, 'you make me a tad nervous.'

Jessica froze for just a second. *Tic.* 'I make you nervous, Detective?' she chuckled quietly. 'And why is that?'

Detective Lubovik slowly rose from the chair, walked out the office door and headed for the front door. 'People drop like flies around you,' he called back at her. 'I can't help but wonder who's next?'

With that, he winked at her, opened the front door, and let himself out.

* * * * *

It was several more months before Declan went to the manor house again. After Lara's death, he had taken some time to grieve, to think, to contemplate life moving forward. Moving on. Moving past what had been his life, but was no more.

He may not have been in love with Lara, but he had loved her. They had started their adult lives side by side. They had supported each other over the years. They had built something together. He was part of a 'couple.' Now he was just himself.

Jessica had extended an open invitation to him to come for dinner any time. If he prefers, they could sit and talk quietly over a bottle of wine. Just a bit of company, should he need it.

At first, he couldn't bring himself to see Jessica. The guilt he felt over his betrayal to Lara had eaten away at him, horribly, terribly. If it weren't for him and the poor choices he had made in his life over these past seven years, perhaps Lara might still be alive.

As time passed, though, he began to soften a little, to forgive himself a little, to like himself a little, and to miss Jessica a lot.

He decided to call her, late one night. He talked for hours. She listened for hours. It was comfortable. It was comforting.

Jessica never pushed him. Never suggested he suck it up and act like a man. Never told him to just get over it. She simply listened, waited. She knew it would come.

A few weeks later, Declan called and asked if he could come over the next afternoon and see her. He had been doing a lot of thinking lately and he wanted to tell her what he had decided about his future, about their future.

Jessica couldn't wait to see him. It was Saturday and Mrs. Powers didn't work on weekends, so she and Declan would have the whole house to themselves.

Before Declan arrived, Jessica enjoyed a long, hot bubble bath. Next, she took a brush and went to stand before the full-length mirror in her bedroom. There, she arranged her long, golden curls, draping them carefully over one bare shoulder, then the other. One solitary strand of soft coils she left to cascade freely down her back, tickling the little hollow at the top of her buttocks. She was giddy.

She chose a sheer white silk blouse, her naked breasts shamelessly exposed beneath. She added a short, teal-colored skirt that suggested the peek-a-boo possibility of something delightful awaiting beneath, if one were so inclined. She hoped Declan would be more than inclined.

One last inspection in the mirror. A fluff to the blonde curls. A fingertip dab to the corner of her mouth where the lipstick refused to hang on. A pretend smile looking back at her.

Tonight is the night. She is ready. She is ready to become Mrs. Declan Fitzgerald. Declan is coming here to tell her how much he wants her. How much he loves her. How they will spend the rest of their lives together. It was her he had wanted all alone. Wished for since the day they first met.

She left her apartment and gracefully walked the long hallway to the grand staircase. At the top, she stopped and looked down...down to the fifth step. She smiled at the memory.

She descended the staircase, taking her time. Relishing the time. She was about to become the true lady of the manor house and she would conduct herself accordingly. All those rehearsals had paid off. Her descent was now flawless.

She went to the big kitchen where she opened a bottle of wine and placed two glasses beside it on the center island. Next, she took a few bricks of cheese out of the refrigerator and set them on a platter to warm, alongside an assortment of crackers, deli meats, and Kalamata olives. There was just one thing missing: Declan.

A half hour later, there was still no sign of Declan. To calm herself, Jessica poured herself a glass of wine. Then a second and a third. It didn't help. The voices that had been loitering somewhere in the background were coming closer, getting closer.

The ring of the doorbell suddenly interrupted the voices. Silenced the voices. 'Declan,' she whispered aloud then placed her again empty wineglass on the counter and ran to the front door. Before she opened it, she took a deep breath and composed herself. This was the moment. The moment she had been working for. The moment she had sacrificed so much for. The moment she had killed for.

She opened the door and greeted Declan with a quiet, sweet smile. 'Hello, Declan,' she said to him, 'please come in.'

Declan looked at Jessica, but there was something wrong with his smile. It was a pretend smile. She would recognize it anywhere. *Tic.*

'Thank you, Jessica,' he said as he entered the house.

'It's good to see you, Declan,' she meant it. 'How have you been?'

'Oh, you know,' he shrugged, 'I'm doing as well as can be expected, I suppose.'

'Come, let's go to the kitchen,' she said as she turned and led the way. 'We can relax over a glass of wine.'

Declan followed her. 'Perfect,' he replied, 'I could use a drink.'

'Well,' Jessica said, 'then you've come to the right place. Please,' she gestured to a stool at the kitchen island, 'have a seat.'

Declan sat down, reached for the wine and topped up her glass before pouring his own. 'What shall we toast to?' Declan wondered aloud. 'What could a person possibly have to cheer about when his or her spouse had been so mercilessly slaughtered?'

Jessica raised her glass, waited for Declan to do the same, before she spoke. 'How about we toast to new beginnings?' she suggested. A new beginning for her. A new beginning for him. A new beginning together. It would have been the perfect toast, had Declan not chosen that very moment to open his mouth and let his words fall untethered.

'Yes,' he raised his glass, 'to new beginnings.' He clinked his glass gently against Jessica's and took a sip before he continued on. 'Speaking of new beginnings, as you are well aware, I've had some time on my hands lately.'

Jessica smiled at him, 'Yes, I know,' she gently replied. 'I'm sorry, I know it's been very difficult for you.'

'Over the past several weeks, I started to think about my future,' Declan began to explain. 'What did I want? What would I like? Should I keep practicing or should I take some time and do some traveling?'

Tic. 'What do you mean travel? Where would you go? How long would you go for if you did go somewhere?' *Was he fucking kidding?*

'I don't know,' he casually shrugged, 'I've always wanted to go to Bali. I was thinking maybe I'd spend the winter there. Get some sun. Figure out what it is I want to do when I grow up,' he smiled meekly at his attempt at humor.

But she couldn't understand what he was saying. What he was getting at. 'Declan, you don't mean it?' she looked at him. 'You're not really going to leave me, are you?'

'Jessica, I put my house on the market yesterday. I just can't live there any longer,' he put his head down. 'I can't get the images of that night, of Lara, out of my head. I thought it would be the perfect time to get away, while the house is on the market. In the meantime, it gives me some time to figure out what I want to do,' he said matter-of-factly.

'Take me with you, please?' she pleaded. 'I won't be any trouble, I promise. I'll take good care of you. You'll see.'

'Jessica,' Declan looked at her, reluctance in his eyes, 'I need some time to myself,' he tried to explain. 'I need to figure some things out and I can't do it with all of the distractions in my life at the moment.'

Tic. 'So, I'm just a distraction to you now, am I?' she could feel the anger starting to burn inside of her. The tears that threatened to spill from her eyes were not the result of wounded feelings, as Declan assumed. They were the result of her effort to keep the rage inside of her from exploding, to keep it contained.

'No, no, Jessica,' Declan reached for her, 'that's not what I meant. It came out all wrong,' he explained. 'You've never been a distraction to me, darling, honestly. I just need some time to think, that's all. Just a little time, I promise,' he soothed her.

Jessica's rage had reached a level that was making her feel nauseous. She thought she was going to be sick to her stomach. She instinctively covered her mouth with one hand, while she placed the other over her stomach. 'Are you alright, Jessica?' Declan asked, for he could see that she was clearly in distress.

It was one of the voices that came to her rescue at that very moment. It was one of the voices that gave her the idea.

She took a deep breath, before she brought her head up and looked directly into Declan's eyes. Her face expressed no emotion whatsoever.

'Declan,' she said to him, 'I'm afraid you can't leave.'

Declan was puzzled. 'Jessica, please,' he insisted gently, 'you're not making this any easier.'

'I'm pregnant, Declan,' she blurted out at him. 'I'm going to have your baby.' She smiled sweetly up at him, took one of his hands in hers, and placed it over her stomach. 'You see? You can't possibly think of leaving me now, can you?'

Chapter Ten

Together, they had decided on a small, civil ceremony. Just the bride and groom, and their only witness, Mrs. Powers, who stood alongside the couple as a proud parent might do. Although, she did nearly fall off her chair when Jessica told her that she and Dr. Fitzgerald were getting married. Why, the first Mrs. Fitzgerald was barely cold in the ground, for heaven's sake.

Declan suggested, just for now, that Jessica not tell anyone she was pregnant. He was still trying to wrap his head around the news, so couldn't quite imagine how others were going to take it. He knew how it looked, of course. 'Wealthy old man loses his wife of 35 years and seeks solace in the body of a very sexy woman more than 20 years younger,' or 'Wealthy old man loses his mind after his wife of 35 years is murdered and he's sucked in by a gold-digging bimbo.'

Mind you, he always did want to be a father, but unfortunately Lara had been unable to conceive. So, Dr. Fitzgerald had thrown himself into his work, while Lara had thrown herself into the world of fundraising, fancy hats and afternoon tea.

Needless to say, Declan was completely stunned by Jessica's news, at first. A baby? His baby? His baby. After all these years. Maybe it was meant to be. Maybe this is what he was supposed to do with his life now. Maybe he was supposed to be a father.

He and Jessica had stayed up for hours talking the night she told him she was pregnant.

'How many months along are you?' was one of the first things Declan had asked.

'Two months,' Jessica had already done the necessary math. Apparently, Declan was doing the same math.

'That means you most likely got pregnant on the night Lara…that night,' was all he could manage. The words were still too awful to think, let alone say.

'Yes, I think so too,' Jessica quietly agreed with him.

'Well, how have you been feeling?' Declan asked. 'Have you been to see a doctor yet?

'No, I um, haven't,' Jessica replied. 'I only took the home pregnancy test a few days ago.'

'Then let me call and make an appointment for you with one of the best obstetricians in the area,' Declan offered. 'She's an old friend and I'm sure she'd be happy to fit you in.'

'No, really,' Jessica quickly declined, 'I, um, I think it should be someone I decide on. I just want to make sure I'm comfortable with that person. I hope you're not offended?'

'Not in the least,' Declan smiled at her. 'I completely understand. But, if you change your mind, let me know.'

Jessica returned his smiled. 'I will, I promise, thank you, Declan.' She picked up her wineglass and put it up to her lips.

'Jessica,' Declan grabbed her wrist, 'what are you doing? You know you shouldn't be drinking now.'

Fuck. 'Oh my God,' Jessica immediately put the glass down. 'Sorry, I guess because it's all so new, I wasn't really thinking,' she explained. 'It won't happen again,' she assured him. At least not in front of him.

It took Declan a few days to come to terms with Jessica's news, but when he did, he decided to embrace the situation wholeheartedly.

In lieu of a big wedding, Declan presented Jessica with a brilliant three-karat diamond solitaire ring and a matching diamond wedding band. Of course, she needed the full set. He also paid for her wedding gown with a price tag of just over $10,000. It's what she wanted. He also bought her a brand new white Range Rover Luxury SUV. After all, she would need something that was safe and reliable to transport the baby in. And yes, it just so happened that she looked fabulous in it, too.

Declan had put his house on the market and moved in with Jessica at the manor house. The only possessions he brought with him were his clothes. He didn't want anything else. He didn't want any reminders. Neither did Jessica, so it worked out nicely for both of them.

Declan had also taken on the task of overseeing extensive renovations they were going to make to the manor house. All traces of the former apartments on the second floor were to be obliterated and replaced by a massive master suite for Jessica and Declan, complete with separate dressing areas, separate walk-in closets and a joint, luxurious en suite bathroom, as well as two guest rooms, each with its own well-appointed en suite. Oh yes, and a nursery with a nanny suite next to it. Jessica forgot to add that in the original design. 'Imagine, a baby without a nursery? Thank goodness Declan caught that oversight.'

While the main floor of the manor house wasn't going to undergo renovations, Jessica had insisted on its complete redecoration. The very first thing on her list was to replace the tile in the foyer with new, pure white-only marble tile.

It wasn't that she minded the old black-and-white tiles. It was that the voices didn't like them. They told her that the tiles were tainted with the blood of that fucking bitch Ms. Müller. They had made a deal with her. Destroy the tiles and they would destroy the memories, which was a relief to Jessica. It was becoming far too crowded up there, in her head.

As the days and weeks passed, Declan was attentive to Jessica's every need. He brought her tea and dry toast with raspberry jam on the side in the mornings. He told her it would help with any morning sickness. She didn't have any, but she enjoyed Declan's servitude, so she decided not to tell him.

He indulged her cravings, which only seemed to be satiated with expensive dinners out three or four nights a week.

Declan gave her a credit card with which to buy whatever she needed for the nursery. She used it to buy whatever she wanted for herself, too.

He also excused her more-often-now-than-not mood swings. They were simply a by-product of pregnancy. She couldn't help it. It wasn't her fault.

He arranged for a personal masseuse to come to the manor house twice a week to give Jessica a massage. She was having a difficult time with the pregnancy and needed something to help her relax. It would do, for now.

He had Mrs. Powers prepare healthier meals. It was important that Jessica get as many good nutrients as she could, so she could pass the benefits on to the baby. Jessica was thrilled to have someone else do all the cooking, the shopping, too, the cleaning up, the housework. She really shouldn't be doing any of those things in her condition, should she?

When Jessica had made it successfully past the first trimester, Declan made reservations to take her out to dinner to celebrate. Jessica chose a slinky black cocktail length dress for the evening. She accessorized it with a beautiful double strand of white pearls Declan's mother used to own. He had given it to her as another wedding present, along with a matching pair of drop pearl earrings.

'They look beautiful on you,' Declan said after he had secured the strand around her neck and stood back to admire her. 'My mother would have approved,' he added with a smile.

'Thank you, Declan,' Jessica replied, as she looked at herself in the mirror and ran her fingers back and forth across the pearls, a smug look on her face.

'You always hear people say that women glow when they are pregnant,' Declan smiled at her reflection. 'They were right. You are positively glowing. Although anyone looking at you wouldn't know you were pregnant,' he commented casually. 'You still look amazing.'

Jessica looked at her reflection in the mirror. She did look amazing. And no, she didn't look pregnant, did she? That's because she wasn't.

* * * * *

'Detective Lubovik,' Declan was surprised when he answered the doorbell late one afternoon a few weeks later. 'Please, come in. What brings you here?'

Detective Lubovik appeared a little anxious. 'Dr. Fitzgerald, I wonder if we could have a word. In private,' he requested.

'Of course,' Declan responded, 'why don't we step into Jessica's office? She's upstairs at the moment, so we won't be disturbed.'

Declan turned and crossed the foyer toward Jessica's office, the detective on his heels. Just before Declan slid the pocket doors closed behind him, he heard his name called from somewhere above. 'Declan, is everything alright?' Jessica asked. She had seen Detective Lubovik as well. 'Should I join you?'

'No, that's alright daring,' Declan smiled up at her on the second story landing, 'the detective just wanted a private word. I assume it has something to do with Lara's death, so maybe it's best that you don't hear what he has to say,' Declan stated. 'I don't want you getting upset unnecessarily.'

'If you're sure,' Jessica replied. *Tic.* 'Well, I was just coming down anyway,' she said as she started to make her way down the stairs. 'I'll be in the kitchen with Mrs. Powers if you need me.'

'Fine,' Declan said as he met her at the bottom of the staircase and reached out to take her hand, gently helping her down the last few steps. 'I'm sure I won't be long.' He gave her a kiss on the cheek and walked back to Jessica's office.

Jessica offered a little wave and a smile to Declan as he slid the doors closed. But she didn't go anywhere. She couldn't make herself walk away. The voices didn't want her to go. They were whispering at her, trying to get her attention. Something wasn't right.

Now behind closed doors, Declan indicated one of the guest chairs to the detective, before he sat in other. 'Is this about my wife's murder, Detective?' Declan asked.

'Sort of,' the detective answered.

'Sorry, but I don't understand,' Declan stated.

'It means that I'm here about your wife, just not the one that was murdered,' the detective replied, his eyes now locked on Declan's.

'Well, now you've completely lost me,' Declan was growing frustrated. 'If you would kindly just get to the point, Detective, perhaps we can then both salvage something of this day.'

'I'm glad to hear you say that, Doc,' Detective Lubovik commented, 'because I've really been struggling with how I was going to go about telling you some interesting things I found out about your wife.'

'Jessica?' Declan was taken aback. 'What does she have to do with any of this?'

'I suspect she has a lot to do with all of this, which is why I'm here,' he explained. 'Look, Doc, I just need you to help me understand a few things,' he continued. 'Maybe there is a perfectly good explanation for all of it. In which case, I'll have no problem admitting that I was wrong and we'll carry on. Besides, I'm sure you wouldn't want us to leave any stone unturned with respect to Lara's death, would you?'

'Of course not, Detective,' Declan agreed. 'Please, ask me what you need to know.'

Lubovik didn't bother to take his small notepad from the inside pocket of his coat. He didn't need it. He knew exactly what he wanted to ask, and exactly what he wanted to say.

'I take it you are fully aware of Jessica's past?' he began.

'Yes, of course I am, Detective,' Declan replied. 'And I am sure you are just as aware that Jessica was my patient when we first met, but there was absolutely nothing inappropriate going on between us during that time,' he insisted.

'So, when did it all start, Doc? When did you and Jessica become more than just the doctor and his patient?' the detective asked. He enjoyed this part of any interrogation, big or small. It's amazing what you can learn from someone who is put in an especially uncomfortable situation. From their body language, the movement of their eyes, the way the tongue labors in a desperate attempt to hydrate their mouth.

'First of all, Detective,' Declan quickly replied, 'I don't like what you are implying. My wife…Jessica and I didn't become romantically involved until *after* she was no longer my patient. I would never cross those ethical boundaries.'

Detective Lubovik nodded a few times, before asking his next and what he felt was an obvious question. 'So, you and Ms. McCallum were having an affair then,' Lubovik stated, 'because Ms. McCallum stopped being your patient about two years ago and your wife was murdered just four months ago. Simple math.'

Declan began to squirm in his chair. 'I'm not proud of it, but yes, we were having an affair.'

'And during that time, were there any discussions about you leaving your wife? Leaving Lara?' he questioned Declan.

'Not specifically,' Declan recalled. 'I knew Jessica wanted more from the relationship, but I made it very clear to her from the very beginning that I would never divorce Lara.'

'Do you know if Lara and Ms. McCallum ever met each other?' Lubovik asked next.

Shit. Shit. 'No, not to my knowledge, Detective,' Declan lied. He didn't see how sharing details of the night Jessica showed up at the charity ball and introduced herself to Lara would make any difference at this point. It didn't seem relevant.

'Before your wife died, you signed the deed to this house over to Jessica. Why was that, Doc?' he fired off his next question.

'You make it sound so conspiratorial, Detective,' Declan countered. 'It was simply a business arrangement between us, that's all.' *Maybe not so simple,* Declan thought to himself, *but it was a business arrangement. Technically.* He felt he hadn't lied. Exactly.

Detective Lubovik wasn't so sure. 'You caught all of us by surprise when you and Ms. McCallum suddenly got married,' he looked at Declan.

'Trust me, Detective,' Declan thoughtlessly revealed, 'it caught me by surprise, too.' By then, it was too late. All he could do was stare at the detective and hope. Hope that he had another question at the ready and they could quickly move along. Unfortunately, he did.

'Funny thing, Dr. Fitzgerald,' the detective began, 'in my day, there was only ever one reason why anyone got married in such a hurry. I doubt very much if that has changed over the years. What do you think?'

Declan closed his eyes and dropped his head. His whole demeanor suddenly changed. 'I suppose you'll find out soon enough,' Declan said. 'We're expecting a baby.'

Detective Lubovik sat there, nodding his head slowly up and down for what seemed an eternity to Declan. 'I just have one more question for you, Dr. Fitzgerald,' he finally said. 'Are you absolutely sure she's pregnant?'

'Don't be absurd. Of course, she's pregnant,' Declan insisted.

Detective Lubovik just shrugged. 'In that case, are you sure it's yours?'

'How dare you suggest such a thing,' Declan raised his voice. 'Jessica wouldn't…couldn't…lie to me about that.'

'When we searched Garrett Armstrong's motel room, we found these on a phone he had in his possession,' the detective said as he passed a Manila envelope to Declan. 'They're pictures of Mr. Armstrong and your wife, together, if you get my drift.'

'I don't believe you,' Declan protested, but took the envelope from the detective anyway. 'There must be a mistake,' he insisted as he opened the enveloped and reached a hand inside. 'Jessica wouldn't,' he started to say as his hand pulled several photographs from inside. While he never did find any words that could defend what he saw in those pictures, he did find his voice. He used it to cry. The magnitude of the whole situation was just starting to hit him, right in the heart.

'I'm sorry, Doc,' the detective offered sincerely, 'but we believe she also had something to do with Lara's death.'

Declan just sat there, his head in his hands, trying desperately to hold on to some semblance of sanity. There were no words to describe how he was feeling at that very moment, so he didn't bother to try.

'I think Ms. McCallum wanted you all to herself, and unfortunately, Lara was in her way, so she manipulated Garrett into doing her dirty work for her,' Lubovik added.

The detective rose from the chair and turned to leave the office. 'I came here today, because I wanted you to know that I'll be back in a day or two and I'll be bringing an arrest warrant for Ms. McCallum with me,' he added. 'I don't normally go around notifying people when we're going to make an arrest, but this is a bit of an unusual circumstance. I just wanted you to be prepared for what's coming, that's all.'

Declan looked up at the detective. 'Thank you, Detective,' Declan managed to say.

Lubovik walked to the pocket doors and slowly slid them open. Had he been faster, he might have caught just the blur of Jessica's back as she turned a corner and disappeared down the long hallway on the far side of the foyer. She was heading for the kitchen, as she had originally intended. Instead, she had crept toward the closed office doors and leaned in, trying desperately to hear what was being said behind. *Why had the Detective come to talk to Declan? Why had he asked to see him alone?*

As it turned out, it was a good thing that she decided to stop and listen. Had she not, she wouldn't have known that the time had come to awaken the third teddy bear candle. The only pure one left.

Chapter Eleven

Mrs. Powers picked up the phone in the kitchen following two quick rings. Someone was calling from another extension within the house. Since Jessica was sitting beside her, it could only be Dr. Fitzgerald.

'Yes, Dr. Fitzgerald, what can I do for you?' she inquired.

'Is Jessica there, Mrs. Powers?' he calmly asked.

'Why, yes,' Mrs. Powers replied, 'she's here, poor thing. I just got her some dry crackers and ginger ale; she was feeling quite poorly all of a sudden.'

'Would you ask her to come and see me right away, please? I'll be waiting for her in her office,' Declan firmly instructed her.

'Could it possibly wait for a bit, Dr. Fitzgerald?' Mrs. Powers asked. 'Only she's looking a little peaked at the moment.'

'No, Mrs. Powers,' Declan answered firmly. 'It can't wait.'

'Of course, then,' Mrs. Powers responded obligingly, 'I'll let her know right away.' She hung up the phone and turned to Jessica.

'Your husband requests the honor of your presence in the office, madam,' she lightheartedly pretended to bow. 'Go on now, you have your marching orders.'

Jessica closed her eyes and reached her hands up, placing one on either side of her head. 'Shhhhh, be quiet,' she barely whispered.

'I beg your pardon?' Mrs. Powers asked, unsure of what it was that Jessica had said.

Jessica rubbed her temples with the tips of her fingers, round and round, before she continued. 'Not you, Mrs. Powers,' Jessica closed her eyes for a second. 'I wasn't talking to you.'

'For heaven's sake,' Mrs. Powers dismissed, 'there's no one else here. Who else would you be talking to, I'd like to know?' she teased back, although she was beginning to sense an awkwardness in the room. 'Did you hear what I said, Jessica?' Mrs. Powers asked. 'Dr. Fitzgerald is waiting in your office for you. He says to come right away.'

Satisfied that she had done what had been asked of her, Mrs. Powers went about her business. Whatever was going on between Jessica and Dr. Fitzgerald was none of her concern. Besides, it was coming up to five o'clock when it would be time for her to leave for the day. She remembers thinking to herself that it was the first time since she started working here that it couldn't come soon enough.

'I heard you,' Jessica snapped at her. 'I heard you the first time, Mrs. Powers.' She struggled to compose herself with one final fleeting rub to the temples. She took a deep breath and walked over to a mirror that hung on the wall by the kitchen's back door. One last inspection: a pat to the hair, a fingertip dab to the corner of her mouth where the lipstick refused to hang on, a pretend smile looking back at her. 'Time for one of Mama's special plays,' she quietly whispered to her reflection.

She turned, and without so much as a look at Mrs. Powers, confidently walked out the kitchen door to the long hallway that led to the foyer. She crossed the still black-and-white tiled floor to her office, its pocket doors wide open.

Declan was sitting in the big chair, her chair. Behind the big desk, her desk. 'You wanted to see me, darling?' she cooed sweetly to him.

Declan was no longer buying what she was selling. That store was about to go out of business. For good. 'Close the doors and sit down,' he insisted.

Tic. Jessica reluctantly did as he asked. 'Is something wrong, my love?'

Declan maintained his composure, barely. This was his opportunity to see just how far she would take things. How far she would go to get what she wanted.

'No, darling,' he smiled at her, 'there's nothing wrong.'

She waited for Declan to continue, but he simply sat there. Looking at her with what she recognized as a pretend smile on his face. *Tic.*

She tried so hard to wait him out, but the voices shattered her concentration, forcing her to break one of her most important rules. She spoke before he did. She gave in before he did. 'Not now,' she whispered aloud, although she had only intended to appease the voices through thought alone. To cover for her mistake, she quickly continued on. 'I have to go lie down,' she added. 'I don't feel very well. Must be the baby.'

'Yes, about the baby, sweetheart,' Declan continued to stare at her, 'I'd really like to go to all your appointments with you. I want to be as involved as possible,' he added. 'If I'm not mistaken, you must be close to having your first ultrasound. When is that booked for, *Jess*? I'll make a note in my schedule, so I don't forget. I wouldn't want to miss it.'

She suspected he was playing with her. 'That would be wonderful, darling,' Jessica easily agreed. 'I believe the ultrasound is next Friday afternoon, but I'll double check my calendar, just to make sure,' she smiled at him, 'and I'll get back to you.'

Declan continued to sit there. 'I must say,' he finally said, 'you look amazing for a woman who is almost halfway through her pregnancy,' he said as he pointed a finger at Jessica's stomach. 'How have you managed to maintain that amazing body of yours?'

Jessica tilted her head sexily to one side, put the tip of one index finger into her mouth, and slowly pulled it out. 'Must be all the exercise we've been getting in the bedroom,' she smiled at him. 'In fact,' she dared to add, 'why don't we go upstairs now and work out?'

Declan never took his eyes off of her, even as he slowly pushed the Manila envelope Detective Lubovik had left with him across the desk toward Jessica. He had enough.

'What's that?' she asked him, her left eye now beginning to twitch.

'It's a surprise,' Declan answered her, 'go ahead, open it, darling.'

Jessica sensed a hint of sarcasm in his tone. *Tic.*

'Don't open it,' she thought she heard a whispered warning in her head, but she couldn't be sure. Things weren't getting through. They were all mixed up. They were talking over each other again.

She slowly reached a hand out and pulled the envelope toward her. She put her hand inside and removed the contents. *Tic.*

She knew Garrett had taken naked photos of the two of them together and kept a few on his phone. She had encouraged him to do it. She wanted him to do it. It was sexy. It was erotic. Often, late at night, when Jessica's mind refused to sleep as it had so often lately, she would call him and tell him to masturbate while looking at her picture. She would listen to him. She would incite him. She would finally beg him to come while imagining he was deep inside of her.

But not that night. That night, she had insisted he leave his phone with her. He believed it was because she didn't want him to accidently leave it somewhere behind at Lara's house and risk getting caught. She knew it was because she had to get her hands on his phone and completely destroy it. The only relationship she wanted there to be proof of was their professional one.

So, where had these photographs come from? Garrett had neglected to mention that he had a second phone. That's because he never intended to use it as a phone. He only wanted it to keep a few pictures of Jessica with him that night. He needed them to remind himself of why he did what he did. She was his reward. He had done it for her.

'Declan,' Jessica began, 'it's not what it looks like. I don't think any of them are even real. If you look closely, they all look like they've been photoshopped, see,' she desperately tried to show one to Declan.

'Stop it,' Declan brought his fist down, heavy, on top of the desk. 'Stop it, Jessica. I've heard enough. It's all lies. Everything's been a lie, hasn't it?'

'No, my love,' Jessica said as she rose from the chair and began to walk around the desk to where Declan sat. 'Why don't we go upstairs and talk about this where we can both be more comfortable,' she seductively suggested as she reached a hand out to caress his face.

Declan's hand suddenly lashed out, grabbing Jessica's outstretched arm by the wrist. 'Don't touch me,' he practically spit at her. 'Don't ever touch me again.' He roughly pushed her hand away.

'You don't mean that,' Jessica smiled sweetly at him. 'Think of the baby. Our baby, Declan.'

Declan sneered at her. 'Listen very carefully, Jessica,' Declan said as he leaned over the desk. 'I'm going to give you two days to pack your things and get out of my house,' he said. 'I never want to see you or hear from you again. Do you understand me?'

'Or what, Declan?' she sneered back. 'What will you do, you pathetic old man? This is my house, not yours.' She could feel herself unraveling. The voices growing louder and angrier.

'Leave me alone, Jessica!' Declan screamed at her. 'Get out. I can't stand the sight of you one second longer!'

Jessica took a deep breath, stood tall, turned, and headed toward the open pocket doors of the office. At the doorway, she stopped, turned around, and began to slide the doors closed. 'Remember, darling,' she smiled at him, 'you made a promise. *Till death do us part.*' With that, she closed the doors hard, ascended the staircase, and walked the long hallway to the end and her apartment.

She locked the door behind her, poured herself a glass of wine, and went to the living room. There, she sat down on the couch, took a gulp of the wine and closed her eyes. 'Shhhh,' she softly whispered. 'You all need to stop talking at once,' she continued. 'You're confusing me. It's all too confusing.' She raised the wineglass to her lips and emptied it, then put the empty glass down on the coffee table in front of her and wiped her mouth with the back of one hand. More, they needed more. They were all so thirsty.

She returned to the kitchen and rather than pour just a glass this time, she brought the bottle back to the living room with her. She sat down again on the couch and tipped the bottle up to her mouth, intent on finishing the contents, which she readily did.

When it was empty, she hurled it across the room where it hit a wall and shattered into pieces, embedding itself into the carpet below like shrapnel.

She rocked herself back and forth, back and forth, on the couch, her arm folded tightly across her stomach. She squeezed her eyes closed. Tight. 'Tell me what to do,' she whispered. 'You have to tell me.'

A few minutes later, she suddenly stopped the rocking and opened her eyes, a sneer appearing on her face. 'See,' she whispered. 'I knew you'd think of something.'

She pulled opened the coffee table drawer, reached into the back left corner, lifted the shawl, and removed the black box that lay hidden under it. She placed the black box in her lap, removed the lid, and smiled down at the three, red teddy bear candles that smiled back at her. She ran her fingers lightly over the first two, coming to rest on the third. The one that had not yet been used.

'Hello, baby doll,' she said as she picked it up and laid it in the palm of her other hand. 'I've got a very special night planned for us. It's time to get ready.'

* * * * *

Several hours later, Jessica, dressed in a sexy white chiffon nightgown, quietly let herself out of her apartment, and made her way along the hallway to the second story landing at the top of the grand staircase. There, she looked across the foyer and out the two-story high arched glass windows that graced the entire front of the house. Outside, she could just make out Declan's car sitting in the driveway that circled the front of the house. He was still here. Somewhere inside this house. She smiled.

'He must be in one of the other two apartments on the second floor, but which one?' She went to the first door and leaned into it. She couldn't hear anything on the other side, so she went to the second door and placed her ear up to it, but an approaching thunderstorm was making it difficult for her to hear much of anything, other than the ominous rumblings that were growing louder, coming closer.

She returned to the landing at the top of the staircase and stood there for a moment watching the flashes of lightning through the windows. She suddenly closed her eyes and breathed deep. In. Out. She gently lifted her arms out to her sides and held them there. In. Out. It was as though she were drawing energy from the storm that now raged overhead.

Her eyes flew open and she dropped her arms down by her sides. She quickly descended the stairs, her ethereal nightgown making it appear as though she simply floated the entire way. She ran across the foyer and flung open one of the main entrance's double doors. Shielding her eyes from the blinding bolts of lightning that were now tearing through the night sky, she made her way through the pouring rain to the side of the house. She could just make out the gardener's shed off in the distance, at the edge of the grounds.

By now, the rain had melted her nightgown to her body like a translucent sheet of skin. There was no peek-a-boo potential here. Absolutely nothing about her was left to anyone's imagination.

Her once carefree curls had melted in the rain, too, replaced by stringy bits that stuck to her face. Her shoulders. Even the little hollow at the top of her buttocks. The depression of night and the dark stain of rain had dyed it a dull brown.

She reached the gardener's shed and began to feel around the top of the door until her fingertips found the key she and Garrett had hidden there. This was a place where they had often met. Where they had often kissed. Where they had quite often fucked each other's brain out. So, she knew exactly what she was after.

She unlocked the door and stepped inside. There, she reached to her left and felt for the small flashlight she knew was hanging from a nail on the wall. She turned the flashlight on and scanned the darkness around her.

In the far corner, she spotted what she was looking for. Two five-gallon containers of gasoline. Each one full. She remembered Garrett telling her that he kept them there so he always knew there was enough gas for the gardening equipment.

She took the containers, one at a time, into the house and placed them on the tile floor in the foyer, making sure she was as quiet as possible in the process. She didn't want to wake Declan. Yet.

She picked up the first container and walked down the long hallway to the left of the staircase and to the kitchen. There, she went to the backdoor and made sure it was locked. She undid the cap on the container and began to back her way out of the kitchen, down the hallway and to the front door, leaving a sloppy trail of gas as she went.

She put the now empty container down and picked up the full one right next to it. She went to the front door and began to pour another trail of gasoline from the front door, across the foyer, up the center of the grand staircase to the very top step where she stopped.

She swished the container around and smiled. She still had about half left and she knew just where she was going to use it. She crossed to the other end of the landing and turned right at the hallway that led to her apartment. Outside the door, she tipped the container and slowly splashed her way back down the hallway until she reached the landing, where she again stopped.

She next went down the opposite hallway, toward the front of the house where the other two apartments were located. Where Declan now lay, fast asleep. 'Sweet dreams, my love,' Jessica whispered before she slopped a path of gas from each of the two apartment doors back to the same spot on the landing where she first stopped. All paths now merged together. And all paths led to and from one door to another, yet there would be no escape.

She calmly walked to the center of the landing where she leaned up against the bannister and looked around her. At the opulence of the foyer. The stunning floor-to-ceiling, wall-to-wall arched windows that offered a variety of scenery, whether from the inside looking out or from the outside looking in. It all belonged to her now, so she could do with it what she wanted.

She reached into a pocket in her nightgown and pulled out the little red teddy bear candle, its wick pure. 'Mama's little baby doll,' she whispered tenderly to it, while she stroked its head with the tip of one finger.

Next, she reached into the same pocket and took out a lighter. She flicked the lighter to life, and before holding it to the candle's wick, she lifted the candle to her lips and kissed it tenderly. 'It's time,' was all she whispered as she ignited the wick, a grotesque grin now on her face, her eyes large and frantic.

She held the candle in front of her, turned and walked to the far end of the landing where the hallway led to the three apartments and where the three paths of gas now merged into one. She bent down and held the candle's flame to the carpet, igniting the small pool of gas. A second later, three tentacles of fire set out on their separate journeys. One traveled to Jessica's apartment door; the second to one of the two apartments at the front of the house; the third to the second apartment at the front of the house.

Still holding the red teddy bear candle in her hand, Jessica went to the other end of the landing and stopped at the top of the grand staircase. There, she calmly bent down and touched the fiery wick to the top step. She watched, mesmerized, as the flame traveled down the stairs, across the foyer to the front door where it met the last path of gas, instantly setting it alight. Its journey then took it down the hallway, through the kitchen and straight to the back door.

Jessica walked to the middle of the second story landing, the only place where she had not poured gas, and stood next to the bannister, the red teddy bear candle still held tightly in one hand. All around her, flames were crawling up the walls, consuming anything that dared to get in the way.

Now it was time to wake Declan. It was time to prove to him that she was right. That they would be together forever. 'I warned you, Declan, till death do us part! Now you'll be mine forever,' she screamed out before she suddenly began to laugh. At first, it was simple laughter like any other, but as the flames rose higher and wilder, it escalated louder, crazier, out of control.

A streak of lightning suddenly lit up the night sky and, out of the corner of her eye, Jessica caught a glimpse of something through the smoke and the flames. There, just beyond the arched glass windows at the front of the house. There it was again, only that time it had moved, back. Away from the flames.

How could that be? It was Declan. Standing in the driveway at the front of the house, his hands up to shield his face from the heat and the smoke that now totally engulfed the once beautiful manor house. It seems he couldn't sleep and had gone for a walk to clear his head, to think, to decide what to do.

But, the decision had been made for him. There was nothing more for him to think about. Everything here would all soon be gone if he didn't do something.

Declan quickly pulled a cell phone from his coat pocket, flipped it open, and entered 911 before he was unexpectedly forced back when the windows across the front of the house began to shatter as the flames forced their way through. For just a brief moment, he caught a flame and smoke framed glimpse of Jessica standing on the second-story landing, staring down at him, the rage on her face making her almost unrecognizable.

'911, what is your emergency?' he heard a voice on the other end of the phone ask. He looked up again and could see that in one hand, Jessica clutched one of the red teddy bear candles, its head half melted from the heat of the wick, wax slithering down her hand like tears of blood.

He simply stood there, watching, contemplating. Finally, he lifted the phone up to his mouth, 'My apologies, operator,' he calmly said. 'False alarm. Everything is fine, thank you.' He closed the phone, returned it to his pocket, turned and slowly walked away.

There was *nothing* here worth saving.